The Age of Worry

The Age *of* Worry

A NOVEL

Steven B. Sandler

Charleston, SC
www.PalmettoPublishing.com

The Age of Worry

ISBN-13: 978-1-64990-146-0
ISBN-10: 1-649-90146-1

Table of Contents

Chapter 1   The Big Fight ···························1

Chapter 2   Cordelia on the Tracks·····················5

Chapter 3   An Awakening ························13

Chapter 4   Flying a Kite····························22

Chapter 5   Not the End of the World ················31

Chapter 6   A Slippery floor ························37

Chapter 7   The Three Fates ·······················43

Chapter 8   Safe and Sound·························50

Chapter 9   Only Mr. T····························56

Chapter 10 The World Walking Tour ················63

Chapter 11 A Trip to Tucson ·····················69

Chapter 12 The First Clue ·······················75

Chapter 13 Don Juan ··························84

Chapter 14 The Christmas Truce··················92

Chapter 15 The Dill Pickle Aisle ·················96

Chapter 16 Brooklyn ·························101

Chapter 17 Emergency Meeting··················107

Chapter 18 A Brief History of the Wingback Chair ······112

Chapter 19 The Lord's Prayer ···················117

Chapter 20 A Missed Opportunity·················125

Chapter 21 A Literary Mystery···················130

Chapter 22 A Hurt Knee ······················136

Chapter 23 Tikkun Olam ······················139

Chapter 24 Bad Dreams ······················146

Chapter 25 Uncle Jack························155

Chapter 26 Sister Agnes Joan · 161
Chapter 27 Martin · 173
Chapter 28 The Day After · 179
Chapter 29 A Daring Escape · 185
Chapter 30 Daniel's Dream · 196
Chapter 31 Montreal · 201
Chapter 32 Silence Can Kill · 207
Chapter 33 Marie-Luce · 216
Chapter 34 Late · 221
Chapter 35 A Balcony Scene · 228
Chapter 36 Cirrhosis · 238
Chapter 37 Carlos · 244
Chapter 38 A Moral Dilemma · 250
Chapter 39 Sinners and Innocents · · · · · · · · · · · · · · · · · · 257
Chapter 40 People Don't Change · · · · · · · · · · · · · · · · · · 261
Chapter 41 Family Therapy · 268
Chapter 42 Irises · 275
Chapter 43 Mrs. Rose · 279
Chapter 44 Who Killed Jesus? · 288
Chapter 45 No Time to Waste · 295
Chapter 46 Syracuse · 302
Chapter 47 The Promise · 310
Chapter 48 A Familiar Face · 315
Chapter 49 An Unlikely Story · 320
Chapter 50 A Family Reunion · 326
Chapter 51 The Source of Clues · · · · · · · · · · · · · · · · · · 331
Chapter 52 Flashbacks · 340
Chapter 53 The End of Suffering · · · · · · · · · · · · · · · · · · 346
Chapter 54 Cast the First Stone · · · · · · · · · · · · · · · · · · · 354
Chapter 55 Last Words · 359

1.

The Big Fight

Daniel Wunsch, Professor of English Literature at the State University of New York in Albany, wanted to pick up his teenage daughter's backpack and throw it through the window. It sat there on the floor in the middle of the family room, despite the fact that he had asked her to move it when she got home from school that afternoon. His daughter stood before him defiantly—not defying him about the backpack, which wasn't even the topic of conversation. She was defying him about his most basic values, ignoring his completely legitimate concerns. How was a father supposed to parent such a child?

"The facts are the facts, Cordelia," he said, looking up at his daughter from where he sat in his favorite chair. "You were seen at a coffee shop when you were supposed to be in school. Why shouldn't I be upset about that?"

"Dad," said his daughter. That was all she said. She stood there with a look of exasperation on her face.

His wife sat on the couch across from him, looking at him with pleading eyes, as if the whole problem were his fault. He just glared at the backpack. For a moment, he could see himself picking it up and hurling it at the window. Since it was full of her school books, it would have significant mass. Mass times velocity equals momentum. It would have terrific momentum. He could almost hear the glass shatter.

For a moment, he thought that Cordelia had tears in her eyes, but then she blinked hard and there were none. He started to feel bad for her, but then he just felt annoyed again. Why should she be so upset, anyway? He was the one who should be upset.

"How do you plan to succeed in life if you can't even meet the minimum expectations and attend class?" he asked.

His daughter took a big sigh—an unnecessarily dramatic sigh, in his opinion—and rolled her eyes at the ceiling.

"Dan, please," said his wife, Abby. "She's just being a kid. She made a mistake. That's all."

He looked at Abby and held his empty palms upward to signify the futility of his situation. He hoped that Abby would read his nonverbal message: *What do you want from me? She's the culprit. Why don't you ask her to fix this mess?* But Abby wasn't getting it at all. She made another comment or two to defend Cordelia, while Dan sat in his chair trying to maintain his equanimity.

"Dad, listen," said Cordelia. She seemed to be relaxing her attitude in response to her mother's support. "You have a point, of course. I should have been in class. No doubt about it. I'm sorry about that. I didn't mean to worry you. But it's no big deal to cut one boring French class, and I'm going to do fine in life. Really, you need to stop worrying. I'll be fine."

"It's not fine," he said in quick reply. "And I'm certainly going to worry when I see my daughter starting down a bad path in life. This can only lead to disaster. You cut classes, you do very little homework these days, and you run around at too many parties.

Drinking parties." He emphasized the word *drinking*, just to make sure she got his point.

Cordelia shifted her stance. He thought she might storm out of the room, as she had done in past arguments, but she stood where she was. She pursed her lips, let out a big breath, and then spoke in a very restrained tone.

"Dad, listen. It's not the Prohibition era. It's 1997. Kids drink at parties. And as far as school goes, I cut one class. Okay, maybe two classes. But I'm in the second semester of my senior year, right? I've got very good grades, and I've already been accepted to a terrific college. So, what's the problem?"

What's the problem? he thought. His daughter couldn't see the problem. His wife couldn't see the problem. No one saw it except for him, and he was getting tired of trying to explain it to everyone.

"What's the problem? he repeated. "What's the problem? The problem is that you're about to throw everything away by your ridiculous behavior now. Everything you've worked for in high school could be destroyed by one reckless decision at one of these parties you go to. Do you want to be a girl who accomplishes something in this life? Or do you want to be a loser?"

She turned her head abruptly to her right, as if she just couldn't stand the sight of him anymore. She tapped a foot rapidly on the floor, gazing out the window. When she spoke again, her voice was unexpectedly loud and strident.

"You know what, Dad? I'm sick and tired of listening to you criticize me all the time! To be honest with you, I'm sick and tired of coming home at all!"

Dan gripped the arms of his big wingback chair. He looked at Cordelia's backpack sitting in the middle of the family room. Was it packed with books? Or was it stuffed with clothing? Was she planning to leave home? He felt himself rising up from his chair to a standing position.

"Well, fine!" he said. "Then maybe you should look for someplace else to live!" He had an urge to walk over to the backpack and give it a good kick. For a moment, he thought he was actually going to do it, but she grabbed it before he could make his move. She stood there staring at him for a moment. The look on her face was a look of shock, total disbelief. Then she turned and ran up the stairs.

"Cordelia, wait!" called Abby.

He heard his daughter in her bedroom as she walked back and forth overhead, loudly opening drawers and slamming them shut. He sat back down in his chair, suddenly feeling self-conscious. His daughter must be thinking that he was behaving like a monster. His wife Abby probably agreed. Worse, he truly felt like a monster. In the moment of rising from his chair, he felt like someone capable of doing terrible things in a blind rage. Was he really going to kick his daughter's backpack? And why did he say such mean things to her?

A few minutes later, Cordelia came back down the stairs. Her backpack was bulging now, obviously loaded with extra supplies. She walked straight out the front door. She didn't say good-bye; she didn't even look back. She slammed the screen door as she walked out. Abby, still sitting on the couch, started to cry. Dan sat in his wingback chair, wishing that he could just disappear.

2

Cordelia on the Tracks

Cordelia circled her neighborhood for an hour or so. As she walked, she kept picturing her father sitting in his favorite chair in the family room. *Well, maybe you should look for someplace else to live!* She thought up numerous responses to his outburst, but none of them brought her any relief. She imagined shouting at him. She would tell him that he was being ridiculous. He was completely unfair in his criticisms of her. But he just sat there in her mind's eye, repeating his hurtful words. *Well, maybe you should look for someplace else to live!* She would plead with him. How could he say such a thing? How could he reject his own child? She would try to scare some sense into him. She was leaving home, never to return. She would be a homeless person because of him! The only response that she could envision was the same image of him sitting in his chair, stubborn, silent, and implacable.

She wanted to talk to her best friend Becky, but Becky was at the movies with her mother. If this had happened a week sooner, she could have talked to her boyfriend—now ex-boyfriend— Logan, but he had cheated on her with another girl. Besides, conversations with Logan only really worked when the topic was about Logan. She went on walking, and when she was tired of walking, she wandered back to her own block again and saw that the lights were out at her house. Good! Her parents always went to bed early, and they must be asleep. She was able to get in through the back door and throw a few more belongings into her backpack. Her mother called to her from down the hall, and Cordelia reassured her mother that she was home for the night. Good night, good night. And then she quietly left again with no intention of returning anytime soon. Maybe never.

But then what? It was dark outside now, and the April evening was getting cooler. Becky still wouldn't be home yet, and Becky was the only person she really wanted to talk to. She turned right toward the railroad tracks that ran just to the south of her neighborhood. She walked along the tracks with no place to go, feeling very lonely, lost in her thoughts. She was pulled back into the world by the distant sound of an oncoming train. She got off the tracks and sat down on a grassy little hill a few yards away. As the freight train slowly approached, she started to cry, knowing that no one would hear her over the sounds of the train. The long procession of freight cars thundered by, and she cried harder, sobbing until she thought she would never catch her breath again. She leaned forward, resting her head on her arms, rocking back and forth as she cried. When it was finally over, she sat there feeling exhausted, limp, and dazed. This just couldn't be happening to her.

When she stood up, she couldn't think of anything to do except to get a drink. Yes, a drink would feel good right now. But where would she get one? She remembered that a girl named Alice was having a party in her backyard. Alice wasn't really a close friend; in fact, she was one of the kids whom her father had recently labeled "the wrong crowd." But there would be plenty of alcohol at Alice's party, and Cordelia needed a drink.

Fifteen minutes later, she found herself standing—and drinking—around a bonfire in Alice's backyard. It was quite dark now, but the faces of the kids were illuminated by the flames. She tried to talk to Alice about the problem with her father, but Alice seemed unimpressed. After all, said Alice, she hadn't spoken to her mother in over a year! Cordelia decided to drop the subject and join in the small talk of the kids standing around the fire. Somebody was dating somebody. The history teacher, Mr. Tremblay, was the cutest man in the school. The New York State Regents examinations were a total waste of time. She did her best to talk like this. Meanwhile, she drank down her vodka and cranberry juice. She drank quickly, defiantly, knowing that it would upset her father terribly if he could see her drinking.

She continued to ruminate to herself about the situation with her father, but as the evening progressed, she found herself keeping an eye on Alice. Alice was known for getting "blackout" drunk, so drunk that she couldn't remember anything after she sobered up the next day. And when she drank, she did stupid things. She once jumped into the deep end of someone's swimming pool, and a couple of the other kids had to fish her out. Tonight, her father and stepmother were out of town, and she was throwing a party in her backyard. There was no limit to what she might do.

Cordelia finished her second drink—or was it her third? — amazed that no one could tell from her face that she was going through the worst time in her life. Not one of them seemed to notice. As she refilled her plastic cup, she noticed Alice. At that moment, Alice was laughing too loudly and drinking too much. She was leading a few kids away from the fire, heading down to a path that led from her yard to a little creek running behind her house. Sometime later—it seemed like a long while—Cordelia saw the kids return on the path without Alice. She felt concerned and asked the others. Alice? Alice was sleeping under the stars, they said, laughing.

Cordelia put her drink down and ran along the path. She was more than a little drunk herself, and she stumbled on a root. She recovered her balance without falling, and she went to the end of the short path. She found Alice lying on the ground, face up, just a couple feet from the creek. The moon was coming up, so Cordelia could see her quite clearly. Alice was a petit girl, short, thin, and light-framed. Her face was round and small, with delicate features. Lying there unconscious, without being able to make dramatic faces or spout rude curses, she looked like a young child asleep in the woods.

"Alice, wake up!" Cordelia tried to shake her, but Alice didn't stir. The evening air was rapidly cooling now, and Cordelia thought about the morning frost that still settled on the ground in early April. She worried about leaving Alice there all night. She ran back to the bonfire and convinced a few of the boys to come with her and carry Alice into the house. When they lifted her up, her body was completely limp. Her head flopped like a rag doll unless someone held it. The boys carried her back up the path and into the house. They laid her on the couch in the living room, and Cordelia covered her with a blanket.

"Poor Alice," Cordelia whispered as she left the house.

She walked outside into the yard, but she couldn't bring herself to rejoin the group around the bonfire. The alcohol was really hitting her now, and it was just making her feel drunk and miserable. All she could think about was her father. She couldn't continue to be part of the silly high school conversations. She picked up her backpack and quietly left the yard.

She only got about a block away. She kept seeing Alice's head flopping around like a rag doll as the boys carried her up the path. She stopped on the sidewalk and debated with herself. Alice was inside the house now, on her own couch. She wouldn't roll over and drown in the creek. She wouldn't freeze overnight on the cold ground. Still, she didn't look good. She was breathing, yes, but was she breathing deeply enough? Cordelia strained to reason things out. She wished there were a way to shake off the alcohol and think straight.

She turned around and went back to the house. The yard was still full of kids. She went inside to the living room and stood over Alice, who was lying motionless on the couch. There was only one small lamp on, but Cordelia could see the girl pretty well. She watched her breathing for a couple of minutes. There was a brief pause now and again, but then Alice would resume breathing regularly. Cordelia tried to shake her awake, but she was limp and unarousable. What to do? If only the alcohol didn't make one's thinking so fuzzy and cumbersome.

If she called for an ambulance, she reasoned, it would probably become a big emergency scene for nothing. Alice would probably be fine medically, but she would no doubt be in big trouble with her parents. The hospital would call them and tell them everything. The other kids would probably be mad at Cordelia for making a big drama about nothing. But if she didn't call, and something bad happened, she would never forgive herself. And all the terrible consequences of alcohol were fresh in her mind from a recent lecture in health class. She finally made her decision.

"Hello?" she said into the phone. "I think I need an ambulance. I'm not really sure. I think my friend has had too much to drink, and I'm really worried about her. Her breathing seems really shallow."

The emergency dispatcher started asking Cordelia questions, but at the same time, things started to happen fast around her in the house. One of the other girls had come inside to get more ice for the drinks, and she heard Cordelia on the phone.

"Are you crazy?" said the girl. "Now they'll send the cops and we'll all get arrested!"

The girl ran outside into the yard, and Cordelia heard the panic through the screen windows of the living room. The word "police" echoed across the yard in many voices. She heard car engines starting, and she saw kids scattering left and right. Tires squealed, and the yard was emptied in seconds.

The ambulance crew showed up in a surprisingly short time. Two men and a woman gathered around the couch. They turned on all the lights in the room, which revealed to Cordelia the glaring, sad truth of Alice: a drunken little girl, passed out on the couch, without a friend in the world. Cordelia was the only kid left on the property, and she was hardly a close friend. The paramedics asked Cordelia a few questions while they examined Alice, and she did the best she could to answer them. How much had Alice been drinking? A lot. Were there any other drugs at the party? Only a little marijuana. Any heroin used? No! Cordelia stood back as they talked amongst themselves. The girl's color was pink at the fingernails and lips, they said. She seemed to be breathing pretty well. Heart rate was fine. They told Cordelia they would take her to the emergency room just for observation until she sobered up. The woman stayed by Alice while the men went out to get a gurney.

But then everything changed in an instant. The woman's voice became loud and urgent as she yelled to the other paramedics to hurry back *now!* Cordelia struggled to make sense of what was happening. The woman was yelling: *She's blue! She's blue!* Cordelia looked at Alice and realized that her lips had become a dusky blue. And she wasn't breathing at all. The men came running back into the room. They all lifted Alice from the soft couch onto the hardwood floor, and one of them kneeled down at her head. He put some kind of tube down her throat. They connected it to a clear plastic cylindrical bag, and one of them started squeezing the bag to force air into the girl's lungs. They talked among themselves, but Cordelia couldn't really follow what they were saying.

Things kept happening faster than she could really keep track of. Somehow a gurney appeared in the living room and Alice was lying on it. They were still squeezing the air into her lungs. They said something to Cordelia about which hospital they were taking Alice to, but she couldn't remember what they said. And then they were suddenly gone, and two cops were standing in front of her. Cordelia couldn't remember when the cops had arrived or how they got into the living room.

One of the cops was very young, and he kept looking at her like the boys at high school looked at her, lunging at her with his eyes. The other one was much older, and he was very nice. He asked her a lot of questions, and she tried to sound sober and sensible as she answered them. She was afraid, of course. They could arrest her for underage drinking, or accuse her of supplying the liquor to the others. She had heard stories. The older cop seemed satisfied with her answers, and then there was a moment of silence. She thought that they would probably put handcuffs on her now.

"Don't worry," said the cop. "I have a daughter who's about the same age as you are. I'm not going to arrest you, honey. You can go home now."

She thanked him, amazed that he had apparently read her mind. She just stood where she was, though, afraid to move lest they see how unsteady she was on her feet. Alcohol is so fast getting into your brain; why is it so slow to leave?

"Go home, Cordelia," said the cop. "Go home before your father starts to worry about you."

She started to cry.

"Don't worry, honey, they'll take good care of your friend at the hospital."

Still crying, she thanked him again and walked out of the house, trying to navigate a perfectly sober straight line into the cool April evening.

3

An Awakening

"**D**an, wake up!"

He was sound asleep when he first heard his wife's voice. He had no idea what time it was, but he knew it was certainly too early to be awake yet. He just wanted her to leave him alone. He often thought that it would be nice if everyone would just leave him alone. He was a man who struggled every day of his life to prevent people from disturbing his peace, a very tenuous peace that was easily shattered.

"Dan! You have to wake up!"

His mind was stirring just enough to remember that this was Saturday, so his wife's persistence seemed particularly puzzling. What could Abby possibly want of him? Why couldn't she have the decency to wait until a more sensible hour to talk to him?

"Wake up, Dan! Cordelia's gone! Wake up!"

There is nothing like fear to counteract the gravitational pull of sleep, and he went from half-asleep to fully alert in a second. He opened his eyes, rolled out of bed, and charged down the hall.

"What do you mean, gone?" he called over his shoulder. "Where in hell is she?"

When he reached his daughter's bedroom, he opened the door and looked in. The first rays of sunlight were giving clear shape to the furnishings in the bedroom: an empty bed; a dresser buried by a messy assortment of books, papers, hair ties, and inexpensive jewelry; a chair holding a pile of hastily folded articles of clothing waiting to be put away in their proper places. There was also a cork bulletin board covered with photos of his daughter and her various friends smiling into the camera without a care in the world. One of the photos was a close-up of her; she looked straight at him from the bulletin board, wide-eyed and innocent. Beneath the photos, there was a hand-lettered quotation:

"Think occasionally of the suffering of which you spare yourself the sight."
—Albert Schweitzer

Dan's eyes were drawn again to the empty bed. It crossed his mind, if only for a split second, that the objects in the room might be the last remnants he would ever see of his daughter's life.

"Where is she?" he repeated.

"I don't know," said Abby, her voice shaking as she stood behind him in the doorway. "When you went to bed after the argument, she came back home. We said goodnight to each other, and I thought she went to bed, too. But she must have gone out again."

Dan left the room, went farther down the hall, and looked in his son's room. He saw that the boy was still asleep in his bed. "What time is it?" he demanded.

"It's almost six. I just got up to go to the bathroom and I happened to look in her room."

"Goddammit!" He went downstairs to the kitchen, Abby following quietly behind him. He turned on the kitchen light. He went into the living room to check the sofa, hoping to find his daughter asleep there, but the empty sofa offered him no relief. He came back into the kitchen and confronted his wife. "Well, come on, call somebody!"

"Call who?" she asked, her brow furrowed with worry.

"Her friends! Her friends! Who do you think?"

"All right, Dan, just stop yelling at me."

"Okay. Sorry, sorry. I'm sorry."

Abby went to the phone on the kitchen wall and turned back to him. "Should I call Becky's house? She's usually with Becky, you know."

Dan shrugged his shoulders and held his hands palms up, feeling helpless and desperate. In the midst of his agitated state, one of his favorite Shakespeare quotes came to mind: *Frailty, thy name is woman!* But this only made him feel worse about being so critical of his wife. Abby dialed the number. As she waited for an answer, he paced back and forth. She was probably just at her friend Becky's house, he thought. That's all. Nothing was wrong. She probably just slept over at Becky's. But his mind raced with images of ambulances and hospitals and wrecked automobiles. No, she was probably safe and sound at Becky's. But who knew in this crazy world? Maybe she had just disappeared, vanished without a trace. There would be newspaper stories, television reports, and vigils held at the high school. The state police would set up checkpoints at the major highways leading out of Albany, just in case they spotted a possible abductor. He felt like he had just entered a terrifying dark tunnel that had no exit.

He had feared this day since the moment of her birth. He could still remember sitting in the hospital with his wife, waiting for the nurse to bring their baby in. He couldn't stop thinking that someone could steal her out of the hospital nursery. After they got home with her, he worried uncontrollably with every minor illness for the first year or two. As soon as she could walk, he was afraid that they would lose her in a shopping mall, or that someone would abduct her. Sending her to school was a terrible experience for him. Why would anyone in his right mind trust a bunch of strangers to protect a helpless little girl? He had to meet her teacher at the beginning of every year, and his questions made his wife feel embarrassed. *They're not criminals*, she would tell him. But he insisted that he had a right to know their background, education, and experience before he was going to trust them with his child.

He had worried about her for seventeen years, and the worrying had only become more intense—almost unbearable at times—since she started her senior year in high school.

"Oh, hi, Sharon," Abby finally said. He could hear her trying to steady herself and sound composed. "I'm so sorry to bother you at this crazy hour."

Dan was pacing back and forth in the family room, and he walked back into the kitchen. "Goddammit," he muttered under his breath, but loudly enough for Abby to hear. "Just ask her. Never mind the pleasantries. Just ask her."

Abby held up a hand which he understood to be a quiet signal. He was momentarily calmed and contained by this. He always felt comforted on those rare occasions when his wife stood her ground against his little outbursts.

"Well, Cordelia never came home last night and we just thought she might have gone home with Becky." There was a pause in Abby's voice. "Yes, if you wouldn't mind checking, that would be great. Again, I'm so sorry to bother you."

"Jesus," Dan said under his breath, annoyed again. "How many times do we have to apologize?" He paced restlessly in the kitchen. Then he stood perfectly still, bracing himself for terrible news. For a moment, he was frozen in place, unable to move, feeling that he was about to fall into a terrible nightmare that would change his life forever. Finally, he heard a voice coming out of the receiver in his wife's hand. He couldn't make out the words, but he could see the muscles of his wife's face beginning to relax.

"Oh, that is such a relief! Thank you so much! I hated to bother you, but we really had no idea where she went. She never called us last night or anything. This is great news. Thanks again." The two women exchanged a few more comments, and Abby put the phone back on the wall. "Thank God, she's just over at Becky's house." Abby came over and gave him a hug. "See, we were worried for nothing."

He was relieved, naturally, that Cordelia was safe, but he was also humiliated by his behavior. And Abby's kindness only made him feel worse. He had just recently promised himself (yet again) that he would rein in his temper, and he had failed again miserably. In fact, he had failed just the previous night when he blew up at Cordelia and she stormed out of the house. This entire mess was his fault.

"Come on, let's go back to bed," Abby said.

He followed her dutifully up the stairs, but he couldn't look her in the eye when they got back to their bedroom. She had seen his abominable behavior again, and he couldn't bear the thought of having her look at him now. He went to the closet.

"Dan, are you all right?"

"I'm fine," he said. At first, he didn't quite know what he was going to do, but he knew that he urgently needed to be alone. He often needed his time alone, and his wife had stopped objecting to it long ago. It was one of those unwritten terms that become tacitly ratified in a marriage contract over time. One person needs time alone; another needs to sleep only on the left side of the bed. He picked a shirt from the closet.

"What are you doing?" she asked.

"I'm getting dressed," he said. "I just need to get dressed."

"Dan, it's not even six o'clock on a Saturday morning. Where are you going?"

"I'm wide awake now. I might as well drive over to the office and grade a few papers." Out of the corner of his eye, he could see her standing beside the bed.

"Honey, she's fine. Why don't you just come back to bed?"

"I'll just grade a few papers," he repeated. He wanted to say something else, but he couldn't think of anything to say. As it always happened after his anger erupted, he was completely inarticulate. In his shame, he became speechless.

Besides, he couldn't possibly go back to sleep. In fact, he couldn't imagine ever sleeping again. Even though he had just heard the good news that his daughter was safe, he couldn't shake the feeling that the dreaded tragedy had actually happened, or nearly happened. The horrible moment that he had feared for the past seventeen years had almost happened. He kept reassuring himself that she was fine, she was just at her friend Becky's house, but some part of his mind just would not believe it. She wasn't in the house, he couldn't see her or hear her voice, so maybe she was really missing. He feared that he was losing his grip on reality, and he needed to go sit by himself in his office at the university.

Abby was standing by the foot of the bed. He looked at her and remembered one of his least charitable thoughts about his wife. Sometimes, he had the urge to tell her to stand up straight. *Stand up straight!* Why did she have such bad posture? Why would a nice-looking woman in her mid-forties choose to slouch like that? He never actually said it—at least he had that much self-control—but he thought it sometimes. He thought it now, and he hated himself for thinking it.

Abby said, "Don't worry, Dan. I'll call Cordelia later this morning and talk to her about calling home next time."

Without looking up from buttoning his shirt, he managed to speak. "When you talk to her, tell her she should come home and help make dinner tonight." That was all he could think of to say. He wanted his daughter to come home.

"Okay, Dan, I'll tell her."

He finished dressing and went downstairs, leaving his wife in the bedroom. He grabbed an apple on the kitchen counter and headed for the door. Before exiting the house, though, he turned back to the kitchen counter and put several scoops of coffee into the top of the coffee maker. Then he opened the kitchen cupboard and took out Abby's favorite coffee mug (the one with the idyllic farmhouse scene) and set it right beside the coffee maker. He pushed the "on" button. She always liked it when he made the coffee for her. Then he went out to his car.

The neighborhood was naturally quiet at such an early hour, except for the sound of birds singing. The sound of the mourning dove caught his ear. Ah-coo, coo, coo. There was no noise from car traffic at all. The sun was just rising in the East, and the crocuses were silently blooming in the front yard. On his drive to the office, he first took the side streets, passing the homes of his neighbors. No one was outside, and he was glad not to be seen.

When he turned onto the main road that led to the university, he realized how angry he was at his daughter. He imagined the fierce hellfire-and-brimstone lecture he would give her when she came home from her friend's house. He even began to rehearse it out loud in the car.

"Have you no concern for anyone but yourself? What were you thinking?" He was so preoccupied with his soliloquy that he suddenly had to hit the brakes hard to avoid going through a red light. "Do you have absolutely no sense of responsibility for anything? Not for your schoolwork? Not for your family? Not for anything?" A police car drove past him, and he was quiet for a minute so he wouldn't draw attention to himself. When the patrol car passed, he resumed his tirade. "Do you have any idea how much you worried your mother by not coming home last night?" He was gripping the steering wheel tightly as he raged at his irresponsible daughter. "For all we knew, you could have been dead!"

As soon as he said this, his mind shifted abruptly to an image of the old kitchen table in the house where he grew up in Detroit. He instinctively pulled himself away from the image and returned to the lecture he planned to deliver to his daughter.

"We knew nothing! You didn't even think to call us!" But it happened again: He saw the old kitchen table, and this time his father was sitting there across from him, looking shaken and exhausted. His anger started to change from righteous indignation to impotent fury. "Goddamn you!" he yelled, pounding on the dashboard with his fist. "Goddamn you!"

He pulled into the university parking lot just in time, as he was hardly able to control himself. He parked the car, turned off the engine, and sat there gripping the steering wheel. He could not have said why he was getting upset at that moment. He periodically muttered aloud ("Goddamn you!") but could not have said whom he was addressing. Was he angry at his mother? The Shakespeare quote crossed his mind again. *Frailty, thy name is woman!* But was it fair to blame her? The question demanded an answer, but he had none. How could it be fair to blame his mother until one knew exactly what had happened? The facts were the facts, of course, but there were so few of them available for consideration. And even if one knew more about the facts, he reasoned, one could hardly assess blame on the basis of an observable set of actions. One must also know the motivation for those actions. Is that not a critical element in our legal system? If one person hurts another by accident, that's not the same as hurting someone by design. We have to know a person's intention before we pass judgment. It was not enough to know that she left; one would have to know *why* she left. And how could anyone ask her about her reasons when no one knew where she was? Before judging her, one would need some explanation to account for her absence over the past thirty years. No, blaming his mother was just illogical and unfair.

Was he angry at his father? And for what? His poor father had suffered as much as anyone, so it made no sense to blame him. The man was weak; no one could argue with that. But his weakness was his constant desire to make everyone else happy. Was that such a terrible weakness? His father was a man who had tried to keep everyone happy, including the wife who finally left him. Maybe it was just an impossible mission to keep her happy, but he tried. He tried to make his children happy, tried to convince them to see the world as an endless series of pleasant experiences and wonderful opportunities. In the end, he made no one happy with his hopelessly idealized version of life, but was that his fault? Maybe the world was at fault for being so badly broken.

No, it made no sense to be angry at either one of them. Still, he was angry and upset. He gripped the steering wheel tightly and took a big breath, struggling to get control of himself before going up to his office.

4

Flying a Kite

Cordelia awoke at Becky's house to the sounds of a crow outside. *Caw! Caw!* screamed the crow, and the jagged sound made her head hurt. The bedroom was a small converted attic space with sloping walls and one little window looking out onto a meager square of backyard. She staggered out of bed and went to the window. The source of the racket was sitting on a branch just a few feet away. "Scat!" said Cordelia through the screen, squinting into the daylight. The crow took flight. She then felt a sudden wave of nausea and tugged frantically at the window screen until she was able to slide it up. She stuck her head out the window expecting to be sick to her stomach, but the feeling passed. She took a couple deep breaths, focusing on the branches of the white pine tree where the crow had been sitting. Looking over her shoulder into the bedroom, she saw that Becky's bed was already empty. She could smell coffee brewing downstairs. Her head still hurt, and she realized that it was the hangover, not the crow. She promised herself that she would never, *never* drink that much again.

She tried to calm herself. There were so many things on her mind, and a plan was required to rank them by priority. First, she would have to call the hospital and check on Alice. Poor Alice! Cordelia closed her eyes and prayed that she had survived the night. Then she would call home and tell her mother where she was. Finally, she would have to figure out where to live, since her father had basically kicked her out of the house last night. Another wave of nausea gripped her. She took a few more deep breaths of the fine spring air. When the feeling passed, she pulled her head back into the room and shut the screen.

She wanted to brush her hair. Where was her hairbrush? When she arrived at Becky's last night, she was carrying her backpack with her hairbrush inside it. She saw her backpack on the floor by her bed, but she couldn't find her hairbrush in it. True, she didn't really need it right this minute, but it troubled her to think that she had misplaced another thing. She was always losing things: keys, make-up, books, pens, papers. Once she left her cello in the school music room and forgot where she left it. *(How do you lose a cello?* Becky asked.) Losing things always made her life more complicated. It seemed to her that she was always losing things and always messing everything up. She got dressed and went downstairs to Becky's kitchen.

"You're up early," Cordelia said, trying to appear composed.

"Crew," said Becky, standing at the refrigerator. "Saturday practice." Her back was turned, and on the back of her T-shirt was written: *Don't bug me. I have to row today.* She abruptly pivoted to face Cordelia, holding out a large glass of orange juice.

How could anyone move that quickly without spilling a drop of juice? Her restless energy only made Cordelia feel weaker and more lethargic.

"Here. Drink this."

"I don't know if I can," said Cordelia, sinking into a chair at the kitchen table. Even in the cloud of her hangover, she felt comforted by her friend's voice. Becky always complained that her voice was too deep and throaty, like a man's voice, but Cordelia found the fullness of it pleasing.

"Drink," said Becky. "You're dehydrated, and your blood sugar is probably low. Besides, you look like hell. Drink!"

Cordelia drank some of the orange juice. She closed her eyes and hoped that the juice would make her head stop hurting.

Becky opened a telephone book and laid it on the table. "She probably went to Albany Med. Here's the hospital number."

Cordelia reached for the phone on the wall but hesitated to dial.

"They're not going to give me any information, you know. I'm not family or anything."

"Give me that phone." Becky took the phone and dialed the number. "Hello," she said, making her voice high-pitched and plaintive. "I'm just trying to get some information about my sister, Alice Weber. She was taken to your hospital last night."

The worst possibilities crossed Cordelia's mind, and she reassured herself that she had done everything she could do.

"They're transferring me to the pediatric intensive care unit," Becky said to Cordelia in a conspiratorial whisper. "Oh, hi. Is this the pediatric intensive care unit?"

Becky repeated her request for information. Cordelia tapped her bare foot nervously on the kitchen floor.

"Oh, sure, that would be great," said Becky. She put her hand over the phone and said to Cordelia, "They're getting her nurse." There was another long pause. "Yes, I'm Alice's sister. I'm just trying to find out how she's doing."

Cordelia sat motionless waiting for the verdict.

"Oh, that's great! Thank you so much!" said Becky. She put the phone back on the wall. "Alice is doing very well, according to her nurse. The doctors have already taken the breathing tube out, and she's awake in her bed. She's going to be just fine."

"Oh, good," said Cordelia. She let out a big breath.

"So, you can stop worrying about Alice. You saved her life. One day, that idiotic girl is going to kill herself, but apparently not today. Thanks to you." Becky turned back to a frying pan with eggs in it.

Cordelia pictured Alice lying lifeless on the couch last night, not even breathing. She tried to imagine her sitting up in bed at the hospital talking to the doctors and nurses, no doubt trying to get as much attention as she could possibly fetch. Alice's parents would surely be mad at her, but perhaps they would help her straighten out. Maybe her mother, who lived someplace in Massachusetts, would re-establish a connection with her daughter. Maybe this was all for the best.

Once she concluded that Alice would be all right, her thoughts went straight to her next problem. His words had been mercilessly plain last night: *Maybe you should look for someplace else to live!*

"Stop worrying about your father," Becky said, standing at the stove. "This will all blow over in a day or two."

Cordelia was pleased, although not surprised, that Becky knew what she was thinking. Since the two of them were joined in that symbiotic relationship of adolescent girls called "best friends," they often knew each other's thoughts and finished each other's sentences.

"Of course, I'm worried," said Cordelia. "He basically threw me out of the family last night."

"That will all settle down," said Becky. "He'll forget all about it."

Becky cooked and Cordelia contemplated her situation. She could stay at Becky's house for a while, but then what? She would be essentially homeless. She wondered about staying at a shelter for homeless people. Would she be safe there? But wait, she was being ridiculous. She wasn't really homeless. She was a privileged white girl, a college professor's kid, who was having a little spat with her father. There were people on the streets of Albany who were truly homeless, a fact that had always troubled her greatly. How could such a wealthy country fail to provide basic housing for its own people? Her little predicament was nothing compared to their suffering.

Still, she might not be able to go home, and that was a real problem. Would he let her come home or banish her forever? She challenged herself to think realistically about this question, without any melodrama. He would probably let her come back home, she concluded. But this brought her no peace of mind. Why not? she asked herself. Because in either case, exiled or not, she couldn't shake the feeling that she was losing her father. She fought back tears. Her nausea was subsiding, but she felt the nervous sensation in her abdomen that she had dubbed *belly worms* as a child. (Secretly, she still used the term when appropriate.) She was losing her father, and she didn't understand why, nor could she seem to do anything about it. Clearly, he was dissolving the family contract; he no longer wanted to be her father.

"Here, you'll need this, too." Becky put a cup of coffee in front of her. "Oh, wait." She handed her a carton of milk and a sugar bowl. "Since you drink coffee like a ten-year-old child, here's your milk and sugar."

Cordelia sweetened her coffee and took a sip. "I need to call my mom and tell her where I am."

"No rush with that. She already knows you're here."

"But how?"

"She called here and talked to my mom. At six o'clock this morning."

"Jesus. She must have been worried sick."

"Your Mom will be fine. Everything will be fine, Cordelia. Your mom said they want you to come home later and help make dinner for tonight."

"Really?"

"Yes, really. Your father's not going to reject you. You're the nicest, most kind-hearted person I've ever met in my life. You told me that everyone else left Alice's house last night, right? So, they all left her for dead, except for you. I'm sure that even your father knows that you're a good kid."

"You're silly. I just did what anybody would have done."

"Okay, I'm silly. You're really not a nice person at all." Becky put a plate of scrambled eggs and toast in front of her. "Here. Eat this, you miserable, selfish bitch."

"I can't eat."

"Eat! Your body needs good nutrition to compensate for your debauchery last night."

Cordelia stabbed at the eggs with her fork and made herself eat. Becky talked as she wolfed down her breakfast, and Cordelia answered with a few words here and there, but her mind was elsewhere. She kept thinking about her father. Sure, he would let her come back home, but nothing could ever be the same after what he said. She tried to imagine how she might resolve the conflict with him, but the more she thought, the worse things seemed. Nothing would ever be the same.

"I have to leave for crew," said Becky.

"Okay," said Cordelia, surprised to see that Becky's plate was already empty. "I have to go to my babysitting job soon anyway. See you later."

"Take your time finishing breakfast. And stop worrying about your father. This will all settle down." Becky patted her on the shoulder as she stood up to leave.

"Sure," said Cordelia. "No problem." She marveled at Becky's positive attitude about things, especially since her parents were divorced and her mother barely made enough money to maintain the tiny house they lived in.

Becky folded a yellow bandana and tied it around her head. As she went out the back door, Cordelia happened to glance at the kitchen counter. There was her hairbrush, sitting next to the toaster. She must have left it there when she and Becky were talking late last night. If only she could stop losing things and stop messing up her life, especially her family life. How did things get so bad with her father anyway? It never used to be like this. It was only for the past year or two that he had become so mean and critical. And when she was very young, he was a terrific dad.

She remembered when her father used to take her to fly kites on Saturday mornings. This was long before he turned into a raving lunatic. The kite flying happened when she was little and he was actually fun to be with. They would go to the town park, just the two of them. First, they went alone because her little brother, Gabe, hadn't even been born yet. And then, for a while, her brother was too little to join the outings, so she still had her father all to herself.

On one of those Saturdays, they lost a kite. It was a big red kite, bright red against a bright blue sky, as she remembered it. The wind was perfect, and the kite went up in the air so easily. They didn't have to run back and forth in the park with it, holding the string and trying to get it to take flight. They just held the kite up, and the wind took it. In a few seconds, it was airborne and they were standing together, watching it hover effortlessly in the sky. Her father let her hold the spool of string, although he had a hand on it, too, as she was only five or six years old at the time. For a minute, he bent down to tie his shoe, and she proudly held the spool all by herself. Suddenly, she felt the tension on the line relax.

"Daddy! Daddy! The string broke!" Horrified, she watched the kite drifting away from the town park, crossing the road, and heading toward the housetops. "The kite's flying away!"

He tried to comfort her, but she was crying and inconsolable.

"But Daddy! We have to get the kite back! It'll bump into the houses and get hurt!"

He smiled and said he had a great idea. "Let's get in the car and chase it!"

And so they did. They drove around the streets of the neighborhood looking for the kite, although they quickly lost sight of it. He told her to keep her eyes open (so she opened them extra wide), and they slowly cruised the little back streets of their town. They rode around one street after another, with no kite coming into view. He told her to watch the sky, check in the trees, and look for a kite all tangled up in a power lines. She looked and she looked, but she saw no kite.

"Daddy, we're not going to find it, are we?"

"Well, you never know. Let's keep looking."

He kept driving past houses on the streets, turning left, turning right, but she saw nothing that looked the least bit like a bright red kite. At some point, in her child's mind, she sensed that something was wrong with him. He began to look serious and unhappy.

"Daddy, it's okay. Let's go home. We can buy another kite, right?"

He kept on driving around the neighborhood. He didn't seem to hear her.

"Daddy, it's okay. I don't want to fly a kite any more today."

He drove and drove, and after a while, he didn't even seem to be looking for the kite. He was just driving around the neighborhood, staring straight ahead in silence. When he finally gave up the search and headed home, she felt a sense of relief. She wanted to go home and see her mom. When she and her father got back in the house, she offered him a chocolate chip cookie to make him feel better. He looked so sad and lonely.

5

Not the End of
the World

Dan was starting to feel calmer, sitting quietly in his office and watching the sun climb in the East. The office was small, but it had a high ceiling, and the walls were buttressed with floor-to-ceiling bookshelves. It helped to sit in his little office and look at the books surrounding him on his shelves. The books were like old friends who never disappointed him. In the pages of his favorite books, the great writers had faced the same struggles he faced, or so he liked to think. They had suffered, surely, but they had taken the suffering and the challenges of this life and converted it all to the spoken word, and then converted the words into symbols that could be printed on a beautiful, tranquil page of white paper. In the hands of these authors, life was not a chaotic tumult of unpredictable events, but a story with a beginning, a middle, and an end. And the best of the stories had a meaning, a message that made this life more bearable.

He sat at his desk reading some of his favorite poetry until his phone rang. It was his wife. Abby had spoken with Cordelia, who had called from her friend Becky's house. Good! She was safe. Abby went on to tell him that Cordelia had saved a girl's life. The girl had passed out after drinking too much at a party last night. The other kids paid no attention to her, but Cordelia called for an ambulance, and the paramedics arrived just in time because the girl stopped breathing moments after they walked into the house. Abby was so proud of Cordelia!

Dan put the phone down. He could barely control himself. He stood up from his desk and began to pace back and forth in his little office. His wife could only see the good side of their daughter, the kind, compassionate side. True, she had done a good deed last night, but Abby was missing the other part of the story. Cordelia had been at yet another party. How could Abby not realize what this meant? Cordelia was drinking again, no doubt about it. The other girl had gotten dangerously drunk, and no doubt the other kids were drunk as well, including his Cordelia.

Something terrible was bound to happen. All the warning signs were there. She wasn't paying as much attention to her studies any more. She was cutting classes, albeit only a few times. Her grades were dropping—not much, but why should he ignore the early signs of trouble and wait until things get really terrible? Better to catch the problem early. And then there was the drinking. If you put the facts together, anyone should be able to see that this was a disaster waiting to happen. His wife couldn't see it coming, but he had been living with this awful foreboding for the past year or so.

He sat down at his desk and tried to calm himself. He heard the words his mother used to say when he was hurt or frightened as a child: *That's okay, Danny boy. It's not the end of the world.* He told himself to calm down. Cordelia was safe at Becky's house. All right, then. *It's not the end of the world.* He could almost picture his mother saying this, sitting in the old kitchen in Detroit. He could remember the feeling of calm that came with the words. No matter what he was worried about, his mother could always settle his fears and make him feel safe again. *It's not the end of the world.*

But then his mother left, and it was the end of the world. So, what right did she have to come into his memory now with such calming words? He picked up the nearest thing, a clear plastic box of paper clips, and threw it against the door of his office. The box split open, and the paper clips scattered on the floor. He restrained an urge to punch the door, instead bending down to pick up the paper clips. Stupid, useless memories. At first glance, they always look like pleasant little souvenirs from a trip, but they quickly turn ugly if you look at them carefully.

His birthday would be coming in a few weeks, and he always thought of his mother on his birthday. And every year, when the phone rang on that day, he had the thought—it couldn't really be called an expectation any more—that it could be her. Not that it *would* be, but that it *could* be. Not that he was disappointed, because his rational mind told him that too many years had passed, but the thought was still there. He had never really stopped thinking that he would hear from her once more before she died.

He glanced up at his bookshelves. A couple of thank-you notes sat on a shelf in front of his books.

Dear Dr. Wunsch,
Thanks for letting me hand in my work late this se-
mester. And I really appreciate that you visited me in

the hospital. What other professor does that??? You're
the best.

Tony

Dear Dr. Wunsch,
Thanks for being such a great teacher. You really
made English Lit my favorite subject.

Laura

On another shelf was a colorful child's drawing placed in a wooden frame, leaning against some of his poetry books. A little girl with bright orange hair was standing next to a tall man with brown hair and glasses. The two of them were holding hands and smiling beneath a circle of yellow sun.

To Daddy. From Cordelia. 8 years old.

Somewhere beneath the surface of the impossible teenager, there was still a sweet kid. He took off his glasses, picked up a tissue, and blew his nose. He told himself to stop getting so maudlin. But he kept seeing her as that sweet, red-headed little girl with freckles. Neighbors said she looked like Abby because they both had red hair, but Dan always saw more of a likeness to his mother, Cordelia's grandmother. He thought of a photograph he kept on the mantle at home, a picture of his mother as a little girl. In recent years, he would sometimes see his teenage daughter out of the corner of his eye and feel startled, as if he were seeing his mother as a young woman.

Would Cordelia lose her freckles as she grew older? He hoped not. He himself had been blessed with an ample endowment of freckles as a boy, but they were fading out with age. It was the only physical feature he shared with his mother, and it would give him great pleasure in childhood when people mentioned it. *You got your freckles from your mother, Danny.* He hoped that Cordelia would never lose her freckles. Well, freckles or no freckles, she was safe at Becky's house. She was still at Becky's house, and then she would go to her babysitting job. And she was certainly safe when she was babysitting in the neighborhood. *It's not the end of the world.*

And she had done a good thing last night, a heroic thing. She had saved another kid's life. Maybe they should take her out to dinner and let her know how much they appreciate her. Maybe she would get some kind of recognition at school for good citizenship. He decided to stop on the way home and buy her a card to congratulate her.

But no! One doesn't congratulate a seventeen-year-old girl for going to another party! God only knows what went on at that party. And how much did Cordelia drink before she called an ambulance for her drunken friend? What kind of dangerous situation was she in last night? No doubt there were boys at the party, too, and how well did she know those boys? Was she safe with them? What else might have happened last night? She was definitely heading for trouble. And whenever he tried to warn her about this, she just reacted with anger and defiance. Not a speck of gratitude. He thought of a quote from Shakespeare's *King Lear. How sharper than a serpent's tooth it is to have a thankless child!*

Still, he reasoned, she had done a good deed last night. She had done what none of the other kids would do, and it made him proud to think of this. She must have had a tough time deciding whether or not to call that ambulance, and she had made the right decision. And that other girl was alive today because of Cordelia's efforts. He tried to stay focused on the positive.

And he had to admit to himself that he wasn't making things any better with his temper. God knows, she provoked him again and again, but he shouldn't have said what he said last night. In his own defense, though, he only told her to go live elsewhere after she said that she was sick and tired of coming home. Still, he should never have said it. But why would she take him so literally? Why couldn't she see that he was only trying to protect her and keep her safe? Well, he said what he said, and it was too late to take it back. He would definitely tell her that he was proud of her for what she did last night, even though it had happened at a party. She would be all right, he told himself. *It's not the end of the world.*

6

A Slippery floor

Even before the first guests arrived on that hot summer evening in 1967, seventeen-year-old Danny Wunsch watched his mother uncork a bottle of wine and pour herself a glass. She stood at the kitchen sink, looking out the window at her flower garden in the backyard. She was quiet, too quiet, and he knew what that meant. She was nervous about hosting the neighborhood gathering. It was only a casual meet-and-greet for the new neighbors who had just moved in, but Danny's parents didn't usually host social gatherings. Some of the other neighbors had come to the door last week to ask his mother to do it, citing her lively personality and her easy social graces as reasons to make her the hostess. She had cheerfully agreed, but now she was obviously uncomfortable about it. As she drank the first glass, Danny saw her begin to smile and relax a bit. She asked him to help her finish making a salad, which he did, watching her the whole time. If only she had stopped there—but she rarely stopped after a single glass.

Danny's thirteen-year-old sister Sarah had been helping in the kitchen, too, but now his mother sent Sarah upstairs to finish her homework. When his mother came back downstairs, Danny's Uncle Jack wandered into the kitchen and sat down at the table with them.

"Hey, Kate, pour me a little wine, will you?"

Danny wished his uncle had not said that, because now his mother would also pour herself a second glass. Uncle Jack sipped his wine and looked nervously over at the first few guests who were assembling in the small adjoining living room. He always looked at people with quick, furtive glances, as if he had been charged with a clandestine mission of surveillance.

"You invited a lot of people, Kate." His eyes darted left and right. Danny felt sorry for his Uncle Jack. He was a nice-looking man with a thick head of red hair like Danny's mother had, but the suspicious eyes made him look peculiar. And whenever Uncle Jack drank alcohol, he smelled like it. The alcohol seemed to escape from every pore of his body and permeate the air around him, whereas Danny's mother never smelled like that when she drank.

With the second glass, more guests began to arrive, and Danny's mother became the perfect hostess. In fact, the second glass seemed the ideal counterweight for the nervousness she had shown before the gathering. Now she was herself again, friendly, talkative, and charismatic. Gracefully moving between kitchen and living room, she walked with a proud, erect posture that always suggested to him a touch of royal lineage. She was obviously trying to make everyone feel welcome, and she was apparently succeeding. Everyone vied for a little time to visit with her. This was always the case with his mother. People were always drawn to her.

"I can't believe you're forty, Kate Wunsch," said one of the women. "I should look so good at forty."

"Kate, you make it look so effortless to host a neighborhood party," said another. "I'd be a nervous wreck if I had to do it."

Occasionally, one of the men would stop to visit with his mother. There would often be a wife close by, smiling broadly but watching the husband carefully.

Danny watched as his Uncle Jack moved surreptitiously from room to room, like a spy monitoring the guests for the slightest signs of treachery. He slinked back into the kitchen for another glass of wine, and there he encountered Danny's mother, who held out her glass for a refill. Danny liked his Uncle Jack, even though he was a bit strange, but now he wished that Uncle Jack would stop pouring wine and go back home.

At some point, Danny lost track of how much wine his mother had consumed, but he observed that it was enough to raise the volume of her voice, enough to inflate her cordiality beyond the limits of socially acceptable behavior. She was starting to be too friendly, too familiar with people. She was standing by the stove, chatting in the kitchen with the new neighbors, who were Italian-Americans, and she made a joke about how she should have made a big pot of spaghetti for them. They all laughed, but Danny prayed that she would not say something insulting. She would never do so intentionally, but once the alcohol took over, she was quite capable of saying things that might sound insensitive or inappropriate. He never knew what to expect.

"I'm Irish-American, and I can tell you that we didn't have it easy in this country," she said to the Italian-American neighbors. "My father had to work two jobs just to make ends meet, and lots of people didn't want to hire the Irish."

The new neighbors said something in a sympathetic vein, but Danny could see that his mother's face suddenly lost all its sparkle and charm. Her eyes became dull, and her gaze drifted downward. "My father died young. I was just a girl."

There was an awkward silence until Danny's father came to her rescue. "I think you'll really like the neighborhood here. It's been very good for our kids. It's a nice neighborhood, and we can get into the heart of downtown Detroit in minutes."

Danny realized that although his father had been socializing in the adjacent living room, he had been monitoring his wife's conversation in the kitchen all the while, just in case there was the need for an urgent intervention.

"My son Danny here has his driver's license, but anything he needs is within walking distance."

His father engaged the new folks in conversation, and his mother recovered her good spirits rather quickly. Everything was going along smoothly now, although Danny noticed that his mother poured herself yet another glassful.

A discussion about the war in Vietnam had started in the living room. His father looked concerned about a possible disturbance, and he drifted back in that direction, hovering in the doorway between the living room and the kitchen. Danny could hear a couple of the men arguing, one insisting that we had to stop the Communists, the other contending that we had no business getting into a war on the other side of the Earth.

"The French military was defeated by the Communists at Dien Bien Phu in 1954," said the anti-war neighbor. "Why can't we learn from history? Why should we go over there and get involved in a war that we can't win?"

"Well, any patriotic American ought to know that we have to go over there and stop the Communists," said the other man. "We've already got them sitting in Cuba, just a stone's throw from Florida."

The discussion was getting heated, and Danny's father was characteristically playing the role of the peace-maker. Both men had a good point, he said, but perhaps President Johnson would find a way to strengthen the South Vietnamese army so our troops didn't have to bear the brunt of all the fighting. Neither man looked mollified by his attempt at diplomacy, and their voices continued to rise.

Meanwhile, Danny's mother was still talking—and still drinking—in the kitchen. A woman arrived with an infant in a stroller, and several of the other women knelt down to smile and coo at the baby. Danny's mother loved babies, so she tried to bend down and join the admiring party. Unfortunately, her balance was not quite equal to her maternal instinct, and she pitched over onto the floor.

"She's fine!" called his father, who had been shuttling back and forth between kitchen and living room, now hovering near his wife, now negotiating a truce in Vietnam. "She's all right!" He was at her side in an instant, and he started to help her up. Uncle Jack also appeared and took her other arm to help her into a chair. Then Uncle Jack looked nervously around at the guests and quickly left the kitchen. As Danny's father did his best to steady his wife and assuage her obvious embarrassment, he simultaneously offered a socially acceptable explanation for the incident.

"She must have slipped! There must be something slippery on the floor! Danny, grab a towel and dry the floor."

Danny stood motionless, watching his mother trying to recover her composure in the chair.

"Danny! Grab a towel!" His father's tone was unusually impatient and demanding.

Humiliated, Danny found a dish towel and bent down to rub it over that perfectly dry patch of kitchen floor that had received his mother's fall from grace. The linoleum tiles were now a monument to her frailty, and he covered them with the cloth in shame. He couldn't look up, feeling that all eyes were now on him, watching him with pity.

The get-together ended without further incident, as all the neighbors did their best to follow his father's lead and pretend that everything was fine. There was no further arguing about Vietnam or anything else. Everyone seemed to be complying with a secret contract binding them to put on a sociable face and exchange pleasantries. The new baby in the stroller was adorably cute, the hors d'oeuvres were delicious, and the local high school was really quite exceptional. After about half an hour of this banter, the neighbors all found excuses to make a graceful exit. (Uncle Jack had somehow disappeared from the house with no farewell at all.) Danny's parents cheerfully bid them all goodnight at the front door as they walked out into the hot, humid summer night.

7

The Three Fates

From that day on, Danny had to mop and dry the kitchen floor before anyone came over to visit. He had to mop the floor to clean up anything slippery on it (although there was never anything slippery to be cleaned), so his mother would not slip again (even though she had never slipped in the first place). Oddly enough, he never complained about it. He never thought to himself that this was the crazy charade of a family living with a shared delusion. In fact, whenever that kind of thought threatened to enter his mind, he mopped and dried all the more vigorously to convince himself that this preposterous myth of the slippery floor was actually a household reality demanding his immediate attention.

Amongst themselves, Danny and his family closed ranks around the myth. As long as it only involved his parents, his little sister, and him, he was fine with it. One day, though, he heard his mother talking on the phone to his Aunt Molly in Tucson, telling her how she had slipped on the floor. How embarrassing! she said to her sister on the phone. She had just slipped on something, and her feet went right out from under her! Danny felt a moment of anger at her. Why did she have to talk about it to people who hadn't even been there? Why did she have to explain it at all, when the other person wouldn't ever have to know about it? Did she think that everyone in the United States knew? Did she think that the whole world needed an explanation from her?

The family stuck with their story, but the situation outside the house was more difficult. His immediate family went along with the myth, but he suspected that the entire neighborhood knew otherwise. He always felt uncomfortable seeing the neighbors out on the street after the incident. They must know that his mother had just fallen down drunk in the middle of a week-night social gathering, right in front of adults and children alike. They had seen his father's bit of improvised theatre, and they undoubtedly saw it for what it was: a sad farce to cover up for his alcoholic wife. Danny was sure that behind the closed doors of all those neighbors' homes, they certainly were not talking about a slippery floor.

As Danny went back and forth between home and neighborhood, there lived in his thoughts these two versions of what had happened that evening. So how did he reconcile these two diametrically opposed realities? He did not. He didn't even try. The two stories co-existed in his mind, sitting stubbornly side by side, neither one willing to concede jurisdiction to the other. When he was home, he was immersed in one story; when he was out in the community, he was confronted with the other.

Beyond the immediate neighborhood, the extended family seemed to take starkly different views, depending upon which side of the family one turned to. On his mother's side, the Irish Catholic side, there were his aunt and uncle in Tucson, Aunt Molly being his mother's sister. They seemed to believe the slippery floor version. Actually, Danny had no way to know for certain what they believed, as they were so far out west and he rarely saw them in person. Nonetheless, when he heard his mother talking to them on the phone, he got the impression that they were not challenging her story. It was comforting to think that they believed his mother. It left him feeling that someone was supportive of her honor and reputation. And there was Uncle Jack, his mother's brother, who lived nearby in Detroit. He was actually in the house when it happened. Oddly enough, he also acted as if the story were true, even though he knew quite well what had happened.

Unfortunately, it was not so easy to find a trusting believer on his father's side, the Jewish side. The Sunday morning after the slippery floor episode, he went with his parents and his little sister to the usual weekly brunch gathering at his grandmother's house. His grandmother and her two sisters had set a long dining room table with the weekly ritual of favorite Jewish foods: bagels, lox, smoked whitefish, and various salads and side dishes. Danny and his family took their seats, as they did every week, surrounded by the bustling hospitality of the three sisters, all widowed. On the walls of the dining room, there were black-and-white photos of various Eastern European Jewish relatives who had fled Europe to come to America, as well as photos of younger relatives who had left Detroit to live elsewhere.

Once the meal began, it took less than half an hour for his mother to start telling the dreaded story again. Why did she have to keep talking about it? If only his mother would just eat and make the usual idle conversation—but no, she had to tell the story. From the minute she started, Danny knew that this was the wrong audience for such a fantasy tale. He looked around the crowded table for signs of a reaction. His father was predictably cheerful, looking like a man whose wife was telling a story about winning a new automobile. Danny's sister Sarah was spreading cream cheese on a bagel, looking up now and then to smile at her mother. He studied the faces of the three old women, who were known to be quite free with their opinions. He hoped they would all behave themselves.

Things went along well enough at first. His grandmother and great-aunts listened attentively to his mother and tried to offer smiles of sympathy for her mishap. Danny could see, though, that they were struggling to mask their concerns. He could see the worrying in their eyes. He hoped that they wouldn't say anything that would embarrass his mother. Maybe they would just listen and refrain from commentary.

He worried most about Tanta Zlata—Aunt Zlata—the firebrand of the three old women, the unpredictable hothead of the family. Physically, she was built short and stout, like a cannon, and she was never known to be shy about expressing herself. When she was annoyed or offended by the behavior of other people, she never hesitated to draw upon her extensive Yiddish repertoire of curses, insults, and rude suggestions. Danny knew quite well the stories of her battles with the world.

To the shopkeeper who refused to refund her money for a broken vacuum cleaner, she had said: *A curse upon your father's father!*

To the well-intentioned doctor who scolded her for not taking better care of her health: *You should lose all your teeth except one—so you can get a toothache!*

To the funeral director who tried to sell her the most expensive headstone to lay upon her late husband's grave: *You should grow like an onion, with your head in the ground!*

And to the hapless evangelist who knocked at her door and tried to convert her to Christianity: *Go bang your head against a wall!* The evangelist could not have understood her Yiddish, of course, but everyone understood her tone of voice, her fiery eyes, and the index finger she pointed at them for emphasis, like she was discharging a bolt of lightning from her fingertip.

Danny thought of the three old women, his grandmother and her two sisters, as the three fates of Greek mythology. One had the job of spinning the thread of life, the second measured the thread to determine how long a person would live, and the third cut the thread. It was Zlata, the fearsome archivist of ancient Yiddish curses, who would cut the thread and terminate one's life with a sharp word and a lethal glare from her piercing eyes. Danny's father often joked that Zlata's husband had died from one of her curses.

As Danny's mother concluded her story about the lovely new Italian-American family and that silly little spot of slippery stuff on her kitchen floor, Zlata sat motionless with a piece of smoked whitefish speared on the end of her fork. Her face became stern and cynical; she looked annoyed that anyone would think her stupid enough to buy such a poorly constructed fabrication.

Danny looked over at his mother, who was just finishing her story. His grandmother and great-aunts listened to the end of it and sat in silence. This itself was a rare event, and he was momentarily comforted by their restraint. They made eyes at each other—big, round, conspiratorial eyes—but kept their silence until his mother left the room to use the bathroom. Then Zlata could no longer hold her tongue. She exploded in Yiddish, and soon the whole room was an impossible cacophony of English and Yiddish. Everyone talked at once. Danny didn't speak Yiddish, but he could understand a fair handful of words and phrases. *Shondeh.* The old women kept saying that it was a *shondeh.* A shame, a shameful thing, a disgrace. Obviously, they didn't buy the slippery floor story at all. They knew what had happened. They were saying that his mother's behavior was shameful. His sister Sarah smiled at him and rolled her eyes at the ceiling.

His mother returned from the bathroom and quietly took her seat at the table, but by that time the heated conversation had picked up too much momentum to be brought to a halt. The old women switched to using exclusively Yiddish now, directing their comments to Danny's father, who replied in their language. He appeared to be arguing back in defense of his wife. The women were yelling—this could no longer qualify as talking—about a doctor. Danny surmised that they were telling his father to take her to a doctor. In the middle of a particularly vehement tirade by Tanta Zlata, Danny's grandmother got up from the dining room table and went into the kitchen. She returned with more bagels and prepared one of them with cream cheese and lox. She put it on Danny's plate and laid her hand on his shoulder.

"Eat, *shain kind*," she said softly in his ear. *Eat, pretty child.* Everyone else kept trying to yell over all the others and be heard, and it was becoming harder to pick one voice out of the din and understand anything.

His mother was sitting quietly in her chair, but now she stood up without saying anything and left the table again. Danny watched her go out the front door. Through the window, he saw his mother walk to their car parked in the driveway and get into her seat on the passenger side. The day looked bright, sunny, and silent on the other side of the window pane. In the dining room, the deafening conversation continued, as if nothing had happened.

"She's fine!" his father shouted over the other voices, switching back to English and glancing at Danny. "She's just tired!"

Danny looked at Tanta Zlata, who was red in the face from yelling. He looked at the other two women, who looked very sad and sorry. Then he looked out the window again at his mother, who was sitting perfectly still, all by herself in the car parked in the driveway, looking straight ahead at no one.

8

Safe and Sound

Dan left his office at mid-morning, after doing some preparation for his classes. Driving home, he was eager to see Cordelia again. No, he was more than eager; he desperately needed to see her in order to reassure himself that she was safe and sound. Abby had tried to reassure him on the phone, but he needed to see her with his own eyes. Seeing is believing, he told himself. Maybe Cordelia hadn't told her mother everything about last night. God knows what might have happened before she called the ambulance for that other girl.

His thoughts took a more ominous turn. What if Cordelia ran away? What if she just changed her mind after talking to her mother, and she just decided to run away? The thought—the fear—was unbearable. He turned down a side street that was out of his way, just to drive by the house where she was babysitting. Maybe he could get a glimpse of her in the yard with the kids. He arrived at the house and pulled his car over to the curb, at a point from which he could see a portion of the back yard. There was no one in the yard, and no one came out of the house. She must be in the basement with the kids. She was just indoors with the kids, safe and sound. He sat for a minute watching the yard, just in case. The yards were getting greener these days, and the flowers were coming up. A few brightly colored balls and tricycles were scattered about.

He continued on his way home, struggling to turn his thoughts toward a more positive direction. Cordelia was safe, and their relationship was fine. The babysitting job was proof of their relationship, was it not? After all, he was the one who steered her into working with kids last year, and she had listened to his advice. He comforted himself by reminiscing about it. He thought of the day when a neighbor saw him mowing his lawn last summer and stopped to ask if Cordelia might be available to watch her little boy. He promised he would ask her, and then he convinced his reluctant daughter to try it. The little boy's mother said she was wonderful with her child, which was no surprise to Dan. The woman was so pleased with Cordelia that she spread the word to her friends. That occasional job quickly led to others, including a regular arrangement to care for a handful of kids between the ages of three and six while their mothers went to a Saturday morning yoga class and then out for coffee. The kids were dropped off at one of the homes, the home Dan had just driven by, where Cordelia had set up a play area in a finished basement.

The mothers often told Dan how pleased they were with Cordelia. Granted, she was a bit forgetful about her own possessions, but they were more than happy to make adjustments for this. They would take her car keys upon her arrival and put them in a little cup on the kitchen table, so she couldn't misplace them. And at the end of her time with the kids, they would run a little check list with her. Did she have everything she came with? Had she left anything in the basement? Did she bring a jacket? They were more than happy to do this, since she was so sweet with the little ones, who all adored her.

And despite her absentmindedness about herself, she was so competent in dealing with the needs of the children. Once, the neighbor woman told Dan, a little boy fell and gashed his head on a table. Cordelia was able to stem the bleeding, settle the other kids, call the boy's parents, and call the pediatrician, and she did it all with a characteristic composure that helped everyone else remain calm. The parents wouldn't think of trusting anyone else to care for their children now. Cordelia was a natural, they all told Dan. They paid her much more than the minimal amount she requested, and they jokingly referred to that finished basement as the Cordelia Center. Other parents in the neighborhood were asking how to get their kids "accepted to the program." Thinking about this, Dan felt proud to be her father.

As he drove into his own driveway, he concluded that she was safe, and there wasn't much that could go wrong while she was watching a handful of kids at someone's house. Still, one never knows in this crazy world. Didn't he just read about a terrible home invasion out West someplace? But that kind of thing never happened in their neighborhood, he reassured himself. It was the quietest, safest, dullest suburb in America, which is exactly why he chose it for his family. His son Gabriel had a basketball practice in the morning, but that should be ending soon, and there hadn't been any serious injuries this season. Or in any season, actually. Abby had no specific plans to drive anywhere today after picking up Gabe at his practice, so everyone should be home, safe and sound, by the middle of the afternoon.

This was the reckoning process he conducted every weekday on his way home from work. If there were activities on a weekend day, like today, then the same tally was required. He always felt a little uneasy until everyone was back home. One shouldn't expect bad things to happen, of course, but one would be foolish not to think that something bad could happen. The world wasn't a bad place overall, in Dan's eyes, but it was definitely an unpredictable place, a random universe where people were like billions of stars orbiting in space, always at risk for colliding with a dangerously destructive asteroid. And sometimes a star could just burn out and disappear from sight, with no cosmological explanation given.

When he got home, Abby asked him if he was all right, and he told her that he was fine. Gabe was excited because he was doing so well in his basketball practices. The coach told him he was the best ninth grader he had seen in a long while. Dan promised his son that he would be at the game next week.

"But please don't put your feet on the sofa with your shoes on, Gabe."

The boy moved his feet off the couch and maneuvered his lanky frame into an upright sitting position with his feet on the floor. "Oh, sorry, Dad."

"No big deal," said Dan.

After lunch, he sat in the family room, reading and waiting for Cordelia to return. He waited till about two-thirty. She finally called and told her mother that one of the parents had asked her to stay a bit longer and help her six-year-old with his reading. Cordelia had agreed, of course.

Dan fretted. He walked outside to the backyard and paced for a few minutes, and then returned to the family room. He sat back down in his chair, his favorite chair, a large, red wingback. His chair was the place where he felt comfortable and safe, his favorite spot in the entire house.

While he waited for Cordelia to come home, he picked up the New York Times and scanned the newspaper crossword puzzle. The clue: Expert. A five-letter word. He sat blankly looking at the page, glancing at the surrounding letters that he had already filled in. *Maven!* It fit perfectly. The old Yiddish word for expert. He penciled the word into the little squares on the page. It made him sad, though, to think about the demise of the Yiddish language, the language of his grandparents, his great-aunts and great-uncles. No one spoke it any more. A whole language lost, indeed a whole culture lost.

He was startled when Cordelia finally appeared in the family room. He thought he would feel a sense of relief when she finally came home that afternoon, but when she walked in, he just felt angry again. What was she doing at another party last night? And how could she put him through hell this morning by staying out all night without calling home to tell them where she was? He struggled to keep all his complaints to himself. He was determined to relax and spend some time with his daughter.

He did his best to give her a friendly greeting. Hi, Cordelia. Hi, Dad. He told her that he was very proud of her for saving that girl's life last night. It was a noble thing she had done. But his words sounded stilted and perfunctory, he thought, and her tepid response to his praise made it obvious that she wasn't buying it. There was an awkward silence. He told himself that he should talk to her about their argument last night. He should tell her he didn't really mean to throw her out of the house. However, he was apprehensive about bringing up the subject. He had the sense that she was avoiding the topic, too. Instead, they talked for a few minutes about Alice, the girl in the hospital. Then he made a comment—one little comment—suggesting that perhaps

Cordelia should use better judgment about choosing which parties to go to.

And that was that. She stormed up the stairs and slammed the door to her room. Dan sat by himself in his chair. He heard his wife go quietly up the stairs, no doubt to comfort his daughter. He had the bad feeling that often plagued him after an argument with Cordelia, the feeling of being a monster. He had tried to make his comment in a casual manner, but she obviously heard the anger in his voice. He had spoiled things again. Somehow, every time he tried to convey his concerns to her, he messed everything up. And he was always left sitting by himself, feeling like the villain of the story. His daughter didn't understand his worries. His wife was always telling him to stop worrying. How was that any help? Why didn't Abby see the problems and help him guide their daughter away from danger? No doubt they were upstairs in Cordelia's bedroom commiserating about how awful it was to live with him. And all he wanted was to see his daughter safe and sound.

9

Only Mr. T

To Cordelia, the situation was obvious. If your own father kicks you out of his life—barely speaking with you, obviously trying to avoid being in the same room with you—he is essentially banishing you from the family, and you have no home. It doesn't matter that you still eat and sleep in the same house where you have always eaten and slept; you no longer have a true home base, a safe haven in this world. And once you leave that house for college, the gap between you and your father will only get wider.

Cordelia tried to explain all this to other people, but they never quite seemed to understand. She started with her mother, of course. Shouldn't one's own mother get it? *But Cordelia, he's not really rejecting you, honey. He hasn't literally thrown you out of the house, you know.* How could her mother sit there and deny what was happening right in front of her eyes? How could anyone be so completely out of touch with reality? And how could her mother be so stupid? He didn't *literally* have to throw her out on the street to reject her. Cordelia could feel the rejection as a physical force, an energy field around her father. Why couldn't her mother feel it? Never mind that Cordelia was still physically in that house; she was excluded, rejected, abandoned, right there in that house. Her father seemed perfectly happy to sit in the family room and chat for hours with her little brother, but not with her. It was all so painfully obvious, and her mother saw nothing, absolutely nothing.

She turned to Becky, where things were better, for sure, but still a bit disappointing. Becky was sympathetic to a point, but then she would resort to her trademark tough-girl, unsentimental attitude. *Parents aren't worth all this fretting, Cordelia. This will all settle down. He'll forget all about it.* Which was Becky's I-don't-care attitude toward her own father. *What a jerk! He makes millions of dollars selling skyscrapers down in Manhattan, while my mother squeaks by on a hairdresser's salary. He pays for my rowing, but that's just so he can brag if we win a regatta. Otherwise, he's useless. Not worth worrying about.*

Cordelia broached the subject with a couple of other friends at school, but they just looked at her awkwardly. She could see that they simply didn't know what to say, so she would change the subject to spare them any further distress. She would have talked to her ex-boyfriend, Logan, before he cheated on her, but he never would have understood, anyway. He would have assumed that his awesome male companionship should cure all problems. In desperation, she even tried to discuss her situation with Alice, as she had done at the party a week ago, just before Alice drank herself into a coma. Predictably, Alice appropriated the topic again and began a loud, shrill, melodramatic rant about her mother, who still lived in Western Massachusetts. *Do I actually have to die to get that bitch to care about me?* This happened in the middle of the hallway at school, and it drew a lot of attention from other kids in the area. Luckily, Becky happened to be walking by at that moment. She grabbed Cordelia by the arm and pulled her away, calling cheerfully to Alice over her shoulder. *We don't want to be late for class again!* And then to Cordelia in a low, scolding voice: *You already saved that idiot's life last week. Do you have to be her therapist, too?*

So, no one seemed to understand what Cordelia was going through. Nor did they seem to understand the sick, lonely feeling she had, no matter where she was, no matter whom she was with. She was always apprehensive now, always uneasy. Belly worms, chronic belly worms. Wherever she was, she always had the urge to leave and go someplace else, hoping that the next place would make her feel better. (She thought about drinking as an escape from the restlessness, but she reminded herself that alcohol only made her feel worse at Alice's party.) She felt unmoored, adrift without a place to anchor her sad little boat. It was like this even at Becky's house, much as she preferred to be there. She didn't know how to explain her unease, so she didn't even try. She kept hoping that someone would just *know*. Why couldn't someone just look at her and know how she felt? She could often read other people's moods. Why didn't it work both ways?

In short, Cordelia was in a state of crisis. And in this state, she wandered into the classroom of Mr. Tremblay, her history teacher, at the end of a long and dreary school day. She often went to visit him after classes, and she would offer to help him with little classroom chores like cleaning the blackboards or making photocopies of homework assignments. They would generally chat while they worked, and she always enjoyed their private talks after school. Today, she wasn't particularly enthusiastic about talking at all, but she hoped it might be a pleasant distraction to see him and help with chores.

They greeted each other, as usual. Hi, Cordelia. Hi, Mr. T. She offered him a big smile, even though she felt miserable. He had some papers that needed to be collated, so she took a seat at one of the empty student desks to help him. He sat at his big oak desk at the front of the room where he was planning his lessons.

"What's wrong, Cordelia?"

"Nothing," she said, without looking up at him. "I'm fine."

"Well, obviously there's something bothering you. But if you don't want to talk about it, that's your choice."

Cordelia was surprised—and relieved—that he noticed right away. (Why couldn't everyone else notice? Only Becky seemed to notice, and she couldn't deal with the whole business of a father rejecting his daughter.) She hesitated for a moment. She had talked to Mr. T about many things during past visits, and she had certainly mentioned the problems with her father. But she doubted that he would really understand her current dilemma. First of all, he was a teacher, not a high school kid. Second, he was older, although not that much older, being the youngest teacher in the school at twenty-four. Third, he was a man. What could he really understand about being a seventeen-year-old girl? Well, she was running out of places to turn. What could she lose by trying?

"I'm having a little problem with my father."

And that was the beginning of a new kind of conversation with Mr. T, a conversation she had never allowed herself to have with a teacher before. She surprised herself by telling him everything that had happened and how terrible she was feeling. And he surprised her by his responses, which were exactly what she needed to hear.

"That sounds awful, Cordelia."

Granted, he also tried to look at the situation from her father's point of view, but that was just Mr. T's tendency to be fair-minded.

"From his point of view, I suppose that he's just worried about his daughter. You know, worried that you're about to graduate high school and go out into the big world."

But in the end, he understood.

"Well, a father shouldn't be saying such things to his daughter. He certainly shouldn't be telling you to look elsewhere for a place to live."

Right.

"Even if he didn't mean it, words can really hurt."

Right again. Somebody was finally getting it right.

"And I'll have to admit, it sounds like he meant it."

Right! She told him more and more, the words pouring out of her in a mad jumble, so badly did she want someone to understand what she had been going through.

"So, your father has rejected you. And your mother doesn't see what's happening, so you can't feel close to her, either. And you're left feeling like maybe you don't belong anywhere. No place feels like home anymore."

He got it! And he understood when she told him how awful it felt to be in the room with her father, even when he tried to say the right things to her.

"Listen, Cordelia. You have good intuitions about people. I'd even say you have a gift of reading people correctly. If your intuition says he's rejecting you, I would trust your gut on that."

Intuition, yes. Trust your gut, yes. His words made her feel better. His trust in her made her feel better. Even the sympathetic look in his eyes made her feel better. Mr. T had large brown eyes that made her think of an animal's eyes—either a contented cow in the pasture or a deer. She thought of a fawn she had once encountered in the woods, noting that Mr. T had similarly large, brown, innocent eyes, and his ears stuck out a bit, like the fawn's. (Somehow, his ears did not in any way detract from his handsomeness, which many of the girls regularly discussed in the hallways.)

The conversation went on this way for about an hour, and then she left his classroom feeling better. In fact, she felt absolutely elated. The belly worms were gone. The restless feeling was gone. The terrible sense of isolation was gone. And she had a hopeful feeling about her future, which she hadn't felt since the big fight.

Prior to that conversation, she had been going to visit with Mr. T a couple times a week, but now she stopped by his office almost daily. He didn't seem to mind a bit, so she sat and chatted with him at the end of each school day. When there were chores to do, she cheerfully did them, and she was happy to be doing something so it didn't look like she was just a needy high school kid trying to monopolize the teacher's time. But even without any chores, he seemed quite happy to talk with her. In fact, he even disclosed a bit of his own family history during one of their chats.

"A tough-minded French-Canadian guy," he said, describing his own father. "We really didn't get along well at all during my teens."

"Sorry to hear that, Mr. T." She wasn't really feeling sorry at that moment, though. She was feeling pleased that he was willing to confide in her.

"Yeah, it was pretty awful for a while," he said. "But we did reconcile eventually, and now we have a terrific relationship. I hope you and your dad can work things out, too."

"That's kind of you to say, Mr. T, but I doubt it will happen," she said.

"Well, either way, you're going to be fine, Cordelia. You're a great kid, and you're going to be fine."

And she believed him. If he said it, then everything was going to be fine.

10

The World Walking Tour

Ever since the big fight, Cordelia spent a lot of time up in her bedroom, reading or talking on the phone. Sometimes, she thought about Mr. T and their recent conversations. She could hear his voice in her head—a mellow, resonant baritone voice—and his words always gave her some comfort. At other times, she could hear her parents' voices drifting up the stairway. Her mother always spoke in a high-pitched, chirping voice; every sentence ended with a rise in pitch, suggesting a question. *We'll have dinner now?* The words always came out tentatively, as if they were submitted to the world in the hope of its approval. Her father's voice sounded tightly controlled, with little variation in range or volume. The cadence was slow and deliberate, like the speech of a man who is announcing a small change in the way the bank calculates interest rates. When her father spoke, even a question sounded like a statement. *Should we cut back on expenses by eating out less often.* It wasn't really a question, and there was no discussion about it. Only on rare occasions, usually during an argument with her, did he speak with more passion. Otherwise, his voice was utterly controlled.

She often kept the door to her bedroom shut to keep out the voices downstairs. Even then, it was an uneasy truce between Cordelia and her father. Shortly after their fight, she had retrieved a small suitcase from the attic and brought it down to her bedroom. She loaded it with enough clothing to last her for few days, and then she slid it under her bed, in case of emergency. She reflected on how strange her life had become. How many kids did she know who kept a suitcase handy for an emergency exit? None, absolutely none. She lived in a family where the tenuous connection between father and daughter could be severed at any moment. Could one still define this as a family? Doesn't the word *family* imply a lifelong commitment to each other?

So, she spent a lot of time up in her bedroom, although she did come down for meals. Most evenings, she sat at the dinner table with her parents and her brother Gabe, and it seemed to her that she and her father were both making an effort to keep the conflict from escalating. He would ask his usual annoying questions about her homework—questions that he rarely asked Gabe, who was a mediocre student, at best—but he didn't press his point as aggressively as he used to do. She would occasionally give him a slightly sarcastic answer, but never anything sharp enough to trigger one of his outbursts. Her words conveyed just enough sass to make her position known and maintain her pride.

One evening, the exchange came dangerously close to unconstrained warfare. He made a remark implying that she was being a bit lazy, and she responded by suggesting that parents with limited information and impossible expectations would do well to withhold their comments. She could see him struggling not to explode. He sat silently glowering for the rest of the meal, and then he retired to his favorite chair in the family room where he would sit reading his magazines or writing his poetry. She had to go into the family room to retrieve a textbook she had left there, and she looked at him in his chair. He didn't look up— didn't seem to notice her at all—and she saw what she had seen many times: her father's suffering. On the surface, he looked angry, distant, and arrogant; but she saw an entirely different image of him, an image of a man suffering. She never knew why he suffered so, but she knew that he suffered. It was palpable. She could sense it at times, no matter what kind of facial camouflage he was wearing at the moment.

In fact, Cordelia could see suffering wherever it occurred. She saw it in a friend whose parents were going through a bitter divorce. She read it in the newspapers that her father left on the kitchen table. She saw it in her mother's face after her parents argued. Often her mother would talk to her at those times, and Cordelia would try to reassure her that things would be all right. *Dad's just feeling stressed about work, Mom*, she would say. *Dad just likes to have everything in its place.* Becky often teased Cordelia about being her mother's therapist, but Cordelia couldn't stop herself from responding to her mother's unhappiness.

Everywhere she looked, there was unhappiness and suffering. Sometimes it seemed that the whole world was suffering. One day, she and Becky were walking into school, and they passed a group of boys. She recognized one of them, a boy from the 11th grade who played on the basketball team. He was a very shy boy who had a thin vertical scar on his upper lip. Probably the result of surgery for a harelip, she thought. She suddenly felt upset. What if none of the girls wanted to kiss him because of that little scar? It was just a short, fine line on his upper lip, but so many high school girls were so vain and stupid. What if they all just shunned him? What if he suffered terribly from their rejection?

When she was about fifteen, it had occurred to her that somebody somewhere was suffering intensely *every single minute.* At any point in time, someone was starving, or someone was in pain from disease or injury, or someone was being cruelly, intentionally hurt by another human being. And that led her to the dilemma that had occupied a place in her mind ever since: How could she feel happy, knowing that another person was suffering intensely *at that very moment in time?* How was anyone supposed to enjoy her life and not think about that? Of course, there were times when she felt happy. There were plenty of times when she would be laughing with her friends and having great fun. But how was it morally right to be laughing and carefree when others were suffering so?

She sometimes dealt with the suffering by conjuring up a fantasy of the world as it ought to be. In this perfect model of human existence, there was no serious, threatening conflict between family members. Indeed, there was no major conflict between people on any level. Gone was the antagonism between countries, political parties, or ethnic groups. She could travel from country to country just as easily as one could walk from the bookstore to the pizza joint in the center of her little suburban village. Wherever she went, people would be friendly and welcoming, eager to show an American girl a generous offering of their food and customs. Whenever she heard about bad things happening in the world, she could always find some comfort by stepping into this ongoing dream of the world as it should be. When her father put down his newspaper one Sunday morning and related a story about a massacre in Algeria, she cringed and went up to her bedroom to find Algeria on her world globe. Then she embarked upon a leisurely stroll to meet the people of Algeria and see their country. When her father talked about a massive earthquake in Iran—why did he have to bring this up at dinner? —she found Iran on her globe and took a promenade to see the modern country and hear stories about ancient Persia.

Over time, these little journeys evolved into a World Walking Tour. Sometimes she imagined walking with Becky, sometimes (rarely) she walked with her family, and sometimes she walked alone. Why not walk alone? She would be safe anywhere in the world, and if she ever needed help, everyone would be more than happy to offer their assistance. It would be unthinkable for a man to attack a girl walking down the street in Algeria or Iran or anyplace else. She could never be caught in the cross fire between gangs or armies or political parties, since there would be no such violence between human beings.

In its final version, the World Walking Tour enabled her to dream about crossing boundaries of time as well as place. She would be able to meet famous people, past and present. She could sit with the Dalai Lama as he considered the plight of his people in Tibet. She could speak with Mother Teresa about tending to the poorest of the poor of India. She could walk arm in arm with Martin Luther King Jr. as he marched for freedom in the streets of Birmingham, Alabama.

On her favorite tours, she met with the Buddha as he sat meditating on the nature of suffering. She had recently borrowed a book about the Buddha, and as soon as she started reading about him, she realized that she had found a spiritual soul-mate. Finally, she had found someone who struggled with the same problem she had struggled with for years. The Buddha was so upset by the suffering of others that he left his father's luxurious palace to search for a way to understand it. He faced the same dilemma that had plagued her: How could he enjoy his privileged life in his father's palace, knowing that others were suffering? All of his meditating, all of his revelations, all of his teaching that would become the worldwide practice of Buddhism—it all started with this one problem.

Before learning about the Buddha, she never thought that her distress could be formulated as a legitimate existential struggle. She had always thought that she was just a bit odd, too sensitive, too easily upset, too fragile to gaze upon the human condition without going weak in the knees. How liberating to meet the Buddha! He saw it, too. He saw the suffering, he felt compassion for the ones who suffered, and he sought for a way to understand and transcend the suffering. Perhaps she could become an "enlightened one" and help others with their suffering. What was the term they mentioned in that first chapter of the book on Buddhism? A *bodhisattva*, one who seeks spiritual enlightenment, not just for herself, but also to end the suffering of others so that they, too, might become enlightened. Yes, perhaps someday she could become a bodhisattva. And then maybe she could help her father with his mysterious suffering.

11

A Trip to Tucson

In September of 1967, a few months after the slippery floor episode, Danny's mother announced that she was going to take a short trip by herself. She was going to visit her sister in Arizona. She had only been on a plane a couple times in her life, and she was obviously excited to make the trip. On the morning of her flight, Danny carried her handbag out to their car in the driveway and put it into the trunk. It was a bright, sunny day, and his mother came out of the house wearing a solid-color emerald green dress and a string of pearls around her neck. Looking at her blazing red hair against the green dress, he thought she looked like pictures of British royalty. Or maybe Irish royalty, if they had such a thing. His sister Sarah joined them at the car.

"Mom, you look pretty," she said. "Your hair looks great like that."

"Well, thank you, honey," his mother said. Danny noticed that she didn't really look at Sarah, though. She didn't seem to look directly at any of them that Saturday morning. She had a smile on her face, but she seemed preoccupied and far away. When his father came out of the house carrying her suitcase, they all got into the car and headed to the Detroit Metropolitan Airport.

Danny had asked why this was not a family trip, but his father had explained that he and his sister couldn't miss school. This answer left him puzzled. Why didn't Mom go to Arizona in the summer, when they all could go together? Well, his father explained, his aunt in Tucson hadn't invited Mom in the summer, and she had to wait for an invitation. None of this made any sense to Danny. She never traveled anywhere without her family, and his father's explanations only confused him further. He thought about this during the ride to the airport.

At the airport, the woman at the ticket counter wished his mother a nice trip. Danny considered that to be an extraordinary kindness that perhaps wasn't offered to every traveler. As they walked through the airport concourse, one of the pilots passed them and turned his head to look at Danny's mother. When the pilot saw that Danny was noticing this, he quickly looked away but then stole one more furtive glance at her. When they neared their gate, an older man who looked Japanese was approaching the check-in counter at the same time, and he stopped to let Danny's mother go first. He even bowed slightly to her.

His mother gave each member of her family a cheerful hug—his father, Sarah, and him. Then she showed her ticket to the check-in lady and passed through the doorway to board the plane. But just before she disappeared through that doorway, she turned to look back. She raised a hand to wave, but her face was not smiling at all. She looked intensely serious, even troubled, and she was looking directly at him. He was absolutely certain about this. His father was standing a few feet away from him, and she clearly was not looking in that direction. Sarah had walked over to give her mother one more hug. There was no doubt about it: His mother was looking only at him in that last moment in Detroit. Then she disappeared through the doorway.

He was quiet sitting in the back seat of the car on the ride home, while Sarah and his father chatted happily in the front. Sarah wanted to know all about Tucson, and all about the family there. How hot did it get in Tucson? When had they last seen Mom's family? She couldn't remember them well. Did Aunt Molly have a job? What would Mom do out in Tucson?

Danny was quiet. He remained quiet for the rest of the day, feeling uneasy and apprehensive. His mother called them that night to say that she had arrived safely. When it was his turn to talk, he could tell by the thin, airy quality of her voice that she was feeling anxious and troubled.

He didn't say what he was thinking: *Why did you look at me like that at the airport? What's wrong with you?* He also noticed that she slurred her words a time or two, so he knew that she was drinking. After passing the phone to his father, he went to sit by himself in the living room. His father chatted on the phone, sounding positive and upbeat as always.

"It sounds like your mother is going to have a very nice time," he said when he had finished the call. "Great weather out there in Arizona. One day, we'll all go out there."

Danny said nothing and went to his bedroom.

He was quiet for the rest of the week-end, and quiet as the school week began. She called again on Monday evening after they had finished dinner. She spoke to him with the same airy tone, but this time her speech was more noticeably slurred. His father had spoken to her first, and he only let Danny and Sarah talk for a couple of minutes.

"Let's not take up her entire vacation with phone calls!" he told his children with a big smile.

The third call came on Wednesday night, just as Danny was finishing up his homework in his bedroom and getting ready to go to bed. Sarah was already sound asleep in her room. He heard his father's voice in the kitchen, and he knew immediately that something was wrong.

"I don't understand," his father said. And again: "I don't understand." Danny came downstairs to the kitchen and found his father looking grim and tense. "Well, where is she? If she left you a note, then you know where she is."

There was a long silence. Danny could hear the strained telephonic tones of his Aunt Molly's voice coming through the receiver in his father's hand, but he couldn't make out the words. His father was starting to look frantic. "Well, read the note. *Read the note!* Obviously, she must have said where she was going. You must have read it too fast. Read it again!"

There was another long silence on his father's part, presumably while Aunt Molly read the note out loud to him. Danny was starting to feel sick. His body felt cold and weak, and he was starting to feel dizzy. He sat down at the kitchen table.

His father talked for another few minutes, mostly just repeating the same few questions in urgent tones. He began to pace back and forth as far as the telephone cord would permit. When the call finally ended, he stood by the phone with a blank look on his face. Danny was sitting at the kitchen table, gripping the edge of the table with both hands.

"Tell me," he said to his father.

His father didn't move or speak.

"Tell me!"

His father sat down opposite him at their kitchen table, his hands shaking and his face pale. He sat in silence for another long minute, and then he spoke.

"Your mother's gone."

Danny let go of the table and held his hands with palms upwards, shaking his head to convey his incomprehension.

"She left a note," said his father. "She said not to worry, and not to look for her. She just needs some time by herself."

"But where did she go?" asked Danny, even though he had heard the answer during his father's conversation on the phone.

"She didn't say. It was a short note, and the writing was messy." His father paused, then leaned forward over the table and looked at him with a wide stare. "She's been drinking." This was the first time his father had ever mentioned his mother's drinking, and in those few words he seemed to be simultaneously making two statements: first, acknowledging her problem, and second, confessing his role as the one who had covered it up for so many years. As if to leave no doubt about his disclosure, he added, "She's been drinking *again*."

"But when is she coming home?" asked Danny.

"I don't think she's coming home," said his father, and then he cried. Danny had never seen his father cry before. The entire process was brief, consisting of two or three audible sobs and a few tears running down his cheeks. Then his father abruptly drew in his breath, wiped his face with his hands, and stood up from his chair. "Go to bed," he ordered.

Danny just sat there at the table, not from defiance, but from shock. He simply could not stand up. He sat there for the next hour while his father made phone calls. He called Aunt Molly again. Had she contacted the local police? Yes, but they said there was nothing they could do. His father called the police in Tucson, but they only repeated what they had told Aunt Molly. If a woman leaves a note and takes her belongings with her, then there is no reason to suspect "foul play" and start an investigation. After all, people do leave their marriages, said the officer, and that's not against the law. Danny's father slammed the phone into the receiver and muttered the first curse word Danny had ever heard him say.

During the next hour, his father called Aunt Molly two or three more times, asking if she had heard anything. Nothing, nothing, not a word. He called Danny's Uncle Jack, who lived just a few minutes away in Detroit. This was equally futile, because Jack was a rather strange man who was prone to strange ideas.

"No, Jack," said Danny's father. "It has nothing to do with the C.I.A. Jack, calm down and listen! She was not abducted by the C.I.A. Just promise me that you'll call me if you hear from her."

He called a hospital in Tucson to see if his wife had been admitted to their emergency room for any reason. They had not heard of her. Last, he called the local bus station in Tucson to ask if she had purchased a ticket. Danny could hear the woman talking loudly on the other end of the phone, and she was neither courteous nor helpful. Lots of people purchase bus tickets every day, and it wasn't her job to track the whereabouts of his wife.

Finally, his father gave up. It was almost midnight. Without another word between them, Danny and his father each went to their separate bedrooms. Danny sat on his bed for a long time, too numb to think about anything in particular. When he heard the sounds of running water in the bathroom, he hoped that his father would come into his room soon and say something hopeful. He wanted more than anything to hear his father do what he had always done: make light of a serious situation and pretend that everything was fine. His father did not come to his room, and finally, a couple hours later, Danny fell into a restless sleep.

12

The First Clue

A couple weeks after the big fight with Cordelia, Dan was sitting at the kitchen table on a spring evening, going through his mail. It was a chore that he never liked. There was never anything good in the mail, only bills and people trying to sell him things that he didn't need. The mail tonight was the usual boring assortment of bills and advertisements. Dan heard a couple of the neighborhood dogs barking. First one barked, then the second answered, then the first again. Dan wondered when their owners would shut the dogs up and take them into their respective houses. Spring was a time to open one's windows and enjoy the fresh air, and his neighbors ought to think about being a little more considerate. He tossed another advertisement into a waste basket. There was one more envelope on the kitchen table. Someone should shut those damned dogs up.

The postmark was from Fairbanks, Alaska, and there was no return address. Dan didn't know anyone in Alaska. He opened the envelope, and a newspaper clipping fell out onto the table. It was old enough to have a yellowish hue, and there was no explanation with it. He unfolded the page and looked at it, feeling puzzled.

The article was about a plant nursery in Denver, Colorado, where the owner was offering visits and horticultural classes to local school groups. Dan read the headline and a sentence or two, still not understanding why he had received this—it was clearly his name printed on the envelope—and then he looked at the accompanying photograph of one of the nursery workers holding up a potted plant.

It was his mother. There was a moment of doubt and disbelief, but only a brief moment. The facial features, the physical build, the upright posture—everything about it was the unmistakable image of his mother. Dan jumped up out of his chair and had an overwhelming urge to take action. It was his mother, and she was in Denver! His normal, logical thinking process momentarily malfunctioned. He must get to Denver immediately. He would call the airlines and catch the next flight.

He forced himself to sit down and breathe slowly, in and out, in and out. *Think*, he told himself, staring at the photo. *Think*. The photo was his mother as she looked many years ago. The newspaper clipping was yellow. It was an old picture of her in Denver. Regaining his composure as best he could, he searched the article for a date. June 22, 1970. The photo was twenty-seven years old, taken three years after her disappearance. God only knows where she was now. She could be there in Denver after all these years, but she could also be in a thousand other places.

He studied the photo. There was no doubt in his mind that it was her. She had her hair pulled back in a ponytail, as she often did. The black-and-white photo gave no hint of the brilliant red color of her hair, but it was undeniably her. It looked as though the photographer had come up beside her and tried to catch an impromptu photo just as she noticed him. The look in her eyes was apprehensive, the look of someone who didn't want to be photographed. That look of anxious apprehension was so familiar to him. If the photo had shown only those eyes and nothing else, he was sure he would have recognized her.

When he was calm again, as calm as he could force himself to be, he got up from the kitchen table and took the article into the family room where Abby was sitting on the couch and reading a book. Gabe was slouching in a chair, immersed in a sports magazine while fidgeting with a basketball. Dan handed Abby the article.

"What's this?" she asked.

"It's my mother," he said. And then to his son: "Gabe, please stop bouncing that ball."

The boy looked up from his magazine. He looked surprised to see his father standing in front of him.

"What?" he asked.

"Why don't you take the ball outside, Gabe," said Abby. "And try not to slam the screen door, honey."

"Okay, Mom." He went out the back door, and Abby focused her attention on the article.

"Look at the photo," Dan said. "It's my mother."

She gazed at the photo for a long moment. "Well, that does look like the pictures I've seen, Dan. Where did you get this?"

"It came in the mail."

"But who sent it?" Abby seemed excited.

"I don't know. It came without a return address. Postmarked from Fairbanks, Alaska." As he said this, he realized that he was hoping that Abby would have an explanation for him. As ridiculous as that sounded in his own mind, he was hoping that she could somehow help him solve the mystery immediately.

"So, what does this mean? Is she in Fairbanks, Alaska?"

"I don't know," he said, disappointed that she was just as perplexed as he was. "I don't know what it means. Except that she was
in Denver, Colorado, back in 1970."

Abby took a couple of minutes to read the article. "She's not
mentioned in here. Just the owner is mentioned by name. But it
really does look like the old photos of her."

"It's her," said Dan. "Absolutely no doubt, it's her." He took
the article and read through it.

"Do you think she's trying to contact you?" asked Abby.

"But if she wants to make contact, why wouldn't she just write
me a letter and tell me where she is?"

"True, true," she said. She looked at him as he stood before
her in the family room. "Sit down, Dan. Sit down, and let's think
this through together."

He took his seat in his favorite red chair.

"No, come sit here. Sit on the couch with me." She patted the
empty spot next to her with her hand.

He immediately stood up and followed her directions, a bit
surprised at how obedient he was, and surprised at how much solace he felt in Abby's presence. He didn't want to be alone at this
moment, and he felt grateful for her company.

"All right," she said. "Let's think about this."

They sat together in the family room, and they thought.
Could the sender of the article be his mother? It could be her,
even though that would be an odd way to reach out to one's son
after so many years. She could be sitting in Alaska and sending
him a newspaper article about a job she held in Denver many
years ago. This didn't make much sense, but one must consider
that she might be mentally ill, and therefore not behaving ratio-
nally. This was Abby's theory; Dan was reluctant to consider it,
although he had no argument to refute it. Or his mother could be

in the grip of alcoholism, which could also explain behavior that would otherwise be inexplicable. Again, this was Abby's theory—he had told her about his mother's drinking—and again, Dan felt himself flinch at the idea, although he couldn't dismiss it.

They considered the other possibility: Someone else had sent the newspaper clipping. If this were the case, it had to be someone who knew his mother and knew Dan Wunsch, or at least knew that he existed. Could it be someone who had worked with her in Denver? But why would they wait all these years? Was his mother in touch with a friend or a family member who sent the mailing? And why would they send it? And why now? But all things considered, both Dan and Abby agreed that the article was more likely sent by someone who knew his mother, and less likely to be coming directly from her.

"Somebody knows something," Dan said. "I just need to think about this."

"Okay, Dan. Let me know if I can help," said Abby, and she left to clean up the kitchen. Again, he was surprised at how much comfort he took in her words.

At that moment, Cordelia came home and walked into the family room, where Dan still sat. He showed her the mysterious newspaper article.

"Apparently, your grandmother worked in a plant nursery in Denver many years ago," he explained.

"Oh, my God!" said Cordelia, looking at the newspaper article. "That's so exciting, Dad! Maybe we'll all get to see her. I'd love to meet my grandma. And I'm sure you'd love to see your mom after all these years."

Dan waited until she finished reading the article. There was still a sweet side to his daughter, he thought, even though she was so difficult to get along with lately. She really cared about other people. She still seemed to care about him, oddly enough.

"So, what do you think?" he asked her.

"I think this is amazing!" she said. "Obviously, someone wants you to find her."

"But I have no idea if she's in Denver or someplace else. This article is twenty-seven years old. I guess I'll just try to call the nursery in the morning."

"But why wait, Dad? Isn't there a time difference between us and Denver? Maybe they're still open. You could call right now."

"Well, I guess I could."

"You should definitely call right now."

He felt comforted by his daughter's suggestion, as he did by his wife's conversation a few minutes earlier. He went into the kitchen where Cordelia handed him the phone. When he called the nursery in Denver, the place was indeed open. He spoke to a young woman, a kid who knew nothing. Could he speak to the owner? Well, the owner didn't usually take phone calls. But this was important, Dan told the kid, really important. Finally, the kid put him on hold for a long stretch, after which an old man took the phone. Dan had to repeat himself several times, at a steadily increasing volume, because the old man kept telling him he didn't hear as well as he used to. Dan was getting irritated, and the old man was obviously getting frustrated as well. Finally, he told Dan that he hires a lot of people, and he couldn't remember every damned one of them.

Next, he called his sister, Sarah, who had never left their hometown of Detroit. He didn't think for a second that she might know something that she had hidden from him; he just called to tell her about the mailing. She sounded just as surprised and puzzled and excited as he had felt when he first opened the envelope.

"God, Danny, do you think there's a chance that we might actually find her?" He heard her slipping into the little sister role, calling him "Danny" and asking his opinion. As the big brother, he should be the authority on finding lost mothers.

"I don't know, Sarah. I don't know what this means. But let's try to find out."

They decided that Sarah would call a couple of older folks who had been their neighbors years ago, before their mother disappeared, just to ask if they might know anything. And Dan would call family members to see what they knew. They ended the call with a promise to keep each other posted.

There were only two family members to call on his mother's side of the family, her sister Molly in Tucson, and her brother Jack in California. Dan called them with the hope that they might know something, but his hopes were quickly dispelled.

"You mean, you've heard from my sister?" His Aunt Molly was beside herself on the phone. She started talking quickly, and she was clearly choking back tears. "So, what did this article say? Where is she now? Have you tried to call her?"

"No, Aunt Molly, I don't think my mom sent this. Please try to calm yourself down. I don't know who sent it. That's why I'm calling you. I thought you might have some ideas for me, some clues." But she had nothing to offer, and he spent the rest of the conversation reassuring her that he would keep in touch if he heard anything more about his mother.

The conversation with Uncle Jack was even more disappointing. Uncle Jack had always been hard to talk to. A little *meshugga*, his old Tanta Zlata would have said. A little crazy. Dan hadn't seen him much since he moved out to California years ago. There was something likeable, even charismatic, about Uncle

Jack, something that drew Dan to his zany bachelor uncle, but his thinking was always suspicious and bizarre.

Dan called and told Jack about the mailing. There was a long silence on the other end of the phone.

"Uncle Jack? Are you there?"

Another silence, and then a reply: "The government."

"What are you talking about, Uncle Jack?"

"The government, Dan. They're spying on everyone these days. You can't be too careful."

Dan tried not to sound frustrated. "Jack, someone knows where my mother is. I'm sure of it. Think, Jack. Someone back in Detroit, maybe. Someone who has moved to Alaska. Do you have any idea who it might be?"

"Hold the phone, Danny." Dan heard a door open and close. "Just checking the locks. You can't be too careful these days. It's the government, Danny boy. I know too much, and they're looking for me. I know how they killed off the plans for building electric cars. I know how they seed clouds to make storms. I know way too much."

"Jack, for God's sake, we're not talking about electric cars and the government. We're talking about my mother. Your sister. Think, Jack. Maybe you know someone who might have kept in touch with her."

"Don't let them fool you, Danny. They're looking for me, and they'll stop at nothing."

Dan took a long sigh. "Okay, Uncle Jack. Just promise you'll call me if you hear anything about my mother. Will you promise me that?"

Another silence. "Did you hear that noise on the line? Got to go, Danny. I think they're bugging my phone." And with that, the call abruptly ended.

Dan paced back and forth, hoping that something would come to him, some sudden insight that would solve the mystery. There must be someone he knew who was behind the mailing. Nothing came to mind. Later that evening, after dinner, he sat in his favorite chair, looking at the old newspaper clipping.

"Dad, why don't you just get on a plane and go out to Denver."

He looked up at Cordelia, who had appeared in the family room.

"Maybe you'll find somebody who knows something," she said.

"No," he said. "I don't think so, Cordelia. The article is a quarter of a century old, and the owner of the nursery is a deaf old man who remembers nothing."

"But somebody sent you that article for a reason, Dad. They must want you to pursue it."

"Well, maybe I'll call again tomorrow and see if I can speak with somebody else. But I'm not wasting my money traveling to Denver on the basis of an old newspaper clipping."

Cordelia stood in front of him, looking thoughtful and concerned. "Well, I think you're giving up too easily, Dad. I really do. I think you should go to Denver. You never know."

"I appreciate your concern, honey, but I'm not sure about that." It seemed to Dan that his daughter looked at him with an odd expression, apparently confused by what he said. Was it so odd that he called her "honey?" Did everyone expect him to be fighting with her at every moment? She looked like she wanted to say something to him, but she just mumbled good-night and disappeared up the stairs. When Abby came into the family room, Dan was still wondering what to do.

"Maybe Cordelia's right. Maybe I should go to Denver."

"Of course, she's right," said Abby with a confidant tone that took him by surprise. "I'll check air fares for you in the morning."

13

Don Juan

When Dan arrived at the nursery in his rented car, it was a warm, sunny, spring day in Denver. Before going inside, he entered the fenced-in yard area to the left of the store and walked the perimeter of it. He hardly noticed the profusion of flowers, shrubs, and vegetable plants around him. He walked by bags of mulch and potting soil stacked five feet high without really seeing them. As he scanned the area, he knew that he was looking for his mother. He couldn't help himself, even though he knew that his search was ridiculous. How likely was it that she had worked at this place for the past thirty years and was still working here at the age of seventy? Still, he looked at every woman in sight among the shoppers and the nursery staff members.

He went inside and looked around, walking down every aisle of seeds and garden tools and bird feeders. Finally, he surrendered to reality. Chiding himself for his heavy sense of disappointment,—after all, what had he expected? —he went toward the counter where a young girl was cashing out a customer. The man had many questions about his vegetable garden, and Dan felt his impatience rising. Why was this guy asking a teenage girl how to grow the best tomatoes? Did he think she was a world expert on the subject? She was a tall, thin girl with a big, toothy smile. He relaxed a bit looking at her. She must be about the same age as Cordelia. They could be classmates. She cheerfully referred the man to one of the "master gardeners" in the yard outside. Finally, Dan was at the counter. He said hello to the girl and asked to see the owner of the place.

"Is there a problem?" she asked, flashing her big, broad smile.

"No, no problem. I just need to see the owner."

"Can I tell him what it's about, sir?"

Dan paused and took a long breath. "I'm looking for my mother."

The girl lost her smile and looked apprehensive, as if she feared that he might be mentally unstable and quite dangerous. She quickly excused herself and disappeared into a back room behind the counter. Through the doorway, Dan could see a small desk littered with stacks of unorganized papers. The girl had her back to him, and he couldn't see whom she was talking to. A minute or two later, she returned with an old man who walked very slowly, leaning on a cane. "This is the owner, sir," the girl said, watching Dan with a wary look.

"What can I do for you, Mister?"

Dan recognized the voice he had heard on the phone from home. The man was short and bald, and there was a large purple birthmark on his forehead. He reminded Dan of the old Russian leader, Mikhail Gorbachev, who had a similar birthmark. Dan reached into his shirt pocket and pulled out the newspaper article. He carefully unfolded it and handed it to the owner.

"I know this may sound crazy, but I'm trying to find my mother."

"You're trying to find your *what?* Can you speak up a little?"

"I'm trying to find my mother," he repeated loudly. "This is her in a 1970 photo of your nursery. She must have worked here, at least for a while."

The man nodded, seeming to understand. He slapped his cane down on the wooden counter, making a loud *crack!* He took the newspaper clipping, staring at Dan for a minute. "You're looking for your mother? You mean, she gave you up for adoption?"

"Something like that," Dan answered. Despite the cane and the hearing problem, the old man looked alert and vigorous. Dan hoped he would remember something.

The old man studied the photo for a long minute while Dan waited. Then his face registered a surge of animation. "Well, ain't that somethin'! I bet my wife will remember her. Louise! Louise! Come out here!"

From the back office, a woman's voice called back, a voice that sounded accustomed to speaking more loudly than the speaker might prefer. "What's the matter now?"

"Nothing! Just come out here!"

An old woman emerged from the office and joined him behind the counter. She was short and stout like her husband, the two of them standing at almost exactly the same height. She had a pencil behind her ear and a pair of glasses hanging by a cord around her neck. Her face bore a look of chronic exasperation, and she looked at her husband impatiently. "Well, what is it?"

"Take a look at this picture," the owner said. "Remember her?"

His wife put on her glasses and looked hard at the photo. "Oh, Lordy, Lordy," she said. "Of course, I remember her. I even remember the newspaper folks coming out and writing that article about us."

Dan felt his heart pounding.

"What was her name?" the old man asked his wife. "I remember her just fine, but I can't remember her name."

"Her name?" The woman frowned and shook her head. The two of them stood together looking at the photo, both of them with pursed lips, their heads shaking slightly back and forth, left and right, in perfect unison. Then the woman opened her eyes wider and looked at her husband, the lines of her forehead relaxing a bit. "Kate! That was her name. Kate."

Dan had an urge to hug the woman.

"Right!" said the man. "That was it. Kate. And this here is her son. She gave him up for adoption, and now he's trying to find her."

"Oh, dear," she said, with motherly compassion in her voice that took Dan by surprise. "Well, I never knew about that story. I never knew she had a kid. That's so sad."

Dan tried to calm himself and sound composed. "Do you happen to know where she might be?"

The woman answered him in a more normal speaking volume than she used for her husband. "Oh, she's been gone many years. I wouldn't have a clue." Then she repeated herself loudly so her husband would hear her.

"Yeah," said the owner. "She was only here for a while. A couple of years, maybe."

"More than a couple," his wife interrupted him loudly. "It had to be a good five, six years. At least."

The old man stared at the photo again. "I suppose so," he said. "Maybe it was five or six years. But then she left. She was a nice woman, though, your mother. And a hell of a good worker."

"Yes, she was a good one," said the woman. "We would have made her the store manager if she had stayed with us."

"But you say that she left," said Dan. "Didn't she say where she was going?"

"Not a word," said the owner. "Remember, Louise? She just disappeared one day. Just like *that*." He snapped his fingers.

"That's right," his wife said to him. "Must have run off with that Don Juan. Remember him? The good-lookin' Mexican fella who would come 'round and take her out to lunch?"

"Oh, right!" the owner answered her, as he and his wife put together their memories, ignoring Dan for the moment. "I do remember that," he continued. "A good-lookin' guy, always dressed sharp, always drove a nice car. And she was a looker, too. A good-lookin' redhead. And Don Juan was always stopping by at lunchtime. A classy couple, they were. And then she just disappeared. Must have run off with him, I'd say."

Dan was too stunned to say anything else for a minute or two. Then he asked, "Would you have any clues about this . . . this man? Any idea how I might track him down?"

The owner's wife gave Dan a sympathetic look. "Sorry, Mister," she said, "but we don't have any idea where either one of them might be. It's been years. I hope you find her, though."

Dan remained standing at the counter for what seemed like many minutes. There was nothing left to ask, but he couldn't make himself walk away. The owner and his wife stood on the other side of the counter saying nothing, just gazing at him, the man with a blank face, the woman with a face full of pity. Dan finally turned and walked away, without saying goodbye. He wandered in the nursery yard for a few minutes and absentmindedly picked out a small potted plant with colorful pink flowers. He paid the girl at the desk inside and left.

When he got back into his rental car, he was too dazed to drive. He sat in the parking lot for a few minutes, unable to think coherently about what he had just learned. He finally started the engine and drove back to his motel. By the time he got back to his room, a theory had begun to form in his mind. This man, this Don Juan, must have known his mother *before* she left Detroit. He must have spirited her away from the family by some devilish cunning. Dan knew it to be a false theory, a preposterous theory, but the hatred rising in his chest gave it the power to overcome all logic and reason. This Mexican charlatan had conjured his mother away from her family and caused immeasurable suffering for them all.

A false theory, of course, but Dan had spent years constructing various theories to explain the inexplicable, and none had lasted over time. His mother had been kidnapped and was unable to escape from her captors. She had fallen and hit her head and lost any memory of who she was. She had gone on a secret mission to help someone in her family, but that person was involved with organized crime, so his mother had to disappear in a witness protection program. He had entertained one implausible theory after another, each one falling apart soon after its desperate construction.

Back in his motel room, he paced back and forth, furious at the Mexican "Don Juan" for taking her away. He felt agitated by the knowledge that he had just stood in a place where his mother had once stood, and frustrated by his inability to pursue the lead any further. Why had someone sent him a clue that proved to be so useless? What was the point?

He picked up the motel phone next to the bed and called home. Cordelia answered.

"Hi, Dad. Any luck? Did you learn anything about Grandma?"

"Not much," he said. "Nothing of any use."

"Oh, no! So, no one remembered her at the nursery?"

"Well, they did remember her, actually. But she left that job years ago, and they have no idea where she went."

"Oh, that's awful. You must feel so disappointed, Dad."

Cordelia was a good kid, he thought to himself. Even now, during these terrible teenage years, she was a good kid. "Yeah, I guess I am."

"Well, don't give up. Somebody sent us that clue, so there must be a way to find her. But hold on, Mom wants to say hello."

He said goodbye to Cordelia and waited for his wife to take the phone.

"Hi, Dan. Did you find out anything?"

He was relieved to hear Abby's voice on the other end. "No luck at all. Just a deaf old man who remembers that she worked at his nursery decades ago."

"Well, that's a start."

"And he remembers some Mexican guy used to meet her for lunch. I just can't believe it. I can't even let myself think that my mother was dating someone."

"Hmm," she said. "Did they have any idea where she went after working there?"

"No, not a clue," he said. He picked up the little potted plant he had purchased and held it out in front of him. "I can't find her." He heard his voice breaking, and he felt like a kid about to start bawling. He vowed to pull himself together immediately. He told himself to stop acting like a damned five-year-old.

"It's okay, Dan. We'll figure this out."

"Really?" he asked.

"Yes, really. You just get a good night's sleep and catch your flight home tomorrow, and we'll figure this out."

He said goodbye and hung up the phone, surprised at how comforting it was to hear his wife and daughter reassuring him from hundreds of miles away.

14

The Christmas Truce

Cordelia's chore for the day was to organize a classroom hand-out on the end of the Revolutionary War. She used three of the student desks nearby to lay out all the pages. There was a soft spring rain coming down outside, and she was quite content to be in Mr. Tremblay's room at the end of the day.

"I don't understand one thing," she said. "I don't understand why history is always about war."

Mr. T was at his desk at the front of the room. He looked up from a textbook he was reading. "I guess it's because there have been so many of them," he said.

"Exactly! But *why* are there so many of them? How can this be happening all the time?"

"Your guess is as good as mine, Cordelia. Power. Competition. Territory. Money. Take your pick."

Cordelia put down her stack of papers and looked up at him. "But *how* does war happen? How do people participate in it? After the first shot is fired, and the first young soldier gets hurt or killed, why doesn't everybody just stop and say, 'Wait! Wait! This is terrible! These stupid old men who rule our countries are

sending us out to kill each other, and it makes no sense!' I don't
see how it can continue after the first guy gets hit by a bullet."

"But let's assume," said Mr. T, "that the soldiers believe
they're fighting for some important reason. To free the American
colonies from the British monarchy, or to stop communism, or
stop Hitler, or stop somebody from doing something evil. So,
they are willing to fight."

"Yes, but the fighting itself is evil!" she said. "And if they
could just put down their guns for a minute and meet the guys on
the other side, they would probably just start goofing around and
having fun with each other."

"Exactly so," said Mr. T, closing his textbook and leaning
back in his chair. "During the First World War, there was a spon-
taneous Christmas truce in Europe, at least in certain places. It
happened in 1914. German and British soldiers stopped fighting
on Christmas morning and started singing Christmas carols to
each other. Then they cautiously climbed out of their trenches
and greeted each other face to face. They shook hands, gave each
other little presents of food and cigarettes, and the Great War
came to a temporary halt."

"That's amazing!" said Cordelia. "Really? They gave each
other gifts?"

"Yes, really."

She imagined two groups of very young soldiers, dirty and
sweaty—not unlike the boys on her high school football team—
climbing out of their trenches and meeting their counterparts on
the other side with grinning faces, recognizing in each other the
innocence and ready humor of young men everywhere.

"But the next day," said Mr. T, "they started shooting again.
You'd think the truce had never happened."

"But that's crazy!" said Cordelia. "How could they sit together and sing Christmas carols, and then go back to killing each other?"

"Cordelia, if I knew the answer to that question, I would probably win the Nobel Peace Prize. Or perhaps *you'll* win it someday. Maybe your compassion for people will lead you to figure out what's wrong with this crazy world and fix it."

Compassion. Mr. T used the word *compassion*. As if he knew about her nascent interest in Buddhism. She smiled, hoping she was not blushing. She looked down at the papers she had spread among three desks and began to collate them. After a few minutes of silence, she looked up at him again.

"I don't even know who we are," she said.

"What do you mean?"

"Well, those soldiers could sing Christmas carols together and then go back to killing each other. So, who are we? What's the real essence of human nature? Are we territorial, bloodthirsty killers? Or are we kind-hearted creatures who want to give each other gifts and help each other?"

"Apparently, we're both," he replied.

"But that doesn't sound right," she said. For a moment, she worried that she was being rude by contradicting her teacher, but his kindly face was reassuring. "One side must be the real story," she continued. "Either we're selfish, aggressive beasts who occasionally fake it and act nice, or we're all basically kind souls who somehow get messed up by life and turn violent and ugly."

Mr. T smiled at her. "Cordelia, you've identified one of the great debates in philosophy. Are we inherently good or evil? I'm no philosopher, but I had a terrific philosophy teacher in college, and he taught this topic very well. I remember him talking about Hobbes, who argued that our basic nature is pretty brutal, and we need a strong government to keep us in check. On the other side, Rousseau wrote that we are basically good. In his view, our political and social institutions lead us to be selfish and competitive."

"I think I'm with Rousseau," she said. "At least, I hope he's right."

"And so do I," said Mr. T. "Otherwise, humanity is in big trouble." He spoke further about the question of human nature, and Cordelia chimed in with her own thoughts, tentatively at first, but then more confidently. After a while, Mr. T glanced up at the clock.

"Oh, I've got to get to a faculty meeting," he said.

"Sorry, Mr. T. I hope I didn't make you late."

"Not at all. And it's no big deal if I'm a few minutes late. We'll just talk at the meeting about some new school policy. And then there will be the usual small talk and gossip." He packed up his briefcase and they both stood up to leave the classroom. "Frankly, Cordelia, I'd rather stay here and talk to you."

Cordelia was both pleased and surprised to hear him say this. He actually seemed to like talking with her. On her way out of the building, she imagined the young men from England and Germany coming out of their trenches in 1914, trading little gifts, making jokes. She had a vision of World War I coming to a peaceful, happy, and permanent end, while she and Mr. T presided over the festivities. And if the philosophers like Hobbes and Rousseau could join the party and spend a little time with her teacher, Cordelia was pretty sure that the good-versus-evil debate would be resolved once and for all. Based on the character of Mr. T, they would surely conclude that human beings are essentially good.

15

The Dill Pickle Aisle

The day after Danny's mother disappeared was a Thursday in autumn, and it was a long, dreadful affair. They all stayed home from work and school, trying to understand something that defied comprehension. His father gave the bad news to his sister Sarah—Sarah, who shared their father's perennially cheerful disposition—and then spent much of the day trying to console an inconsolable thirteen-year-old. Mom was just taking a few days by herself to go sight-seeing, he told her. No doubt, they would hear from her soon, and she would be flying home. To Danny, this all sounded pathetic. He recognized the highly edited story of life that his father had always told them, a narrative in which anything distressing was simply denied or omitted. Danny left the living room and went up to his bedroom to listen to The Beatles on his record player.

The phone in the kitchen rang a couple of times during the day, and they all jumped up and ran to the kitchen, but it was never anything important. A neighbor wanted to borrow their rake. A charity called to solicit money. His father called Danny's aunt—Aunt Molly—in Tucson every couple of hours, but there was nothing to report. Sometimes, Aunt Molly called them, and when Danny answered the phone, he could hear her crying on the other end of the phone. In fact, everyone could hear her crying over the phone, and this threw his sister Sarah back into another round of crying and begging their father to *do something!*

More than anything, Danny wanted to get out of that house and get away from his father and the unbearable sounds of his sister crying. He wanted to go see his friends, but they were all in school. Besides, he didn't dare leave for a minute, lest he miss some news. As the day dragged on, his father continued to placate Sarah with empty promises and false reassurances. He kept telling his children that he was going to make them a nice dinner, but he never did anything about it, and no one had an appetite anyway. Finally, they all went quietly to bed, exhausted and miserable.

That was Thursday. Danny and Sarah stayed home from school on Friday as well. Outside, the day looked sunny and pleasant, but they all sat inside. The weather outside had become irrelevant. Friday passed so slowly that Danny kept checking the clock to see if the hands had moved at all. Saturday was a boring repeat of Friday, and Sunday a hazy mirror image of Saturday. On Sunday night, their father said that they would be better off returning to school and seeing their friends again. On Monday morning, his father found Danny sitting in his room after it was time to leave.

"You're going to be late for school," his father said.

"I'm not going."

There was a long pause while his father stood in the doorway looking at the floor.

"You have to go to school, Danny."

"I'm not going."

After another long silence, his father walked away. At that moment, Danny knew that his father would never again exert the authority of a parent. The situation had obviously left the man completely powerless, and Danny could see no particular reason to obey him anymore. As his father walked away, Danny caught himself wishing for a second that he would turn around and sternly order his son to go to school, but it didn't happen.

His father left for work, and Sarah left for school. Danny spent the day going from room to room, unable to settle in any one particular spot. He tried to read but couldn't concentrate, tried to eat but had no appetite, tried to nap but couldn't sleep. He wandered in and out of the kitchen, glancing at the phone on the wall and hoping it would ring. He stood at the sink, where his mother had often stood washing dishes, and looked out the window at her flower garden. Most of the flowers were gone for the year, except for the brilliant orange marigolds. They made him think of his mother's hair, so he had to leave the kitchen. After several hours of wandering in the quiet house, he went to the living room and turned on the television for distraction. He kept the volume low so he could hear the phone, just in case it rang. It did not.

When the mailman delivered the mail in mid-afternoon, Danny sat down at the kitchen table and went through the envelopes several times, almost convinced that there must be a letter from her. He checked the mailbox to see if he had failed to take everything out of it. He wondered how long it would take for a letter to arrive from Tucson, or anyplace out West. He would allow a couple more days.

He spent Tuesday and Wednesday in the same way with the same results. He finally went back to school on Thursday, a week after her disappearance, not because he gave up hope, but because he decided that she would most likely communicate with him by mail, and the mail didn't arrive until two or three in the afternoon. School would be a useful distraction until that time. Each day for the next week, he would rush home and grab the mail with shaking hands, checking every envelope several times. It seemed unbearably cruel to him that the mailman would raise his expectations daily by delivering a stack of envelopes, only to dash his hopes with the disappointing sight of electric bills and fundraising letters and automobile registration forms.

Sometimes, Danny would go to local stores that his mother had frequented. Along the way, he would tell himself that this was a ridiculous waste of time, but he couldn't resist the urge to go. He went to Grunt's food market, a tiny little Jewish grocery store where his mother would buy dill pickles and other Jewish foods that his father loved. He never really expected to see her, but then why did he feel so crestfallen when she wasn't there? On the way home, he chided himself for his foolishness. What did he expect? Did he really think that she was hiding in the narrow aisles of beet borscht and dill pickles?

Once he got on a city bus and traveled downtown to his mother's favorite Catholic church. That particular church, she had told him, always made her think of her father. (*He's the one who really loved me.* And then, in answer to his unspoken question: *My mother? Well, she did the best she could.*) On rare occasions, she had taken him and Sarah there for Sunday mass. Danny's father never objected, but he never could bring himself to go with them. This time, Danny went by himself. Once inside, he scanned the wooden pews for a red-haired woman who might have stopped in to kneel and pray on her way back home. When he didn't find her, he glanced up at the image of Jesus on the cross and wondered how any God could allow such suffering on His Earth. He got on another bus and went back home.

As time passed, Danny became accustomed to his new life. It was not that he accepted it, or understood it, or overcame the sense that the world had dealt him a near-fatal blow; he just got used to it. He didn't stop waking up in the morning with the hope that his father would have exciting news for him about his mother's imminent return, but he was less and less surprised when it didn't happen. He saw his friends again, did his homework again, ate dinner again, but he did all this without any genuine enthusiasm. It had to be done, so he did it. At least, it was better than those first few terrible, clock-stopping, shapeless days of sitting in that house with his father and his sister. Better to have a routine, any routine.

16

Brooklyn

As time passed, Danny felt happy to be with his friends again, and he even enjoyed some of his classes. His favorite was his English class. His teacher, Mrs. Patton, was a lean, no-nonsense, middle-aged woman who talked about her profession with an idealism that appealed to him. The kids in the class had nicknamed her "General Patton."

"If you can't speak your own language well, you're not going to go very far in this life," she would admonish the class, standing at the front of the room looking very much like a general reviewing the troops. "And it's my job to make sure that you go far. So, pay attention!"

General Patton had recently added sentence diagramming to her lessons. Danny hadn't seen sentence diagrams since elementary school. He liked the subject then, and he was glad to see it returning to the curriculum.

"You people are about to graduate high school," his teacher declared, "and you're not leaving my classroom until you understand the structure of your own language!"

Sentence diagramming was so logical, Danny thought. Why were the other kids groaning about learning it? How could anyone not like it? He looked forward to the class every day, and he even practiced the diagramming at home.

He heard his father on the phone with his Aunt Molly in Tucson, and he began to make a sentence diagram on a scrap of paper. First, he put the subject on a horizontal line:

$$\underline{|}$$

The verb came on the other side of a vertical line that intersected the horizontal:

$$\underline{|\text{have heard}}$$

The direct object came after another vertical line that sat atop the horizontal:

$$\underline{|\text{have heard}\,|\,\text{nothing}}$$

The prepositional phrase was added via a diagonal line for the preposition (*about*) and a horizontal for the object of the preposition (*Kate*).

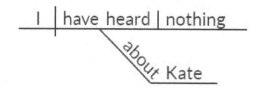

Diagramming a sentence brought a sense of order to the apparently random outpouring of words that comprise human conversation. When he found a particular conversation to be upsetting, it brought him great comfort to parse a sentence and map it on the page. He also found it calming to see that in the diagramming of a question, the word order was rearranged to put the subject first, and there was no punctuation in the diagram. When his grandmother asked his father a question, it became a statement.

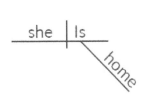

The only way to know that it was a question was to notice that the first word of the original question—*Is*—started with a capital letter. He found the diagram far preferable to the question:
"Is she home?"

Danny would sit with a pad of paper and draw sentence diagrams at home, telling his father that he was doing his homework. Sometimes, though, he would draw the same diagram many times over, until he felt uncomfortably compelled to continue the repetition. He would have to force himself to put the paper down and do something else. Still, he usually enjoyed the sentence diagramming, and he usually looked forward to school.

The only thing he did not look forward to was the weekly Sunday brunch at his grandmother's house. His father had not yet told the truth, and his grandmother and his two great-aunts were looking more suspicious with each passing week. Occasionally,

Danny tried to tell his father that he didn't want to go, but Sarah would talk him into it. It was fun to see their grandmother and great-aunts, she said. Tanta Zlata was hilarious, and besides, the food was great. Why would he want to stay home? Danny was skeptical.

"She decided to spend another few days with her family," his father explained on one of their visits after his mother's disappearance. "She doesn't get to see them very often, you know."

Nothing was said about his explanation, and the meal went along without incident. His grandmother passed around the usual plates, filled with the usual Jewish foods. The old women talked about the price of smoked whitefish.

"Her sister is ill," Danny's father said at the next weekly brunch. "She just wants to stay a bit longer until her sister feels better."

Everyone at the table was unusually quiet on that Sunday, without the constant exchange of sentences concocted from a random mix of English and Yiddish. The plates of food circulated around the long table in silence.

"She wants to see the Grand Canyon before she comes home," he told them the Sunday after that. "It's really an amazing thing to see, you know."

They were all sitting around the long dining room table. Tanta Zlata put her bagel down on her plate and looked over at her sisters with her steely gray eyes. She had heard enough.

"The Grand Canyon? The Grand Canyon is a big hole in the ground!"

Danny wrote on a paper napkin.

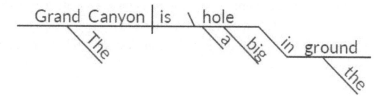

The two other sisters tried to mollify Tanta Zlata, but without success. Zlata persisted. "She needs to see a big hole in the ground more than she needs to see her family?" With this, the table erupted into chaos. The other two women began to argue with Zlata, obviously trying to silence her. Danny's father was trying to talk over them to explain how this was a once-in-a-lifetime opportunity to see one of Mother Nature's great wonders.

"She needs to see the Grand Canyon like I need a *luch in kup!*" Zlata shouted.

As always, Danny missed a lot of the Yiddish, but he knew that a *luch in kup* meant *a hole in the head*. Zlata was stabbing at the air with her index finger as she said this. The other women were trying to settle her down.

Finally, Danny's grandmother, who was always the kindest of the three, took advantage of a momentary pause in the conversation. She stood up at the long dining room table and spoke loudly.

"Traveling is good," she announced with absolute authority, as if daring the others to contradict her. "She wants to travel and see the Grand Canyon. This is good."

Zlata glared at her.

"Traveling is good," Danny's grandmother repeated. And looking right at Zlata, she added, "You like to travel to Brooklyn."

Zlata sat quietly for a moment, and Danny felt apprehensive about what she might say next. To his surprise, she nodded. "Brooklyn is different," Zlata said. "Brooklyn is not a big hole in the ground. Brooklyn is *someplace.*"

"So, let's go make a visit to Brooklyn some time," said his grandmother quickly. "We haven't been back in years." As she talked, she reached over and put a generous piece of smoked whitefish on Zlata's plate. "Remember when we first came over? Remember our little apartment on Powell Street?" Turning to

Danny, she added, "We came over from the Old Country, our parents and us three girls. We were young. I was just a teenager."

Zlata smiled. "Five people!" she added to her sister's story. "And we lived in three rooms. Like the sardines in a can!" She broke out laughing.

"That's all we could afford," said Danny's grandmother. "Our father was a tailor, and he was no millionaire."

"Some tailor!" said Zlata. "One time, he made pants for a man. One leg this long," she said, holding her hands far apart, "and one leg this long." She held her hands close together.

"But the man took the pants and wore them anyway," said his grandmother, laughing too.

"Of course, he did," said Zlata. "It was Brooklyn!"

Everybody laughed, and Danny's grandmother winked at him. The crisis was over, at least for the moment.

17

Emergency Meeting

D anny knew that the day of reckoning was coming with his grandmother and the tantas, and he didn't have to wait long. The week after the Grand Canyon alibi, the old women arranged a big family reunion. Relatives drove up from Ohio for the occasion. There was even a contingency that flew in from New York City. The officially stated reason for their long trip was to celebrate the birthday of Danny's grandmother, but that was never a sufficient reason for such a journey before. He knew that this gathering was all about his mother.

By the time Danny arrived with his father and sister, the house was full of food and family. On the long dining room table, there were the usual offerings of lox, bagels, smoked whitefish, and other Jewish staples. His grandmother had even made her famous *lukchen kugel*, her noodle pudding, a dish generally reserved for the holidays. The kugel was made with cinnamon, and the smell of cinnamon mingled with the usual smells of onions and garlic and chicken soup simmering on the stove.

Long-lost cousins were scattered throughout the little house, and they all pressed their way toward the dining room. Danny saw them all staring at him and Sarah, eager to see the freaks with no mother. His grandmother came out of the kitchen and took Sarah by the arm.

"Come, come, shaina maidele." *Come, come, pretty girl.* "Come help me in the kitchen. We'll bring out the rest of the food."

As soon as Danny's father took his seat at the table, the old women, with Sarah in tow, returned from the kitchen and pounced on him with questions.

"So, Chaim?" asked the grandmother, calling his father by his Yiddish name. "We know something?"

"No, Ma. We don't know a thing," said his father, looking tired and worn, making no attempt at excuses now.

"Nothing?" asked Danny's grandmother.

"No news?" asked Tanta Esther, who tended to be the quietest of the three.

"You heard him!" bellowed Tanta Zlata, already impatient. *"Bubkes!* Nothing!"

Danny saw Sarah smiling, but fidgeting nervously with a hair clip, putting it in, taking it out, putting it in again. And he saw his grandmother blinking back tears. She had always liked his mother, and the feeling had been mutual. His mother had often told him that his grandma always made her feel welcome in the family. He struggled not to cry when he saw his grandmother's face now.

"But Chaim," his grandmother asked, "there must be something we can do. Someone we can ask."

His father shrugged, looking lost and helpless. His grandmother asked him if he had called the police. Yes, he told her, but the officer in Tucson had no information.

"You tell the policeman that he should marry the daughter of the Angel of Death!" snorted Zlata.

The grandmother asked if Danny's Aunt Molly in Tucson might have some clue. Nothing, Danny's father told her. Not a thing, except a short note that his wife had left behind. Aunt Molly said she would call if she heard anything.

"She'll call you?" asked Zlata, nodding sarcastically with her lower lip stuck out. "Oh ya, she'll call you. When the *Meshiach* comes, she'll call you!"

Meshiach, thought Danny. The Messiah. When the Messiah comes. In other words, they'll never get the call.

As if on cue, the three old women broke into loud conversation simultaneously. Three voices warbled all at once, while six hands waved in the air to illustrate the words. Other family members from out of town joined in, wagging their fingers at Tanta Zlata. Danny surmised that they were scolding her for making trouble. Zlata fired back, her eyes wild, her speech becoming harsh and more guttural. She hurled her Yiddish invective at all who dared to challenge her, punctuating her sentences with bits and pieces of English, as well as pretending to spit on the dining room floor to ward off the Evil Eye. Her two sisters tried to rein her in.

"Zlata, *zy shtille!*" ordered Esther, the quiet one. *Be quiet!*

But Zlata was defiant. "Don't you tell me *zy shtille!*"

"Zlata, *genug!*" pleaded the grandmother, the sweet one. *Enough!*

"Don't you tell me *genug!*"

At this point, Zlata shifted into pure Yiddish to vent her wrath about this dreadful situation. Danny couldn't follow it all, but he knew that *schvartz* meant *black*, and *yor* meant *year*, so *schvartz yor* must mean *black year*. Tanta Zlata was wishing his mother a black year, along with a litany of other blood-curdling curses that he could not decipher.

And he understood one other word: *Shikker.* Drinker. Drunkard. She was standing right there in the dining room telling everyone that his mother was a drunkard. She also said something about the Irish.

Danny's face grew hot, and he felt himself rising from his chair at the dining room table.

"You're calling my mother a drunk?" The room fell silent, and everyone looked at him where he stood. "You're calling my mother an Irish drunk, aren't you, Tanta Zlata?" The adults at the table were staring at him, some with mouths gaping wide open. A few of the younger children stood in the doorway between the dining room and the kitchen, and they looked frightened as they watched him. "So, all the Irish are drunks, right, Tanta? Just like all the Jews are greedy, right? So, let's just throw out all the Irish and kill all the Jews! Okay?"

He looked around the room and saw the shock in their faces. Only Sarah smiled at him, and it was a stiff, frozen, mask-like smile.

"Come, Danny, sit down," said his grandmother, taking his arm.

He jerked his arm away from her and stood his ground.

"Danny, please," said his father.

But Danny ignored his father. He looked around the dining room and saw that everyone was looking at him with horror, staring at the monster. They all looked stunned, adults and children alike. They were speechless, obviously appalled by the sight of the loathsome beast standing before them. A moment ago, he had felt so righteous, so justified in speaking out. He spoke out to defend his mother, so what could be wrong about that? He had thought that his biting sarcasm would be the perfect retort to the bigoted attacks of his crazy Tanta Zlata. But now he was reviled by his own family, and he began to shrink into himself. He saw in their eyes that they were horrified by what he had said, and he felt despised. He wished that he could take back his words, but he just stood before them, mute and humiliated. He turned and left the house without another word. He was still angry at Tanta Zlata for what she had said. He was still humiliated by the image of the family looking at him with that look of shock and revulsion. And he was angry at them all for making him feel so humiliated. He passed a couple of kids on the street, but he couldn't look up at them. He walked ahead with his eyes on the sidewalk before him, hoping that no one in the neighborhood was looking at him, but suspecting that the whole world saw him in his shame.

18

A Brief History of the
Wingback Chair

For Dan, his favorite red chair was the key element of his house that made it feel like a home, and he sat there on a Sunday evening after returning from Denver. He and Abby talked at length about his visit to the nursery, and he again found it comforting to hear her thoughts. And the simple act of sitting in his chair gave him the sense of an orderly world in which one might actually have some peace.

Unfortunately, that peace was disrupted as soon as Cordelia came into the room. There was another argument and another frown of disapproval from Abby after the argument. Dan's wife and daughter both withdrew from the family room—Abby to the kitchen, Cordelia to her bedroom—and he sat by himself in his favorite chair in the family room.

As bad moods bring bad thoughts, his mind turned to the nursery in Denver, in particular to the discovery of the "Don Juan" who met his mother for a daily lunch. He had stopped imagining that this man had known his mother before she left Detroit, but he couldn't stop thinking about the situation as it was told to him. He couldn't quite grasp the thought that his mother would do such a treacherous thing, but he really had no reason not to believe it.

He put down the book he was reading and tapped on the arm of his chair. He tried to think of happier times, which quickly led him to think about the day when he and Abby had purchased his chair years ago, in the early days of their marriage. He had voiced a wish to have a nice comfortable chair for reading, and Abby had taken him to a furniture store that very day, a pleasant Saturday in the spring, much like today had been. They wandered through the store for a few minutes while she suggested this or that chair to try. Then a certain blue armchair caught his eye, and he went straight to it and sat down. As far as he was concerned, the shopping trip was over.

"Can I help you folks?" A salesman had appeared from behind Dan, just as his newly-wed wife caught up with him. Dan was a bit startled by the salesman, a portly man dressed in a rumpled brown suit and a brightly colored necktie decorated with pineapples. He looked to be in his late forties. Dan, from the vantage point of his twenty-nine years, thought him to be rather old. His basic view of salespeople was distrustful. They were always trying to sell him something he didn't really want.

"Do you like that one, Dan?" Abby asked.

"Yeah, I like this one," he said to Abby. Then he forced a smile to the salesman. He braced himself for the sales pitch to buy something else, probably something more expensive.

"This chair is called a wingback," said the salesman, smiling and obviously trying to be friendly.

"Yes, I know that," said Dan.

"Dan." Abby spoke in a concerned tone with a hint of a reprimand in her voice.

He knew that she was always worried about his behavior in public, always concerned that he might be less than perfectly charming to people. But he wasn't trying to be rude. He just happened to know what a wingback chair was. And he hated it when salesmen followed him around in a store trying to tell him about the merchandise. They never knew anything about the goods they were hawking, and it would be better if they would just leave him alone. This salesman, however, was undeterred.

"Do you know the history of the wingback chair?" he asked cheerfully.

"I do not," Dan said, looking at the man's pineapple tie.

"It was actually developed in England during the 1600s. The side panels or 'wings' extend forward from the back of the chair for the purpose of keeping warm on a cold night. For the person seated, the wings were designed to block some of the cold drafts, as well as to trap some of the heat from the fireplace. Obviously, one would ideally sit right in front of the fireplace in those days."

"Well, that's interesting," said Dan. He could see Abby studying him, probably trying to assess whether or not his tone was sarcastic. In fact, he was finding this little history lesson of great interest. "I didn't realize it was so functional."

"Absolutely!" said the salesman. "Very functional. But it wasn't always so comfortable. This type of chair was initially built solely of wood. Eventually, upholstery was added, and then horsehair for padding. There are many types of wingbacks, but this model is known as the Chaucer wingback. I suppose it must have been named for the author. Maybe you had to read Chaucer in school?"

"Actually, I'm a college English instructor, so yes, I know Chaucer."

"Oh, that's great! Then this must be your chair. A Chaucer wingback for the English professor!"

Dan was rapidly warming to the salesman. The man actually knew what he was talking about. And he knew who Chaucer was. For Dan, literature was always a bridge across the moat. If another person knew a bit about a great writer, then there was something to share, a mutual friend to discuss.

"You seem to know a lot about your merchandise," he said.

"Well, the history of furniture is really quite interesting," said the salesman. "Old furniture tells you so much about how people used to live."

"Yes, I suppose it does. I never thought much about it before."

"Oh, yes, I would much rather learn history from an old antique wooden chest than from a history book full of dry facts."

"You have a point there," said Dan.

The salesman sat down in a chair opposite Dan. "The wife and me, we like to go shopping for antiques when we're on vacation. We talk about opening up an antique store one day. We don't have the money right now, but maybe someday."

Dan chatted with the salesman for a while, and then he became aware of Abby standing by patiently. "Do you have a chair like this in red?" Dan asked the salesman.

"Oh, you can order it in many colors and styles. It takes about two to three weeks for the finished chair to come in. Let me bring you a book of styles to choose from."

"I just want a red one," Dan said quickly.

The salesman looked at Dan with an indulgent smile. Dan felt a moment of embarrassment, realizing that he probably sounded a bit childish. "I just think it would be very attractive in red."

"No doubt, it would," said the salesman. He disappeared behind a counter and returned with a thick book of upholstery patterns. Abby helped Dan find a plain red fabric, and the deal was done.

"Good luck with that antique shop," Dan told the salesman as they left the store. "I hope you get your chance to have it."

"Well, thanks! And I hope you enjoy your Chaucer wingback."

And he had indeed enjoyed his chair all these years. He had spent many a happy hour reading and writing in that chair. But now, sitting in the same chair in his quiet house, he felt unhappy. Family life was just too damned hard, and he didn't know how to fix it. He thought wistfully of the early days of his marriage, and he wondered how things had become so terribly complicated.

19

The Lord's Prayer

On a rainy Saturday afternoon in May, Cordelia chose a corner of her bedroom and placed a big cushion there. She sat down on the cushion, made herself comfortable, and closed her eyes. She breathed in and thought, *I am breathing in.* She breathed out and thought, *I am breathing out.* But her next thought strayed from this binary script. She thought about the newspaper article about her grandmother. She had taken the article to school (with her father's permission) and made a photocopy of it, so she could pin it to the bulletin board in her room. She had taken down a few photos of herself and her friends to make room for the article. Along the bottom of the bulletin board was the latest quote she had pinned up, thinking of her father as she did so.

"In whom there is no sympathy for living beings: know him as an outcast." – The Buddha

She forcibly pulled her mind back to her breathing. *I am breathing in. I am breathing out.* Would they eventually find her grandmother? And what would that meeting be like? The newspaper article about the Denver nursery was sent from Fairbanks, Alaska. Was her grandmother living in Alaska? *I am breathing in.* Maybe she should just save her money and make a trip to Fairbanks and track her down. *I am breathing out.*

This was hopeless, she thought. She couldn't keep her mind on her breathing for sixty seconds in a row. She had attended a discussion on Buddhism at a meditation center in Albany, and the teacher had called it "monkey mind." The mind just makes a lot of noise like a bunch of monkeys in the jungle. You just have to return patiently to your breath. *I am breathing in. I am breathing out.*

She tried again, but her mind just wandered all over the place, particularly in the direction of the grandmother she had never met. When she blocked those thoughts out, Mr. T drifted in. She kept seeing his face, especially his big brown-cow eyes, looking at her with such kindness. She couldn't get that image out of her mind, and she vaguely realized that she didn't really want to. Absolutely hopeless. She just wasn't in the right mood to meditate today. Or perhaps she was doing it wrong. But how could one get it wrong? She was simply supposed to pay attention to her breathing. Maybe she couldn't meditate. Maybe she could never be a Buddha. But the people at the meditation center had told her this was all part of the journey, so she tried not to be discouraged.

She decided to give up on meditating for the day and work on finishing her senior paper. She picked up the pages piled on her bedside nightstand and thought about poverty in America. That was the topic she had chosen for her paper, and she just had to finish her conclusion. She read the last paragraph, in which she repeated the figure of twenty per cent. That was the number she had read in her review of the research, although it seemed impossibly high. Twenty per cent of American kids were living in poverty. How could this be true in such a wealthy country? And why wasn't this being addressed immediately? The thought of little kids going to bed hungry made her feel miserable. Kids were going to bed hungry right here in the United States in 1997. In fact, kids were going to bed hungry in Albany, New York, just a few minutes down the road from where she lived in her comfortable middle-class suburb. Why didn't the high school administrators just close the school for a few days and mobilize everyone to deliver food to those families?

When she first began to research the subject of poverty, she had the same sense of shock and disbelief that she had felt many times before. Whenever she heard about a major tragedy affecting other people—war, poverty, natural disasters—she always felt astonished that no one around her seemed to share her sense of urgency. No one felt the need to drop what they were doing and take action to remedy the problem. People just seemed to go about their business as if they had never heard the news at all. Shouldn't people all react in unison to help other people in distress?

There was always a jarring dissonance for her between the world as it should be and the world as it actually was. Sometimes she felt like a misplaced person, a person living in the wrong place at the wrong time. But when in history were things any better? Where would she fit in better? Apparently, the world had always been a place where terrible calamities befell people, and many of those calamities were ignored by one's neighbors. Or worse, caused by them.

No one seemed to react to any of this, except her father, but his reaction was always one of outrage. He would sit with his newspaper in the evening and protest to no one in particular. "Why the hell don't those idiots in Washington do something about this?" His anger was always unpleasant, always unhelpful, but at least he saw the problems of other people and he reacted. At least it bothered him. As difficult as he was, Cordelia sometimes felt a secret bond with him in their reactions to the troubles of this world. At least they both cared.

She could hear her father talking downstairs. Earlier in the day, her parents had been talking again about her father's trip to Denver, although there really wasn't anything left to say. They had dissected it from every angle, but they still couldn't see any path forward. There was simply no lead to follow after the visit to that plant nursery. No one knew where her grandmother had gone after working at the nursery, and no one knew the name of the "Don Juan" who would come to have lunch with her. Her father seemed so disheartened, but Cordelia still felt hopeful. Someone wanted them to find her grandmother.

She found it hard to concentrate on her senior paper, and she decided to go downstairs and see if her parents were still talking about the Denver clue. There they were, sitting together on the couch in the family room. This by itself was a startling sight, since her father always sat by himself in his favorite red chair, and her mother usually sat by herself on the couch. Her parents were looking at a piece of paper and talking together.

"What's up?" Cordelia asked.

"It's another clue about our grandma!" said Gabe, who was sitting cross-legged on the floor opposite her parents. "It looks like we're going to find her!"

"I'm not so sure about that," said her mother to Cordelia, "but the mail just arrived, and your father received a second message from Alaska. We're trying to figure out what it means."

"Oh!" said Cordelia. "What is it?"

Her father was looking down at the paper, but then he looked up directly at her. She realized how rarely they actually made eye contact since the big fight a few weeks ago. He held out the paper to her. It was a copy of a prayer, printed in an Old English font. At the top of the page was an image of two hands together in prayer. She read the first couple lines.

Our Father who art in Heaven,
Hallowed be thy name.

"I don't get it," she said. "What's this got to do with my grandmother?"

"Keep reading," her father said.

She read the rest of the prayer. At the bottom of the page was a hand-written message.

Take care of yourself. Kate

"Wow!" said Cordelia. "So, you think she wrote that?"

"It's definitely her handwriting," said her father.

"I'll bet we find her soon," said Gabe.

Cordelia took a seat in her father's favorite chair. No one ever sat in that chair except him, but he was on the couch beside her mother, and his chair was the closest seat facing her parents. It was odd to see them sitting side by side on the couch, with smiling family photos hanging on the wall behind them. To their left, on the mantel piece above the fireplace, there was a small framed photograph of her grandmother as a little girl. Cordelia looked again at the paper she held. "But it's obviously not written to you, Dad, or she would have signed it 'Mom' instead of 'Kate.'"

"Obviously," he replied.

"Dad, I wasn't trying to hurt your feelings. I'm just trying to help figure this out."

"Of course," he said.

"Let's all get along," said her mother in her cheerful, sing-song voice. "We just have to think about this." Her mother picked up the envelope and studied it carefully. "The same postmark. Fairbanks, Alaska. But nothing else on the envelope that might help us."

Cordelia handed the prayer back to her father, and they all took turns looking at it and rereading it. When it was passed back to her, she said, "The paper is definitely old. Not as yellow and parched as the newspaper article from Denver, but definitely old."

Her father frowned. "But old paper is not a clue. There's nothing on the paper to indicate the time when she signed it, or where she was when she did. The newspaper article at least led me someplace. This is worthless."

Cordelia read the prayer again. "Maybe there's a clue in the wording of the prayer itself," she said. She read aloud: "'And lead us not into temptation, but deliver us from evil.' Maybe Grandma was dealing with some kind of temptation. Struggling with some kind of demons."

Her father was silent. Sometimes, it seemed to Cordelia that nothing she said was any good to him. If Gabe had said the same exact thing, it would have been fine, but every word out of her mouth seemed to make his mood darker. She sat there opposite her parents for a while longer, as they all passed the prayer back and forth. Finally, she found it intolerable to sit in the room with him, and she went back up to her bedroom.

Her father was right about one thing, she thought. This second clue was pretty worthless. Still, the clues were being sent to him by someone, and that person must know where she was. And she must be alive or they wouldn't be sending the clues at all. At least, Cordelia hoped so. It therefore seemed possible—even probable?—that she was going to meet her grandmother one day soon. But what would that be like? Would they sit together and have wonderful conversations? Cordelia would love to have a grandmother to talk to. Her paternal grandfather had died before she was born, and her mother's parents had died when she was just a little girl, so this would be her only living grandparent. She eagerly imagined sitting and talking with her long-lost grandmother. Everyone said she looked like her grandmother, and photos certainly buttressed that opinion. The photo on the mantel piece left people marveling over the similarities between the two of them. Maybe they would have a lot in common.

But what if her grandmother was just a crazy old homeless lady who left her family because she was mentally unstable? That wouldn't be much of a reunion. And Cordelia thought about her great-uncle Jack, who was clearly not in his right mind. Jack and her grandmother were brother and sister, so maybe her grandmother was also mentally ill. Maybe they would find her in a psychiatric hospital, all drugged up and barely able to converse at all.

Cordelia's mind did a quick turn-around to the more positive possibilities. She and her grandmother would sit together and have long, leisurely chats. She would tell her new-found relative all about her life in upstate New York. She would talk about her family and her friends, her recent interest in Buddhism, and her college plans. They would become soulmates. And her grandmother would listen attentively and offer worldly wisdom as a wise ancestor.

But Cordelia would also want to ask about her grandmother's life. Why had she abandoned her family? If she was not mentally ill, then what other reason could there be? From what little

Cordelia knew, she had left voluntarily. She had even left a note. But why? Cordelia's father had always described her grandfather as a very kind, gentle person, so she couldn't have been fleeing a violent husband. Who would just pack up and leave her husband and two kids? Cordelia would definitely want to ask her about this, and she would press her for an answer. After all these years, her grandmother owed her an explanation. And maybe, after they got acquainted with each other, Cordelia would even bring up the topic of her father. Someone definitely owed her an explanation for *that* crazy situation.

20

A Missed Opportunity

Cordelia would be eighteen in a couple days, but she was feeling too angry to be happy about her birthday. When she first stormed away from the house, she was energized by her hatred of her father. Once again, he had to start the day by questioning her about her homework and implying that she wasn't doing as much as she could. Why did he have to start the morning by antagonizing her? Why did he have to spoil such a beautiful spring morning? Everything was starting to bloom, but she couldn't appreciate any of it. One of their neighbors grew beautiful lilac bushes which were just starting to display their purple flowers, but she couldn't enjoy them as she walked by. She added this to her growing list of grievances against him: He had ruined the lilacs for her.

Cordelia walked down the street at a furious pace, never looking back. She was sick of her father and sick of his moods. If she could know ahead of time when he was going to be difficult, that would be almost bearable, but she never knew what kind of a mood he would be in. She hated his moods. It seemed to her that one person's bad mood should affect only that one person.

He ought not to spread it around. When her father was in a bad mood, it affected everyone in the house, like a plague spewing vicious little microbes around until everyone was sick. Oh, how she hated his moods!

She walked down the street with a bold, confident step, and a mind cleared for the single purpose of battle. She thought only of how she would get back at him. She imagined all sorts of clever, devastating things that she could say to him, things that would not only demolish his arguments against her this morning, but also wound him so badly that he would never, *never* be able to attack her again.

By the time she got to school, though, she was miserable. Somehow, the fortress built with righteous indignation had collapsed, and her armamentarium had been destroyed. She couldn't think of any other indignities to hurl at him. And what difference would it make if she did say something to him? She would never win an argument with him, anyway. And there was nothing she could ever do that would be good enough in his eyes, so his criticism would never stop. Her mind filled with negative thoughts about herself. She probably wasn't working up to her potential in high school; she probably didn't deserve to go to such a good college; she probably wouldn't succeed in life, just as he seemed to think.

She went to her first period class, but she really paid no attention to the math problems the teacher was reviewing. She was engrossed in another line of thought: What if she were to die today? Not by suicide, exactly, but what if she just absentmindedly walked in front of a car because she was so upset about her father's awful behavior? Would he feel guilty? Would he feel that it was his fault? That would be just what he deserved. He *should* feel guilty. He should live the rest of his life with horrible, unrelenting guilt about being such a crappy father. She imagined people gathering at her funeral and talking amongst themselves. *She just walked out into traffic? My Lord, she must have been terribly distracted by something, terribly upset. Do you have any idea what might have been troubling her, Dan?* A good dose of guilt would be perfect justice. And maybe then he would actually appreciate her. *What a shame! You had such a great kid, Dan.*

Her thoughts continued in this manner, and her mood was unremittingly miserable until she thought about visiting Mr. T after school. The thought of him lifted her gloomy mood almost immediately. With this in mind, she was able to endure (barely) the vocabulary review in her French class. (Why didn't her teacher speak more French in the classroom? she thought. How would they ever really learn to speak it? She would be totally lost in Paris.) In fourth period, she weathered a dreary session of her English class, which consisted of a boring discussion of a boring novel. Lunch, gym, and the rest of the day passed slowly, very slowly.

Her last class ended, and she could finally visit Mr. T. She was eager to tell him that she was turning eighteen. She felt a bit silly for wanting to tell him, but she needed him to know that she wouldn't be a seventeen-year-old high school kid for much longer. She would be eighteen, a young woman who was capable of carrying on an adult conversation with him.

She went upstairs to the second floor, walking quickly toward his room. Just opposite his classroom was the science lab, and she realized that she had left her physics book there earlier in the day. She stepped into the lab and saw her book sitting on the counter where she had left it. She complimented herself for at least remembering where she had forgotten something. Unfortunately, her sense of satisfaction was short-lived.

"Hi, Dee!"

She turned around to see Perry, one of the only kids in school who ever called her "Dee." It was a nickname he had chosen for her without actually asking if she went by nicknames. It always seemed to her that the kids who gave her a nickname—Dee, Delia, Cordy—were the kids who felt left out. They always tried too hard to create a special connection with her by using a nickname.

"Hi, Perry." The boy standing before her reminded her of a big, shaggy dog. His uncombed hair spilled over onto his forehead, and his clothes always looked like he had slept in them. She silently prayed that he wouldn't go off on one of his endless monologues, but her prayers went unanswered. He began with his reflections about their physics class—"too elementary," which he considered to be a hilarious pun—but he quickly digressed into an unsolicited lecture on the physics of light and the human eye, replete with a physiological treatise on the function of rods and cones in the retina. He went on to tell her (not for the first time) about his plans to go to medical school and become an ophthalmologist. Cordelia listened as well as she could, knowing that other kids would routinely just walk away from Perry mid-sentence. He always seemed so desperate to have someone listen to him, so she couldn't really just cut him off. What harm would it do to give him a minute or two of her time?

She told him that this was all very interesting, although she managed to maintain eye contact with Perry while turning herself so that she could see the hallway. She was worried that Mr. T might leave before she could talk to him. Perry, of course, was unaware of her concerns. When she told him politely that she was hoping to catch Mr. T before he left for the day, he cheerfully continued his discourse without acknowledging her words at all.

In fact, he moved seamlessly from his career plans to the history of his mother's gall bladder attacks. Apparently, she was in the hospital right now, and he was on his way to visit her. Cordelia wanted to interrupt him, but how could she interrupt when he was talking about his mother's illness? He spoke about her problems in the same pedantic way he described the human retina, but she could sense that he was worried about his mother. She reminded herself that she wouldn't want someone to interrupt her if it were her mother in the hospital.

From the hallway, she heard the sound of a door closing. Mr. T walked by the science lab with his briefcase. He didn't happen to look into the lab, so he didn't even notice her. For a moment, she hated Perry. She absolutely hated him. And in that moment, she also realized that visiting Mr. T was more than a pleasurable pastime at the end of the day. The visits had become—*he* had become—an essential part of her happiness. This was a discovery both exciting and confusing to her.

21

A Literary Mystery

Ever since his mother left home, Danny took solace in books. When he lost himself in a novel, he could temporarily leave his own world and join another. He would often read after school, if he didn't have homework that needed his attention. When his father called him for dinner, he was jarred by the harsh re-entry into his own life. He couldn't wait till dinner was over and he could return to his novel. He had his favorite chair in the living room, the big red comfortable chair where his mother used to sit and read. She, too, had loved to read, and she always had a book in progress. She had a larger vocabulary than other adults he knew. The neighbors at the end of the block were a bit "ostentatious" in their choice of clothing and cars. Uncle Jack was "taciturn." The politician speaking on the television sounded "disingenuous" to her.

Before her disappearance, Danny's mother used to sit in her chair and do the *New York Times* crossword puzzle. After breakfast on Sunday mornings, she would invite her family to solve the puzzles with her.

"You, business man!" she would say to Danny's father. "A legal claim on another person's property. Four letters."

"Lien, maybe," his father said.

"Sounds good!" his mother announced, writing down his answer.

"You, bird-watcher girl!" she said to Sarah. "A bird upside down. Eight letters."

"Nuthatch!" Sarah said.

"Great!" said his mother, penciling in the word. "Now, you! English Professor! The clue is this: In literature, Nathaniel's colored letter. Seven spaces."

Danny thought for a long minute. "Scarlet?" he said. "From Nathaniel Hawthorne's *Scarlet Letter*."

"Terrific!" said his mother, smiling proudly at him.

Now that his mother was gone, Danny would sit and read in the same chair. (It was called a wingback, she had told him, because the sides were called wings.) In fact, he developed the habit of leaving his bookbag and a favorite book on the floor by that chair, and his sister and father never questioned his claim to the chair, his personal territory where no one else would dare to trespass.

In school, General Patton told the class to read *To Kill a Mockingbird*. He enjoyed reading the story at home in his favorite chair, but what impressed him the most was the fact that the narrator, a little girl named Scout, was being raised by her father. Early in the book, Danny learned that Scout's mother died of a heart attack when Scout was only two years old. Other than this isolated, cold fact, there was no further information about this terrible loss. Danny was puzzled that the author had virtually nothing to say about it. Nothing was said about what kind of person the mother was, or about the effect of her absence on

Scout. In class, he was even more perplexed. The discussion was mainly focused on the issue of racism; occasionally, there was some conversation about the characters in the book, especially Scout's admirable father. But no one ever mentioned the loss of her mother! Danny was dumbfounded. No one even seemed to recognize that this little girl had lost her mother. The author had nothing much to say about it, his teacher was mute about it, and not a single student brought it up. Apparently, the entire world had joined in a conspiracy of silence about the worst thing that could ever happen to a kid.

One Saturday afternoon, he was at home thinking about this, and he suddenly realized that *To Kill a Mockingbird* was not the only book about a child without a mother. What about *The Adventures of Tom Sawyer?* Wasn't Tom being raised by his Aunt Polly? Where was his mother? Danny ran up to his room and pulled his copy of the book from his bookshelf. He spent the rest of the weekend re-reading it, searching the pages for any mention of Tom Sawyer's mother. In the first chapter, he read that Tom's mother was dead. Aunt Polly referred to Tom as "my own dead sister's boy, poor thing." But how did the mother die? When did she die? How did Tom take it when he lost his mother? Nothing was said about any of this. Mark Twain had nothing else to say about her. Another member of the Conspiracy of Silence.

Later in the week, another revelation: Huckleberry Finn had no mother either! There was a father—the drunken, brutal character of Pap—but again no mother. Danny reread this book, too, searching for Huck's mother in the pages of the book. Again, he found only scant mention of her. In an early chapter, Huck's illiterate Pap was scolding him about getting an education and learning to read.

Your mother couldn't read, and she couldn't write, nuther, before she died. And that was that. The rest of the book had nothing to say about the matter.

The theme of the motherless child in literature took hold in his mind. It was a great mystery to him that these authors had written about a child without a mother, and no one, neither reader (his high school classmates and teacher) nor writer, seemed willing to discuss the mother's absence. And the more he thought about this puzzling phenomenon, the more he saw it. He found this theme at every level of writing. He noticed that several popular television shows had this theme in their plots. When he pulled out his book on Greek mythology from last year, he was stunned to confirm his memory of the goddess Athena, who sprang fully formed from the head of Zeus. No mother! A couple months ago, he had read Shakespeare's *King Lear* for class. Again, the same theme: Old King Lear had three grown daughters, including the kind-hearted Cordelia, but there was no mother in the story. Why would all these writers be telling stories about a child without a mother? Had they gone through an experience like his? And if so, why did none of them talk about it in their writing?

Early in his discovery of missing mothers in literature, he decided that he would speak up in class and bring this problem to the attention of his teacher and the other kids. He imagined how surprised his classmates would be, and how impressed his teacher would be. After all, here was a glaring mystery in English literature—and world literature, for that matter. He sat down in his English class to listen to General Patton discuss the ending of *To Kill a Mockingbird*. Kids talked about what they considered to be the most important themes in the book. He started to raise his hand but felt paralyzed. It occurred to him that his comment might not be well received. What if he had just missed something in the books he had read? What if he were wrong? If this were such a problem in literature, wouldn't someone have noticed it before? Or maybe he was right, but no one else would think it was a significant issue. Sitting at his desk in class, he felt strongly that he was right, but he just couldn't take the risk of having his idea rejected by the others. Besides, kids were already talking about the disappearance of his mother, and he dreaded bringing attention to himself.

He continued to think about the problem at home. One evening, he came up with a secret theory. These authors often wrote that the mother had died, but their adult readers would understand that this was just a socially acceptable pretense. Everyone reading such a book would understand that the real story was about a mother who had abandoned her family. Like Moses, for instance. He reread the Old Testament story of Moses, who grew up without his mother. That was a story that made sense. The mother was alive, but she feared that her Hebrew infant would be killed by Pharaoh's men. She put him in a basket and left the basket at the banks of the Nile River to save him.

All those stories about mothers who died made no sense, unless the writers were following a time-honored literary convention of sparing the reader the ugly truth. Mothers sometimes leave their families. Apparently, it happens more often than anyone wants to admit, so the great novelists craft their stories about motherless children without actually describing the unthinkable abandonment.

This theory made sense to Danny for a few days, until he compared it to his knowledge of real families in his neighborhood. He only knew one kid who had lost his mother, and the mother had actually died about two years ago. Danny attended the funeral. He listened to the eulogies in a church. He saw the poor woman in her coffin. Aside from that one kid, he could think of no one else who had lost a mother, and certainly no one whose mother had simply left the family for no apparent reason whatsoever. His theory started to fall apart, but he struggled to hold onto it, even in the absence of evidence. After all, without it he was left with the alarming reality of what had happened to him and *only* to him.

22

A Hurt Knee

Late one evening, Dan sat by himself in his favorite chair in the family room. He couldn't stop thinking about his mother actually dating another man in Denver. And he couldn't figure out how to deal with his daughter's terrible attitude toward him. Today had been better, but only for a short time. Cordelia had seemed very interested in the clues about her missing grandmother. They actually had a nice chat about the subject. By the end of the evening, however, she was angry with him again because of one little innocent comment he made about her responsibilities around the house. She had gone up to her room after the argument, and he hadn't seen her since.

Abby was clearly upset with him, too. There was no problem with his son, but Gabe was just fourteen, and a young fourteen indeed. Gabe was just a kid. Cordelia was older and more mature, but Dan couldn't relate to her. Abby somehow seemed to understand Cordelia, and they obviously had a very close relationship. He felt like an outsider in his own home.

When he stood up to get himself a bowl of ice cream, he accidentally knocked his reading lamp over. In his attempt to catch it before it hit the floor, he banged his elbow against the little side table that held the lamp.

"Damn it!" He had hit his elbow at just the wrong place, at the "funny bone," and he moaned in pain. When the lamp hit the floor, the bulb shattered, so he went to get a broom and dustpan. His elbow was still smarting, and the pain brought a memory to mind.

He remembered the afternoon of Christmas Eve years ago, when Cordelia was only about five years old. She was sitting at the kitchen table eating a snack he had made for her. It was peanut butter on crackers. How odd the things we remember! She only liked peanut butter on a certain kind of cracker, and he would make it for her, with just the right amount of peanut butter on it. He had been trying to fix a leak underneath the kitchen sink while she ate her snack and cheerfully chatted away about her day. When he got up to look for another wrench, he accidentally banged his knee against the open cabinet door to the pipes under the sink.

"Damn it!" He bent down and grabbed his knee, wincing.

"Oh, Daddy! When your knee hurts, my knee hurts, too."

He looked over and saw Cordelia, his five-year-old child, holding her knee in her little hands. Her face wore a pained expression, and she looked like she actually felt the pain.

Another memory came to mind as he swept up the shards of the shattered light bulb. When Cordelia heard about a clothing drive for needy kids in Albany, she insisted that her mother take her door to door in the neighborhood to ask for secondhand clothing. When was that? She was probably in the seventh grade, only twelve years old. But she acted like someone who had been waiting for twelve years to get such an opportunity to start her own grassroots community event. By the time she was done, their kitchen looked like a warehouse for a clothing exporter, with large piles of shirts, pants, socks, and coats, all sorted and neatly arranged. He brought home a pint of her favorite dessert (Roberta's Orange Sherbet) to celebrate her industriousness.

Maybe he should talk to her tonight. He went up the stairs and along the hall to Cordelia's room. He could see that the light was still shining under her door, so he knew she must be awake. For reasons he couldn't fathom, he felt a bit nervous. What would he say to her? She never wanted to listen to anything he said. She was a good kid, though, really. She did help her mother in the house, although not as often as she should. She helped her little brother with his homework. She could be difficult, for sure, but he couldn't deny that he was a big part of the problem.

There must be some way to make things right again. He had an idea. He went back downstairs and wrote a little note on a scrap of paper. As he wrote, he thought about more pleasant times when he and Cordelia would read together from the comic strips in the newspaper. Their favorite was Calvin and Hobbes, a comic about a little boy named Calvin and his stuffed tiger, Hobbes. Sometimes they would get a pair of scissors and cut out a favorite episode to post on the refrigerator.

He found her shoes where she had kicked them off in the family room. He put the note into one of the shoes, went back upstairs, and left the shoes right outside her bedroom door. When she was younger, this had been his little routine to help her start her day right: her shoes by her door and a note inside one of them, usually with some reference to the comic strip. He knew that she often felt frustrated with herself for being so disorganized, and this was his fatherly effort to help. At least she wouldn't have to search the house for her shoes.

Hobbes found your shoes again. Have a nice day.   *Dad*

23

Tikkun Olam

The only time Danny went to the synagogue was in the fall for Yom Kippur, the Day of Atonement. He would go every year to keep his father company, since his sister and his Catholic mother had no interest in attending the lengthy services. Typically, the two of them walked to the synagogue—driving was prohibited on Yom Kippur, the holiest day of the Jewish year—and his father chatted the entire way, extolling the virtues of the synagogue, the neighborhood, and life in Michigan overall. He always found something about the weather to commend. A sunny day was beautiful, a cloudy day was a nice break from the sun, a rainy day was good for the farmers.

The year that Danny's mother disappeared, they walked to the synagogue in silence on a cool, overcast day in October. Danny's father said nothing, and Danny felt bad that he couldn't think of anything to say to cheer his father up. They walked past a row of shops, including his father's favorite Jewish bakery, without a word. Danny had an urge to go into the bakery and buy his father one of his favorite treats, but the bakery was closed for the holiday, and his father was fasting, anyway.

When they arrived at the synagogue, a man greeted them at the door and gave them each a *yarmulke* and a *talis*—a skullcap and a prayer shawl. Danny put the yarmulke on his head and the talis around his shoulders. His father brightened up enough to greet friends in the congregation, but Danny could see that they all looked at his father—and at him—with pity in their eyes. He couldn't wait to take his seat and escape the scrutiny. He looked away from the men talking to his father and scanned the large sanctuary. He hadn't seen the place since Yom Kippur a year ago, and he was struck by the plainness of it. He thought of his mother's church, with its colorful stained-glass windows, dramatic arched ceilings, and carved wooden pillars. By comparison, the synagogue seemed utilitarian. The walls were plain white, the seats were comfortably cushioned but unadorned, and the windows were clear glass. The only craftsmanship in the building was the "ark" at the front of the sanctuary, the wooden cabinet that held the scrolls of the Old Testament. Standing twelve feet tall, the ark was ornately hand-carved with intricate designs on every side. The Hebrew letters of a prayer ran across the top.

As soon as they were seated and the service began, Danny wished it would end. In the past, it felt comforting to sit beside his father and chant the Hebrew prayers. Now, it just felt tedious and boring, and the service on Yom Kippur always dragged on for hours. Since people often left the sanctuary for short breaks during the long service, he began at once to plan his exit. Perhaps the rabbi's sermon would be a good time to slip out and get some air.

After about an hour of the prayers, Rabbi Greenbaum finally stood at the pulpit and got ready to deliver his sermon. He stroked his neatly trimmed beard and looked down at his notes before beginning. Danny closed his prayer book and laid it down on an empty seat. He was about to make his exit, but his attention was drawn by the rabbi's opening remarks.

"During these High Holy Days," said the rabbi, "it would be a good time for us to reflect on the Jewish concept of Tikkun Olam. We translate this from the Hebrew as *repairing the world* or *healing the world*. Say it with me: Ti-KOON o-LAM." The congregation murmured together:

"Tikkun Olam."

"And the world surely needs healing. We have always known this, of course, but periodically we get a reminder. We pick up the morning newspaper and read about some injustice, some suffering in the world. Or perhaps something has happened to you *personally* over the course of the past year, something that should never have happened. And this event—this loss, this injustice, this outrage—jolted you into remembering that the world is broken."

Danny remained in his seat, engrossed now in the rabbi's words.

"We think, at such moments, that God does not seem to be following any sensible plan. The Universe is ruptured, and it stands in sore need of healing and repair." Surely, the rabbi must know. Rabbi Greenbaum must be speaking directly to him. Danny looked at his father. Had he told the rabbi about his mother? He could read nothing in his father's face. Had someone else told the rabbi?

The rabbi knew who Danny was, because his father was friendly with the rabbi—his father was friendly with everyone—and Danny had often stood with his father while he talked to the rabbi before and after the services. When Danny was younger, he used to come with his father to the weekly services on Saturdays, and the rabbi always remembered him and he seemed to like him. The rabbi must know.

"Tikkun Olam. Healing the World. Today, we use the term when we speak of social justice. We use it to refer to the good works of synagogues and other organizations that raise money for orphans or send food to the needy or speak up for the oppressed. It applies to any group activity that helps those who are less fortunate. Tikkun Olam. Say the words with me."

The congregation responded: "Tikkun Olam."

"But there is another sense to this powerful little phrase, another meaning that has nothing to do with committees and fundraising campaigns. I refer to the individual meaning of Tikkun Olam. I speak now to each one of you individually."

The Rabbi paused to sweep his gaze from left to right across the seats of the crowded synagogue. Danny sat up ramrod straight, with full attention. *Does he see me? Is he scanning the crowd to find me? Is he talking to me?*

"It is not solely the responsibility of groups and committees to heal this fractured world. It is the responsibility of each one of us. You and me. Each of us. And we don't have to ship tons of food to the other side of the planet. All we have to do is perform the smallest acts of loving-kindness, and then we are contributing to the enormous project called Tikkun Olam. We are healing a broken world. Someone is lost on the street and you stop to offer him directions. This is Tikkun Olam. You give up your seat on the bus to an old woman. This is Tikkun Olam. You take time out of your busy day to visit a sick friend. This is Tikkun Olam. Say it with me."

"Tikkun Olam," said the congregation.

The rabbi continued with his sermon, but Danny was distracted by his own racing thoughts. He began to imagine all the

little things he would do to help others. He would help a class-
mate who was struggling with math. He would help his father
with chores around the house. He would help his grandmother in
the kitchen on Sundays when she made her chicken soup. He felt
so excited by all the possibilities before him that he could barely
stay seated. He was determined to make his life a continuous series of small acts of kindness, knowing that someday his benevolent deeds would add up to a big change in the world around him.

The service continued as his feverish plans continued to
evolve in his head. At some point, he realized that the rabbi had
finished his sermon and everyone was chanting a prayer. He sat
next to his father and looked at him. He tried to figure out what
he could do to help his father deal with the loss of his wife. He
couldn't think of anything at the moment, but never mind, he
would find a way to help. Not a day would go by without some
charitable action toward another human being.

When Danny came out of his private thoughts and looked up
toward the front of the synagogue again, he saw the cantor join
the rabbi at the pulpit and pick up the shofar, the ram's horn. It
was time for the annual blowing of the shofar, a traditional part
of the service of repentance and reflection.

"In a moment," said Rabbi Greenbaum, "we will have the
blowing of the *shofar*. But first, I have one more thing to say about
Tikkun Olam and fixing this broken world of ours. It's a very
personal thing that I want to say to someone whose world was
shattered this year." The Rabbi paused and scanned the faces
of the congregation again. Danny sat up straighter and held his
breath. *He knows. He knows all about it. He's going to mention me
now. He's going to call my name and talk to the whole congregation
about me. He's going to tell everyone what happened to me, and then
he will ask them all to keep me in their thoughts and prayers while they*

practice Tikkun Olam. And he will ask me to practice Tikkun Olam to help heal the world. And I will promise him that I will do it every day. I promise. I promise. There was a long minute or so while the rabbi continued to look around.

There was a bit of coughing and throat clearing from various points in the synagogue. The sounds were gently muffled by the carpeted floor throughout the large sanctuary. Danny always felt that it was only natural to speak softly in there, as the sounds were always muted when they reached one's ear. When he was young, he used to think that it would sound like this if all the people in the sanctuary could sit together on a huge cloud and talk to each other in the sky. A baby cried out with a single cry. A woman coughed a muffled cough. From the other side of the chapel, a little girl blurted out: "Mommy I have to pee!" People laughed quietly. Finally, the Rabbi spoke.

"Mr. Max Ginsberg. Are you here with us today, Max?"

Danny was bewildered. What was the rabbi doing?

"Max Ginsberg. Will you please stand?"

An elderly man slowly got to his feet on the other side of the aisle. He stood with the help of a cane. Danny looked at the old man and looked at the Rabbi. What was happening? Why wasn't the rabbi mentioning him?

"As many of you know, Max lost his wife Sylvia earlier this year after fifty-eight years of blessed marriage. A terrible loss. Max has always been a staunch supporter of our synagogue, and he decided to continue to support us after his beloved Sylvia's death. In a wonderful act of Tikkun Olam, he has donated seed money for our new campaign to feed the underprivileged children in Israel. I want you to know, Max, how much your contribution is appreciated by everyone here today." The old man dabbed at his eyes with a handkerchief and sat down. "And now we will proceed with the blowing of the shofar."

Danny was stunned. What had the rabbi done? How could he ignore the fact that a kid had just lost his mother? How could it be more important to honor some rich old man who sent money to Israel? None of this made any sense. And the next part of the service seemed equally senseless. Everyone rose to stand. The cantor put his prayer shawl over his head and picked up the ram's horn. He blew one long note, at the direction of the rabbi. Then the rabbi gave the next command, and he blew three shorter tones. Then a series of very short sounds. All of this was familiar to Danny as part of the yearly service, but it all seemed strange now. He remained standing by his seat for another minute, and then slowly started walking toward the exit.

"Danny?" his father whispered after him. "Where are you going? They're blowing the shofar."

He ignored his father and walked out into a chilly October rain. The business in the synagogue was absurd. A grown man with a cloth over his head making noise with a ram's horn. He started walking toward home in the rain. Absolutely ridiculous. They all sat there mumbling prayers in Hebrew for hours and hours. For what? The rain started coming down harder, and his clothing was soaked almost instantly. He considered going back into the synagogue, but he couldn't force himself to turn around. Tikun Olam. Ridiculous! He could help old ladies cross the street all day long, and it would never accomplish anything at all. It wouldn't fix anything at all.

24

Bad Dreams

For Kate Wunsch, the past started to intrude into the present during the summer of 1967, not long after her fall on the slippery floor. It began as dreams. The content varied from one night to the next, but the theme was always the same. There was a tragedy about to happen, and no one seemed to notice, except for her. One night, it was a burning house, and she was the only one who saw the blaze. She stood on the street outside, watching the flames engulf the little wood-frame house that looked a lot like her childhood home. She wanted desperately to rush in and save the occupants, but it was too dangerous to enter the building. She stood idly by, feeling overwhelmed with horror and guilt.

In another dream, a dam ruptured and released a torrent of water. She saw a house—the same house that she saw in the fire dream—about to be washed away by flood waters. There were other houses nearby that were safe, but that one house was right in the path of the oncoming disaster. She tried to call out to warn the occupants, but no one could hear her over the roar of the water.

She would wake with a start after each of these nightmares to find herself lying next to her husband. He was always sleeping peacefully, not the least disturbed by fire or flood. She lay next to him, trembling and alone in the dark. Even after she pushed the specific images of the dream out of her thoughts, she found herself distressed by other abysmal ideas. What if her husband lost his job? What if he got sick? What if someone robbed their home? So many awful possibilities came to mind as she lay awake by herself in the middle of the night. What if one of her children got sick or hurt? What if her son Danny—but here she couldn't even allow herself to think at all. Some thoughts were too terrible to entertain.

One night, after a particularly troublesome dream, she got up and went softly down the stairs to the kitchen, where she poured herself a glass of wine. She sat at the kitchen table, waiting for the alcohol to bring the desired relief, trying to think absolutely nothing while she waited. She was more than a little worried that her dreams might be harbingers of things to come. To distract herself, she picked up a pencil and started a list of things to do the following day. As she often told her children, *Let's just try to deal with today.* When they asked about tomorrow or next week or a birthday coming up, that was always her answer. *Let's just try to deal with today.* She tried to focus her attention on the list, which was the usual: shopping, cooking, doing laundry, and generally caring for her family.

She poured herself another glass of wine and thought about how peaceful her husband had looked, asleep in bed beside her. He was a good man, she thought, and she tried to think only that. She swept away a brief intrusion: *My husband is trying to protect me by making up ridiculous stories to excuse my drinking. He's afraid to confront me about my problem.* He was a good man, and that was that. She did think for a brief moment about how he invented the story of the slippery floor to explain the time when she drank too much and fell down, right in front of their guests. She thought of it, but then swept it out of her thoughts as she might shoo away a noisy fly that was buzzing around right in front of her face. She definitely did not let herself think: *I must protect my husband by retelling the story of the slippery floor in order to convince everyone that it's true, lest people see him as a liar and a fool, a man who doesn't have the courage to confront his own wife.* No, she didn't allow this thought at all. He was a good man, she thought.

She went into the downstairs bathroom. She stood before the mirror and examined her features. At forty, she could see a few thin strands of gray hair creeping in here and there, but her hair was still, for the most part, a vivid red. She had a few wrinkles—"crow's feet"—at the outer corners of her eyes, but otherwise her skin still looked young. So why did her husband seem so uninterested in her at night now? Did he not find her attractive anymore? Certainly, other men still seemed to find her attractive. She could sense it immediately, and she loved to flirt with them, just a little. So why wasn't the man she married attracted to her? In truth, she was no longer attracted to her husband, either, and she had absentmindedly rebuffed his advances for several months, but she didn't think about that. She picked up a brush and ran it through her hair with long, slow strokes, like a woman preparing for a romantic liaison. Did she marry the wrong man? Had they fallen out of love with each other? Were they ever really *in* love? Was there someone else she was supposed to marry? As she brushed her hair, she focused on her own eyes in the mirror, but she could find no answers. She finished her drink in the kitchen, rinsed the glass twice with soapy water, and poured a bit of milk into the glass. She left the milky glass on the table, confident that the ruse would fool her husband, and she went back to bed.

After a week or two of the bad dreams, the troubles began to invade her daytime thoughts. Little things seemed to bring up old memories that had lain quiescent for many years. Danny talked about turning seventeen in a few weeks, and she began to feel tension in her neck and shoulders. She heard her mother's voice: *Oh, now you're seventeen and you think you're too good for this family. Well, let me tell you something, Missy!* She tried to ignore it, but it would happen at the most random times. Right in the middle of doing the dishes: *And where do you think you're going with those friends of yours? Are you too good to stay home and help your mother?* She reminded herself that she was standing in her own kitchen in 1967. There was no reason to dwell on memories and voices from 1944. Still, the intrusions continued. She heard her mother talking to her father. *I suppose you're just going to sit there and let your little princess daughter go spend your hard-earned money at the movies. A fine father you are!*

Soon, the leaves would start to change colors, and autumn was always an unsettling time for her. If only she could just go to sleep in September and wake up at Christmas time. Standing in the kitchen doing dishes one afternoon, she could see her family from her window over the kitchen sink. Her husband and two children were in the yard, and the kids were helping their dad with his vegetable garden. Her own flower garden was just beyond the vegetables, and she heard her husband ask the kids to pull a few weeds from among her flowers. They looked so happy, her husband and children in their pretty little yard.

Go ahead! Ignore me and drink another beer while your daughter acts like a little slut and runs around town with every boy in the high school!

Oh, give it a rest, will ya?

They were good children, she thought. Her Danny and her Sarah were good children, which must mean that she was a good mother, right? How else could they be such sweet kids? No one could look at these beautiful children and accuse her of being a bad mother.

Oh, I see, Mister. Kate's got you wrapped around her little finger! I tell you, that girl will come to nothing! She doesn't give a hoot about her own mother!

Shut up, woman! Just shut your damned mouth!

These irregular fits of memory would startle her at random times during the day, spurting forth like blood from a wound that has burst open after a bandage has been roughly removed. Even the wine she drank in the evening was little help. She was drinking at least a full bottle every evening, which helped her fall asleep, but then there were the dreadful images in her dreams, and she would wake up alone in the middle of the night. In one dream, her town was surrounded by Nazi soldiers who were hunting for her, and no one would hide her and give her refuge. She awoke dripping in sweat, lying next to her Jewish husband who slept peacefully, out of reach of the Nazis.

"Why would they come for me?" she whispered to herself in the middle of the lonely, scary night. "Why would I have a crazy dream about Nazis? They wouldn't have come for me! I'm not even Jewish!"

The whole world seemed to be conspiring to torment her with memories. One day, the family cat got herself stuck up in a tree in their backyard while they were all sitting on the back porch after dinner. Her husband propped a ladder against the tree, and Danny started to climb it. She watched the scene from her seat in the screened porch.

"Be careful!" called her husband, watching Danny climb the rungs.

"Don't scare her!" called Sarah to her brother. "Don't worry, Kitty! Danny's coming up to get you!"

Kate began to shake uncontrollably and went into the kitchen. She spilled some of the wine as she poured it into her glass.

Shut up, woman! Just shut your damned mouth!

You want me to shut up, Mister? I bet you'd like me to shut up. You just can't stand to hear the truth, can you? You're no damned good and neither is that daughter of yours!

I don't have to listen to this crap!

She went to the sink to busy herself with dirty dishes, but she saw a familiar scene again: Her father stormed out of the old kitchen, and she followed him outside to keep an eye on him. That was her job, after all, her unofficial but all-important job in the family. She kept an eye on her Dad. When he drove off in the car after one of these arguments, she watched him go down the road to see if he was driving in a straight line. When she came home after school and found him passed out on the sofa, she would bend down and make sure he was still breathing. When he disappeared into the garage after dinner, she would seek him there.

I can't take much more of your mother, Kate. I just can't take it.

It's all right, Dad.

That woman is just plain evil. I never saw such a mean streak in a woman.

I know, Dad, but it'll be okay.

If it wasn't for you, Kate, I'd have left a long time ago. No other man would put up with her shit. He would sit there in a lawn chair in the garage, taking another draw on his cigarette, another swallow of his beer. Then he would move some of the tools aside on his workbench and light a candle, and Kate would take a seat near him in a second lawn chair.

The two of them would just sit there together as the light outside faded and nightfall set in. He didn't usually say much. He just sat there in the garage, smoking and drinking, and she sat nearby. Sometimes he would complain out loud to himself. Occasionally, he would speak directly to her. *You're a good one, Kate. Don't listen to all that nonsense your mother says about you. Don't you listen to anybody. You're a good one.* He only said it a few times, but she always kept those words in her memory.

Mostly, they sat in silence. Now and then, he would say—speaking to himself—that he was a good man, a hard-working man, that he didn't deserve this. She would immediately agree. *Of course, you're a good man, Dad.* It wasn't always clear that he heard her. Nonetheless, she sat near him by the candlelight into the middle of the night, until he finally took himself into the house and fell asleep on the sofa in the living room.

"Danny got her down safe, Mom! Danny got her!" Startled, Kate looked out the kitchen window to see her daughter waving happily to her from the backyard. She opened the window a bit wider and forced a smile, but she didn't look in the direction of the ladder.

"That's good, Sarah. Very good, honey."

I don't have to listen to this crap! Again, she saw her father storm out of the kitchen. She saw him going up the ladder to finish cleaning out the leaves in the rain gutters. She tried not to see this, as she had tried for years not to see it, but the image was clear in her mind. He was wearing a green flannel shirt, and he moved very slowly, clumsily, from one rung to the next. At the time, she didn't call out what was in her mind: *Dad, be careful!* She was afraid that he would turn to look at her and lose his balance. She stood motionless, barely breathing, watching him reach the level of the gutters. Her mother opened the front door and stuck her head out, saying nothing, but glaring at Kate and her father. He began angrily throwing fistfuls of leaves and twigs to the ground, as if he hoped they would land on his wife and bury her in a pile of righteous indignation.

"Mom! I got her!" Now it was Danny standing outside the kitchen window, holding their cat over his shoulder, a wide grin on his face. She tried to smile again but couldn't force her facial muscles to perform this time, and Danny's grin faded as he saw her face in the window. He looked puzzled, confused by the face he saw. She wanted to smile for him but simply could not. He had survived the ladder, but what about all the other dangers of this terrible world? He was seventeen now, and he had his driver's license. Her husband had taken him out for all of his practice driving. There was no way she could sit there in the passenger seat without feeling panic-stricken.

"That's great, Danny," she said, and quickly turned from the window to busy herself in the kitchen.

I don't need your bullshit, woman! Her father glared down at her mother from his perch on the ladder. He reached to his left, far to his left, to clear the next stretch of the gutter. And then Kate saw the fall. It seemed to be happening in slow motion, as if her father had been walking on the moon, not bound by the pull of Earth's gravity. She saw him floating downward slowly, like a maple leaf making its graceful aerial journey from the branch to the earth. He fell so slowly for most of the trip, but then it was suddenly over. He had been standing at the top of the ladder, but now his body landed with a thump on the brick walkway leading to their front door. At first, she couldn't comprehend what she was looking at. It was her father, but not her father. It was certainly not a sick father, or a hurt father, not a moaning-in-pain father; just a no-father, a lump of lifeless protoplasm deposited on the brick walkway. It was not a father who could tell her: *This is why I fell.* He couldn't explain to her: *This is why I climbed up the ladder drunk.* He couldn't say: *This is why I lived my life the way I did.* It was a perfectly still no-father, lying in a silence that was finally broken by her mother's hysterical screaming. And in that moment when the screaming started, Kate learned something about the way life works. In that moment—if one can call such a violent, immeasurable rent in the structure of time a "moment"—she learned a lesson she would never forget. The world can change suddenly, dramatically, and irrevocably, without warning and without reason.

25

Uncle Jack

"Don't you worry, Kate. I won't tell him where you are."
The author of these words spoke them aloud to an
empty kitchen, a very small, very dirty, empty kitchen on a quiet
street in Big Sur, California. He was a man in his mid-sixties, but
he looked much older than his years. His face was worn and tired
looking, deeply etched with lines that spoke of constant vigilance.

"I can't tell him where you are, Kate, but I can tell him where
you were. I never promised not to tell him where you were. And
I have to tell him something. Poor Danny has told me more than
once how much he'd like to see his mother one more time if she's
still on this Earth."

He sat on the only chair that provided companionship to a
small kitchen table. He alternately sipped a beer and inhaled a
cigarette, although sometimes he became lost in thought and the
ash from the cigarette just fell to the table or the floor.

Spread over the table were piles of papers in no particular
order or system. Interspersed between the piles were empty beer
bottles of varying brands and shapes. He picked up a greeting
card from his sister and glanced over the lines.

Dear Jack,
Thanks for the news about Danny and his family.
I really appreciate it. I can't believe that Cordelia
is graduating high school! And thanks for sending
the photos.

Kate

"No problem, Missy," he said aloud, putting the letter back on a messy pile of mail. "I'm happy to keep you posted. After all, what's a brother for?"

He turned to another pile on the table and studied several of the papers in it. "Let's see," he said to himself. "What shall I send to Danny boy this time? Poor fellow keeps calling me, wants to see his mother before she gets old and passes on." Jack consulted his memory. He had already sent Danny the little newspaper bit about the nursery in Denver. And the words to The Lord's Prayer. He picked up a pamphlet from a convent in New Mexico. Yes, that would do nicely. That would make a good clue, one that might help Danny see the pattern and find his mother.

He folded the pamphlet and put it into an envelope addressed to Fairbanks, Alaska. Then he added to the envelope the note he had already written.

Hi Suzanne,
Please send this along to my nephew Danny, just like
the others. Do NOT put a return address!

Jack

P.S. Don't trust your mailman. I think the Postal
Service is involved in a government cover-up.

It never occurred to Jack that there were no patterns to be found in his clues, and no patterns to be discerned from the random movements of his big sister, a woman who repeatedly disappeared without a trace, without a discernable motive, without any pattern at all to her recurring flight from town to town. But Jack was a man who lived in a world of connections that were not obvious to other people. In his world, the election of Tony Blair as England's new prime minister was obviously related to the U.S. space program. Blair was collaborating with the U.S. government to help put surveillance cameras into orbit and spy on U.S. citizens from outer space. His upstairs neighbor (a sweet, frail, old Italian man of ninety-two) was obviously and undeniably linked to a Mafia crime family in New York City. The decline in public etiquette was no doubt caused by mercury pollution coming from industrial smokestacks and the effect of that mercury on the human brain. These connections were obvious to him, and he was just waiting for his nephew to catch on to the obvious clues arriving in the mail. Then "Danny boy" would surely be able to find his mother.

"Don't you worry, Missy," he said aloud. "I'll keep your secret, I promise. I'll take it to the grave with me. I ain't tellin' Danny where you are. I can tell him where you *were*, of course, but I ain't tellin' him where you are. I ain't tellin' him, and I never told Mom, either. I remember how you liked running with that older boy in high school, but I never told her a word."

At that moment, the phone rang. The sound startled him badly, and he jumped up from his chair, staring at the phone on the wall. He glared at it with eyes that were both fearful and angry. After it rang several more times, he stood up and answered it.

"Hello?"

"Hello, Uncle Jack." It was his nephew Danny in Albany, New York. The same nephew he was just thinking about! This could not be a coincidence. No way was this a coincidence.

"Well, hello there, Danny boy! How are you doing?"

"I'm okay, Jack. How are you?"

"I'm fine and dandy," said Jack. "Of course, my doctor says all this smokin' and drinkin' is going to kill me, but he won't say when." Jack laughed a hard, wheezy laugh into the phone.

"Well, Jack, maybe you should listen to your doctor and cut back a little, don't you think?"

Jack took a sip of beer. "Don't you worry about me, Danny boy. Your Uncle Jack can handle himself."

There was a short silence on the phone. "Jack, the reason I'm calling is that I received another one of those weird clues in the mail. Clues about my mom. But it's just like the first one. There is no return address on the envelope, just a postmark from Fairbanks, Alaska."

Jack said nothing.

"This one was just a copy of The Lord's Prayer, Jack. And on the bottom, it says, 'Take care of yourself. Kate.' And that's it. It's definitely her writing, but it's old, just like the newspaper article from the nursery in Denver."

Jack took a long pull on his beer bottle. "There were clues about Richard Nixon, too, Danny, but nobody paid attention. All that fuss about Watergate was just a distraction, so nobody would see what he was really up to. But the whole time, he was in cahoots with China to knock Russia out of the space race. And guess what he wanted to do up there in outer space?"

"Jack, for God's sake, I'm not talking about Nixon and China! I'm calling about my mother. Do you know anything about this copy of the prayer with her name on it?"

"Nixon's people were trying to get me involved, but I wouldn't have anything to do with it. Thought control, Danny boy. Nixon and the Chinese were planning a thought control station in outer space. Then he could control us all!" He heard Dan take a long sigh on the other end of the phone.

"Jack, please. Just think about it. Someone is trying to give me a clue about where my mom is. Maybe something will come to mind. Maybe there is someone you and my mom grew up with in Detroit who moved to Alaska. And maybe that person could help me. If my mom is still alive, I'd really like to see her again. Just think about it."

"All right, Danny boy. All right. I will think about it. And meanwhile, you keep your wits about you when the mailman comes to your door. I have reason to believe that the Postal Service is involved now. It's an international plot, and it just keeps getting worse. Be careful, Danny."

"Okay, Uncle Jack. Okay. I'll be careful."

"Bye, Danny."

"Good-bye, Jack. And Jack, please go see your doctor. Are you even taking the medicine he prescribed?"

Without another word, Jack put the receiver back into the cradle on the kitchen wall. He let out a big sigh and began a survey of his little kitchen. That phone call was no coincidence. Someone must be eavesdropping on him; someone must have heard him talking about Danny, and then that person was able to manipulate Danny's mind (via the usual thought-control radio frequencies) and get him to call. Poor Danny would never even realize what was going on.

The kitchen must be bugged. He looked suspiciously from the sink to the oven, from the oven to the toaster—the toaster! Of course! It sat right there on the kitchen counter, directly across from his seat at the table. The toaster was bugged! He opened a window, violently yanked the toaster's electrical cord out of the wall, and threw the toaster out of the second story window. He heard it smash on the sidewalk below and slammed the window shut.

He took his seat at the table again, darting his eyes around the kitchen, listening carefully for any suspicious electronic sounds. The silence gradually reassured him that all was well, and he resumed his afternoon ritual of drinking and smoking. It took him two beers and a full cigarette to settle himself.

"Anyway, don't you worry, Missy. I never told Mom where you were, and I won't tell Danny, either." He sat for a while, smoking, drinking, skimming a newspaper on the table. "Don't you worry," he repeated. "I won't tell. A promise is a promise."

26

Sister Agnes Joan

Dan sat in his favorite chair, holding the latest clue in his hand, the third such mailing in a month. It had arrived in the same format as the others, an envelope from Fairbanks, Alaska, without a return address. It was a small pamphlet about a convent in New Mexico. The print was a bit faded.

"Maybe it means that Grandma joined a convent," said Cordelia. She was sitting opposite him on the couch with her mother.

"No, that makes no sense, Cordelia," Dan said. "When she married your grandfather, she really became interested in Judaism. She never converted, but she read a lot about being Jewish." He thought for a minute and added, "But she did take us to a Catholic church once in a while. So, I guess I just don't know what to think."

"Don't worry, Dad. We'll figure it out."

He was puzzled by the mailing, but relieved to see that he and Cordelia were getting along better. Leaving the note in her shoe had definitely helped.

Abby said, "Well, maybe things didn't work out with that Mexican guy in Denver, so she went to a convent."

Dan said nothing in reply. The thought of "Don Juan" always put him in a foul mood.

He called the number on the pamphlet. The nun who answered was not very helpful. Dan thought she clearly sounded suspicious about this male caller. When he mentioned the purpose of his call and told her his mother's name, there was a pause on the other end of the phone. The woman then stated that she was not allowed to give out information about the sisters. He could leave his phone number with her, though, and they would call him back if they had any relevant information. He asked if he could visit, and she politely (if coldly) repeated herself. He could leave his number.

"She knows something," he told Abby after ending the call.

"Maybe," said Abby. "Or maybe she's just following their policies."

"No, it's more than that," said Dan. "She definitely knows something. I think I should go out there."

Abby had her doubts, but they decided that he should visit the convent, just in case he was right.

Ten days later, he was sitting at a convent in northern New Mexico. The nun who met him at the door was stiff and unfriendly. He recognized her voice from the phone call. She tried to tell him that he couldn't just drop in and visit, but he insisted that he had to find out about his mother. She finally relented and deposited him in a small study, not much bigger than his office at the university. It was lined with bookshelves on three of the four walls. The southern wall had large windows that let in plenty of natural light. He sat by a window in one of several well-cushioned chairs. He realized that he had expected very uncomfortable straight-back chairs, in line with his belief that nuns would prohibit any type of furniture that might make a person feel at ease. Apparently, these particular nuns thought it wouldn't be a bad idea to sit in a nice over-stuffed chair and relax while reading a good book. He glanced at a few of the book titles on the shelves closest to where he sat: *Mere Christianity* by C.S. Lewis, *The Confessions of St. Augustine*, John Bunyan's *Pilgrim's Progress*. It occurred to him that perhaps the nuns at this place got as much comfort from their books as he got from his. His attitude softened. In fact, he found himself drawn to the titles, wondering if these Christian texts might bring a person some peace of mind. Perhaps he should have been raised as a Christian, he thought, rather than with a hodgepodge of Jewish and Christian traditions. He remembered the rare times when his mother would take him and his sister to church in Detroit. Jesus was portrayed on the cross in a beautiful stained-glass window. Dan would look up and wonder if Jesus could somehow overcome his own suffering and make his mother happier and calmer.

He read his pamphlet about the convent until he heard footsteps coming along the hall. He imagined a petite woman with fine, delicate facial features and round wire-rimmed glasses, the ascetic type of woman, too delicate to survive in the world outside the convent. Instead, the woman who entered the room was somewhat portly, with a round face and bright, mischievous eyes. Her physical features seemed incongruous with her classic nun's habit: a black robe and hood, with a white cloth covering her head underneath the hood.

"You must be Danny!" said the nun, taking his hand and giving it a vigorous shake. "I'm Sister Mary Margaret. It's so wonderful to meet you!" She was probably at least seventy, his mother's age, but she had a husky, booming voice to match the healthy handgrip.

He was surprised at her extraverted, worldly comportment, and yet more surprised that he was obviously familiar to her. She even called him "Danny."

"I would recognize you anywhere," she said. "You look just like the photos I've seen."

"Photos?" asked Dan eagerly. "Then you know my mother! She's here!"

"Oh, no, no. She was here, but that was long ago." She looked at him with a sympathetic expression. "Please sit down, Danny. I'm sorry. Your mother's not here. She left us years ago."

He sat down hard in the chair behind him. Sister pulled a chair closer to him.

"So, it sounds like you didn't know for certain that she used to live here, and you obviously didn't know she was gone. Then how did you know to contact us?"

Dan tried to tell her about the clues, but he stumbled over his words, and he just couldn't organize his thoughts.

"That's okay," said Sister kindly. "You must be very disappointed that she's not here." She offered him a cup of tea, which he willingly accepted so he could compose himself. She disappeared down the hallway. She was gone for about ten minutes, and then she returned with a tea set on a metal tray. She poured the hot water into two cups.

"You've seen photos," he said.

Sister nodded. "Oh, I shouldn't be telling you anything without consulting with our Mother Superior about our policies." She winked at him. "But yes, indeed I have. I've seen photos of you as a little boy. And I've seen a few photos of you as a young adult," said Sister. "Even a few pictures of your family. Your daughter is such a pretty little girl, and she looks so much like your mother. But I'm talking about old photos from years ago. Your daughter must be all grown up now."

"Yes, Cordelia's about to graduate high school. And my son is fourteen. But I don't understand. How would my mother get photos of us? My mother hasn't been in touch with anyone in the family for the past thirty years."

Sister's face changed. Her contagious smile faded, and she looked disappointed and sad. "No contact with you or your family? Oh, dear." She sighed a heavy sigh. "When they told me you were here, Danny, I hoped that she had gone back home at some point. You know, she just disappeared from here years ago. It's been fifteen years and three months exactly since I last saw her."

Dan was impressed that she knew exactly how much time had passed. He realized that his mother must have meant a lot to this elderly nun sitting across from him.

Sister continued. "I figured that you came here—well, I guess I had no idea why you came here. But I assumed that she must have returned home at some point and told you about her time with us, and that somehow you were bringing us good news about her. Or maybe bad news. Any news."

"No, sorry, Sister. No word from her in thirty years." It seemed odd to Dan that he was apologizing to her; after all, it was his loss. But he realized that they were both feeling disappointed, each one hoping that the other would have news. He wanted Sister to help find his mother, and she wanted him to bring greetings from her old friend. "But those photos," he said. "I don't understand how she would get those photos."

Sister shrugged and held her palms up. Dan wondered if she was hiding something.

"She would have to get those photos from somebody," he said. Sister shrugged again, and he realized that she wasn't going to say anything else about the subject, whether she knew or not. But how could his mother get those photos? He occasionally sent photos to her two siblings, his Aunt Molly in Tucson and his Uncle Jack in California. Aunt Molly would certainly have told him if she had heard from his mother. And Uncle Jack was too crazy to keep anything like that to himself. He would definitely blurt it out, along with some irrational tirade about the government. Dan also sent pictures to his sister Sarah back in Detroit. Was she sharing them with someone else who was secretly in touch with their mother? That seemed the most likely possibility. He would definitely check with Sarah when he got home.

"So, what brings you out here, Danny?" Sister asked, her face brightening up again.

"Well, as I say, she never did come back home or contact any of us. But I've started getting clues mailed to me about where she's been." He pulled the pamphlet out of his pocket and showed it to her, along with the postmarked envelope from Alaska.

"Curious," said Sister.

"Does it make any sense to you?" he asked. "Did my mother mention anyone in Alaska?"

"No, not to me," she said. "No one I can think of."

Dan wondered why someone was sending him clues that always led to a dead end. What was the point? "Well, perhaps you could tell me something about her time here at the convent. Anything might help." He felt like a beggar on the street. Anything might help.

"Well, Sister Agnes Joan worked in the kitchen and the garden," she said.

"Sister Agnes Joan," he repeated.

"Oh, it must be hard to hear that name," said Sister. "She came here as Catherine Wunsch, of course, but after the initial period of being a postulant—a candidate—she was given a new name."

"Of course," said Dan.

"She did well for the first year or two. She took her first vows—we take a vow of poverty, chastity, and obedience. She was doing so well, and everyone really cared so much for her."

"And then?"

"Well, then the troubles began. She seemed increasingly tense and withdrawn. Eventually, she found it hard to function normally, and our Mother Superior sent her away for a while."

"Where did she go? Do you know?"

"Oh, yes. She went to an alcohol rehabilitation center in Albuquerque."

Dan fell silent and looked at the floor.

"Oh, Danny, I hope I'm not telling you something you didn't already know. Did you not know that your mother had a drinking problem?"

He looked up at her and saw great kindness in her eyes. "I knew," he said, confessing the sin of his own silence to this nun.

"I assumed you knew," Sister replied. "During the years she spent with us, she would drink pretty heavily at times, and I know it didn't start here. She'd be sober for a while, and then she'd relapse. When she couldn't hide her drinking any longer, she went away to Albuquerque for a month or so. Then she came back, and she was fine for a while. Until her next relapse. There was more than one trip to Albuquerque, you see. She was such a good woman, Danny, but a tortured soul. And she tried to numb her suffering with alcohol."

He made no reply to this, and Sister seemed content to sit in silence for a while. She poured a little more hot water into his cup and offered him milk and sugar. Dan took a spoonful of sugar and slowly stirred his tea. He hadn't found his mother, but he was glad to be in the company of someone who had known her, and he was in no hurry to leave.

"I appreciate your telling me all this," he said. "But how would she get alcohol? According to what I just read about your convent, you have very little contact with the outside world."

"Well, that's true, except for a couple of us. I'm one of the externs. It's my job to interact with the surrounding community. Somebody has to call the plumber when the faucet drips, you know."

She laughed a hearty laugh, and Dan understood how this cheerful extravert would be chosen for her job.

"But we are a monastic convent, as you've read. We don't do a service in the community. We're not out there teaching children or helping the poor. Our only mission is to be here and pray for the world. And your mother was here for eight years, during which time she had little opportunity to leave the convent. But as I say, she worked in the kitchen and the garden, and she was in charge of ordering groceries to be delivered to the kitchen. And it's easy enough to add wine to the shopping list." She laughed again.

"And no one noticed?"

"Well, Danny, you have to understand that in a community like ours, each sister has a job, and no one looks over your shoulder to check on you. Each nun does her job to the best of her ability, and she doesn't put her nose in someone else's business. If you're the one who greets the man delivering supplies to the kitchen, no one is checking the receipts every week. And if you decide to order a case of wine and hide it in the cellar, then it's not hard to do."

Dan mulled over the information. "But after the first time in the rehab program, wouldn't your Mother Superior give her a different job? Wouldn't she take her out of the kitchen?"

"Oh, I don't think Mother Superior ever knew where the wine was coming from."

"But you did," said Dan.

Sister smiled and made no reply. Instead, she talked about life in the convent, and his mother's comings and goings between the convent and the rehab center. She spoke about their Mother Superior, and it sounded like Sister Mary Margaret was instrumental in convincing Mother Superior to let his mother back into the convent after each relapse of drinking.

"The rehab center wasn't the easiest place to be," said Sister. "There were some kind people working there, but a few of them were less than kind. They were former addicts themselves, and some of them had a get-tough approach that bordered on cruelty. There was a staff member named Bonnie who was particularly lacking in compassion, and she really gave your mother a hard time. In the group sessions, she was very sarcastic and confrontational. It seemed that she just wanted to humiliate the patients, especially your mother. Your mother wasn't really able to admit she had a problem, Danny. She always told herself that she just drank too much on occasion, but she could never really admit that she was an alcoholic. Such is the nature of alcoholism. Denial everywhere. But this Bonnie would just blast away at your mother's denial. *How many drinks do you typically have during an evening? And you don't think you're an alcoholic? Oh, really, Kate? And you expect us to believe that?* It was tough for your mom, that's for sure."

Dan looked down at the floor, feeling a wave of anger at the woman named Bonnie. He didn't want Sister Mary Margaret to see him glowering with resentment. When he looked up, she seemed to be lost in her memories. She was quiet for a while, sipping her tea, and Dan thought she looked a little sad. He had an urge to say something comforting, but he couldn't think of anything that sounded quite right. After a couple minutes of silence, Sister looked up cheerfully and launched into another story, and another, and another. Most of them were little stories about some good deed or kindness his mother had done for one of the other nuns. A few of the stories were about the rehab center. All of them revealed a genuine fondness for his mother, and Dan was happy to sit and listen for the next hour or so.

When there was another break in her talking, he forced himself to ask the question that was festering in his mind.

"I've been told that there was a man she was seeing out in Denver. A Mexican man, I believe. Do you know anything about that?"

"Carlos," said Sister.

Dan winced to have the story confirmed. Now it would be registered forever in his mind with a man's name attached to it. How could his mother do that? How could she possibly do that?

"Oh, yes," said Sister. "I heard about Carlos. But she left him, too. That's just how she was. She suffered terribly from her demons, and she had to leave everyone and every place, eventually. The poor woman never knew peace." And with that, she turned to another story. Dan suspected that Sister changed the subject in order to protect him from too much information, and he couldn't gather the courage to ask any more about it. It seemed to him that Sister was beginning to look tired, and he searched his mind for any other important questions he might want to ask before she decided to end the interview.

"My mother was here for eight years," he said. "Why did she leave after all that time?"

"It was all about the final vows," said Sister. "After being with us for seven years, she was eligible to write a letter to Mother Superior asking to take her final vows. This is a very serious commitment. You are making your final commitment to a life of poverty, chastity, and obedience. And a final commitment to this little community. I watched your mother struggle with this terribly. She wanted to do it, but she seemed afraid to do it. She drank more and more, although somehow she managed to hide it better. She even requested a one-year extension on the vows, which only prolonged her suffering. When the end of that eighth year approached, she disappeared. She left me a little note, and she was gone."

"She left so abruptly?" he asked.

"Oh, yes. Literally overnight. I awoke one morning and found her note. And that was the end of her. I never heard another word from her."

"I'm so sorry," said Dan. He picked up his teacup for something to do, but it was empty. They sat in silence for several minutes. He realized that she was probably accustomed to sitting in silence and praying for hours at a time, but it was awkward for him. He finally glanced at the large clock on the wall. He and Sister had been talking for nearly two hours. The rays of sunlight coming in through the southern window now entered at a slant, and they were less vibrant. She made a comment about some chores she had to tend to.

"I can't thank you enough, Sister. I really appreciate hearing about my mother. She must have trusted you very much to tell you all this. Especially the stories of the rehab place."

Sister Mary Margaret smiled. "Oh, she didn't tell me any of that."

Dan was puzzled. "Then how did you hear it? From someone else? Is there someone else I should be talking to? Maybe someone at the rehab center in Albuquerque?"

Sister laughed a big ho-ho Santa Claus laugh. "No, no, no. There's no one else."

"Then how did you hear about it?" he asked.

"I didn't hear it. I was *there*. Every time your mother relapsed, so did I." She paused, smiling at him. "I followed her right over the cliff every time. They sent us packing several times to that rehab place. And little good did it do for us." She laughed again. Then her face became serious, and her voice dropped in volume. "The day she disappeared from the convent here, I stopped drinking, and I've been sober for fifteen years and three months since. Fifteen years and three months, Danny. And every day I pray that the same is true for your mother. Wherever she is, God bless her."

27

Martin

Cordelia was preoccupied as she helped Mr. Tremblay tidy up his classroom. She kept thinking about her father. For a while, he had been much better, even kind at moments. After she found his little note in her shoe a couple of weeks ago, life at home became easier for a while. His kindness allowed her to feel more relaxed and less defensive. But over the past few days, the old tensions had returned. Any discussion of her college plans seemed to make him irritable. And the mere mention of a graduation party could set him off and ruin the entire evening. She tried to stop ruminating about her father and help her teacher.

Mr. Tremblay's classroom had been rearranged for the annual Open House event on a Thursday evening in June, just a couple weeks before graduation. All the teachers had opened their classrooms to parents of current students, as well as the incoming ninth-graders and their families. The usual speeches were made, and information sheets were passed around to the new families about what to expect in high school. Now it was over, and everyone had left. Cordelia helped Mr. T by moving the chairs back to their usual places, throwing out a few paper coffee cups that parents had left on desks, and gathering up some information sheets that families had neglected to take with them. When they finished, Cordelia went to the doorway and put her hand up to the light switch, waiting for Mr. T to close his briefcase and follow her out.

"Go ahead. You can shut the light," said Mr. T. "I'm all set."

Cordelia shut the light off, leaving the room behind her in darkness. In front of her, she saw that someone had already shut off most of the lights in the hallway outside the classroom. There was only one small light visible at the far end of the hall. Standing in the doorway, she turned to make sure that Mr. T could see to find his way out. He was already at the doorway, right behind her, and he stopped abruptly to avoid bumping into her. There was just enough of a moon shining in through the classroom window so that she could see him in silhouette. As she turned to face him fully, she moved one foot to step backwards into the hall and let him pass through the doorway, but then she returned that foot to where it was. She kept both feet planted where they were, and she didn't move again. He made a similar half-step, as if he was going to step back into the room and create some distance between them, but he did not.

"I shut the light," she said.

"Okay," he said.

And then they stood there, close to each other in the doorway, without moving and without speaking. Cordelia could see the shape of him, but she couldn't see his face very clearly. There was only the moonlight at his back. She knew he was looking at her, but she couldn't see his big, brown-cow eyes at all. It was strange and exciting to be standing this close to him in a dark room. For another moment, she still had the notion to turn away and walk through the doorway so he could exit the classroom.

But then she realized that her body had decided not to move. Her mind knew what she should do, but her body was going to stand right where it was. It wasn't going to do what it was supposed to do.

Mr. T was still holding his briefcase in his right hand. He put it down on the floor and he seemed ready to say something, but he said nothing. He picked up the briefcase again and put it down again. She couldn't see his face, but it seemed to her that he was struggling with himself, and she imagined the struggle as it might appear on his face in the shadows: a furrowed brow, narrowed and serious eyes, pursed lips. That's how he looked when he was serious in class. She wanted to say something, but no words came to her mind.

She should leave the doorway, she told herself. She should turn and walk away, calling a cheerful "Good night, Mr. T!" over her shoulder. She should walk out to her mother's car, get in it, and drive straight home. Then she should look at her homework for a few minutes and go to sleep. But she stood where she was, unable or unwilling to move at all. They were only a few inches apart from one another.

She heard a couple of car engines starting outside. She was afraid for a moment that the headlights of a car would come shining straight into the window and expose them where they stood. The whole moment would be ruined, and whatever was about to happen would never happen. The next step that was ordained to take place would be sabotaged by the silly, random intrusion of a car's headlights, and the course of her life would be forever changed by a missed opportunity. When it didn't happen, when the headlights didn't come blazing into the room, she realized that nothing was going to pull them apart in this moment.

When the cars drove away and the sound of the engines faded, there was complete silence in the room. She could hear herself breathing. She could hear him breathing, too. It was clear to her now that whatever was happening was understood by both of them. He obviously had no more intention of walking away from it than she had. They had only been standing there for a minute or so, but she had the feeling that everything had changed between them forever in that minute.

When he finally kissed her, he did so very lightly. He quickly pulled his face back. "I'm sorry. I shouldn't have done that, Cordelia. This is so wrong."

"It's not wrong," she said.

"Yes, it is. I'm your teacher."

"But I'm graduating soon."

"Look, Cordelia, we shouldn't do this. We can just pretend it never happened."

She knew that he meant it. She could step away, if she chose to. She could just say, "No problem, Mr. T," and run out of the building and pretend it had never happened. She could step away from him, and move away from this moment, and go back to her life as it was two minutes ago. In truth, though, nothing about her life felt right any more. So many things had felt so wrong for the entire year: the teachers in high school treating her like she was in kindergarten (*Do you have permission to be leaving the building early, Cordelia?*); she and all the other kids playing the game to get the A instead of the B in Biology class, instead of actually thinking about Biology and marveling about the science of all living things; the girls gossiping about which boy was seen with which girl, and whether they were really "together" or not really "together;" the boys giggling in class like they were ten-year-old children hiding in the bodies of seventeen-year-old young men;

her mother asking when she was coming home in the evening, and her father ranting and raving like a lunatic about his doomsday visions of her disastrous future; and—worst of all—her own theatrical retorts to her father, which seemed so childish to her afterwards. All of this felt like an old coat that she had outgrown, a coat that she was still forced to wear, no matter that it was too tight, no matter that it restricted her movements, no matter that she could barely breathe in it.

Her eyes were getting accustomed to the dim light, and she could see his eyes upon her, wide open and guileless.

"We can just say it never happened," he repeated. "You can go home, and I'll see you in class tomorrow."

"I don't want to go home," she said in a voice not much above a whisper." She said nothing more, but stood her ground, blocking the doorway with her body. She felt a surprising flicker of defiance. If he was considering a change of plans, she was determined not to let him walk past her and end this encounter. She was blocking any escape route that love might take, blocking any chance that love might slip away before she could know what it really was. Steadfast, she held her post until he kissed her again. This time, she leaned in and kissed him back.

"Cordelia, I'm not supposed to feel like this about you."

Which sounded true to her, of course. Her teacher was not supposed to feel like this about her, and she wasn't supposed to feel what she was feeling for him. But she knew now that she did feel this way about him, and she had been feeling like this for a very long time, even though she hadn't been able to talk about it or even admit it to herself until this moment. It was simply against all the rules. But who makes up these rules about what one is supposed to feel toward another person? Who appointed himself the Chief Justice of the Supreme Court of Feelings, with the power to outlaw a particular emotion felt toward another human being?

"Mr. T," was all she could say.

"Martin. Call me Martin."

"I can't. I can't!"

"Okay, fine. Call me whatever you want. It doesn't matter."

But it did matter. She saw this moment as a challenge to step out of childhood and enter the brave new world ahead of her. In the face of this challenge, she could still break away, of course. She could easily remove his arms from around her waist, unwrap her own arms from around his neck, and rush out the door. She could go running back into her girlhood and spend a little more time—perhaps a lot more time—in a space that was safe, albeit boring, and familiar, even though suffocating. For a moment, she regarded this as a choice she had to make, a fateful decision that would lead her in one of two directions, with consequences that would linger for the rest of her life. Yes, she thought, she had to make a split-second choice, a critical, irreversible, epochal choice, even though she knew quite well that there was really no choice at all to be made this evening. She had made her decision about him long ago, without knowing at the time that she had made a decision, without imagining that her nameless, forbidden stirrings could ever have a name.

"Martin," she said.

28

The Day After

By the time Cordelia came to school the next day, her world had changed completely. High school was no longer high school, but a dreadful play in which she had to act a role that had nothing in common with her actual identity. She had to feign interest in people and things that suddenly meant nothing to her, and she had to hide her feelings for the most important person in her life. Fortunately, she ran into Becky in the hall, and they walked along together toward their first classes.

"Oh, my God, my parents are so crazy!" said Becky. "They decided to have another fight over who's going to pay my college tuition. My father is making a trillion dollars selling buildings in Manhattan, and my mother has about fifty cents in the bank. And he's stingy enough to pick a fight over my tuition, and she's wimpy enough to engage in such a stupid argument instead of hanging up the phone. I could kill them both, really. Would I go to prison if I just killed them both? I think a judge would understand, don't you?"

"I'm sure any judge would understand," said Cordelia, happy for the distraction of Becky's chattering. They had a few minutes before they would have to go to their separate classrooms, so they stood talking for a while. Cordelia forced herself to attend to her friend's story, hoping to block out thoughts about the absurdity of high school. If it weren't for Becky, she thought, she would probably just turn around and walk out of the building. Behind her in the hall, she heard one voice rise above the others.

"Hi, Dee!"

She didn't have to turn around to know who it was. "Please hide me," she said quietly to Becky. "Just hide me. I really can't deal with this today."

"Too late," said Becky.

"Hi, Dee! What's up?"

"Hi, Perry," she answered as she turned around. She tried to smile politely at the sadly disheveled boy standing in front of her.

"Hey, Dee, are you coming to the party for the school yearbook staff? I think it's going to be awesome."

"Yeah, Perry, I think I'll be there."

"Great! That'll be so much fun!"

Cordelia could find nothing else to say, and Perry just stood there staring at her with wide, eager eyes. She usually felt sorry for Perry, with his disheveled looks, his boring monologues, and his uninvited nickname for her, but today she felt annoyed and impatient.

"I have to go, Perry. I have to get to class a little early today."

"Okay, Dee. Have a great day!" He stood there without moving an inch.

Cordelia turned and walked away, waving at Becky as she left. She felt annoyed at Perry for interrupting her conversation with Becky, and even more annoyed that she had to walk away because Perry was too stupid to sense that he was intruding. Why couldn't he walk away and just leave them alone?

Her sense of irritability only increased when she saw her ex-boyfriend Logan standing between her and her first classroom in the hallway. After cheating on her earlier in the year, he had recently been trying to talk to her again at school, like nothing had ever happened. At the moment, there was no way to avoid him.

"Hey, Cordelia. Want to hang out after school?"

"No, sorry, Logan. I'm busy after school today."

"That's cool. Maybe tomorrow?"

"I think I'm going to be pretty busy till graduation, Logan. I'm really sorry." She didn't feel sorry at all. She felt amazed that he could look right at her and not see any difference in her. He obviously didn't recognize that she had gone through a change, a total metamorphosis, nor could he realize that he meant no more to her than a mosquito landing on her arm. She continued down the hall to her first class.

She dragged herself reluctantly from class to class, feeling restless and apprehensive about going to history class. She felt terribly nervous when it was time to approach that room. She thought she might have to leave the building or go to the girls' bathroom to vomit. Nonetheless, she was drawn to that room, and she knew she would never be able to convince her feet to turn around and walk away from it. When she first entered, she looked quickly at him—at Mr. T, at *Martin*—and he met her gaze. They only looked at each other for a second, but it was enough to reassure her. Last night was not a crazy dream or a desperate creation of her wild imagination. What happened last night was reality, and she reassured herself that they both knew it and felt it. She looked away and took her seat next to Becky.

Mr. T was talking about American history, wrapping up the semester's work on this topic. Today, he drew comparisons between American and Canadian history.

"As you know," he said, "I grew up in Canada. And we Canadians know all about your history. But you Americans know very little about us. Perhaps we can finish the semester with a bit of Canadian history."

Cordelia felt that he was speaking directly to her, and only to her, albeit in code. He wanted her to know about him and his background, and she was ready to memorize anything and everything he chose to tell her. If she could steal away from home and see him later in the evening, she would talk to him privately about what she learned of his country. She started scribbling furiously on a sheet of paper, making notes about John Cabot landing on the coast of Newfoundland in 1497. She wrote that The Hudson's Bay Company opened in the 1600s, and she imagined one of Mr. T's ancestors trading furs up north. For the most part, she sat looking at her desk and her notes, only occasionally daring to look up at him. She did her best to play the role of just another student, but she was sure that she must be failing to hide her feelings. She felt certain that every kid in the class would be able to tell at a glance that something was dramatically different about her. She glanced left and right at several of her classmates, and she was surprised to see that they were not staring at her. Stranger yet, those who returned her gaze revealed not a flicker of suspicion or interest in their faces. Even Becky, seated right beside her, seemed oblivious to her state of romantic agitation.

Such was the state of this crazy world, she concluded. People always seem to notice trivial things of no consequence, while they miss the important things. The entire class would notice if she cut her hair short. The entire school would notice if she dared to walk down the halls barefoot. But no one seemed to notice what was happening between her and Martin. How could they not notice? *She* noticed when Becky was upset about losing a race in crew. Why did no one else seem to notice things? Was everybody else in the world deaf, dumb, and blind?

Mr. T finished his class, and Cordelia plodded through her other classes until the day was finally over. She walked down the hall with Becky, relieved to be done, and thinking about an alibi to tell her parents after dinner. She was determined to see him tonight.

"What's the matter with *you*?" asked Becky.

"Nothing. Nothing's the matter with me."

"Bullshit. You're acting weird."

Cordelia felt a sense of relief to know that her friend was not actually oblivious to her changed state of being, but she was also caught off guard.

"I'm fine."

"You are definitely not fine. You were not your usual little Mother Teresa self with Perry in the halls. You actually looked annoyed, like a normal human being would look. And sitting next to you in Mr. T's class was like sitting next to a caged animal."

Cordelia pivoted around to face Becky. She started talking in a mad rush of words, waving her hands in the air for emphasis.

"You want to know what's the matter with me? Okay, I'll tell you. I can't stand this place any more, okay? I can't stand high school. I can't play this stupid little game. I don't want to go to any more high school classes. I don't want to see stupid, annoying people like Perry and Logan in the halls. I don't want to pretend any more. I can't stand even being in this building right now. I have to get out of here right now! Okay?"

Becky looked at her with a bewildered expression. "But it's only a few weeks till graduation," she said. "What's the big deal all of a sudden?"

"Right, you're right. It's only a few weeks. And then all this nonsense will be over, and we'll all graduate, and Martin will go home to Canada—to Montreal—for the entire summer, and I'll never see him again, and that's the end of that!"

Becky stood looking at her with a blank expression on her face, as if she had just heard someone speak to her in a foreign language and she was waiting for the interpreter. But then her eyes opened wide.

"What? What did you just say? Did you say *Martin*? Oh, my God, Cordelia! Oh. My. God."

29

A Daring Escape

"**I**'m done!" Cordelia announced as she got into Becky's old Toyota. "I've listened to enough of his craziness, and I'm done!" She banged on the dashboard three times with her fist. "Bastard! Bastard! Bastard!"

"So, what did he say?" asked Becky, driving away from Cordelia's house.

Cordelia struggled to stop crying so she could talk. "Just the stuff I told you about on the phone. He found an empty vodka bottle in my backpack, and he went nuts."

"Oh, Jesus. So, what did you tell him?"

"Well, I couldn't tell him that I brought it to the graduation party last weekend to share with everyone. So, I told him it belonged to someone else. I told him that Cheryl passed it to me when her parents came to pick her up at the party because she was afraid her parents would see it."

"Oh, how clever of you," said Becky. "That's just the oldest excuse in the world. 'I was only holding the vodka bottle for a friend.'" Then the expression on her face changed. "Sorry, sorry. This is no time to make fun of you."

"No, it's not," Cordelia said sharply. "He found the bottle in my backpack and he absolutely went crazy. I mean crazy!"

"But wait," Becky said. "What was he doing in your backpack, anyway?"

"Oh, he claimed he was looking for the car registration that I borrowed from him a couple of days ago. But I think he was just snooping." She couldn't get the image out of her head: her father, standing there in the kitchen, holding up an empty vodka bottle. The look in his eyes was intense and disturbing, the look of a fanatic unhinged, the glare of a victorious lunatic who had discovered proof, at last, to confirm his paranoid delusions. His daughter really was the embodiment of evil, a totally worthless creature, essentially a no-good drunk.

Becky turned the car toward her own street.

"You wouldn't believe the way he talked to me," added Cordelia. "He kept yelling that I'm a drunk. A drunk!" She struggled to compose herself. "And that I'll never amount to anything in life. That I'll never succeed in college."

"That sounds awful," said Becky. "I thought he's been better lately."

Cordelia sniffled and tried to collect herself. "Yeah, he was. He was a lot better for a while. But no more. This was the worst. Listening to him, you'd think I sit home alone all day and chug vodka in my bedroom."

Becky drove the rest of the short way to her house. She parked the car in her driveway, and they both sat together quietly for a couple of minutes. It was a warm day in June, so they put the car windows down to let the breeze blow through. In the front yard of Becky's little house was a huge Northern Catalpa tree in full bloom. The sweet scent of the blossoms drifted into the car. Cordelia heard the song of a red-winged blackbird. It seemed odd to her that the world would just continue with its usual spring merriment when she was so unhappy, so completely unable to enjoy it.

"I just want to get out of here," said Cordelia. "I wish I could go to Canada and see Martin."

Becky was playing with her key chain, but then looked up at Cordelia. "So, let's go!"

Cordelia looked at her. "What do you mean?"

"Just what I said. Let's go to Montreal! You know that my grandma still lives in Montreal, so I can stay at her house. And you can visit Mr. T. Okay: *Martin*. Whatever you call him."

Cordelia opened her car door. "Are you crazy?" she asked.

"Not at all."

"You're not kidding?"

"Why would I be kidding?" asked Becky. "School is over. We've graduated. You already told your neighbors that you're not going to be running your little one-woman daycare center over the summer. So, we're free. Let's go!"

"But your mom would have something to say about that. You can't just pick up and leave like that, with no warning. Won't your parents object?"

"Oh, no," said Becky. "I'll just call my mom and tell her that I'm sure Dad won't mind. She never wants to be the bad one, so she'll agree right away. Then I'll call my dad and tell him that mom has approved our trip, and he'll be afraid to be the bad guy, so he'll agree, too. And then we'll hit the road."

Cordelia sat thinking about this for only a brief minute. "Oh my God, let's do it!"

"Great! Call him and tell him we're coming."

Cordelia hesitated. He had invited her to visit, but would he really be happy if she drove up to Montreal to see him? What would he say on the phone if she called?

"Never mind," said Becky. "Let's surprise him!"

"Great!" said Cordelia.

They went into the house so Becky could pack a bag and make two phone calls, one to each parent. Cordelia heard the end of the first conversation:

"Thanks, Mom. You're the best mom in the world!"

And the end of the second conversation:

"Thanks, Dad. You're the best dad in the world!"

Becky bragged that the calls had gone exactly as she predicted. The girls then waited for about an hour, because Cordelia knew that her parents were going to be out of the house at that time. Then they went back to Cordelia's house so she could run up to her bedroom and grab the suitcase that sat ready for just such a daring escape. She went to her bulletin board, unpinned the photocopied clues about her grandmother's life, and lay the papers on top of her clothing in the suitcase. She wrote a brief note, addressed only to her mother. At the last minute, she remembered to grab her purse and her money from her babysitting job, and she ran out to Becky's waiting car.

"Let's go!" she said to Becky, and they headed off to Canada.

For the first hour of the ride, Cordelia gave Becky more details about the ugly scene with her father. Becky offered her sympathy, as well as her assurances that one can lead a perfectly happy life despite having a despicable father. Cordelia was still badly shaken by the incident, but gradually she began to settle down as Route 87 unfolded before them. She was actually leaving home; she wouldn't have to see him later in the day. Perhaps she wouldn't have to see him for a very long time.

After another hour on the road, they were looking at the Adirondack Mountains, and Cordelia felt a sense of relief getting away from her life back home. She saw the image of her father standing in the kitchen with the vodka bottle, but he looked smaller now with every mile they drove.

Becky turned to Cordelia. "You do have your driver's license, I hope. You'll need it to get through the border check."

"Yeah, I've got it," said Cordelia.

Becky drove another few minutes. "And by the way, how are we going to find Mr. T?"

"That's easy," said Cordelia. "He gave me his address before he left for the summer. Just in case I could find a way to visit him."

"Sweet!" said Becky.

Cordelia opened her purse and started to fish around in it, looking for the folded piece of lined paper with Martin's address on it. She was happy at first to find a slip of paper, but it was the wrong one.

> *Hobbes found your shoes again. Have a nice day.*
>
> *Dad*

She crumpled it up and threw it out her window. She hated it when she saw other people littering the road, but in this case, an exception seemed warranted.

"What the hell are you doing?" asked Becky.

"Nothing. That wasn't it." She continued to search, but her mood quickly darkened.

"You have the address?" asked Becky.

"It's got to be here someplace," said Cordelia, continuing to look in the purse.

"I hope you didn't leave it at home," said Becky.

"No way. I always keep it in my purse with me." She pulled everything out of the purse and spread it on her lap: hairbrush, make-up, wallet, spare keys to her mother's car, a pen, a pack of gum, and several little notes she had written to herself so she wouldn't forget things. There was also an overdue notice from her local library regarding a copy of Tolstoy's *Anna Karenina*. (Oh no, where in the world did she put that book?) She found everything except Martin's address.

"Oh, my God, Cordelia. Please don't tell me you've lost his address."

"No, I haven't lost it. I just can't locate it this exact *second*."

"You've lost it, haven't you? Don't lie to me. You lose everything. How did you ever get through high school? How do you even get through a single day of your life, Cordelia?"

Cordelia felt terrible, as she often felt when she lost things. She tried to make light of the problem. "It doesn't matter," she said. "I know where he hangs out."

"Oh, really? Where does he hang out?"

"There's a bookstore. He knows a guy who works there. His name is Charles. They're friends and they like to talk. It's called Tous Les Livres," she said in her best French pronunciation. "All the Books. We'll just find him at the bookstore."

Becky snorted. "Oh, sure. We'll just stake out some random French bookstore in the middle of Canada, like undercover detectives looking for a fugitive, and no doubt we'll catch him in about fifteen minutes. Unless, of course, he decides not to buy any books this summer, and his buddy Charles doesn't work there anymore. In which case we're driving four hours to Montreal for nothing."

Becky drove along, and the two girls sat in silence for the next half-hour. Cordelia knew that her friend was angry with her, and she was angry with herself for losing things. But the material objects of this world never seemed to stay where she put them. There were so many objects, and so many places where one could put them! How was she supposed to remember all those things and all those places? Still, everyone else seemed to remember where they laid things when they didn't want to hold them in their hands. Why couldn't she ever seem to remember?

Finally, Becky spoke again. "You're really crazy in love with Mr. T, aren't you?"

"Totally. Completely."

Becky let out a big sigh. "Okay. But are you sure about the name of the bookstore?"

"Absolutely certain. I swear to God. Tous Les Livres."

"All right," said Becky. "I believe you. You do seem to have a good memory for facts, even though I wouldn't trust you not to lose a grand piano. So, here's the plan. We'll go to this bookstore and find this guy Charles—you better pray that he still works there—and we'll ask him where Mr. T. lives. If they're really friends, he ought to know the address."

"Right!" said Cordelia. "That's a great idea, Becky! Thanks a million!"

"No need to thank me. I feel sorry for handicapped people. It's my Buddhist compassion, you know."

And they continued their journey north.

Cordelia was relieved to settle the rough spot with Becky, but the peace between them left room for thoughts of her father. His words drifted across her mind again, and she felt distressed again. She wanted to cry, and she wanted to scream at him, but most of all, she wanted never to see him again. In the note she left for her mother, she said she would be in Montreal with Becky's grandma for a week or two, but she daydreamed about setting up residency in Canada for a lifetime. She was sick and tired of trying to figure out what was wrong with her father. She was exhausted from wondering if part of the problem was her fault. His behavior had become so outrageous that she found it toxic to be in the room with him. She took some comfort by reminding herself that every mile they drove was one mile farther away from him, and one mile closer to Martin.

They were on the road for several hours when the U.S.-Canada border came into view. Cordelia's mood began to lift. She had the exciting sense that she was escaping from America, the land of her irrational father. Becky drove the car up to the inspection booth, where they were greeted by a woman in two languages.

"Bonjour. Hello."

Becky said hello and handed the woman two drivers' licenses. Cordelia was thrilled by the thought of Martin speaking French, which added to her sense of a great adventure. She and Becky answered the inspector's questions.

Where do you live? And you? Where are you going? What's the purpose of your visit? How long do you intend to stay?

As the inspector gave them the approval to pass through, Cordelia called out, "Au revoir!" The woman smiled at her.

About an hour later, the two girls walked into Tous Les Livres.

Cordelia had imagined a small, dimly lit shop with narrow aisles stuffed with books, and a single staffer—Martin's friend Charles—sitting behind a dusty old wooden desk wearing a black beret. Instead, the store was large and bright, and there were several people working there. For a moment, Cordelia felt sick with dread as she faced the possibility that the entire trip was ruined because she had lost Martin's address. She couldn't imagine that any of the people she saw could be his friend Charles. But then she saw a man behind a counter who looked like he was in his mid-twenties. He was a thin fellow, with wire-rimmed glasses and a short, sparse beard. She pulled Becky in that direction.

"Pardon," she said in her best French. "On cherche Charles."

He smiled at her. "You are looking for Charles?" he asked in heavily accented English. "You find him."

Cordelia felt her heart pounding in her chest. "You're Charles? That's great! I wonder if you could help us. We're looking for Martin Tremblay. I think he's a friend of yours, right?"

"Ah, Martin," said the man, smiling. "Yes, of course."

"Great!" said Cordelia. "Do you happen to know his address? We're trying to find him."

"His address?" Charles shrugged his shoulders. "No, I have no address."

Cordelia felt her mood sinking so quickly that she could think of nothing else to say to Charles.

Becky, who had been standing just behind Cordelia, stepped up to the counter beside her. "Are you sure? It's really important that we find him, and we figured that you would have his address."

Charles studied them both for a long moment. "I don't know the address for Martin, but I think you two girls must have an address in the U.S., yes?"

"Right," said Becky. "We're from New York State."

Charles looked directly at Cordelia and began to smile broadly. "And I think that perhaps one of you is called Cordelia."

"Yes! That's me! I'm Cordelia!"

He held up an index finger. "Wait, please. Une minute." And he turned away from the girls to pick up the phone on the wall behind him. He dialed a number, and after waiting a few seconds, he spoke. "Salut, Martin. Ici Charles." He chatted happily for a minute or two, and then put the phone back in its receiver.

"What did you tell him?" asked Cordelia, feeling breathless.

"I told him that I have a new book that he must see. I told him to come now to see the new American book before someone else will steal it from the bookshelf."

"So, he's coming here to meet us?" asked Cordelia in disbelief.

"Yes," said Charles. "He come now."

She thanked Charles and ran outside to stand on the sidewalk and watch for Martin. She was only vaguely aware of Becky standing beside her and stuffing a piece of paper into her purse.

"Here's my grandma's phone number," said Becky. "Try, try not to lose it!"

"Yes, yes, of course," said Cordelia, never taking her eyes away from the street and its many pedestrians.

In the distance, far down the street, her attention was drawn to a figure who briefly appeared separate from the crowd, then disappeared behind other walkers, then reappeared, a figure with a familiar easy-going, long-legged stride. Cordelia stood perfectly still, as if any approach on her part might expose the sight of him to be a mirage, a hallucinated oasis in the middle of a desert. But he emerged again from the other people on the street. As she watched him grow bigger and closer, the drama of the day receded into the distance: her father's attack, the daring escape with Becky, the stress of losing Martin's address, the border crossing, the encounter with Charles. At a certain moment, she could clearly see his face, and he raised a hand to wave to her. And it seemed to her that everything she had always thought impossible was possible, and everything she had ever dreamed about in her best fantasy life was actually just a mental representation of the way the real world works. At least in Canada.

30

Daniel's Dream

I am standing at a train station on a cold, cloudy day. Cordelia is standing on the platform, too. I suddenly realize that we are here for different purposes: I have come to meet someone, although I'm not sure who that is; she has come to take a train. I don't want her to go, but I can't bring myself to talk to her and convince her to stay. Besides, she won't even look at me, so I can't get her attention.

The train pulls into the station, but she just stands there. I know that she is about to board the train, but she doesn't move. The train is going to travel west, although I don't know its exact destination. Cordelia stands where she is. I know that her departure is inevitable. There is nothing I can do to stop her. Why won't she get on board? I feel terribly agitated by the situation. Go already, I think. Just go! The waiting is unbearable. If you're going to leave, then leave! The doors open to the train, but she still doesn't move. In a moment of impulsive fury, I push her into one of the cars. She stumbles a bit as she lurches into the car. I feel bad about shoving her, but she recovers her balance quickly and doesn't even look back at me. It seems as though she is unaffected by my push, untouched by my life entirely, as if I don't matter to her. Standing alone on the platform, I am starting to cry, but she doesn't notice.

The doors close, and I can see her through the window. She sits down in one of the seats, and now she turns to look at me. She has no particular expression in her face, but she is clearly looking at me. It occurs to me that there are many other people gathering on the platform, and some of them now seem to be relatives of mine, but Cordelia looks only at me. Then the train pulls away from the station, and I lose sight of her.

I start running along the platform, chasing the train, but I can barely move. My legs feel weak and heavy, my steps are small and sluggish, and I realize that I can never catch the train.

Dan awoke with a start, feeling scared and shaky. He was breathing hard. He sat up in bed and looked at Abby asleep next to him. He focused on her in order to ground himself in the reality of his sleeping wife and disavow the terrible shadow of the dream. It was just a dream. He was in his bed, next to Abby, and there was no train pulling away from the station.

He got up and went downstairs. He stopped at the refrigerator to pour himself some orange juice, and then he went to his chair to sit by himself. He turned on a small lamp and looked around at his books and magazines. All of this gave him some comfort, which he badly needed, because he was still shaken by the dream images. The most persistent was the image of Cordelia looking at him from inside the train. She wouldn't stop looking at him, but he couldn't make out any particular expression or message in her gaze. He tried to distract himself so he would stop remembering this scene.

His mother. He suddenly saw his mother at the airport when he was seventeen years old. She stood looking at him, and only at him, not at his father or his sister. And in the dream, Cordelia looked only at him, even though there were other unidentified relatives on the platform. So, was the dream about his mother?

Cordelia was leaving at the train station, as his mother had left at the airport. And the train was heading west. Of course! His mother had gone west to Tucson. The whole thing was actually about his mother. One didn't need to be a Freudian psychoanalyst to see that. But why was his mother not in it? Why do dreams so often travel in disguise? Why did the dream substitute Cordelia for his mother? Surely, he had dreamed many a dream about his mother before this night. She had entered his dreams repeatedly over the years, sometimes in the backyard, sometimes in the airport, sometimes sitting at the kitchen table with the family.

He reached over to the small table next to his chair and picked up the envelope with the latest clue. It was a menu from a diner in Albuquerque, New Mexico. He had called on the phone the day before, but no one knew anything about his mother. Now he looked again at the menu. The owner seemed to be someone who was aware of current news events and fond of putting them into his menu.

> The Berlin Wall. A huge garden salad with walls of Romaine lettuce, a celebration of fresh vegetables, and free crumbles of feta cheese. No passport needed.

The Berlin Wall. The Berlin Wall came down in 1989. So, this culinary wit must have been putting this item on his menu at about that time. Which means it was only eight years ago. And the other clues were in chronological order. The first—the Denver nursery article—was dated 1970, just a few years after she disappeared. Her stay in the convent ended fifteen years ago, in 1982. The menu was from 1989 or so. Maybe there was some sense to these seemingly random clues, after all.

He sat there alone in his wingback chair, mulling this over. Gradually, his thoughts drifted away from the clues, the dream, and the memories of his mother, and he was left with the stillness of the house in the middle of the night. He sat there confronted with his life as it was. He wondered about his daughter up in Montreal. It had been three days since she disappeared, and he still couldn't believe that she had run away like that. She left a note for her mother telling her where she would be staying, and she talked to her mother on the phone after arriving. Still, he was shocked and distressed by her sudden absence.

Obviously, he was to blame. That much seemed clear in the dark stillness of the night. He had driven her away from home with his outbursts. Since she had left, every day was a torment to him. Every time he thought about her, which was dozens of times a day, he felt guilty and ashamed about his temper. Then he would feel angry at her for making him feel so bad, and finally he would scold himself for holding his child responsible for his own despicable behavior. When she called home, he couldn't even talk to her on the phone, much as he longed to hear her voice again. And whenever Abby looked at him with that sad look in her eyes, he felt wretched.

He found himself in the insomniac's world of worst possibilities, where every thought becomes a disaster about to happen. Was Cordelia safe in Montreal? Was she living in a safe neighborhood? What if she got involved with the wrong kind of people and got hurt? If anything bad happened to her, he would never forgive himself.

He forcibly steered his mind away from his darkest thoughts. She would be home later in the summer, and she would be fine. And he would try yet again to be kind and understanding, without the flares of his temper. He closed his eyes. *Please*, he whispered.

He had long ago abandoned the concept of the Judeo-Christian God who answers the prayers of wayward mortals, but he prayed anyway. *Please help me.* He silently prayed that someone— Anyone—would help him before he lost his daughter forever.

31

Montreal

When Cordelia walked the streets of Montreal with Martin, she was free. She was no longer the high school girl who was trying to hide a secret crush on her teacher. She was Cordelia, and he was Martin, and they were a couple. No one looked at them with the slightest hint of suspicion or disapproval. And why should they? People should be allowed to be in love, and they shouldn't be bound by the silly conventions of middle-class American society. Here in Canada, things were different.

She knew, of course, that their physical appearance, walking hand in hand down Rue St. Denis, would not raise any eyebrows unless someone knew them from back home. Martin, wearing shorts and a T-shirt instead of a dress shirt and necktie, looked a bit younger than his twenty-four years; she, on the other hand, had often been told that she looked older than her years. Given these obvious facts, she might well have surmised that they would be an acceptable sight on the streets of any city in the world. However, for Cordelia, the more compelling explanation for their new, happy life could be summed up in one word: Montreal.

For her, Montreal was the City of Love, where each of its citizens was a champion of the heart, every street a promenade for lovers, every café a sanctuary for outlawed romance. By day, she strolled the streets with Martin and learned her way around his neighborhood. By night, she explored the geography of the human body, continuing the experiment that they had begun together back in Albany. She discovered that any particular point on her skin surface could be transformed, by a simple touch from Martin, into a direct conduit for the passage of love. She had no such experience with her self-centered ex-boyfriend back home, and she wondered how she had ever lived without it.

Her new love life was intoxicating and exotic, as was the entire city. When Martin took her on the Metro train to Old Montreal—Vieux-Montréal—she felt like she was in Europe. And they spoke French! For years, she had taken French classes in school and suffered through the boredom of the weekly quizzes on vocabulary, verb tense, and how to order a salad in a restaurant. But to hear it spoken on the street was quite another thing. And to hear Martin speak French added a whole new layer to his attractiveness.

Cordelia was in love with Montreal. And she was in love with Martin, which meant that little characteristics of his appearance and behavior became imbued with special value. For instance, she was in love with his style of conversation. He always tried to give fair consideration to both sides of an issue. One evening, a friend complained that the price of apartment rentals was too high in Montreal. Martin first commiserated with the friend, but later looked at the issue from the landlords' point of view.

"Put yourself in the owner's place," he said to Cordelia when they got back to his apartment. "He's probably thinking to himself, 'My taxes are going up. The cost of maintaining the building is going up. I just have to raise the rents.' So maybe he has no choice."

Martin had his own principles and beliefs, to be sure, but he always tried to balance the scales before taking sides in a controversy. Cordelia loved his habit of stepping into the other guy's shoes, speaking the part of the imaginary adversary in a debate. It was more than a style of speaking, she knew. It was his defining personality trademark: a fair-minded, even-handed temperament, quick to listen and slow to pass judgment.

She was in love with his voice, too, a pleasingly resonant baritone that sounded to her ear like the human equivalent of the cello, her favorite instrument. She was in love with his eyes (large, brown), his chin (square, no cleft), his ears (slightly forward-jutting), and his smile (wide and relaxed). He walked with big, easy strides, never seeming to be in a rush to get where he was going, and she loved this, too. For Cordelia, Martin's personal traits had been completely transformed by the process of falling in love. His individual qualities, from the trivial to the grand, had coalesced to form an island of perfection in an otherwise imperfect world.

Cordelia had no idea what would happen when she first arrived in Montreal, but she and Martin quickly came to an understanding. His parents were spending the summer in Europe, and he had already planned a trip to join them for a family reunion in early August. That would be about five weeks from the day of her arrival. He was also scheduled for an annual fishing trip with old friends from college, but he decided he would rather stay with her and see his friends some other time. They both agreed that they would spend that month-plus-a-week—thirty-six days exactly, by her tally—together in Montreal, at which time he would leave on his trip and she would return home to get ready for college.

They quickly developed a little routine. He had his graduate classes at the Université de Montréal, and she signed up for an intensive French class to match his schedule as closely as possible. In their free afternoons, they would stroll in the neighborhood or do a little grocery shopping. Occasionally, they did some sightseeing in Old Montreal. Wherever they were, they were often talking, and Cordelia found their conversation to be one of life's great pleasures. She marveled at the complexity of human speech. What a miracle that we humans can converse like this! We put all manner of intricate ideas and emotions into words, the words come forth in logical sequence and orderly sentence structure, and the entire process is improvised on the spot, like jazz musicians playing their ad lib solos.

In the evenings, they would sit together on the little balcony of his apartment and watch people stroll along in their quiet, tree-lined neighborhood. Occasionally, they got together at a café with Martin's friends, including Charles from the bookstore. (Becky sometimes joined the group, although she also spent time with friends she had made during previous summer trips to visit her grandmother.) Martin's friends were all his age, give or take a year, but Cordelia had no trouble getting along with them. This didn't surprise her. It had never been difficult for her to talk with older people. The challenge was always to fit in with kids her own age. How do you talk to boys who call it sport to hit each other with hockey sticks? How do you get close to high school girls with their cliques and make-up and perfect sun tans? She got along quite well with Martin's group of friends. They spoke mostly English when she was around, and they seemed to accept her very easily.

At home in Martin's apartment, he quickly tried to accommodate her. He made space in his closet for her clothes. He asked her about favorite foods to add to his shopping list. When she told him of her interest in meditation, he bought a big cushion and put it in one corner of the bedroom for her. He also surprised her with a little hand-carved figure of the Buddha, made in Cambodia.

On Sundays, Cordelia called home, as she had promised her mother. On her second such call, she was already annoyed by her mother's chirping, sing-song voice, already tired of making the usual inane talk about the weather in Montreal and how much fun she was having with Becky. And her mother said the same things she said on the previous Sunday.

"But when are you coming home, Cordelia?"

"I told you last week, Mom," she said in her usual reply. "We'll be home in early August."

"But why wait till then? Why August?" asked her mother.

Cordelia paused and considered what she could not say. *Because that's when Martin, my teacher-turned-lover, leaves on a trip to Europe. That's why.* She felt suddenly exhausted by this weekly pretense on the phone. "Because that's when Becky wants to leave, Mom. And she's the one with the car."

"I'll come get you any time, sweetheart."

"Mom, I just need a little more time away from Dad. I'm fine, and I promise we're coming home in August. In about a month."

"But what are you doing for money, Cordelia?"

"Mom, I told you last week. I'm spending my own money. The money I made at my babysitting job."

Her mother sighed deeply on the other end of the phone. "You know, your father is very upset about you running away."

"Mom, for God's sake, I didn't run away! I went for a trip with Becky because I needed a break from him!"

"I know he can be difficult, Cordelia, but he only wants the best for you."

Cordelia pursed her lips together tightly and kept herself from speaking until she could compose herself.

"Sure, Mom. Anyway, is Dad there? I should probably say hello to him. I haven't talked to him since I got here."

"I think he's a little preoccupied right now. He just received another of those strange clues about your grandmother. A library card from Santa Fe, New Mexico, with your grandmother's name on it. He's just sitting in his chair, trying to figure it out."

"But he can take a break for one minute and come to the phone, Mom."

There was a pause on the line. "Well, no, honey, he won't come to the phone. He's still pretty upset with you."

Cordelia felt her body get tense. Her belly felt funny—belly worms. Her father was still causing her to have belly worms, even from a couple hundred miles away. She fought against an urge to cry. "That's fine, Mom. I didn't really want to talk to him anyway!"

She said an abrupt good-bye, hung up the phone, and turned around to see Martin standing in front of her. She could tell by his face that he was feeling sorry for her, and that he understood what was happening without even hearing half of the conversation. Martin seemed to understand everything about her. When he came over and put his arms around her, she cried about her father, and she said a secret prayer of thanks for having a man like Martin in her life.

32

Silence Can Kill

An old saying came to Cordelia's mind.

Stick and stones can break my bones,
But words can never hurt me.

She heard it when she was a kid in elementary school. She always considered it to be nonsense, pure bravado invented by some sassy kid who was trying to stand up to a schoolyard bully. After all, everyone knows that words can hurt. But worse than name-calling is silence. Silence can kill.

Sticks and stones can break my bones,
And words can really hurt me,
But silence can kill.

Silence can kill any relationship, even a bond that was originally good and innocent once upon a time, even a lifelong family relationship that was once in full bloom. Silence can starve it for air and water until it inevitably succumbs and withers away to nothing.

She hadn't heard a word from her father since she left home two weeks ago. Whenever she called home, her mother would answer and her father would refuse to come to the phone. Her mother was forwarding her mail up to Becky's grandmother's house, but there was never anything from him. She would wait anxiously for Becky to bring her mail over to Martin's apartment. She would take a seat at their kitchen table and tear open the large manila envelope with her home address on it, eager to see what her mother had put inside it. She would find mostly letters from Marist College about the dormitory she would be living in, or who her college advisor would be, or what kinds of clubs were available to join on campus. Nothing from her father. She would look inside the manila envelope again, just in case a little note from him was stuck in there, but there was nothing else but silence.

Since he had dropped out of the conversation, Cordelia's mind was left to interpret the silence. Nothing good came of this. First, there were practical worries. Would he pay for her college tuition? Would she have to get a job—*any* job—and forego her chance to attend a good college? She struggled with this for a while, until she struck a defiant stance in her thinking. He could keep his damned money! She would work to earn her own tuition, and she wouldn't lower herself to be dependent on him. But then she did some quick math, based on what she earned in her babysitting jobs, and her prospects looked grim. She had seen the tuition that Marist College charged. Even though the neighborhood parents paid her far more than she asked, she could never come close to supporting herself through college. She thought about her grandmother and the clues from Alaska. Maybe she was about to meet her long-lost grandmother, who would come to the rescue and pay for her college bills. But one of the clues had led her father to a convent. She scolded herself for her silly fantasy. Did she really think that her grandmother was a religious recluse who secretly made a fortune in the stock market and hid the money in her nun's habit?

"Don't worry," Martin said, when she talked to him about her concerns. "My dad was as difficult as they come, but he helped me through college. I'm sure your father will do the same for you, Cordelia."

Hearing Martin say this was calming. Hearing Martin say *anything* was calming, because he was always so thoughtful and kind, and his voice was so soothing. But ironically, his reassurance also made things worse, because assuaging her fear about tuition exposed the deeper fear lurking behind it. What if her father simply never spoke to her again? What if he wrote the tuition checks, but refused to engage in the relationship with her ever again? She remembered hearing stories about her father's old great-aunt, crazy Tanta Zlata, who would get angry at a family member and stop talking to that person for years. Years! Maybe her father had inherited a Crazy Old Jew gene from his Eastern European Jewish ancestors.

The silence continued, and the effect was devastating. Finally, she had sent him a letter, a very carefully worded letter trying to let him know she was still open to having a father-daughter relationship with him, but there were things that needed to be addressed. Perhaps they could talk by phone soon and resolve these issues.

The response: more silence.

So, Becky continued to bring over the mail, and Cordelia continued to search through it, looking for something from him.

"Don't sweat it," Becky said, obviously knowing what she was looking for. "He'll get over it."

But he apparently wasn't getting over anything, and the lack of contact was wearing her down. Sometimes it was hard to enjoy her time with Martin in Montreal. Her father's silence was becoming a permanent presence in her life, like a fugitive criminal who sneaked across the border with her and followed her to Canada. She woke up to his silence in the morning; it followed her when she walked along the street to her French class. It would appear and disappear, like a bandit darting in and out of the shadows of a dark alley. When it disappeared, she would be fine for a while, but it was always around the next corner, waiting for her. Sooner or later, she would sense its presence again, and she would feel hopeless and hollow.

She woke up one morning and felt the presence of the silence. To make matters worse, she had a terrible hangover. Martin and his friends generally preferred a café to a bar, but there had been a party at a friend's house. She drank too much and awoke feeling achy and thirsty. She had a throbbing headache. While he was getting dressed for class, Martin made one single comment to her.

"You drank quite a bit last night."

She sat on the edge of their bed feeling sluggish and nauseated. She was afraid that he was going to say something else. When he did not, she vaguely realized that she *wanted* him to say something else. She wanted him to say something stern, something forceful. She wanted him to tell her, in no uncertain terms, to stop drinking *now*. Why didn't he get in her face and yell at her about her idiotic drinking? Martin was so sweet and easygoing, but sometimes he was just too sweet, too easygoing, if such a thing were possible. Too passive, she thought, as she entertained (for the first time) the possibility that Martin might have human shortcomings. And his passivity left her alone with her own inner voices, which were merciless. Maybe she was ruining everything with Martin, the voices screamed, as she had ruined everything with her father. She fought back against the voices. She reminded them that she had only been drunk once in Montreal. And in truth, she had no great desire to drink since coming to Canada.

When he left for class, she sat by herself drinking her coffee on their little balcony. Gradually, she began to feel better. The neighborhood was typically quiet, and it was a beautiful morning, sunny but cool, a welcome respite after several days of hot, humid weather. A breeze waved the branches of the trees overhead, and the sunlight stole through the moving leaves to make dancing patterns on the sidewalk below. She watched a couple squirrels chasing each other up and down a tree. She heard a familiar *rat-a-tat-tat*, and turned her head just in time to see a woodpecker with a bright red cap pecking away at a maple tree across the street. If not for the silence of her father, she would have been content to sit there on the balcony all morning until Martin came back home. But she had to do something about this murderous silence. She sat brainstorming about ways to force her father back into contact with her. There must be some ploy she could use that he couldn't resist.

Her thoughts turned to her grandmother. There had been that one recent clue, a library card from Santa Fe, New Mexico. Would she actually get to meet her grandmother? Was she even alive? She thought again about what she would want to say to this woman who had abandoned her family so long ago. She went into the apartment and sat on the bed, looking at the clues she had brought with her from home. She tried to imagine her grandmother as a nun in New Mexico.

Then she realized that this was the answer. Her grandmother was the answer. Her father would never be able to ignore that topic. Besides, she really did want to say something to him about the search. She considered her strategy in more detail, and then she went into the little living room, sat down in a chair, and dialed the phone. While she waited for an answer, she looked at a drawing that lay on the coffee table in front of her. She and Martin had posed for a street artist who sketched the two of them sitting together at a sidewalk café in Old Montreal.

"Hi, Mom."

"Hi, Cordelia! How are you, honey?" Her mother's familiar voice was comforting.

"I'm fine, Mom. I just wondered if I could talk to Dad for a minute. Is he home?"

"He's home, but you know he won't come to the phone. I'm sorry, but I just can't get him to talk to you when you call."

Cordelia found herself looking again at the artist's sketch. She looked so happy sitting with Martin. How could one person be so happy and so unhappy at the same time?

Her mother continued. "I'm sure he'll get over it one of these days, though."

Cordelia hesitated. She could have used her mother's answer as an excuse to give up and avoid a possible confrontation with him, but she pushed ahead. "Tell him it's about Grandma."

"Grandma?"

"Yeah. Just tell him I have to talk to him about Grandma."

"I don't understand, honey. We haven't heard anything new since I last talked to you. Just that one new clue, the library card."

"Mom, just tell him. Please."

"Well, all right. Hold on, and I'll tell him. But I doubt he'll come to the phone."

There was a long silence. Cordelia wondered what it would be like to be home again. She had a moment of intense longing to see them, but then she found herself dreading the reunion. What if he acted completely crazy again? How would she ever stand it? She hoped he wouldn't take the phone, after all.

"Hello." The voice sounded flat and dull.

She tried to sound cheerful. "Hi, Dad!"

"Hello, Cordelia."

Maybe she shouldn't have called. If he was going to act so cold, why should she bother? But she had called, so she might as well go through with it. "Dad, I'm sure you're mad at me for leaving home, but I want to say something about Grandma."

There was such a long silence on the other end of the phone that she thought he might have put the phone down and walked away. Then he spoke. "Your grandmother?"

"Yeah."

"Okay. What do you want to say?"

She fought an urge to tell him to go to Hell, and then hang up the phone. "Well, Mom told me last Sunday that you received another clue. I don't know if you're going to travel more and trace the clue, but I have one request. If you find her, you have to let me know right away."

"I would have your mother call you, of course."

"No, I mean I want to know right away. I want *you* to call me as soon as you find her."

"What's the rush?"

"If she's still alive and you find her, I'd like to meet her. I would come to wherever you find her."

Did she hear him snort in contempt on the other end of the phone? Or did she just imagine it? She could see him tip his head back dismissively, as he was inclined to do when they argued.

"You'll come to see your grandmother, but you won't come home?"

"I am coming home, Dad. Of course, I'll be coming home."

"Good. When?"

She registered the word. He said the word *good*. She heard it with her own ears. He said *good*. "August first," she told him.

"August first," he repeated. "That's almost a month away."

"I know, Dad, but that's when I'll be home. August first."

"Ah ha," he said.

She pictured her father sitting back and thinking in his red armchair, and she suddenly missed him. She missed seeing him mulling over a book he was reading or a poem he was writing. She missed hearing his contemplative *Ah ha*. Emotions are crazy, she thought. One minute you hate somebody, and the next minute you miss him terribly. Having emotions is like being buffeted by waves on the ocean, tossed back and forth like a pitiful little piece of driftwood with no free will.

"Ah ha," he said again.

"Dad, are you going to travel again to track the latest clue?"

"No, I don't think so. It was just a library card from Santa Fe, New Mexico. I called the library, but no one seemed to know anything about your grandmother."

"Oh, that's too bad. You must be so disappointed. But don't give up, Dad. Maybe you'll find her."

There was a long pause on the phone, but this one didn't feel arrogant or dismissive at all. Funny, how much you can sense on the phone without even seeing the other person, and without a single word being spoken.

"Okay. Thanks, Cordelia."

"You're welcome."

Another pause. He started to say something, then halted. Then his voice again: "Are you all right?"

"Yes, I'm fine, Dad. Are *you* all right?"

He made no answer for a few long seconds. "I'm fine. See you on August first."

She wanted to say so much more. She wanted to thank him a thousand times for talking to her. She wanted to tell him that she was sorry, and that she still loved him, and that he was the best father in the world. But she also wanted to tell him that she was terribly hurt by his cruel silence since she left home, and his malicious words before she left. She wanted to ask him why he would ever say such mean things to his own daughter. She wanted to yell at him for making such a mess of things at home, and for making everybody feel so tense and upset all the time. She wanted to tell him that he was the worst father in the world. And most of all, she wanted to ask him what was wrong with him. What in the world was really wrong with him?

"See you on August first," she said.

33

Marie-Luce

With that one phone call to her father, Cordelia had vanquished the silence. True, she hadn't completely solved the problem with her father. She still couldn't really forgive him for some of the things he said to her. She would forgive him if he would simply apologize, but that wasn't likely going to happen. And she didn't really trust him now. What would stop him from rejecting her again the next time they got into an argument? She still worried about their relationship in the future. But at least they were on speaking terms again, and this left her free to pursue her life in Montreal. And part of that life was a secret self-improvement project she had undertaken.

She stared wide-eyed at her purse, as a person might stare at a rainbow, hoping that it wouldn't disappear too soon. "My purse is on top of the bedside table," she said to herself aloud. She studied the little purse for a long minute, and then she focused intently on the other items on top of the little table, which she also named out loud. "My hairbrush, a pair of earrings, a pen, and a pad of paper."

She sat down on her meditation cushion in the corner of the bedroom and closed her eyes. She drew in a long, slow breath. She tried to focus only on the breath. Then she breathed out, focusing on the out-breath. A thought intruded: she had told Martin that she would make him a nice dinner, and she should go shopping for food. *Not now,* she thought to herself. *I am only breathing right now.* And she took another deliberate breath in and out. And another, and another.

After about fifteen minutes of meditating, she opened her eyes and went to the bedside table. She opened the drawer to the little table, where she saw her book, *Wherever You Go, There You Are.* It was her new Bible. She had decided to get serious about the practice of mindfulness as a means to combat the chaos of her disorganized life. "Everything has its place," she said to herself, as she had said many times over the past few days. It was her way of reminding herself that she had lived a life of scatterbrained disorder for long enough. Now she would be mindful.

She closed the drawer and put her purse on the floor. "I'm putting my purse on the floor by the bedside table," she said quietly to herself. She decided she would go shopping at two o'clock. Yes, two o'clock would be a good time to shop. And now her day was organized. She had a goal and a time frame.

Much to her surprise, her little experiment in mindfulness was working. She was becoming much better at keeping track of her belongings. True, she had lost—*misplaced* was her preferred term—a necklace earlier in the week, and she and Martin had searched the apartment top to bottom until they found it, lodged in-between the cushions of the sofa. Still, she was making good progress. She was much more attentive to what she was doing and where she was putting things. She was delighted one evening when Martin, who never lost anything, couldn't find his watch.

"I think I saw it in the kitchen, right by the toaster," she said.

"Oh, right," he said, as he retrieved it in the kitchen. "I remember now. I left it there when I took it off to wash the dishes." Then he looked at her quizzically. "Hey, how did *you* notice that?"

She just beamed a proud smile. "If you have trouble finding anything else, just let me know."

So, Montreal became the place where Cordelia conquered her maddening tendency to lose everything. It was also the place where she loved Martin and studied French. All in all, Montreal was a wonderful place.

There was only one minor irritation. Martin had a friend named Marie-Luce, whom he had known since childhood, and Cordelia soon began to feel uncomfortable about their friendship. When Marie-Luce joined them at the café, even though other friends were also at the table, Cordelia noticed that there were so many references to past memories that she and Martin shared. To be sure, the whole group of seven or eight people had stories to tell about shared experiences, but when everybody at the table laughed about one of the old stories, it always seemed that Martin and Marie-Luce laughed longest, looking at each other with the knowing gaze of two people who felt very close to each other. After the first few meetings with these friends, Cordelia began to feel tense whenever Marie-Luce joined the group.

One evening, Cordelia was cooking spaghetti at Martin's apartment.

"Shouldn't you drain it now?" he asked.

"Why should I do that?" she asked, feeling annoyed by his question.

"Well, you don't want to overcook pasta," he said. "It should be *al dente*, according to the Italians. A bit firm."

"Oh, excuse me! Sorry to ruin your dinner."

"Cordelia, I didn't say you were ruining anything. I was just making a comment."

"Right, Martin. A comment implying that I'm ruining your dinner. Maybe you can get someone else to cook your dinner." *Maybe Marie-Luce can cook it*, she thought to herself. *Maybe Marie-Luce can cook your damned spaghetti al dente.* Cordelia stirred the tomato sauce in a pot with a wooden spoon. She made a considerable amount of noise by picking up the pot, stirring it vigorously, and banging it down on the stovetop. Martin took a step closer to her, but she held up a hand to keep him away.

Martin was characteristically docile and good-natured in response to her eruption. He tried to ask her what was bothering her, but she wouldn't tell him the truth. He reassured her that he hadn't intended to criticize her cooking. He stepped away from the stove, and she was finally able to calm down. Later that evening, she considered telling him how she felt about Marie-Luce, but chided herself for being so petty. She kept quiet.

Fortunately, Marie-Luce was not at every gathering of the friends, but when she did show up, Cordelia couldn't help feeling annoyed and resentful. Nor could she ignore the fact that Marie-Luce was quite attractive, with dark hair and dark eyes not unlike Martin's eyes. Cordelia caught herself wondering if Martin might prefer such dark good looks to her own fair-skinned red-headed package. Sometimes, he would hold her hand as he sat at the table, and she would feel reassured. But the next minute, he would lean toward Marie-Luce and bring up some old story (all those stupid stories!) about something that happened back in high school, and the two of them would laugh as if they were the only two people at the table. As for Marie-Luce, she always seemed very friendly toward Cordelia. Marie-Luce even took her aside one evening and told her that she was pleased to see Martin looking so happy, implying that Cordelia's presence was the cause of such happiness. Cordelia did her best to look friendly and kind in return, but she couldn't wait for the evening to end when Marie-Luce was there.

"I can see what you mean," said Becky, after joining the group one evening. Cordelia and Becky were walking some distance ahead of the others as they left the café. "They do seem connected in some way. But Martin seems head-over-heels in love with you, so I don't really see a problem."

"Well, it's a problem to sit there and watch her making sugary eyes at him every time he opens his mouth. I'd call that a problem!"

"So, why not just ask him? Ask him what's going on."

Cordelia hesitated. "No, I can't do that."

"And may I ask why not?"

"He'll think I'm jealous."

"Excuse me, but you are."

"Yeah, but I don't want him to know that. He's always so calm and loving. I don't think he would be jealous, if the tables were turned. And I don't want him to think I'm crazy."

"Don't be stupid," said Becky. "Everybody's jealous. And everybody's a little crazy."

"I'm not so sure that's true of Martin." And she decided not to say anything to him about Marie-Luce.

34

Late

Cordelia hurried along the street to meet Martin at a café, and she was worried about how he might react.

"I'm late," she said, as she took her seat at the table opposite him.

"No, you're not. We said one o'clock and it's just a couple of minutes after one. You're fine."

Cordelia took a deep breath and tried to calm herself. "I don't mean that. I mean . . . I'm *late*."

"Oh!" he said. There was a long silence. He reached across the table and took her hand. She clutched his hand tightly.

"I'm usually very regular," she said in a low voice, "but I'm definitely late. A few days late."

"All right," he said. "You're late."

"Yeah. Just a few days, but definitely late."

"I see," he said. "Definitely late." He took a long, slow, deep breath and exhaled through his mouth. "All right."

And that was that, as far as she could tell. He blew out one long breath, and with that breath he had apparently taken in the information and reconciled himself to the new situation they now faced. She felt surprised, but then she realized that she should have expected him to react in exactly such a calm manner. Did she expect him to jump up and run out of the café? No, not with his tranquil disposition. But she had worried that he might have a very negative reaction to the news. She watched him for any sign of trouble, but he seemed fine, as far as she could tell. They had their coffee and then went back to the apartment. He asked her how she felt, and she said she felt fine. He asked her if she was scared, and she said yes. He gave her a kiss, and that was that.

As the afternoon passed, she could tell that he was worried, just as she was worried, but he was obviously trying his best to hide it. Sometimes, he would pace from room to room for a few minutes, but then he would settle down on the couch with her. He was overly solicitous toward her. Did she want anything to drink? Did she need to rest? She found his questions unnecessary, but endearing. He was quiet, though, much quieter than usual, and this worried her.

That night, he fell asleep before she did, and her mind was free to think about herself, rather than about Martin. She didn't *feel* pregnant, but can a girl feel it this early? She closed her eyes and tried to get in touch with her body. If an egg cell and a sperm cell join together and start to collaborate in the process of building a baby, wouldn't she be able to sense it? She tried as hard as she could to be aware of what might be happening in her body. She felt nothing unusual, but was this because she didn't want to feel it? Certainly, she didn't want to get pregnant, so maybe she was just refusing to let herself know the truth about her body's workings. But, she argued with herself, how could she not feel it if there were a baby beginning to grow in her uterus?

And what about a baby's soul? When did that happen? If a girl was a few days pregnant, would that mean that there was a little soul inhabiting that little ball of cells? Or did that happen later? And if so, how much later? When does a little clump of cells become a person with a personality and a soul?

She wondered what she would do if she were pregnant. Martin was Catholic, so he might have strong feelings about this, although he had said nothing so far. (His silence bothered her, even now as he slept.) She had always believed that a woman should have the right to choose an abortion, and she still felt this way, but would *she* choose it? And would he support her decision? Suppose she decided instead not to have an abortion. Her mind raced to grapple with the consequences of having a baby. College would have to be postponed, at least for now. She tried to imagine having the baby and raising it—it? him? her? —with Martin. For a moment or two, a pleasant scenario unfolded. She saw herself pushing the stroller down Rue St. Denis, chatting with other young mothers, stopping for a cup of coffee on her way to the park. Then she saw herself coming back to a sweet little house where Martin returned from his day at the University.

But wait. There would be no university, no Montreal. Martin had a job teaching high school in upstate New York. She would have to return to the U.S. and have her baby in her hometown, where everyone would be gossiping about her. She would be the talk of the high school for decades to come. *What? You haven't heard about that girl who got pregnant by her history teacher?* She couldn't imagine facing such a future.

The next day, he went off to a class, and she found herself unbearably alone. She picked up the phone at the apartment and called Becky at her grandmother's house. When Becky answered, Cordelia wasted no time.

"Hi. Listen, I think I'm pregnant."

"Oh, Jesus, how'd you do that? Well, I guess I know *how* you did it. But don't you use protection? And please don't tell me you lost it. Just don't tell me that you lost a birth control pill or you lost a condom."

"No, I didn't lose anything! And yes, of course we use protection. But I'm late, and I think I'm pregnant." Her voice quivered with the last few words.

"Okay, okay, okay. Sorry, didn't mean to criticize at a time like this. It's going to be okay. We just have to think about this." There was a silence on both ends of the phone.

Cordelia said, "I guess I need to buy a pregnancy test at the drugstore."

"Right!" said Becky. "That's exactly what you need to do. Then we'll know, either way."

"Right. I'll go and get one right now."

"No, wait!" said Becky. "They're not accurate right away. You have to wait a while."

"Oh, right. But how long do I have to wait?"

"I think it's ten days," said Becky.

"Ten days!" Cordelia felt weak and scared. "I can't wait ten days. The waiting will kill me."

"Sorry, but I'm pretty sure it's ten. You know Karen on my crew team, right? Karen, the slutty girl who sleeps with every boy she meets. Well, she always thinks she's pregnant, and she's always taking the test. And I'm pretty sure she said ten days."

"That's so long!"

"I know." There was another silence. "Does Martin know?"

"He does now. I just told him yesterday."

"And how is he taking it?"

"Great!" said Cordelia. "He's amazing. I'm not kidding. He is truly the nicest guy in the world." She said nothing about his long silences and his pacing around the apartment. She tried not to think about it.

They talked for a while longer, and then Cordelia hung up the phone. She tried to read a magazine, but she couldn't concentrate. She sat down in her meditation corner and tried to meditate, but that was absolutely impossible. She cleaned up the apartment a little, but she knew she was being absentminded and ineffective. (She caught herself washing their coffee cups by hand and then putting them into the dishwasher to be cleaned.) It was a relief to see him return, even though he was still strangely quiet. When he first walked in, he saw her standing with the vacuum cleaner and immediately took it from her and finished the job she had started. He insisted that she sit down and rest, even though she didn't feel tired at all.

They joined some of his friends for lunch at a restaurant, and Marie-Luce was among the group. Again, Cordelia noticed the connection they seemed to have, and it seemed to her that Martin became more animated over lunch, more talkative. She felt a relief when the lunch was over and the two of them were alone again. For the rest of that afternoon, he had no classes, so he spent the rest of the day with her. She did have her French class, and he walked her to the class.

"You don't have to do that," she said.

"No problem," he said.

When her class was done, he was standing outside, waiting to walk her home. Later in the day, when she went out to buy milk, he went with her. When she went to the basement of their building to do laundry, he tagged along. Wherever she went, he went with her, always looking pensive and a bit preoccupied, but always there. She felt like she had her own guardian angel watching over her.

After dinner, she called home and talked to her mother for a few minutes. She wanted so badly to tell her mother what was going on, but obviously she couldn't tell her the truth. What could she say? *Oh, by the way, Mom, I've got great news: I'm pregnant! Yeah, isn't that terrific? And you'll never guess who the lucky guy is. Mr. T! My old history teacher!* No, she thought, her mother would never be able to handle this kind of thing, no matter who was involved. If she told her, then she would have to go right home to keep her mother from falling to pieces.

She asked to speak with her father. Not that she could tell him, either, but she felt the need to hear his voice.

"Oh, he's not here, honey. He took your brother to the library to work on his term paper."

"Oh, I see." Cordelia felt ambivalent about this. On the one hand, she still found it awkward to talk to him. On the other hand, she wanted to hear his voice on the phone. Maybe it would somehow be comforting.

"Any more clues about my Grandma?"

"No, not a thing, honey,"

She found herself thinking of her lost grandmother. She wished that she had a grandmother to talk to. "I hope he finds her, Mom."

"I do too," said her mother. "I hope all these crazy clues are not a waste of time."

She hung up the phone and sat with Martin in their little living room. The summer evening was long in Montreal, and by eight o'clock, Martin looked restless and unsettled. He paced in the little apartment for a while, and then he suggested that they go out for a walk. She was more than happy to go back out. It was too difficult to stay in that apartment, sitting with her own fears and watching him pace.

The evening was warm, but not humid, so they walked for a long while. They passed the familiar shops and restaurants in their neighborhood, but everything seemed strange and different now. He asked her if she wanted to stop for a coffee, but she just wanted to keep walking. She wanted to walk until Fate revealed itself and ended the mystery of the unknown. Each time they turned a corner, Cordelia imagined that someone would be standing there, someone who was the human incarnation of Fate or God or Whatever, someone who would give her the answer. Several times, a random bit of conversation on the street made her wonder if she had just heard the answer. An old woman passed them by and Cordelia heard her say something about "la vie," life. For a second, Cordelia thought it must be a message indicating that she was carrying new life in her. Then a disheveled man passed by and she heard him muttering to himself in English, "It's all the same, pal." Maybe he meant that her life would soon be the same as it was before. This was too silly, she told herself. No one was going to get a message about her fate from idle snippets of street conversation. But then she immediately argued with herself. Was it so silly to think that God (if there is a God) might send a message to us via an unlikely messenger? Wasn't it possible that this happens all the time, but we are deaf to the messages? "C'est domage!" said a man to his wife on the street, gesturing with his hands as Cordelia and Martin passed by. *It's a pity!* But what could that mean? Was it a pity that she was going to have a baby? Or was it a pity that she and Martin were not going to have a baby? How was one supposed to interpret these messages, if indeed they were messages at all?

Cordelia decided just to walk side by side with Martin, who seemed quiet and unaware of the chatting of other people on the street. Likewise, he seemed barely aware of her.

35

A Balcony Scene

On the fourth day of her lateness, Cordelia was getting quite worried about Martin. He was still kind, of course, still attentive to her every need, but he barely spoke over breakfast. He still looked at her with his wide-open, guileless eyes, but the luster was gone from them. His eyes seemed dull and vacant, and this alarmed her. She tried several times to ask him if he felt all right, but he always deflected the attention back to her.

"Don't worry about me. Let's just take care of you."

After they cleaned up the breakfast dishes, he was obviously restless again. He paced for a few minutes in the apartment, and then he took her by the hand and silently led her out onto the street again to walk. The walking, she decided, seemed to be his way of dealing with the stress of the situation. He was quiet and uncharacteristically distant, but she was reassured by his physical presence with her at every turn. When she wanted to look at a store window, he waited patiently for her to finish looking. When she needed to stop at the library to get a book, he followed her into the library. Wherever she went, Martin was with her, and that was reassuring, no matter what was going through his mind.

Every now and then, they separated for a few minutes. She went into a shop to look at clothing, or he stopped at a newsstand. But when she emerged, he would always be waiting for her, loyal and true, her guardian angel. Martin was everywhere, oddly quiet, but always there for her.

Until he was suddenly gone. She went into a bakery, at his suggestion, to get a loaf of bread for dinner. He said he would wait outside because the bakery was crowded. When she came out with the bread in hand, he was nowhere to be seen. She looked up and down the street, but there was no Martin. She tried to tell herself that the best thing would be to calm herself down and stand outside the bakery, but her apprehension quickly mounted. After a few minutes of standing there alone, she was solidly in the grip of her anxiety. Another few minutes passed, and the anxiety broke loose into panic. Surely, he would appear, she told herself, looking up and down the street. But he did not appear, and she came to the conclusion that something was seriously wrong. The fear went into her feet, and she began to wander down the street looking for him. She retraced their steps, hoping that he might be at the last shop she had looked at. But this made no sense, as she knew. After all, why would he go back to a dress shop?

She found herself looking desperately at every young man on the street, hoping that one of them would be hers. She was surprised to notice that there were many young men of Martin's approximate height (six feet), build (medium), and hair color (brown), but none of them were Martin. She clutched her loaf of bread and walked ever faster, rounding several corners until she had walked the perimeter of a large block and was heading back in the direction of the bakery. Her mind filled with dire scenarios of being a single teenage mother without Martin by her side.

He must have gone back to the bakery to find her, she decided. She went into the bakery and found it quieter inside now, with fewer customers. A woman behind the counter asked her in French what she wanted.

"Rien du tout, merci," said Cordelia. *Nothing at all, thanks.* She thought about asking the woman if she might have seen Martin, but the idea seemed futile. She stood right outside the bakery for another half-hour or so, darting her gaze back and forth, looking for him. Then she circled the block a second time, with similar results.

Finally, in despair, she turned and headed back to the apartment. There was no particular reason to think that he would be there, but he didn't seem to be anywhere else, so she went back to the place where he must return at some point. She kept hoping to run into him on the way home, but every young man with dark hair and his general physique was one more disappointment.

She got back to the apartment building and walked up the stairs to the second floor. She fumbled with her key and then managed to open the door.

"Martin? Martin? Are you here?"

There was no answer. Then she saw the closed suitcase sitting on the sofa. There was a note on top of the suitcase:

> *Martin,*
> *A bientôt à Paris!*
> *Marie-Luce*

Martin, See you in Paris! Marie-Luce. She felt lightheaded and weak when she read the note. She checked the rest of the little apartment—the bedroom and the kitchen—but he was not at home. She was still holding the loaf of bread, which she now recognized as an accomplice to the scam. She threw it against a wall and started to cry. After a minute or two, she got up and ran into the bathroom, thinking that she was going to be sick to her stomach. Kneeling on the bathroom floor, she wondered how this could possibly be happening to her.

Looking back, she tried to put the pieces of the puzzle together in some sensible order. She appeared in Montreal several weeks ago, unplanned and unannounced. Martin took her in, charmed, perhaps infatuated, perhaps flattered that his pretty little high school student had fallen in love with him. Meanwhile, he must have had nascent feelings for Marie-Luce that were put on hold when Cordelia arrived. Or perhaps she was an ex-girlfriend, and they had been considering a reunion. In any case, there was obviously something between them that had started long before Cordelia arrived. The family trip to Europe? An alibi to get rid of her after a few weeks, in case he didn't really want her. And once the pregnancy scare happened, he was done. He tried to look caring and concerned, but he had obviously put together his escape plan—with Marie-Luce's help—and now they had planned their big rendezvous in Paris. He got Cordelia out of the apartment, sent her into the bakery, and made his getaway from his pregnant teenage girlfriend, like a man escaping prison. Where was he now? He must have run out to get some last-minute necessities for his trip. Apparently, he hadn't planned on her returning to the apartment so soon.

She wandered into their kitchen and found a pile of money on the table, several hundred Canadian dollars in small bills. She tried not to jump to the obvious, inescapable conclusion: abortion money. He was fleeing the country with Marie-Luce, and leaving her a stack of bills to get the abortion. She sat down at the kitchen table and felt her body shaking.

But how could any of this be true? He had always seemed like such a sincere, honest person. He seemed so genuine back in New York as "Mr. T," and he had been the same here in Montreal. Even after she announced her lateness, he never faltered in his kindness toward her. He was so good, so gentle and solicitous. True, he had been weirdly quiet and withdrawn for the past few days, but wouldn't any man be? When she thought of everything she knew about Martin up to this day, nothing about this terrible turn of events made any sense. Was nothing as it appeared? If Martin could be so duplicitous, then her ability to judge people (a capacity in which she took great pride) was seriously flawed, and the world was frighteningly chaotic and unpredictable. The events of the past hour simply could not be true, she told herself, but neither could she deny the tangible evidence: a packed suitcase, a pile of money, and a treacherous note.

She went out onto their little balcony and looked down at the sidewalk below. She gripped the rail tightly with both hands as a thought crossed her mind. It was not that she wanted to jump, but the possibility suddenly occurred to her that one could jump. One could easily clear the railing and land on the pavement below. But their apartment was only on the second floor. Would she die from such a fall? Or just get badly hurt and lie on the sidewalk groaning pathetically in pain? She looked up at the balcony above her in the three-story building, and other possibilities emerged—not that she would execute any of them, but one could go upstairs and ask the neighbors to see the view from the third story balcony.

She thought she heard his voice. No, she must be hallucinating simply because she wanted to hear it. For a moment, she feared that she was really losing her mind. But then she realized that she did indeed hear him.

"Cordelia!"

And there was Martin, coming along their street holding a cup of store-bought coffee in his hand. He was walking more quickly than usual, but it was unmistakably his easy-going, rambling gait.

"Cordelia! Where did you go? I've been looking all over for you!"

He looked surprisingly the same as he always looked. He was Martin, looking kind and concerned, without a hint of guilt on his face. The last hour of her life—possibly the worst hour of her life—was absolutely inexplicable when she looked at Martin sauntering down the street toward her with the coffee in his hand.

"What are you talking about?" she called down from the balcony, disoriented by his sudden reappearance, choking back tears. "You left me! I came out of the bakery and you were gone!"

He arrived at the house and stood directly below her, looking up at the balcony.

"No, *you* left," he said, looking quite perplexed. "I just went to a café a couple doors away from the bakery. You said you felt tired, so I thought I would get you a coffee. I had to wait on a long line. And when I came back, you had left. I've been searching all over for you."

Cordelia felt completely bewildered. "Martin, stop playing with my mind! I saw the packed suitcase on the sofa. And I read the note!"

Martin looked surprised and even more confused by her comment. "The suitcase?"

"Don't pretend you don't have a suitcase packed for Paris!"

"Oh, the suitcase! I don't own a suitcase for my trip to Europe, so I asked my cousin Marie-Luce to loan me one. She knows that

I keep a key under the mat, so she must have brought one over while we were out."

Cordelia struggled to comprehend what she was hearing. "Your *what?* Your cousin?"

"Yes, my cousin Marie-Luce."

She shook her head forcefully left and right, trying to shake off her confused state of mind. "Why didn't you tell me you were cousins? I thought—"

Martin's face suddenly assumed a pained look. "Oh, no! It's not like that at all, Cordelia! She's my first cousin! Our fathers are brothers. We're family! And she's going to travel with us to Paris for the reunion. I'm so sorry if you thought something else!"

For a moment, Cordelia's mind became so clouded with conflicting bits of information that she couldn't speak at all. The only way she could free herself of the turmoil in her head was by raging at him. "Then how dare you not tell me that she was your cousin!" she yelled. "How was I supposed to know that you weren't just flirting with an old girlfriend?"

"But we *did* tell you!" he protested.

"You did not!" Cordelia shouted at him. Two old women wearing head scarves walked by arm-in-arm on the sidewalk below and glanced up at her. She suddenly became aware of how she must look to these immigrant passersby: a hysterical American girl standing on a balcony, shrieking at her boyfriend in a childish fit of jealousy. Her outlandish flaws were on display for the entire world to see. She wished she could disappear.

"We did tell you!" insisted Martin, seemingly oblivious to the old women passing behind him. "It was the first time we were all together after you arrived. I introduced you, and Marie-Luce spoke to you in English. I told her you had studied French in school, and she switched to French. *C'est mon cousin.* He's my cousin. I remember her saying that, and I said something in French, too. And you nodded, so I thought you understood us. We both assumed that you understood."

Cordelia was mortified. She remembered the exact moment that Martin was talking about. She remembered how she had nodded and smiled and pretended that she understood, because he had just told all his friends that she had studied French, and she was too embarrassed to admit that she hadn't understood a word of what they said. She struggled now to save face.

"Well, you should have known that I didn't understand!" she said. "You should have checked with me later, after we left the café!"

"You're right," he said sympathetically, lowering his voice. "I should have checked."

She stood there staring dumbly at him from the balcony, trying to digest all the contradictory facts in her head. "And the money?" she asked. "What about the money?"

"What money?" Martin asked.

"The money on the kitchen table."

"Oh, yes, I told Marie-Luce that if she left me some money, I would go to the bank and exchange it for French currency. It's hard for her to get away from her job to do that."

"French currency," she repeated mechanically.

"Yes. Francs."

Standing on the little balcony, she realized that she had composed in her mind a colossal Shakespearian tragedy, using the few meager props available upon her stage: a loaf of bread, a one-sentence note, a pile of Canadian dollars, and an empty suitcase. She saw that she had written her script in a tour de force that began within seconds of her exiting the bakery. Clearly, her mind had been waiting for any opportunity to create such a narrative of sorrow and betrayal. She wondered how in the world she could have been so suspicious and untrusting. And here she was, exposed in her foolishness as she stood on the balcony. A Shakespearian balcony! she thought. But the balcony scene in *Romeo and Juliet* was a love scene, and hers was a painful scene of abandonment, written in her own hand.

She looked down at him, and she could clearly see now that he was still Martin, still the same person she had fallen in love with. He was standing there looking up at her, holding a cup of coffee for her, purchased because she made an offhand remark about feeling a bit tired. He was obviously relieved to have found her, and their misadventure had brought the light back into his eyes. Looking back at the last hour, she felt like she was emerging from a brief period of mental illness. It seemed like a paranoid delusion to think that a man like Martin was planning to abandon her for another girl.

"Well, I'm sorry I wandered away," he said. "Really, I just wanted to buy you a coffee. Sorry to cause you such stress, Cordelia, especially at a time like this."

"Martin, I'm not—"

She stopped mid-sentence, deciding that she would tell him in a minute, and then she would step back into the apartment and run down the stairs to emerge from the first floor and throw her arms around his neck. But not just yet. She wanted to tell him what she had just discovered five minutes earlier in the bathroom: she wasn't pregnant anymore. That is, she wasn't *late* anymore, so she had never been pregnant at all. She would tell him and then run to him, but not just yet. She was reluctant to let him out of her sight by stepping inside to use the stairway. She wanted to hold onto this moment and burn this image of him into her head forever: Martin, the man who had searched the streets of Montreal to find her, was standing below on the sidewalk, holding a cup of coffee he bought for her. She wanted to look at him—and see him looking up at her with his placid, brown-cow eyes and his charmingly protuberant ears —for another long minute. She knew that in his mind, she was probably pregnant, and *definitely* vain, jealous, and foolish. And yet he just stood there, apparently quite content to be standing under their balcony, looking at her instead of looking at any other girl in the world.

36

Cirrhosis

Doctors should talk plainly, she thought to herself. Otherwise, how can anyone understand them? Instead, they talk gibberish, a maddening patois of nonsense words that only doctors can understand. He should make himself clear so she could get whatever treatment he ordered and get discharged from the hospital.

"The bilirubin level is high," he said, looking at the reports in his hand. "Very high. Transaminase levels are low." He spoke in a quiet voice. He said something about "hepatic damage." He was a nice-looking young man, standing tall and confident in his freshly pressed white coat, but he was simply incomprehensible, as far as she was concerned.

She sat in her hospital bed looking at him blankly. She was in a hospital in St. Louis, and she could hardly believe that two years had passed since she arrived to attend a program for alcohol treatment. She dropped out of the program long ago, but she never left town. She suddenly felt nostalgic for the past, particularly for a convent in New Mexico and the sisters who lived there. How did she end up in St. Louis?

And why couldn't they make hospitals more welcoming? Her room was such a drab little square, with nothing on the walls except a calendar. Did they think she didn't know what day it was? And what was this doctor trying to say? He was talking directly to her now, but she didn't understand him. She brushed a wisp of hair from her forehead. For much of her life, a simple gesture like that was enough to disarm any man and bring him running to her aid. Now it meant nothing to him, as she could clearly see. It was obvious to her that he simply saw an old woman fussing with her hair, a thick, unruly mop of white hair to cover an empty head.

"I don't understand," she said in a thin voice that she recognized as her scared voice. She vaguely realized that she *did* understand but didn't want to understand because she was frightened.

He stood there, looking at her in her hospital bed. "Liver damage," he said, holding up the papers in his hand as evidence. "You have serious liver damage, Ma'am."

She involuntarily turned her face away from him. She put both hands up to smooth her hair, but without the desired effect. He was not charmed into softening his cruel message. He didn't tell her that it really was nothing serious, nor did he try to comfort her in any way. He just kept standing there in silence, watching her struggle with the merciless news that he was delivering.

"Are you a drinker?" he asked. In her day, men were not so callously blunt. A man should be more circumspect; he should show a little delicacy, a bit of chivalry, a little respect for a woman. Any gentleman should know this.

"Once in a while, I'll have a bit to drink."

He didn't even pause to give her words a chance to influence his next question. "How much do you drink?"

At least she was in a single room. This discussion would be even more humiliating if she had a roommate. She drew in a deep breath and sighed. "Sometimes, I've had too much to drink. It has happened at times."

"Ma'am, it's time to be honest about this."

She wished he would stop calling her "Ma'am." It just made her feel older and sicker. "My name is Kate," she said pointedly.

"Fine. Kate. It's time to be honest. You have a serious alcohol problem, yes?"

She said nothing, but her silence couldn't stop him any more than fussing with her hair could stop him.

"You have an alcohol problem. That's obvious. That's what caused you to get admitted to our hospital in the first place. You were vomiting blood because of bleeding in your esophagus. We were able to stop that bleeding. But the liver damage is also from the alcohol, no doubt. It's called alcoholic cirrhosis."

This was not the first time someone had confronted her about the drinking, of course. Every time she went into one of those alcohol "rehabilitation" programs, she had to participate in the dreadful ritual of the group meetings and recite the initiation mantra: *My name is Kate and I'm an alcoholic.* She would dutifully say the word—*alcoholic*—even though she secretly rejected it. How could anyone describe a human being by such a demeaning little word? How does one take the complexity of a human life and reduce it to a cold, clinical label like *alcoholic*? Certainly, she didn't see herself as an alcoholic. She was a woman who had seen troubles in her life, and sometimes she drank when she felt distressed. True, sometimes she drank a lot, but that doesn't give anyone the right to delineate her existence with such a meager, four-syllable slander.

"Do you have any family, Kate?" asked the doctor standing by her bedside.

She looked away from him as she searched for an appropriate answer. "No one close by," she said.

"Well," he continued, "I'd suggest that you might want to let your family know that you're here. You should tell them about your condition, which is quite serious, Kate. And if I were you, I wouldn't wait too long. I would call them today."

These last words frightened her. He wasn't even suggesting another rehab program. The implication was clear: He thought it was too late for that.

"Thank you for your advice," she said weakly. He surprised her by leaning over and patting her on the arm. She fought back an urge to cry, and he left the room.

Within the hour, she got herself dressed and told her nurse that she was leaving. The nurse tried to convince her to stay, but she insisted. The nurse asked her to sign a form stating that she was leaving "against medical advice." Kate signed and thanked the nurse for her care.

When she left the hospital, she stopped at the first bar she came to and ordered a Scotch on ice. She felt so humiliated by the nice-looking young doctor in the freshly pressed white coat. Did she look *that* old and pathetic that he would talk to her that way? Not an ounce of sympathy in that cold, clinical young man. Not a shred of chivalry for a lady. She looked up at her image in a mirror behind the bar. Did she look that bad at seventy? And why would they put that huge mirror right there, right behind the bar, giving her no choice but to confront her image in the glass?

"My God, I look like hell. My body is just rotting away," she said out loud to herself.

"You look fine, honey," said the bartender, who was standing a few feet away. She was a woman who appeared to be in her mid-forties, wearing heavy eye make-up, still pretty despite a worn, lined face. She had a husky voice and a harsh cough.

"Thanks, but I don't look fine," said Kate. "I look old and wrinkled and sick."

"Well, we all get old and wrinkled," said the bartender. "That's just the way the human body is. It's like a party dress. It looks so wonderful and attractive at first, when you put it on. But as the evening goes by, it starts to get wrinkled. When you get home at the end of the evening and step out of it, and you let it fall to the floor, what do you see? A crumpled old rag. That's the way it is with our bodies. But you look fine, anyway."

Kate smiled at the woman, but suddenly she missed Carlos, even though she hadn't seen him in a quarter of a century. She was scared, and she wanted to be with him again. He knew how to read her, and he knew how to comfort her when she was scared.

"I miss Carlos," she said, half to herself and half to the bartender.

"Who's Carlos, honey?" asked the bartender.

"A man I used to know," said Kate. "A very nice man."

"Men are pigs," said the woman bluntly. "If he's a man, then he can't be all that nice."

"But not all men are bad," said Kate. "It depends on who you meet."

"Well, if you met my two jackass ex-husbands, you'd come to the same conclusion I came to. Men are pigs."

Kate sipped her drink, feeling afraid and alone. She wanted to be back in Denver with Carlos.

"So how did you meet your Carlos?" asked the woman.

Kate looked up at this woman with the overdone eye make-up, feeling grateful for the opportunity to talk.

"I met him at a market," she said. "I had just come to Denver, and I met him quite by accident at a farmers' market."

"Oh, that's nice." But the bartender had to step away to serve another customer, and Kate was left sitting alone at a bar in St. Louis.

37

Carlos

A few days after leaving her family in Detroit to visit her sister in Tucson, Kate left again. She got up before dawn, wrote her sister a brief note, and left the house. She had no particular plan in mind, but after several days of bus rides and cheap motel rooms, she found herself in Denver, Colorado. When she arrived in Denver, she rented a tiny apartment with the little bit of money she had with her. On her fourth day there, she was strolling at a farmers market when a man started a conversation with her.

"Are you sure you can take the heat of a habanero?" he asked.

She was buying a chili pepper at one of the stands.

"I'm trying to make a Southwestern chili, but I'm from the East and I don't know what kind of hot pepper to buy," she said to the man. He was quite handsome, with thick black hair and a neatly trimmed mustache.

"Well, if you're a newcomer to Southwest cuisine, you'll want the jalapeno. It's plenty hot enough, but not so hot that it will ruin your meal."

"Okay, thanks for the advice," Kate said.

His name was Carlos. She chatted with him for a while, and then they left the farmers market and had coffee together. Carlos was originally from Mexico, but he had come to the U.S. with his mother and his eight older siblings, and he was obviously proud of the successful life he had built. He was the founder and president of a trucking company in Denver. The only blemish in his tale of success was his unhappy marriage, he told her. He mentioned this in a matter-of-fact manner, and then passed on to other topics. He didn't seem to be telling her about his marriage as part of a subtle seduction scheme. He spoke like a company president who was simply providing a business update at a meeting of his shareholders. One of his products—his marriage—was doing poorly, and he was open to ideas for a new venture. Kate felt neither intimidated nor pressured by him. In fact, she found his candor reassuring.

Things happened quickly with Carlos. He seemed like a man in a hurry, yet he never made her feel rushed into something she didn't want. They had lunch together, and then a dinner or two, and then they stayed together one night at her little apartment. After that first night, the relationship progressed without any need for discussion or explicit planning. It was understood that they were going to spend time together whenever they could. He set her up with a larger apartment, a car, and an ample bank account. As he arranged all this, he explained to her that although he was in a dead marriage, he could never leave his wife. She was too weak emotionally, he explained. Besides, it would hurt his kids. She could see that he was telling her all this in an obvious attempt to justify his double life and ease any discomfort she might have about the arrangement. He didn't seem to realize that she was relieved by his commitment to his wife, as it limited the risk that he would make too many demands on her emotional life.

She became accustomed to his visits. Sometimes, he would spend a part of the evening with her, and then leave to return home to his wife and children. Other visits were longer. He would tell his wife that he had business out of town, perhaps back in Mexico, and then spend the weekend with Kate. He was a bit full of himself, no doubt. He loved to talk about the company he had started, and how he had created such success despite an impoverished childhood; yet he was also surprisingly attentive to her needs. She saw him as a curiosity among men. He could be obliviously self-centered and shamelessly boastful, yet at other times so gentle and giving and selfless.

When he was around, she found that her mood was definitely better, and she would drink less. When he was gone for a few days, things would fall apart for her. She would often sit up by herself late into the night, praying and drinking and crying all at once, hoping that the praying would excuse the drinking, the drinking would numb the crying, and the crying would carry the praying straight up to the merciful ear of Our Father Who Art in Heaven. Sometimes, she turned to the Bible for comfort. She would read and read again the story of Moses, whose mother left him in a basket on the Nile. It was clear from the text that as a mother, she had to do this to save him from the Pharaoh. But Kate wished the story of baby Moses could be longer and more detailed. The few sentences about it said nothing of how his mother felt about leaving him. Surely, she must have thought of him often after the Pharaoh's daughter found him by the river and raised him as her own, but the Bible was silent on this. And there was no mention of a reunion when Moses was a grown man. Did he understand why she did it? Did he understand that she had to leave him in order to save him? Did he suffer because of her actions?

At night, she dreamed of ladders. There was someone climbing a ladder, and she was standing below. Sometimes Carlos was climbing the ladder. Sometimes it was her husband. Occasionally—this was the worst—it was Danny. In a typical dream, she was standing at the bottom of the ladder, holding it steady for the person above. She was always gripping the upright side rails tightly, and she would try not to move an inch, lest she cause a terrible accident for the person on the ladder above. She would hold her breath and stand in silence, fearing to look up.

She would wake from these dreams trembling and sweating. She would turn to Carlos' side of the bed. If he was there that night, he would wake up immediately in response to her distress. He would put his arms around her and say comforting words in Spanish. *Cálmate, mi amor. Calm down, my love.* She would shake and shiver for a while. *Cálmate, mi amor. Cálmate.* After a while, she would relax and fall back to sleep. If he was not there, the rest of the night was a terrible stretch of tossing and turning.

To her surprise, none of her troubles ever seemed to threaten the relationship at all. At first, she was sure that he would get sick of dealing with her restless, tortured nights, and her daytime nervousness, but his patience seemed limitless. When he saw how easily she was startled by unexpected sights or sounds, he put a little bell just inside the door to her apartment. He would ring it as soon as he entered, so she would know it was him. When she felt withdrawn and distant, he would sit quietly looking at the stock market reports in the newspaper while she sat by herself in a corner chair, hour after hour, reading a novel. He seemed quite content to be in her presence. A curiosity among men. He clearly had insatiable appetites for money, power, food, and sex, and yet he could put all his own needs aside just to give her the space she needed.

Generally, things went along well for them, although she eventually began to feel uncomfortable with the financial arrangement. She was relieved to have the security of the money, but she felt terribly guilty about it. She didn't mind being the "other woman," but she couldn't stand feeling like a "kept woman." One day, she told him that she needed to work. She needed to earn her own money.

"What kind of work?" he asked. They were sitting at her kitchen table over breakfast on a Sunday morning. "What do you want to do, Kate?"

"I don't know," she said, feeling a sudden sense of gloom. "I don't really know how to do anything." What had she ever done? She had been a housewife back in Detroit. She knew how to shop and cook and do laundry. She knew how to grow flowers in the backyard. She had been a mother, a very good mother until she left home—but one must not think about that.

"I've got plenty of connections, honey," he said. "I can get you a job. Just tell me what you want to do. Try something new. Anything you want."

No, one must not think about having been a mother. She had to leave Detroit, no doubt about it. Had she stayed, something terrible would have happened. Why should this be true? She had no idea. She had asked God many a time, but she had never received an answer. All she knew—and she knew it with unshakeable certainty—is that there would have been a terrible catastrophe if she had stayed, and it would have been her fault. Her mind drifted to the most recent letter from her brother, Jack. She was always grateful for his letters, brief and disjointed though they were. Jack's letters reassured her that the kids were all right.

"Are you listening to me, honey?"

"Sure. I'm listening. You can get me a job."

Her daughter, Sarah, had undoubtedly gotten along fine, she reassured herself (for the thousandth time). Sarah was a positive, optimistic kid from the time she was a toddler. She would be fine. It was Danny who always troubled her. He was so sensitive, so delicate. How had he fared? Thanks to Jack, she had the basic facts. Danny was doing well in high school, and he had been accepted to college at the University of Michigan. Thank God for that. But was he all right? One mustn't think too much about this. It was no good to dwell on it. One mustn't dwell on his face at the airport, or the way he had looked at her with those innocent eyes on the day she left. He had known something was wrong. Oh yes, he knew. But what could she possibly have said to explain it to him? *I'm no good, Danny. No good at all. I'm the child of sin and badness. Something terrible will happen to you if I stay here.*

She suddenly became aware of the fact that Carlos was holding her hand, for how long she didn't know.

"Hey, are you all right?"

"Yeah. I'm fine."

He was looking at her with genuine concern in his eyes. "So, what kind of work would you like to do?"

She looked down at her half-eaten plate of eggs and toast, and then pushed it away. "Nothing, I guess. What could I do? I know how to grow flowers in a backyard. Other than that, I'm really no good for anything."

"Oh, sweetie, don't say that. You're an amazing person." He dabbed at her wet face with his napkin and put his arms around her. He held her for a while, pulling his chair close, and then he stood up and led her to the couch. She thought that he was going to start making love to her, but he did not. It would have been all right with her either way, but he just sat with her on the couch, his arms still around her. Carlos was a good guy, she thought. A very good guy. A curiosity among men.

38

A Moral Dilemma

O n the day of the big departure, Cordelia managed to pack her few belongings. She remembered, at the very last minute, her book in the drawer of the bedside table. *Wherever You Go, There You Are.* Everything started to seem unreal to her as Becky appeared, ready to drive them both to the airport. They would drop Martin off and then head home to Albany. Time seemed to move too quickly. Cordelia had no idea how they arrived at the airport. Once there, Martin checked his luggage without a word. Cousin Marie-Luce went ahead to the gate to give them time alone. Becky said goodbye to Martin and told Cordelia that she would be waiting in the car. Cordelia said okay, without ever taking her eyes off Martin.

They said all the usual things that lovers say to each other when they are being parted, things that have been said for centuries, for millennia, even though these things sound quite new and unique to someone who is saying them for the first time in her young life. Cordelia spoke with Martin about writing letters, calling on telephones, and planning reunions in the future. Naturally, all these things were said with an economy of words necessitated by the waiting airplane and the breathlessness of imminent separation. A casual passer-by, if he could get close enough to hear anything, would hear only short bits of pedestrian vocabulary that would hardly attract any interest.

"I'll write to you, Cordelia. From Europe. Every day."

"Me, too. Every day."

The passer-by would not be likely to take much notice of the two young people standing perfectly still with their arms wrapped around each other, motionless in the midst of the frenetic rush of people trying to catch planes.

"Don't forget me, Martin."

"Never."

"Promise?"

"Promise."

The passer-by would take no notice, as Cordelia took no notice of all the passers-by whose itineraries brought them within a few feet of her in the crowded airport. She saw none of them, nor would she ever believe that any of them could understand what she and Martin were saying to each other, even if one of them came close enough to hear their conversation. After all, they were essentially speaking about *love*, a secret code word that she and Martin had invented as part of a private language known only to the two of them. The rest of the world would never understand, neither in English nor in French. And they certainly wouldn't understand the significance of a particular date.

"September 13th," he said.

"September 13th," she said.

That was the date they picked for their reunion in the fall. He would drive down to her little college town, and she would slip away from her new roommates to meet him.

They stood together for a few more minutes, until the dreaded moment arrived. Cordelia felt him forcefully jerk himself away from her, and she watched him go running toward the gates. He kept turning and waving every few yards until he disappeared into the crowd. She stood by herself for a minute or two, trying to see him in the distance, hoping to see him running back to her. When it didn't happen, she turned and started walking toward the exit. An older woman walking toward her stopped to address her.

"Are you all right, dear?"

Cordelia didn't stop and didn't answer. She couldn't have spoken, even if she had wanted to. She walked outside and stood on the sidewalk, lost and confused and crying. She couldn't remember anything that Becky had said about where they were supposed to meet. She had lost Martin and now she had lost Becky, and she was standing outside a huge airport in a foreign county. The French conversations around her only increased her sense of isolation.

"Cordelia!"

She turned to her left and wiped her eyes.

"Come on, Cordelia!"

Her eyes following the sound of a honking horn, and she saw Becky's old Toyota a few car-lengths away in a long line of cars waiting to pick up passengers. She ran to the car and got in.

Becky drove out of the airport, but she soon pulled the car off to the side of the road.

"Okay, let's get this crap over with," Becky said. "If you cry, it makes me want to cry, and then I can't see the road in front of me, and I'll just crash the damned car and kill us both. So, let's just sit here for a while. You can cry, and I'll probably cry, too, which I hate, and then we'll both feel better and we'll go home."

Cordelia laughed a one-syllable "Ha!" and resumed her crying. The girls sat together in the car for the next half-hour, as Cordelia cried and talked about Martin. Becky was alternately comforting and silly, which seemed to Cordelia the perfect blend of responses. She couldn't imagine being with anyone but Becky during that time on the side of the road near the Montreal airport—except, of course, for Martin. She could imagine being anyplace in the world with Martin and being the happiest person who had ever lived.

Finally, they got back on the road. The first leg of the trip brought them down to the Canada-U.S. border within less than an hour. At the customs station, the young man at the booth asked them the usual questions about where they had been born, where they were going, and so on. He seemed very innocent and very sweet, Cordelia thought. She could tell that he was looking at her and Becky the way the boys back in high school looked at them. It seemed to her that he was slow to let them pass through the gate. He looked at their drivers' licenses and handed them back. Then he added one more question, looking at Cordelia.

"Are you all right, Miss?"

Cordelia felt herself getting tearful again and couldn't answer. Becky came to her rescue.

"Oh, don't mind her. Her boyfriend just left for Europe, and she's a total mess."

"Sorry to hear it," said the young inspector.

Becky added, "She'll be in tragic mourning for the next few months. But I'm available any time. I live right outside of Albany."

The young man blushed, clearly abashed and uncomfortable. "Okay," he said. "Have a nice day." And he waved them through.

Becky drove away from the booth, and they crossed back into the U.S. She drove only as far as Plattsburgh, the first U.S. city south of the border. By this time, Cordelia felt calmer, albeit exhausted from crying. Becky pulled off the highway and turned into the parking lot of a fast-food restaurant.

"You're probably critically dehydrated from all your dreadful blubbering," she said. "We need cold drinks."

The two girls got out to stretch and buy cold sodas. They sat together at a picnic bench outside the restaurant and talked for a while.

"I was going to apply to college here," said Becky. "They say it's a really good school, but they don't have crew. That's why I picked Oswego instead."

Cordelia nodded, but she already knew all about Becky's college deliberations. And she knew that her friend was just trying to make distracting conversation. Cordelia was able to listen and comment now and then, without ever taking her mind off Martin. It would only be about five weeks, and then he would have to come back to upstate New York to teach history. She would be close by at Marist College. Only five weeks. She tallied the days in her head. When the two girls got back in the car and headed south again toward Albany, Cordelia actually felt happy for a while. She thought of his trip to Europe and realized that he would be home in a few weeks. Plattsburgh became marked in her mind as a place of great hope. Plattsburgh, City of Hope.

Gradually, however, bad thoughts began to creep in. She struggled to keep them from entering her mind. The thoughts took different forms, but they all converged on one central question: Would she and Martin survive as a couple in this world? She tried to reassure herself. It would be hard at first, but each year going forward, their love would be less objectionable. In three years, for example, things would look quite different. The world, in all its glaring stupidity, would begrudgingly acknowledge that a senior college student, a woman of twenty-one years, could certainly be dating a man who was a few years older. But would they survive the first year as an eighteen-year-old girl and a twenty-four-year-old man? The distance alone—about eighty miles to Marist College— could destroy them, as everyone knew that long-distance relationships rarely survive.

But distance was not the only problem. He could easily get in his car and visit her, but what would they do? She would have a new group of friends, all college freshman. How would Martin ever fit in with a bunch of eighteen-year-old freshmen? And she could come home for weekends to see him, but the rumors would fly. The girl who was barely out of high school was coming home on weekends to sleep with her high school history teacher. She would rather die than live with all the stupid rumors.

She shared her thoughts with Becky for a while, and then they sat in silence as the Adirondack Mountains came into view. She decided to close her eyes and meditate. Buddhist teachings came to mind. According to a book she had read, the root of all suffering is our attachment to people and things. We should experience compassion, not a possessive craving. When we get attached, we cause ourselves so much suffering. She had trouble with this notion of "non-attachment." Was it wrong to have a strong desire for someone? Her mind drifted to thoughts of Martin.

She craved Martin. Was she attached? Absolutely! She was attached to his big, brown eyes. She was attached to his stick-out ears. She was attached to his chin, his hands, the way he walked, the way he talked—she was attached to everything about him. So, should she try to overcome this "attachment" to the man she loved? Maybe so, she thought. Maybe the way she loved Martin was a selfish way. The Buddhists thought (if she understood them correctly) that one should love all people—indeed, all *sentient beings*—with the same boundless, universal love. She should care about all people and all animals, as she did care, of course. But she cared more about Martin.

She presented herself with a moral dilemma: If a ship were sinking and she had to choose between saving Martin or saving a thousand other people on the ship, whom would she choose? Without a moment's hesitation, she knew the answer. Obviously, she would choose Martin, much as it would distress her to see the others perish. And why would she save Martin? Because she loved Martin and she wanted him in her life. It was totally selfish, she had to admit. She would let a thousand people die because she, Cordelia Wunsch, wanted this man named Martin Tremblay in her life. Because of her selfishness, she would intentionally, knowingly cause the death at sea of one thousand souls.

So maybe the Buddhists were right. But what would it be like to love Martin in the Buddhist way? She tried to imagine that she loved Martin as she loved all sentient beings. She tried to imagine herself like the Buddha: calm, serene, and unattached. She told herself that all the tangible things in this world (including a man named Martin) are temporary, and we must not get too attached to them. That's what causes our suffering; we get attached to all the impermanent people and things of this world. But she kept seeing Martin's face in her mind, and her thoughts quickly turned to their plans for a rendezvous.

She opened her eyes. It was no use. She craved Martin, and she was completely incapable of renouncing her selfish desire for him. And she couldn't stop her thoughts from buzzing around in her brain.

"I'll never be a successful Buddha," she said to Becky. "I love Martin too much."

"Shocking news," said Becky.

39

Sinners and Innocents

There were two directions in the world: toward Danny (east) and away from Danny (west). She tried to keep her bearings by watching the sun. Occasionally, the road would bend north or south for a stretch, and she would feel angry at the Greyhound Bus driver. *What are you doing, fool? Stay east! Just keep going east!* They were pulling into a town, but she had been dozing, and she had no idea where they were. Someplace between St. Louis, Missouri and Albany, New York. She must get to Albany. There was no room for doubt in the message of that cold-hearted doctor back in St. Louis. Her time was short. She wanted to see her son. She thought of calling Danny to tell him she was coming, but she was afraid of his reaction. What if he didn't want to see her? What if he slammed the phone down and refused to see her? One couldn't blame him after all these years. No, it would be a mistake to call him. She would get herself to Albany and find him, somehow.

The bus passed by a small synagogue, and she thought about the suffering of the Jewish people. She knew that life was full of suffering, and she divided people into two types: the sinners and the innocents. The sinners would ultimately suffer eternal damnation, no matter how deftly they had escaped punishment in this earthly life. The innocents, no matter how much they suffered here, would finally reap their eternal reward. In her private, unofficial census, she had counted Christians pretty evenly between sinners and innocents. (Surely, she had met some shockingly mean-spirited people who made a regular habit of attending church and saying prayers.) The Jews, however, were another matter. All the Jews, those alive today as well as those long dead and those yet to be born, belonged to the innocents. Jesus himself was a Jew. All the historical troubles of the Jews—the ancient expulsion from the Promised Land, the pogroms of the nineteenth century, Hitler's Holocaust—were simply God's re-enactment of the crucifixion over and over again.

Modern day Israel presented her with a problem, though. The more she heard about it, the more she saw the Palestinians as the innocent sufferers. But then who was making them suffer? The Jews? This thought was in direct conflict with her lifelong view of the Jewish people, and it was an intolerable idea. She finally found a way out of the dilemma: A small handful of Israeli politicians were causing great suffering for the Palestinians, while most of the Jews worldwide were still in the category of the innocents.

All of this was firmly established in her mind before she ever met Harry Wunsch. When she met him, and he took a fancy to her—what man did not take a fancy to her? —she saw an opportunity for eternal redemption. She would marry into the Jews and join the innocents! She, the miserable sinner who had failed so tragically to be a good Catholic, would join the family of the innocents, the Chosen People. And perhaps, over time, God would come to see her as one of them, deserving of forgiveness. (Perhaps God would even forgive her for the wicked pleasures she took with that boy in high school, the boy she would meet at night in the cemetery—the cemetery, for God's sake!—where she would slip out of her Catholic high school uniform and surrender to the sinful demands of the flesh.)

Her mother had been so appalled when she married a Jew. But why so shocked? Our Lord Jesus was a Jew, as were all of his disciples. Wasn't the last supper their Jewish Passover meal? So, she had married a Jewish man. He was a gentle man, as Jesus was a gentle man, even if her husband had been a disappointment in many ways. He always wanted to please her, always wanted to give her everything she could possibly need. But somehow, he never seemed to know what she really needed. When she needed comfort, he gave her advice. When she needed advice, he gave her a hug, accompanied by the reassurance that whatever the problem was, it didn't really exist, or it would soon be over. He was so determined to give her a perfect life that he never really saw her as she was. She never wanted a perfect life without a moment of suffering; she wanted someone to see her suffering, to bear witness to it.

Her mother-in-law, Yetta, saw her suffering. She always knew that Yetta saw it. Yetta was obviously familiar with suffering, as all the Jews were. Some of them had been driven mad by it, like crazy Aunt Zlata, always pounding on the table and venting her incoherent rage about the mailman and the price of smoked salmon and the *galem*—the fool—who sat in the White House in Washington, D.C. Yetta seemed to know the suffering of life, yet she was neither broken by it nor hardened by it. On the Jewish holidays, Yetta would give her a dish of her noodle pudding. (What did they call it in Yiddish? Oh, right, *kugel.*) Yetta would put the dish in front of her, and her eyes would say, *Don't be afraid of the suffering. Stay with me. We'll get through this together.* She suddenly missed Yetta terribly. And she suddenly needed a drink. Maybe the bus would stop for a break soon and she could find a little tavern.

40

People Don't Change

The bus didn't stop in the town with the synagogue, so she couldn't get a drink. As the main street of the town turned into highway, her thoughts turned to her time with Carlos back in Denver, a time when she at least had someone who comforted her when she needed comfort. Maybe he didn't really understand her suffering, but he was kind and patient.

She had complained to Carlos about not working, so he used his influence to get her a job in a plant nursery. She was terribly worried at first, because she had never really held a job, but she quickly acclimated and learned what to do. In fact, she was surprised to see how happy she was to be surrounded by plants. If she had thought about her life back in Detroit—which she adamantly refused to do—she would have realized how much she missed her flower beds in the old backyard. All she knew was that she felt happy to be working with plants of all kinds. There were the annuals (marigolds, pansies, geraniums), the perennials (columbine, hollyhock, blue wild indigo), and the succulent plants with new names that she had to learn (red yucca, blue chalk sticks, Parry's agave). Every time she learned the name of a new plant, she felt the delight of a young child who learns a new word and wanders about the yard repeating it for the sheer pleasure of making the sounds.

At first, she was quite cautious around her boss. He was a man in his fifties, short and muscular. He could be rather volatile in his dealings with his employees. His bald head was decorated with a large purple birthmark which somehow made him more intimidating when he had one of his tantrums. He would yell and curse when things went wrong, but the storm always passed quickly, and then he could be surprisingly kind and generous. As she learned more about the plants, he seemed to notice how much she knew and how hard she worked. He told her she was doing well, and he gave her more responsibility and a decent pay raise. Customers began to ask for her and seek her out for her opinions and suggestions. All in all, she was quite pleased with her first job in the world.

One day, a newspaper crew came to the nursery to write an article about the place. They took a photograph of her, and she sent a copy of the article to her brother Jack in California. She made it her habit to send him little bits of information about her new life in Denver. It was the least she could do for him, knowing how troubled and lonely he was.

For a brief time, there was a problem at work. One of the other women became jealous of her popularity with the boss and the customers.

"Well, it's nice that you know so much now, isn't it, Kate?" She said it with a sing-song lilt in her voice that was a perfect parody of kindness. Her face produced an exaggerated smile of the mouth that was contradicted by the cold slits of her eyes. "You must be very pleased with yourself, Kate." It wasn't the first time that a woman had used this death-by-sweetness method to express bitter resentment toward her, and she knew exactly how to handle it.

"Can you tell me again what this cactus is called?" she asked the other woman. "I just can't keep the name in my head." Of course, she knew quite well that it was a prickly pear cactus (genus Opuntia). "And what about this one over here? Will this plant grow best in shade or sun? I always get that mixed up." She wasn't mixed up at all; the plant required full sun. "Honestly, Gloria, I don't know how you remember all this stuff!"

The strategy worked, as Kate knew it would. The woman was quickly mollified, and she dropped her campaign of sarcasm and scowling. Kate's time at work continued in the most pleasant way, surrounded by plants and sunshine.

Her life with Carlos also continued smoothly for the next five years, with his "business weekends" becoming more frequent. When the weather was nice, they would sometimes get an ice cream or take a walk in the evening after dinner. She knew that he was very careful about where they went, so he wouldn't run into people who knew him and his wife. He was clearly trying to be subtle about this strategy, but she was not offended at all. His preference for anonymity was more than matched by hers.

One evening, they were sitting in the living room of her little apartment eating a dessert, a Mexican flan she had made for him. Carlos said he wanted to talk to her. He said it in a very serious tone, and it made her feel uncomfortable. In fact, something about him had made her uneasy all evening. Something about the way he looked at her. Even his posture worried her. It was always his custom after dinner to sit back in an easy chair and put his feet up on an ottoman with the air of a man who had conquered the world. Now he was sitting on the edge of his chair, leaning forward, looking at her. He put his unfinished dessert on the coffee table. He wanted something, and she was afraid to know what it was. His shiny black hair looked beautiful, as always; he was undeniably a very handsome man. But she felt an inexplicable urge to move her chair further away from him.

"Kate, I can't go on like this. You see—"

She interrupted him immediately. "It's okay, Carlos. I understand. You have a wife and children." She tried to convince herself that he was about to announce the renewal of a monogamous commitment to his wife. That would be terribly painful to her, but she felt in herself an urgent need to believe this. Something in his demeanor—the way he leaned forward and held her gaze—told her that this was not his mission. There was something else, and it was alarming her.

"No, no, Kate. You see, I don't want to go back to my wife. Not ever. I can't go on like this, pretending that I care for her. I just want to be with you."

She put her dish down next to his on the coffee table, and then she froze in her seat, unable to move or speak. It seemed like he had just moved closer to her, much closer, even though he hadn't moved an inch.

"I can't keep pretending with my wife. I can't."

Her chest felt tight, and she could barely breathe. She forcibly took a deep sigh to draw in air.

"I only want *you*, Kate."

He was changing before her eyes, and this confused her. They had spent the past five years in a certain arrangement, a comfortable rhythm of coming and going. She had his company to enjoy, and there was no commitment, no expectation of her. It was hard when he was gone, terribly hard, but she knew that he would return. And when they were together for too many days in a row, and she started to feel trapped and claustrophobic, she knew that he would soon be leaving again. Now everything was changing.

"When I'm away from you, I'm unhappy, Kate. I only feel like myself when we're together."

She had often heard it said that people don't really change, and no one in her own life had ever disproved that proposition. Her boss at the nursery would always be prone to childish fits of temper. The jealous, insecure co-worker named Gloria would always be jealous and insecure. People didn't change. This belief in the permanence of an individual's character had become one of her most basic convictions about human beings. But Carlos was changing right before her eyes.

Of course, Carlos had been different from the start. A curiosity among men. It seemed to her that most men could be divided into two camps: the bullies and the wimps. (She had long ago assigned her husband in Detroit to the latter group.) Men either ruthlessly competed with each other to conquer the world and enjoy the spoils of the victors, or they sat back, helplessly watching, lacking the pluck to join in the battle. But Carlos was different. True, he wanted what he wanted, and he didn't hesitate to fight for it, but he was not ruthless in his efforts to get it. He would not hurt others to get his way. And he had a certain tenderness toward women and children—she had seen it in his behavior at restaurants and markets—that set him apart from so many men. Now he sat across from her, perched on the edge of his chair, reaching out to her with his eyes. She heard herself stammering in futile attempts to refute his words and block his advance. Nothing seemed to have any effect on him.

"I know that I told you I would never leave my wife," he said, "and I meant that when we first met. But things have changed for me."

She didn't want him to change. She never had any illusions about him, and she was comfortable with him just as he was. And he never seemed to make any pretense to be other than himself. He was Carlos, the little Mexican boy who came across the border into Texas with his mother and a bunch of older siblings. He had made a successful life here in Denver, here in America. He had overcome the poverty and xenophobia and bullying of his childhood. Now he had mastery over the world and its resources, including women. She knew where she fit into his world. She sensed that he had resolved long ago that he would never again suffer from deprivation of any sort, that he would have all the creature comforts any man could have. He had obviously stayed with his wife because a divorce would cause him discomfort, and he seemed determined to avoid discomfort at all costs. All his little acts of kindness and all his caring gestures were laudable, but they didn't prevent her from seeing what she saw in moments of quiet between them: a man who had never really loved anyone but himself. And she knew very well that their arrangement, in his mind, was simply an exchange of goods. He supplied her with material goods (apartment, car, etc.), and she supplied him with the feminine comfort that he couldn't get from his wife. Until this moment, this had been their mutually accepted bargain, but now all that was changing.

"Kate, I feel so different about you now."

She knew what he meant, and it frightened her. He loved her now, and this changed everything. She thought briefly about her husband back in Detroit. For all his foibles and shortcomings, he had really loved her, too. Did she love her husband in the same way? She was never really sure about that. She had loved her children, of course. Her Danny—but one mustn't think about that.

One mustn't think about Detroit at all. She had to stay focused on Carlos now. He loved her, and this changed everything.

"I'm not the same man you met five years ago."

She saw what was happening. It was all writ large in his eyes. She saw, in an instant, that he was completely engulfed in a process of change; that he was surprised (as she was) by the nature and depth of the change; that he was discovering in himself, after forty-seven years of benevolent self-absorption, an immense, untapped capacity for love.

She was frightened. It terrified her to know that she was both the stimulus for this nascent love and its only object. She got up from her chair to clear the dessert dishes, and her hands were trembling.

"I need to think," she muttered.

He jumped up from his chair with a sudden movement that startled her, and he stood between her and the kitchen. He took the dishes out of her shaking hands and placed them back on the coffee table. He took her hands gently in his. "Yes, of course, Kate. Take all the time you need. I know this must come as a surprise. Just please think about it. Think about us." Then he kissed her once lightly on the cheek and left her apartment.

As soon as he was gone, she went straight to the refrigerator and took out a bottle of wine. Her hands didn't stop trembling until the bottle was half-empty. She cried for a few minutes, and then sat down to write him a note, which she left on the kitchen table before going to bed.

The next morning, she packed her car, emptied the bank account he had established for her, and drove away from Denver.

41

Family Therapy

As soon as his daughter returned home, Dan insisted that she must see a psychiatrist. For the first visit, the three of them—Dan, Abby, and Cordelia—got in the car and drove to a psychiatric hospital that provided out-patient psychotherapy. (Abby tried to convince him that driving forty minutes out of town was not necessary to protect their privacy, but Dan insisted.) The psychiatrist gathered a lot of information from Dan and Abby for part of the session. Then he met alone with Cordelia.

On their second visit, Dan was still trying to understand why he and Abby had to attend the sessions at all. He was also trying to decide whether or not he liked the psychiatrist. He approved of the fact that Dr. Burgess was an older man, rather than a kid fresh out of training. And he seemed to be a man who was still energetic and intelligent; no sign of decline in a fellow who must be in his early sixties. Dan was not sure whether the tweed sport coat and wire-rimmed glasses were an obsolete cliché or the perfect image of what a psychiatrist ought to look like. And he couldn't decide what he felt about the thick Southern accent.

The room was a generous space, furnished with well-padded easy chairs and a sofa. There were homey rugs on the floor and a few colorful landscapes on the walls. Dan gave them credit. They had at least taken some pains to create a welcoming space for families to meet. Dan took a seat in the same comfortable armchair he had chosen for the first visit, and Abby sat down next to Cordelia on the sofa.

"Nice to see y'all again," said Dr. Burgess. He took a seat in the one rocking chair in the room and rested a clip board on his lap, with a pen ready in one hand. "So how have things been since we last met?" he asked.

Dan wasted no time in expressing his concerns.

"We're still worried about our daughter," he opened. "We still don't understand why she ran away from home earlier this summer and stayed with a girlfriend in Montreal for over a month. And she seems depressed. Staying in her room a lot, not her old self. We're very worried." Dan saw that Abby quickly teared up, and Cordelia reached over and patted her arm.

"It's all right, Mom. It's all right," Cordelia said quietly. She reached over to the round table in front of them and handed her mother a tissue.

"I see that you're real sweet to your momma," said Dr. Burgess. Dan recoiled at the term *momma*. It sounded like an uninvited bit of intimacy, an intrusion into the inner life of his family.

"Cordelia is a very kind girl," said Abby, wiping her eyes with the tissue.

"That's real nice," said Dr. Burgess. "Real nice."

Dan couldn't help but feel suspicious of the Southern accent. Was Burgess putting it on a bit thick? He pronounced nice as "noss," almost rhyming it with the first syllable of *posse*. Second, anyone with a fourth-grade education ought to know enough to say 'really nice' instead of 'real nice,' *really* being the adverb that modifies the adjective *nice*. Dan could imagine his wife telling him not to be so critical of people, as she often told him. Well, all right. He would give this guy Burgess a chance.

"She's an exceptionally kind girl," said Abby.

"Um-hm," intoned Dr. Burgess. He nodded and smiled at Cordelia and her mother. Then he turned to Cordelia. "And how long have you been takin' care of your momma like this?"

Cordelia looked a bit apprehensive. "Oh, I don't really take care of my mom. She takes care of me."

Ignoring her answer, Burgess turned to Abby. "Do you find yourself confiding in Cordelia?"

Cordelia jumped in to answer on her mother's behalf. "No, she doesn't really confide in me," she said. "We're close, but she doesn't confide like that," she said.

"I do," said Abby. "I do confide in her. I probably lean on her too much."

"So, how come you don't confide instead in this nice fella right here?" asked Burgess, tipping his head in Dan's direction.

Dan was feeling apprehensive about this whole line of questioning. "Abby does confide in me," he said to Burgess. "We confide in each other, and we have a very good marriage. Besides, we're not here to analyze our marriage. We're here to help Cordelia. I'm really worried that she has depression, and I think she would benefit from an antidepressant medication."

Burgess looked at Dan patiently to let him finish his thought. Then he laid his clipboard and pen on the round wooden table in the middle of the seating area, and he sat back in his chair. "Now listen to me, son. This little darlin' of yours doesn't have a disease called depression. She's got a life"— he pronounced *life* almost like a rhyme with the first syllable of *mafia*—"and right now that life is a little sad. We're here to help her to feel better."

Dan was taken off guard by Burgess calling him "son." The term sounded so kind and caring, but he was wary of dropping his guard. And he wanted to press his point.

"She has all the signs of depression, and I think an antidepressant medication makes perfect sense."

Burgess listened again and paused before he answered. He glanced at Cordelia, and Dan had the sense that the two of them shared some kind of secret from the first appointment.

"Well, let's talk a bit more and we'll see," Burgess said.

"Okay," said Dan. 'I'm not trying to tell you how to run your business."

"I understand," said Burgess, nodding and smiling. Dan admired him for his composure. He was obviously a guy who would stay calm under fire, and this was reassuring.

"Cordelia," Burgess said.

"Yes?" she answered.

"Cordelia. That's a real nice name. A name from one of Shakespeare's plays, as I recollect."

"It is," answered Dan.

"King Lear, I believe," said Burgess.

"Correct," said Dan. Dan was always surprised and pleased when someone turned out to be unexpectedly well-read. Burgess knew Shakespeare, and this gave them some common ground to stand on together. Dan felt that now he could forgive him. Forgive him? he thought to himself. Forgive him for what? For the accent? What if the man had a Southern accent? He was from the South. Did he need to forgive him for his intrusions into the life of this family? He was only doing his job as a psychiatrist.

"Dan's an English professor," said Abby.

"Really?" said Burgess, looking impressed. "Then you know more about old King Lear than I do." He rocked in his rocking chair for a minute, tapping a finger on his chin, apparently lost in thought. "Isn't that the play where the crazy old king exiles his own daughter from the kingdom? Kind of a silly story line, if you ask me."

"That's the play," said Dan, surprised again that Burgess knew this much. In fact, he had always used Shakespeare as one of his many yardsticks for measuring the people he met. He had divided most of the world into two camps, based on one's knowledge of Shakespeare. There were those who knew nothing about Shakespeare, and there were the pretentious academics who worshipped him. Burgess was perfect, right in the middle, in neither camp, knowledgeable but not blindly adoring.

"And Cordelia in the play is the good daughter, right?" said Burgess. "Lear gives his kingdom to his other two daughters, who are mean and nasty. But Cordelia's a real sweet girl."

"And that's why we named her," Abby interjected. "The character in the play was a good person, and Cordelia turned out to be just as good."

"Um-hm." Burgess sat quietly mulling this over.

Dan didn't say what he was thinking: that he named his first child for the sweet, innocent daughter in the play, and he secretly vowed that he would never, *never* be separated from her like King Lear separates himself from his daughter by banishing her. Burgess looked at him and held his gaze for a moment, saying nothing. Dan thought to himself that maybe Burgess would know what he was thinking just by looking at him, but then he dismissed this as nonsense.

Dan looked at his daughter. Cordelia. She had been such a sweet little girl, just as Abby said. And still sweet, sitting here trying so earnestly to answer the psychiatrist's questions, trying to keep her mother from getting upset. But here she was, here they all were, sitting in a psychiatrist's office because she had run away from home. The whole situation was just unfathomable.

"I suppose you've both been terribly worried about Cordelia," Burgess said. He glanced at Abby, but then focused his gaze on Dan.

"Dan worries about all of us," Abby volunteered. "But he worries most about Cordelia, especially over the past year or so."

"Well, of course I do," Dan said. "Fathers always worry about their daughters."

"Yes, we do," said Burgess. "Yes, we do."

Dan felt comforted by the comment. It felt like an invitation to join a group of like-minded sufferers, a fellowship of worried fathers. Burgess sat quietly for a moment, looking at his clipboard. Then he looked up at Dan again.

"So, Dan, what was your life like growing up?"

"It was fine," Dan said quickly.

Abby spoke up again. "But Doctor, I think you should know that Dan's mother left the family when he was still a kid."

"Really?" he said to Dan. "What happened?"

Abby began to answer, but Burgess held up a hand to stop her. He obviously wanted to hear from Dan.

"We don't really know," said Dan quietly. "She just disappeared."

"Just like *that*?" Burgess asked, snapping his fingers.

"Just like that," said Dan.

"I'm really sorry to hear that," said Burgess. He paused to scribble a note to himself.

"So, how old were you when she left, Dan?"

"I was in my teens," said Dan.

"In your teens," Burgess repeated. "A tough age, even without such a terrible loss."

Dan fixed his eyes on the rug on the floor in front of him, but he could feel that Burgess was still looking at him.

"And what's your biggest fear for your Cordelia now?"

Dan suddenly felt panicky, as if something terrible were about to happen. He was lightheaded, and he felt his heart pounding. The room and its furnishings seemed somehow unreal. He tapped his fingers on the arm of his chair, thinking to himself: *It's real. This chair is real. Everything is all right, and this chair is real.*

"We don't have to talk about it if you don't want to," said Burgess in a very calming voice. "It's completely up to you, Dan."

"Are you okay, Dad?" asked Cordelia.

"Yes, I'm fine," answered Dan, but it seemed like he was listening to his voice from a position outside of his own body. He rubbed his palm against the upholstered arm of his chair and took a deep breath. He was going to say something else, but then he couldn't remember what he was going to say. In fact, he couldn't recall what Burgess had just said. He got up and stood in front of his chair for a long minute, just to make sure that he felt steady on his feet. "I just need to use the men's room. I'll be right back."

"Maybe somebody should walk with him," he heard Cordelia say.

"He's fine," said Abby's voice. "Just give him a little space."

"But Mom—"

"He's fine, honey. Just let him be."

42

Irises

Once outside the family therapy room, Dan wandered down the hallway. His mind felt dumb and sluggish, but at least his heart stopped racing and the lightheaded feeling was resolving. The hallway was empty and quiet, and he was grateful for that. He paced back and forth for the next few minutes, and his thoughts began to clear.

He wandered farther down the hallway, passing the closed doors with names of psychotherapists on them. He found himself at the end of the corridor, where he came to a large picture window looking out onto a tidy little flower garden. There was a small couch placed by the window, facing outward to the garden. He took a seat, transfixed by the flower bed. His mind ran a critique of the garden. The flower bed was too perfect, the plants laid out in flawless rows, the rows meticulously separated by layers of dark mulch, the entire effect rigid and sterile. It seemed wrong to make living plants look so regimented and lifeless. Still, he couldn't take his eyes off the flowers. He sat on the couch, feeling tired, looking at the neat rows of flowers, thinking of nothing for a quiet few minutes.

His mother had a flower bed in the backyard every summer. Not a neat, linear array of captive plants like those in this hospital garden, but a more natural arrangement, a loosely strewn collection of brightly colored flowers, each variety freely spilling over into its neighbor's territory.

Flowers always cheer a person up, Danny. She dug a hole with her shovel, and gently placed a new plant in the hole. Danny gathered into his cupped hands some dirt from a big mound and began to fill the hole around the plant.

That's right. A little more, honey. Now pack it down nice and firm. That's right.

He patted the soil. They moved over a bit and planted another of the same variety. His mother bent down and whispered in his ear. *These are called irises. They're my favorites. But don't tell the other flowers! It would hurt their feelings.*

Don't worry, Mom. I won't tell.

She kissed him on the forehead, as she did every night after tucking him into bed. They continued their garden work. It was warm and sunny, and he saw their shadows on the ground right next to them.

Mom, are you sad that Grandma died? He had heard his parents talking about this over the past few days. They would talk after he went to bed, but sometimes he could hear them downstairs talking in the kitchen.

Well, she was getting old. It was her time to go. His mother had stopped smiling now, and she looked so serious.

Are we going to Grandma's funeral? He had heard them talking about a funeral for her.

His mother was quiet for a long time. Then she spoke. *No, honey, she lived far away from us.*

Is that why I never met her?

Your grandmother was a hard woman, Danny. So, we're not going to her funeral. Here. Put some more dirt on this one now.

His grandma was a hard woman. But what did that mean? His grandpa, whom he had never met, used to build things with stones—*a stone mason*—so maybe it had something to do with the hardness of the stones. His grandpa's name was Daniel. Just like his name, except that his name always got changed to Danny.

He scooped more of the soil into his hands. His mother's motions seemed rough and jerky now, not gentle like they usually were. She patted down some of the soil he added, but she seemed to be slapping the ground rather than patting it. She was not looking at him anymore. He began to ask more questions, watching her face to see if she would start looking at him again.

And Grandpa, he died a long time ago. Right, Mom?

That's right. A very long time ago. I was very young. Only seventeen years old.

But that's pretty old, Mom.

It sounds old to you, Danny, because you're only five. But seventeen is not that old.

How did Grandpa die, Mom?

She was quiet again. He thought maybe she hadn't heard him.

How did Grandpa—?

He fell off a ladder. Her words sounded sharp and short.

He thought of the small step-ladder that his father kept in the garage. *Was the ladder bigger than Daddy's ladder?*

His mother sighed loudly. His questions were not having the desired effect; she was only getting quieter. She wasn't looking at him, and she wasn't smiling at all. *Yes, it was a very big ladder.*

How big was it, Mom? Was it as big as our house?

His mother put down the iris plant in her hand and stood up abruptly. *I have to start making lunch now.* And she went into the house, leaving him kneeling alone in the middle of the flower garden.

"Are you waiting for someone, sir?" Dan's thoughts were interrupted by a young woman who was leading a group of five or six teens down the corridor.

"No, no. I mean yes, I'm just waiting for my daughter to finish a therapy session."

"And do you know where she is having her session?"

"Yes, I do. They're just down the hall."

"All right. Have a nice day."

"Thanks."

The young woman and the kids vanished around a corner. He could hear the kids talking and laughing as their voices faded out.

He sat looking out at the hospital garden. His mind returned to the memory of his mother's garden, but the memory had changed now. It began as a wonderful, happy memory of a sunny day in the garden with her, but now it looked dark and sad. Was it a happy memory or a sad one? he asked himself. It seemed to depend upon which part of the memory you focused on. Memory seemed so fluid, so malleable. He wished it could be made of more solid stuff. It seemed that one could shape a memory this way or that way, as one pleased, or—more correctly—the memory could shape itself into various renditions. Memories should stand firm in their original form, like great books fixed in black ink on the page, constant and dependable, no matter when you decide to revisit them.

43

Mrs. Rose

The difficult second visit to the psychiatrist was the last one, since her father refused to go back for any more sessions. As the end of the summer approached, and her September college launch was only a few weeks away, her father seemed to be getting ever more distant and irritable. She tried to avoid him whenever possible. Either she went out with friends, or she spent time alone in her bedroom.

No one spoke about the visits to Dr. Burgess, and no one spoke about her time in Montreal. Much of her time at home was spent in writing letters to Martin and waiting for letters from Martin. In accordance with their previous agreement, he sent his letters to Becky, because Becky always brought in the mail before her mother got home from work. Then Becky would give the latest letter to Cordelia, who would run home, shut herself in her room, and devour the letter word by word. The letters came every few days, and she wrote to him at least that often.

> *Dear Martin,*
> *Every day, I look at a map of the world to find Paris.*
> *With you in Paris, the world seems so much bigger,*
> *my life so much smaller.*

She sat in her room and wrote in the evenings.

> *Life without you is half a life. I can't wait to be with*
> *you again. Then I'll feel whole again.*

The words flowed effortlessly, and her letters ran to three or four pages.

> *God, I hate Paris! Paris is my rival because she gets to*
> *see your face and hear your voice every day.*

At first, she felt happy writing, but she soon began to feel a nagging discomfort triggered by her own words.

> *I hope you're having a wonderful time with*
> *your family.*

Writing that sentence confronted her with the fact that he was a twenty-four-year-old man traveling in Europe with his family, and she was an eighteen-year-old girl who was not part of that family. She was a high school kid writing to her teacher.

> *Dear Martin, I had a wonderful dream about you*
> *last night. I can't wait till you get back home.*

But then what? she thought. When he got back home to Montreal later in the month, it would be time for her to pack up for college. And when September arrived and he returned to the U.S., her classes would be starting at Marist College, and he would have to start his new year of teaching history at the high school. Some days, every line she wrote brought her into closer contact with the terrible reality of their separate lives. She couldn't see how the relationship with him would ever last.

She needed some distraction from ruminating about Martin. She had resumed some of her childcare for the neighbors, and she also decided to work at Albany Medical Center as a volunteer. She enjoyed interacting with the patients, even when she was only taking someone down to the X-ray department in a wheelchair. She appreciated the positive feedback she received. Patients told her that she was very kind, and the nursing staff seemed to like her.

She liked going down to Albany Med despite the little annoyances on the job. On her second day at the hospital, she heard someone call out, "Hi Dee!" It was Perry, of course. He, too, was a volunteer at the hospital. She wanted to tell him to stop using the uninvited nickname, but she couldn't see the point of hurting someone's feelings just to fuss over a name. Soon, however, everyone on the ward was calling her "Dee," despite the fact that she wore a name tag with *Cordelia* on it. Oh, well, she thought. She knew that Perry already had a hard time feeling accepted by other people, so she wasn't about to embarrass him by telling everyone that she hated nicknames.

One afternoon, she saw a nurse helping an elderly woman get out of her bed. The nurse held the patient by one arm. The old woman seemed pretty steady on her feet at the moment, but Cordelia thought she looked frail nonetheless. She ran into the room and took the woman's other arm. She noticed a small bruise on her forehead.

"Well, thank you, my little angel," said the woman.

"You're welcome," said Cordelia.

"Mrs. Rose, this is Dee," said the nurse. "Maybe Dee can help you get in and out of the shower today."

"Hello, Dee," said the old woman, flashing a big smile. "If you can get this old lady to clean up and look better, maybe we can go out on the town tonight."

Cordelia liked her at once. She had been taking care of an old woman down the hall who was always complaining bitterly about her life. It was refreshing to have an older patient with a sense of humor and a charming smile. "Sure," said Cordelia. "Then we can go out dancing."

"Dancing!" said the old woman. "Sounds delightful! But first, let's see if you can help me get this old body from here to the bathroom."

The nurse left to help another patient. Cordelia held onto Mrs. Rose carefully, even though her balance seemed fine. Slowly, the two of them walked arm in arm for a few feet to the bathroom attached to the patient room. Cordelia could feel how light and brittle the old woman's body was. Mrs. Rose's skin had an unhealthy yellowish tinge to it, and the whites of her eyes had turned yellow, too. The only feature that still seemed vibrant and healthy was her hair, thick and white. Cordelia felt happy for her that at least one part of her anatomy had escaped the ravages of disease.

Mrs. Rose picked up two small tubes that were sitting on the sink in the bathroom. "I can manage just fine in the shower," she said. "But you'll have to tell me which one of these is the shampoo. They seem to have lost my few belongings in the Emergency

Room, including my glasses, and I'm blind as an old bat without them. I can't even read without them, and what good is this life without a good book to read?"

"This is the shampoo," said Cordelia. "This one is the hair conditioner."

"Thanks, Dee."

While the old woman was showering, the nurse motioned Cordelia into the hallway and gave her some background. The patient had been found on the street a few days ago, not far from the hospital, wandering around looking sickly and weak. When she was brought into the Emergency Room, she was confused and disoriented. She had a bruise on her forehead, so the doctors assumed she had fallen down on the street. Now, she was clear-headed again, but she was quite ill and her prognosis was poor.

Soon, Mrs. Rose was getting back in bed with a towel wrapped around her head.

"So, tell me about yourself, Dee," she said. "How old are you? And what are you doing with your life these days?"

Cordelia helped adjust the hospital bed to a sitting position with the head up, and she pulled a chair closer to the old woman's bedside. She shared with Mrs. Rose a few basic details about herself and her family, as well as her plans to attend Marist College. Mrs. Rose listened politely and smiled often.

"And what about young men in your life?" she asked with a raised brow. "I don't have my glasses with me, but even a half-blind old woman can see that you're a beautiful girl. And kind-hearted as any girl I've ever met."

"Thank you," said Cordelia. "There were a couple of boys in high school, but they didn't last. They were a little immature."

Mrs. Rose removed the towel from her head and started to pull a hairbrush through the thick white hair. "And what's the rest of the story?" she asked.

"Why do you think there's more to the story?"

Mrs. Rose smiled. "Oh, I don't imagine that a girl like you would be alone for five minutes before another young man took an interest. So, if it's not one of the immature boys from high school, then there must be someone else, right?"

Cordelia was caught off guard. "Well, there is," she answered. She hesitated for a moment. No one knew except Becky, and she had planned to keep it this way. But why not tell an old woman who wouldn't be on this earth for much longer? Besides, Mrs. Rose seemed very kind and motherly.

"There is someone else. His name is Martin."

The old woman looked interested. "And that's it? His name is Martin?"

Cordelia wanted to say much more, but she held herself back. "I visited him in Montreal this summer. He lives in Montreal. At least in the summers. He comes from there."

"I see," said Mrs. Rose. "And how did you meet this Martin of yours?"

Cordelia paused, but her need to talk overpowered her instinct for caution. The story came out faster than she had anticipated.

"He was my teacher. I know it's not right, Mrs. Rose, but there's nothing wrong about it, really. He's only twenty-four—not that old, really, and I'm eighteen. And he's the kindest, most wonderful man I've ever met, and we just get along so well. We're soul mates, really." She felt surprised that she was telling all this to a sickly old woman whom she had just met.

"Oh, your teacher! I see." Mrs. Rose paused to arrange the items on her bedside tray—tissues, a pitcher of water, a container of juice. "Let me ask you a few questions about your Martin," she said.

"Sure," said Cordelia.

"Is he truly kind to you?"

"Oh, yes! He's so kind, Mrs. Rose. He really has a good heart."

"And does he think about what you need? Or is he self-centered like most men?"

"Oh, he's very giving."

"You're sure he's not one of the skirt-chasers who try to get us into bed and then disappear?"

"No, no, not at all. He's the real thing."

Mrs. Rose sat quietly for a minute or so. "Well, you say so, but would he sacrifice for you?"

Cordelia had to think about this for a minute. "Yes, I think he would. In fact, he did. Last month, when we were together in Montreal, he gave up an annual fishing trip with his college buddies just to stay with me."

"I see," said Mrs. Rose. "Not exactly a heroic battlefield sacrifice of blood and courage, but a sacrifice of sorts. That will do." She reached for a small container of apple juice and pulled the foil top from it. "I have another question, but perhaps you haven't been together long enough to know the answer to it. How is your Martin when there's a bump in the road? Still kind and caring? Or is that just his behavior when things are going well?"

Cordelia moved her chair a little closer to the bed and lowered her voice. "We actually did go through a couple of scary days. I thought I was pregnant."

"Oh, dear!" said Mrs. Rose. "And how was Martin?"

"He never flinched," said Cordelia proudly. "He stayed right by my side. I thought once that he had abandoned me, but that was just me being silly. He was right there with me. He knew I was really scared, and I could tell that he was scared, too, but he was just as sweet as ever."

"Really!" Mrs. Rose looked impressed. "A young man in his twenties thought that his eighteen-year-old girlfriend was pregnant, and he didn't run for the hills. I'm beginning to like this young man, Dee. I think you might be right about him. I think he might actually be the real thing."

"He is! He definitely is! He's the best." Then Cordelia felt sad to think of him. "But it will never work. I'm leaving for college in a few weeks, and he's coming back to teach high school in my home town. I don't see how it can ever work."

"You go ahead and cry if you want to cry, honey," said Mrs. Rose in a maternal voice. "It's fine to cry over a good man. We don't want to waste our tears on the rascals, but a good man is worth a good cry."

Cordelia didn't let herself cry. She just sat there, thinking about how happy she was up in Montreal, making dinner with Martin, strolling down Rue St.-Denis with Martin, or doing *anything* with Martin.

"You know, Dee, in my day, this would not have been a problem. A young man with a steady job would meet a slightly younger girl, and they would get married. Of course, you would not be going off to college, and your opportunities would be much more limited, but being with Martin would be quite acceptable. And he sounds like a fine young man."

"Thanks, Mrs. Rose," said Cordelia. "But it's nineteen ninety-seven, and girls do attend college, and it will never, never work."

Mrs. Rose sat quietly. She picked up her little cup of apple juice and took a sip. Then she reached out and patted Cordelia on the cheek. "Well, Dee, maybe it will work out for the two of you, and maybe it won't. It's in God's hands now, my dear. You just have to leave it in His hands."

"Yeah, I suppose so," said Dee. She envied Mrs. Rose for her belief in the old-fashioned Judeo-Christian God, a God who had nothing better to do with His time than to worry about an eighteen-year-old girl and her boyfriend. She wished she could believe in that. And meanwhile, she was left wondering where Martin might be at that moment, hoping that he was thinking of her.

44

Who Killed Jesus?

"I realize it's a technicality, Kate, but I think it's only fair." Jack sat alone at his small kitchen table in Big Sur, California, writing on a scrap of paper. As he wrote, he chatted aloud in the empty kitchen. "I promised not to tell Danny where you are, but I never said I wouldn't tell his little girl, Cordelia, now did I? And if she goes and tells him, then there's nothing I can do about *that*. But technically, I still haven't told him, right? I just don't want you to be mad at me, Missy. You're pretty much all the family I've got left, except for Her Highness Miss Molly in Tucson and her husband, Buck." He stopped to light a cigarette and take a drag on it. "Buck? Why don't they call him Buffalo? Or Antelope? Or Big-Horned Sheep? Why Buck?" He chuckled to himself and finished writing a hospital address on the scrap of paper.

Upstate Medical Center
750 East Adams Street
Syracuse, N.Y. 13210

He thought about the phone call he received from his sister earlier in the day. He was happy to hear from her, as always, but distressed by the way she sounded from the hospital in Syracuse. "You don't sound so good, Missy. Not good at all," he said to his empty kitchen. He drew a little box around the hospital address. "I don't really get it anyway, Miss. Why should I have to keep your whereabouts a secret if you're on your way to see Danny? You're traveling cross-country to see him, but I'm not supposed to tell him. I swear, you're getting crazier than I am. Well, okay, I'll keep my promise and I won't tell him. But if Cordelia wants to tell him, that ain't my business."

He added a short message to the hospital address: *No time to waste!* Then he picked up a blank sheet of paper and wrote a note.

> *Hi Suzanne,*
> *Please send this along to Danny's kid, Cordelia Wunsch. Same address. Do NOT put a return address! And please send this by Express Mail! It's urgent! I'll pay you back, I promise.*
>
> *Jack*

He put both notes—the hospital address and the note to his friend Suzanne—into an envelope addressed to Fairbanks, Alaska.

"Done. Now young Cordelia will have the note, and the rest is up to her." He took another pull on his beer bottle and sat back in his chair, looking quite pleased with himself. He picked up a copy of yesterday's newspaper and started to read an article, but then put it down on his lap. "Imagine. Danny's little Cordelia has grown up. Already graduated high school and ready to ship out to college. And she's just the spittin' image of you, Missy. I swear, the photos that Molly sent me look just like you looked at seventeen. I'll bet the boys are chasin' Cordelia just like they chased after you." He paused and sat quietly for a while. "I wonder if her little brother is covering for her like I covered for you."

Suddenly, his expression became dark and brooding. He stood up, dropped the newspaper onto the floor, and paced around the table a couple of times. He opened a kitchen cupboard door and closed it very slowly, very gently. Then he opened it again and closed it again, but this time with a bit more force. He repeated this several more times with increasing energy until he was slamming the cupboard door as hard as he could. He abruptly spun around to face an imaginary person behind him, and he spoke in a shrill, high-pitched voice.

"Jack! You come over here and tell me where your big sister is! Jack!" He roughly pulled his belt off his waist, raised it in the air, and brought it down on the table with savage fury. Whack! Piles of papers scattered to the floor. Several of the beer bottles toppled over on the table. He swept them off the table with his free hand. As they went crashing to the floor, the belt struck again. *Whack!* "Where is she! You know where she is!"

In his own voice, he said loudly and plaintively: "I don't know, Mom! How would I know?"

In the woman's voice: "Don't lie to me, Jack! You know plenty!" *Whack!*

In his own voice: "Mom, stop! I really don't know!"

In the high-pitched voice of the inquisitor: "Tell me, you little bastard! Where is that little whore of a sister of yours?" *Whack! Whack! Whack!*

He started to pace silently back and forth in the kitchen, not speaking in either voice, perhaps not sure about whether he was in the role of the enraged, violent mother, or the beaten child who is seeking revenge. Perhaps, at this moment, he was an inextricable fusion of both, like a storm raging over the ocean, a cyclone in which one can no longer say that this wind joined the storm from the west and this wind came from the east, because all winds were now joined in a violent, malevolent spiral that threatened to destroy anything in its path. He circled the perimeter of the dirty little kitchen and vented his fury at anything in reach of his belt: the refrigerator, the sink, the kitchen table, and a small, delicate coleus plant that sat on the windowsill leaning toward the sun for succor. *Whack! Whack! Whack!*

After a couple minutes like this, he dropped the belt on the floor and sat down on the chair—fell onto it, really. He was breathing hard, and his hands were shaking badly. He did his best to steady his hands and pick up the cigarette from its ashtray.

"Calm down, Jack," he said to himself in his own voice. "Calm yourself down now." He took a long drag on the cigarette, rocking slightly back and forth on the hardwood chair. "Calm down, Jack." He stood up and pulled another beer from the refrigerator. With some difficulty, he wrestled the cap off and took a long drink from the bottle. Gradually, he felt himself beginning to settle down. "But I kept your secret, Missy. I never told her where you were. I knew you were chasing around with that older boy from the high school, but I never told on you, no way. I knew she would give you a good beatin' if she knew what you were up to, so I just took the beatin' myself." He took another drag on the cigarette and put it down on an empty plate that had survived the belting. "You really ran wild back then, didn't you, Kate? You just ran wild with the boys back then, and you always picked the bad boys. How funny that you ended up marrying that boring little Jewish guy with the carpet business." He gathered a few of the papers that remained on the table and coaxed them into a neat little pile. "Not that I have anything against the Jews, 'cause I don't. All that crap in church about the Jews killing Jesus. What a bunch of garbage! For Christ's sake, Jesus was a Jew! You always said that, I remember. And all his apostles were Jews! If a man hates Jews, then he hates Jesus. That's what you always told me." Another long swallow of beer, another deep drag on the cigarette. He had stopped rocking now, and the shaking in his hands had started to diminish. He scanned the room suspiciously. One could never be too cautious these days.

"So, who did kill Jesus? That's the question, Missy. Who did kill him?" He got up and walked over to the window. A delivery truck was parked across the street in front of a restaurant. He watched the driver get out and bring a large cardboard box into the restaurant. A harmless delivery, but one can never be too cautious. He moved away from the window and took his seat.

"Hey, I have the answer! Mom killed Jesus! That's who did it, Missy! Mom killed Jesus!" He broke into loud, brassy laughter. When the wave of laughter subsided, he stood up from his chair and assumed a serious, statesmanlike pose as he addressed an imaginary audience. "May I have your attention, my dear members of the clergy. As you are all priests, all men of the church, I know you will be interested in the announcement I am about to make." He coughed a rough smoker's cough, which interrupted his speech. He held a hand up to signal to his audience that a momentary intermission was required in order to catch his breath. He drank the last of the contents of his beer bottle, belched loudly, and continued. "Holy fathers, I have solved the mystery of the ages. I have the answer to the question that has never before been properly answered: Who killed Jesus? Yes, yes, that is the question. Who really killed Jesus? A question that you blessed priests—with all due respect—were too stupid to ask. You assumed you knew the answer. Most of you assumed that the Romans killed Jesus. And a few of you assumed that the Jews killed Jesus, which is ignorant bullshit. In Latin, holy fathers, that would be *bullshitus ignoramus*. The truth is simple. My mother killed Jesus. Look no further for your answer. My mother killed Jesus!"

With this, he broke up laughing again. He laughed and he laughed, laughed until tears rolled down his face. Then he cheerfully grabbed a broom and tended to the job of sweeping up the broken beer bottles he had whipped off the table with his belt. He collected the papers that had been swept away in his rage. Every so often, he would repeat his ecclesiastical announcement aloud: "My mother killed Jesus!" This would trigger another round of hearty belly laughing. Finally, the laughing was overtaken by a more serious round of harsh coughing, which brought him down onto the solitary kitchen chair again. He drank from a new beer bottle, coughed again, and finally settled into a spell of quietude.

"That's the answer, Missy," he said reflectively, nodding his head in somber agreement with himself. "Mom killed Jesus. And she tried like hell to kill us, too. Always beatin' on us for somethin'. You more than me, and me more than her precious little Molly. She did beat on me a lot, but don't you worry. Your secret is safe with me. I didn't tell her where you were. Hell, she's dead anyway, and probably not thinking about you a bit. Probably just trying to keep the devil's flames off her backside.

"And that other business, too. Don't you worry. I'll keep quiet about *that* little secret, too. I'll definitely take that one to the grave with me. And you were right not to tell anyone. If Dad had found out, he surely would have killed him and gone to prison. Would have murdered him. Mom, on the other hand, would have done absolutely nothing against her own brother, but Dad would have killed him for messin' with you like that. Hell, I would have killed him myself, if I had been bigger at the time. Too bad. By the time I was grown, he was dead in that damned car accident. Too bad. I never got my chance.

"Imagine. Our own uncle doin' something like that to you. And why the hell did mom ever send you up to his house to baby-sit his kids? Didn't she know he was slimy like that? How could she not know? But then again, she never seemed to have much use for you. She only ever made a fuss about her little pet, Molly. But don't you worry. A promise is a promise. I'll keep your secret forever, Missy."

45

No Time to Waste

Whenever she was at home, Cordelia would go straight to her bedroom to get away from her parents. On her bulletin board was a new quote:

> **"Doubt thou the stars are fire;**
> **Doubt that the sun doth move;**
> **Doubt truth to be a liar;**
> **But never doubt I love."**
> **- Shakespeare**

She didn't want to sit downstairs in the family room with them and fall into the role of the teenage daughter again. She had been a free woman in Montreal, a woman living with her man. She didn't want her mother to ask her what she wanted for dinner. She didn't want her father to ask her about her plans for the evening. She just wanted them to leave her alone so she could read letters from Martin and write back to him.

Other pieces of mail arrived, too, but she ignored them until she had read Martin's latest letter two or three times. After this ritual, she would open the other envelopes that her mother would put in a neat pile on her bed. The first ones she had found when she returned from Montreal had already been opened. She felt exasperated by this. One of them was a tuition bill, so it made sense that her parents would have to open this in order to pay it on time. Still, she felt annoyed. Her mother should have asked her permission during one of their phone calls. Then she remembered the sad tone of her mother's voice during those calls, and she felt sorry for her. But she didn't want to feel sorry for her mother. She wanted to feel the righteous indignation of someone whose mail has been opened without permission. When would it ever be possible to sit in this house and have a feeling of her own without worrying about her mother or her father?

One evening in early August, she sat on her bed after dinner and went through the day's mail. Most of it was junk mail from other colleges that she had applied to. She crumpled them up, one by one, and threw them across the room toward a waste basket by her desk. Half the time, she missed her mark, even though her bedroom was small, and the mail landed on a pile of clothes that she was sorting for college. She tried to imagine what she would be wearing during her first day walking across campus. Not a sweater, of course, since it would be too hot. Jeans and a T-shirt, she imagined. Perhaps a T-shirt with her high school name on it, so people would know where she was from. No, that would be ridiculous. High school was over. Time to grow up and look more mature. She started to think about what she had worn in Montreal, but that made her think of Martin, and it just made her sad.

She went back to her mail on the bed. One envelope had information about her dormitory, which only made her think more about Martin. It was depressing to think about being in a dorm room with a total stranger instead of being with Martin at his apartment in Montreal. Another envelope had an invitation to the various clubs at the college. She was about to throw it on the floor with the others, but she had a better idea. She would join a club, she thought, and that would help her adjust to college at Marist. She tried mightily to cheer herself up and muster a more positive attitude about college, but her efforts were not very successful. She listlessly looked at the last of the mail, but without bothering to open anything. There was nothing from Paris today (via Becky), so what was the point? She could tell by the return addresses what the remaining letters were about: student loan offers, other colleges, a message from the campus churches. She tossed them onto a chair in the room and went to sleep.

She awoke early the next morning and went downstairs to get some coffee. She immediately regretted this, because her father was sitting in the kitchen. Her brother Gabe had already left for his summer basketball camp, so she was alone with her parents. Her father didn't say anything to her, but just the way he looked up from his newspaper made her feel miserable.

"Good morning, Dad," she said.

"Good morning," he said. Then he disappeared behind his newspaper again.

"What's your schedule today, Cordelia?" asked her mother, standing at the sink.

"I told you yesterday, Mom. I have to work at my babysitting job this morning. Then I'm at Albany Med for the afternoon."

"Well, that's a nice full day, dear."

"Yeah. At least I won't be bored." Cordelia added milk and sugar to her coffee and paged through a magazine. She heard her parents talking, but paid little attention to their conversation.

"It's been a while," said her mother. "I suppose we'll get another clue one of these days."

"Maybe not," he said. "Maybe whoever sent them has decided to stop sending them. I don't know. I don't understand any of it."

Her mother stepped away from the sink. "Cordelia, I packed you a lunch."

Cordelia broke away from her magazine article. "Oh, thanks, Mom."

Her mother turned to her father. "Don't give up hope, Dan. You never know."

At that moment, Cordelia tuned into their conversation and thought about her mail upstairs. She put her coffee mug down on the kitchen table.

"Oh, wait a minute!" she said out loud.

"What's wrong, Cordelia?" her mother asked.

"Wait!" she said. She ran up the stairs to her bedroom. She pawed through the unopened mail sitting on her bedroom chair until she found what she was looking for. As she remembered it in her mind, one of the envelopes had no return address on it. It was addressed to "Ms. Cordelia Wunsch" in a handwriting she had seen someplace before. She could hear her parents calling to her from downstairs. "Just a minute!" she yelled. The envelope had an Alaska postmark, and it was marked "Express Mail." She ripped it open and pulled out a wrinkled stub of paper with an address on it.

Upstate Medical Center
750 East Adams Street
Syracuse, NY 13210

Just beneath the address was a phone number and a brief message:

No time to waste!

She went running back downstairs with the letter in hand.

"Dad! Dad! I know where Grandma is!"

"What are you talking about?" her father asked.

"She's in a hospital in Syracuse!"

She handed him the note and the envelope, and he studied them both.

"Damn," he said. "It's the same handwriting. That's for sure. And the Alaska postmark."

"But this one was sent to you?" Cordelia's mother asked.

"Right," said Cordelia. "And it was sent via Express Mail. Somebody's trying to tell us to get there fast. 'No time to waste.' She must be there right now, Dad."

Her father began to pace back and forth in the kitchen with the letter in his hand. He stopped by the stove, staring at the paper.

"She's right, Dan," said her mother. "I think they're trying to tell you to get over there."

"So, what should I do?" he asked.

"Let me call the hospital," said her mother. "You just sit down and finish your coffee."

Cordelia's father immediately sat back down and picked up his coffee cup. She was surprised to see her mother taking charge of the situation, and more surprised at how easily her father allowed this to happen. He looked relieved to have her mother's help.

"Okay, great," he said. "Thanks, Abby."

Her mother took the paper from him and went to the phone. They heard her asking about a room number for Catherine Wunsch. There was a pause. Then: "Oh, don't tell me! Well, how soon do you expect everything to be back in order? I see. Well, thanks anyway." Her mother put the phone back in its receiver and sat down at the breakfast table. "They're having problems with their computer system, and she has no way to look up your mother's name. They have no idea when the computers will be working again."

They all sat together at the kitchen table now.

"What should I do?" asked her father, looking quite lost and docile.

"Just go!" said her mother. "The note says there's no time to waste. Just get in the car and go, Dan. You can be there in three hours or less. It might be your last chance to see her."

"But I was going to pick up Gabe at basketball camp," he said.

"I can pick up Gabe," said her mother. "You just go."

"I want to come with you," said Cordelia to her father. "I want to meet my grandma, but I can't cancel on my babysitting this morning. Can you wait till this afternoon? I could easily cancel on Albany Med."

"Your father needs to leave right away," said her mother with surprising authority.

"You're not likely to miss anything," said her father. "These clues never amount to anything, anyway. And if I find her at the hospital in Syracuse, I'll call home and let you both know right away."

Cordelia sighed. "Okay, but you have to call *right away*."

"Okay, everybody. Listen up," said her mother, her voice coming out in a lower pitch than usual, her tone firm and confidant. "Dan, you go pack an overnight bag for your trip to Syracuse. You call me as soon as you know anything. Cordelia, you call Becky and ask if she might want to take a road trip to Syracuse this afternoon, just in case. I'll drive you over to your babysitting job. Go get ready. It's only a few hours of work. If your father finds your grandmother, he'll let us know and you can cancel your afternoon at the hospital. I'll be here at home to answer the phone and relay any news about your grandmother. Now both of you, go!"

Without another word, Cordelia and her father got up and left the breakfast table to do as they were told.

46

Syracuse

Dan felt excited for the first half-hour or so of his trip. He turned on the car radio and imagined a happy, animated conversation between the two of them, filled with news he would give her about his life as an adult. And she would sit there in her hospital bed, beaming with pride about her son, the English professor. But after another hour-long stretch of Interstate 90, his mood began to collapse. What if he was rushing out to Syracuse to find that his aging mother was critically ill, unconscious, and breathing only with the help of a respirator? Maybe there would be no conversation at all. What was the point of going to Syracuse? Still, he had to see her, no matter what shape she was in. After thirty years, he had to see her.

It occurred to him, not for the first time, that his life was different from other people's lives. Most people grow up having mothers in their lives. They call their mothers, they visit their mothers, they bring their children to visit on holidays. All through his adult years, when people asked about his parents, he had a well-rehearsed answer. *My father died years ago.* And his mother? *We're not in touch.* That was his laconic answer, and no one seemed eager to press him for details. The message he wanted to give the listener was that there had been a mutual agreement to stop all contact. But now, if he saw her again—*when* he saw her again—it would reawaken the painful reality of the abandonment.

Interstate 90 took him westward, running parallel to the Mohawk River. Sometimes he could see the river to his right, but at other times the road veered away and he couldn't see the water. Then it would reappear. He had an urge to pull the car off to the side of the road and sit by the river for a while, but that might be foolish. No time to waste. He had to get to see his mother.

But what would he want to say to her? He once heard a couple of colleagues talking at work, and one of them posed a question to the other. If you knew that a parent of yours was about to die today, and you had one last chance to say something to that parent, what would you say? Apparently, this question was asked on some silly television talk show, and his colleagues found it interesting. But what would he say? *Mom, I love you.* Too trite and sentimental. *Mom, I forgive you.* No, that made no sense. Forgive her for what? He didn't even know why she left, so how could he forgive her? *Mom, my daughter Cordelia ran away from home this summer.* Oddly enough, that was what he wanted to tell her. And he wanted his mother to comfort him over this terrible, dreadful experience he had suffered. But why would he turn to his mother, who had also run away from home? How could she possibly be comforting? But that was all he could think of saying, whether it made sense or not.

When Dan saw the sign for the Syracuse exit, he was surprised that he had arrived. Lost in thought, he hadn't even noticed the last part of the trip. He got off the highway and stopped at a gas station to get directions to Upstate Medical Center. By the time he found the hospital parking lot, he caught himself silently praying. *Please, God, let her be here.*

When he got to the hospital, he went straight to the information desk and asked for his mother's room number, hoping that the computers were up and running again. A pleasant young woman at the desk told him that her computer was back in action. However, she searched her screen and shook her head.

"I'm sorry, sir, but there is no one here by that name."

"There must be some mistake," he said. "I'm sure that she's here."

"I'm sorry, sir," repeated the woman.

"She *must* be here," said Dan. He reached into his pocket and took out the stub of paper with the hospital address on it. He held it out for the woman to read.

"That's our address, sir, but I see no listing for your mother. I'm sorry." The young woman seemed very kind and patient.

Dan gave his mother's birthdate, but that didn't change the woman's reply. He slowly, carefully spelled *Wunsch* to no avail.

"Then maybe she was recently discharged?" he asked.

"No, sir," said the woman. "I see no record of her being here at all."

Dan walked away from the information desk and shoved the piece of paper back into his pocket. He was tired from the drive and deflated by the futile effort. He simply couldn't understand what was happening. Most of the other clues had some merit to them; they pointed him to the trail of his mother, even if the trail was decades old. How could this clue be any different? He wanted to shoot whoever was sending the clues.

He called Abby and gave her the news.

"I'm so sorry, Dan," said Abby. She sounded disappointed, too.

"I don't get it," he said. "She's not here, and she never was here. So why the clue?"

"I don't understand either," said Abby. They talked for another few minutes. She was obviously trying to sound encouraging, but he could tell that she, too, was feeling pretty pessimistic about the whole search. He told her that he was going to stop for a cup of coffee and then head home. He walked toward the hospital doors but stopped before going outside. He had an idea. He headed back to the information desk and spoke to the young woman again.

"Would you mind searching for my mother under a different name?"

The woman at the desk looked puzzled by the request, but she seemed willing to oblige him again.

"If you could try it this way, I'd really appreciate it," he said.

The woman looked again on her computer screen. "Oh, there she is!" she said, looking truly pleased. "Let me write down the room number for you."

"Thank you so much!" Dan said. He took the piece of paper from her and went jogging down the hall to the elevators she pointed to. Once he got on the elevator, he felt his heart pounding. He had wondered what he would say when he found her, but now he couldn't think of a single word.

He got off the elevator and turned right, as the woman at the information desk had told him to do. He heard a commotion ahead of him. Someone was talking to the nurses at the nursing desk, and the voice was growing louder. At first, he saw only a group of several nurses, and he couldn't see who was speaking. He walked ahead and stopped just a few yards from the group.

"I want to see my baby!" said a woman's voice.

"You're on the wrong floor, dear," replied a nurse. "This is not the floor where the newborns are kept."

"I want to see my baby!" said the voice.

Dan came closer to the scene. A young woman, barely out of her teens, was standing at the center of the group of nurses. She was barefoot and dressed in hospital gown. Her gown had fallen open in the back, exposing a large tattoo on her left buttock: *Daddy's Little Girl*.

The nurse who spoke to her was an older woman. She tried to calm the young mother down. "Let me call the maternity floor and see where your baby is, honey."

"Well, fine!" snorted the barefoot young woman.

The nurse spoke on the phone for a minute or two. "Okay, I see. Yes, I'll tell her. Thanks." As she talked, Dan noticed that a second nurse—farther from the patient, but closer to him — picked up a phone and talked with her hand held up in front of her mouth, as if she didn't want to be overheard by the angry woman. He heard her asking the operator for the security guards.

"Well," said the young mother, "where's my baby?"

"Your baby wasn't breathing easily when the nurse checked him a little while ago," said the older nurse, "so they've taken him over to the Neonatal Intensive Care Unit. Remember? They told you where he was going. You can see him as soon as the doctors examine him and decide what to do to help him."

The young mother exploded. "That's bullshit! There's nothin' wrong with my baby! He's fine and I'm takin' him home!"

"Now honey," the nurse said, "I know you're upset, but you just have to stay calm. You'll see your baby as soon as they're done." The young woman continued to make her demands, and the nurse continued to make every effort to calm her. After a couple minutes of this interaction, three of the hospital's security guards came down the hall and stepped in front of Dan to confront the woman. She became only more agitated.

"Why are these clowns here? What's goin' on? You people don't know what you're doin'! I'm takin' my baby and goin' home!" She looked at the three young men in uniform with a wild look, as if she might have to defend herself against them in a hand-to-hand, life-and-death struggle.

One of the young men said, "Come on, ma'am, you have to go back to your room now."

She looked at the three men, then at the nurse, then back at the men. Dan was standing beside a large cart with medical equipment on it. Suddenly, the woman charged at the security guards, pushing between them and heading toward Dan and the elevator beyond. There wasn't much room between Dan and the medical cart, so the young mother ran right into him, pushing him hard to get past him. Knocked off balance, he staggered to right himself but was bumped again, this time by one of the security guards. Dan fell to the floor as they raced past him.

"Are you all right, sir?" said one of the nurses, rushing over to where he lay on the floor. "Oh, my God, I'm so sorry, sir!"

"I'm fine, I'm fine," he said, picking himself up off the floor. "Really, I'm fine." He saw the security guards disappear around a corner, chasing the woman. "I'm just trying to visit my mother," he said, getting to his feet. He handed the nurse his paper with the room number on it, and he gave her the name.

"Oh, yes, she was here. She was my patient, and a sweet old lady she was. But she left a few days ago."

Dan was crushed. "But that's impossible!" he said in a pleading tone. "The woman at your information desk downstairs told me that she's here."

"She was," said the nurse, "but she left. We've been having some computer problems, so the patient list hasn't been updated properly. Your mother was in the room right here," she said, pointing to the nearest patient room, "but she's gone now. She signed out A.M.A.—against medical advice. And she is so terribly sick. She really should have stayed. The doctor said she doesn't have much time left. She shouldn't have left, but we have no legal right to keep her in the hospital against her will. I'm so sorry, sir."

Dan peered into the room that the nurse pointed to. He saw an elderly man struggling to get a spoonful of food to his mouth without spilling any.

"Do you know where my mother is staying?" he asked. "She must have given you an address."

"Sorry, but she didn't." The nurse looked uncomfortable and apologetic. "I think she's homeless."

"Homeless," Dan repeatedly flatly.

"Yes, sir."

Dan mumbled a thank-you and walked back to the elevators. He went downstairs and headed toward the pay phones on the first floor, but he couldn't bring himself to call Abby again. Instead, he went to the hospital cafeteria and bought a cup of coffee. He sat down by himself to think. His mother had been here a few days ago. He had just missed her! But she had signed herself out of the hospital. She was homeless and wandering the streets, very ill. She didn't have much time left. What was he supposed to do? Call the police? They surely had more to do than go looking for one homeless old lady? He could call Abby, but what could she suggest? He could go down to the hospital emergency room and see if his mother got re-admitted, but how long would he stand around and wait for that to happen? It was just as likely that she would come wandering into the cafeteria to get a bite to eat. Yes, he thought, that was as likely as anything. He would just sit for a while and see if his mother came walking into the hospital cafeteria.

He drank a cup of coffee. He bought a newspaper and read it cover to cover, glancing up now and then to check for new diners in the cafeteria. He had a second cup of coffee, followed by another newspaper. He kept his vigil in the cafeteria for a couple of hours, until he finally surrendered and headed for the pay phones to call Abby again with an unhappy update.

47

The Promise

Cordelia spent the morning in the neighbor's finished base-ment with the children she watched, but her thoughts were about her grandmother in a Syracuse hospital. She watched the clock and calculated how close to Syracuse her father was at any given time. It was only two and a half hours to get there, but the time seemed to drag. She called her mother a couple of times, only to be reminded that her father could not possibly have ar-rived yet, and no, he had not called home yet. Finally, on the third call, her mother had news for her, but it wasn't good news at all. Her grandmother was not at the hospital in Syracuse, nor had she ever been a patient there.

When parents arrived to pick up their children, they all stopped to talk with Cordelia. Her father's search for her grand-mother had been a hot topic of conversation ever since the first clue arrived in the mail, and every parent had a theory about the source of the clues. When Cordelia had arrived at the house that morning and told them about the Syracuse trip, they all joined her in her excitement. Now they were all kindly sympathetic about the disappointing news coming from her mother. She thanked them and took a bus into Albany to do her volunteer work at the hospital.

At Albany Medical Center, she went about her chores without much enthusiasm until she heard that Mrs. Rose had taken a fall. She made a quick path to that room and found the old woman in bed talking with a young nurse from the Philippines.

"Mrs. Rose decided to get up and use the bathroom without letting us know," said the nurse in a tone that was playfully scolding. "She's just lucky she didn't get hurt."

The old woman smiled at Cordelia and addressed the nurse. "I was just practicing my dancing steps so Dee and I can go out on the town later," she said.

"Just as I thought," said Cordelia. The nurse left the room, and Cordelia pulled a chair up to the bedside.

"They treat me like I'm a child around here," complained Mrs. Rose. "Do they really think I'm going to call them every time I want to use the bathroom?"

"But we're just trying to take good care of you," said Cordelia. "And you did fall, you know."

"I'm fine," said Mrs. Rose, sitting up straighter in the bed. She had a way of sitting and walking, a certain posture and carriage that Cordelia saw as classy and worthy of respect, even in her current hapless circumstances. The old woman picked up a cup of tea and took a sip. Cordelia imagined her lifting a cup of tea and sipping it with great dignity at a royal dinner for the queen of England.

"So, you'll be leaving for college soon," said Mrs. Rose, putting the cup down.

"Yes," said Cordelia. "I leave in a month."

"Well, that's nice." Mrs. Rose took another drink of her tea. "But I hear there's a lot of drinking on campus these days. Do you drink alcohol, Dee?"

Cordelia was taken off guard by the question. She wanted to say no, but found it impossible to lie outright. "Well, sometimes I drink a little."

Mrs. Rose raised her eyebrows. "A little?"

Cordelia found herself looking at the floor. "Well, to be perfectly honest, it's sometimes more than a little."

"Dee, listen to me. The doctors tell me that I've ruined my health by drinking. Completely ruined it. I was young and pretty like you once upon a time, and I don't want you to wind up like me, sitting here in this hospital bed. You really should stay away from alcohol, you know."

Without looking up, Cordelia quickly replied, "I will, Mrs. Rose."

"Now, I want you to look at me," said the old woman.

Cordelia looked up.

"Dee, this is important. I don't want you to ruin your life like I've done. I want you to promise me that you won't drink."

Cordelia sat speechless.

"Promise me, Dee."

"I promise."

"Promise me that you won't drink. Say it."

Cordelia thought to herself that this was exactly what she had needed all along. She didn't need her mother to ignore her drinking. She didn't need her father to yell at her hysterically. She didn't need Martin to be so passive and silent. She just needed this, exactly this. How odd that it was coming from Mrs. Rose, an old woman in the hospital whom she had only met a couple of days ago. "Okay, Mrs. Rose. I promise you that I won't drink. I really do promise." And she meant it. How strange, she thought, that this sickly old woman had drawn from her a vow that she gave so earnestly.

"Good," said the old woman. "Now I won't have to worry about you. And how exciting that you're going off to college! Your parents will be sad, of course, but how exciting for you!"

"Well, my mom will be sad. I think my dad will probably celebrate. He'll be glad to get rid of me."

"Oh, no! I can't believe that. How could he be glad to see his little girl leave home? And such a sweet girl you are."

"Thank you," said Cordelia, "but I don't think he sees me that way. Not at all. He never seems happy with me. During this past school year, he wouldn't let up on me. He always looks for things to criticize."

"Well, how sad! It must have been hard to grow up with a father like that," said Mrs. Rose.

"He wasn't always like this, though," said Cordelia. "That's the really sad part of the whole thing. He was the best dad in the world when I was little. We used to go everywhere together. He would read stories to me every night. It was great. But the last couple of years, as I got a little older, he turned against me."

"So, you had him, but you lost him."

"Exactly!" said Cordelia. "I had him, but I lost him."

Mrs. Rose said, "I lost my father, too, Dee. I really lost him, permanently, when I was still a girl. But I carry the good memories of him with me always, and that helps. And maybe someday you'll carry good memories of your father."

"I suppose," said Cordelia skeptically. "Maybe someday. But right now, all I can think about is how nasty he is to me."

"I understand, dear, but things might look quite a bit different as the years go by."

At that moment, a nurse stuck her head in the doorway. "Anything I can get you, Mrs. Rose?"

"Yes," said the old woman, smiling. "You can tell the doctors to finish up their business and get me out of here. I need to go to Albany."

The nurse smiled. "You're in Albany, Mrs. Rose. This is Albany Medical Center." The nurse disappeared down the hallway.

Mrs. Rose turned to Cordelia, looking perplexed. "I'm in Albany now?"

"Yes, this is Albany, Mrs. Rose. When you were admitted here, you were very confused, and you didn't know where you were. Now you're in Albany, New York."

"Oh! Well, that's wonderful! I have arrived."

Cordelia thought she looked troubled, though, even as she declared herself happy.

"So, why did you come to Albany?" Cordelia asked.

Mrs. Rose made no answer and didn't seem to hear the question. She sat staring straight ahead with a blank look in her eyes.

"Mrs. Rose? Are you all right?"

"Yes, yes. I'm fine, dear."

The nurse returned and asked Cordelia to help take a patient to another floor.

"I'll check back with you as soon as I can, Mrs. Rose."

"Okay, Dee," said the old woman, looking preoccupied and distant.

48

A Familiar Face

Cordelia went off to do her next task. She thought briefly about Mrs. Rose, but then her thoughts turned to her father. He would be coming home in a bad mood, *another* bad mood, and she dreaded seeing him. She felt sorry for him, too, of course. She could easily imagine his excitement as he arrived at the hospital in Syracuse with the clue in his hand. And she could see the painful disappointment in his face when he found out that the trip was all a waste.

About an hour later, Cordelia returned to Mrs. Rose's room and stopped in the doorway. The bed was empty. The door to the little private bathroom was open, and the bathroom was also empty. She went down the hall until she found the young Filipino nurse assigned to Mrs. Rose.

"Oh, I think she must have gone down to the cafeteria," said the nurse. "She's got a bit of the devil in her, you know," she added, smiling. "We all got involved in an emergency with another patient down the hall, and when we finished with that, she had left her room. We figure she sneaked out to the cafeteria against orders, so we've called the security guys to look for her there.

The good news is that they finally found her belongings in the Emergency Room and brought them up to her in a plastic bag. And a second bag of her stuff arrived right after she disappeared."

Cordelia had a bad feeling about this. She went into Mrs. Rose's room and looked around. As she suspected, there was nothing left—not a hairbrush, not a single article of clothing, nothing. She ran back out to the hallway.

"Where is that second bag of belongings?" she asked. The nurse pointed to the far corner behind the long countertop of the nursing desk.

Cordelia imagined old Mrs. Rose wandering the streets until she fell down and died all alone in a strange city. She went behind the nursing desk and grabbed the plastic bag that was stuffed with the old lady's possessions. She ran to the elevator. After waiting for just a few impatient seconds, she went to the stairway and ran down several flights of stairs to the main entrance. She exited the building and stood under the white pillars of the old entrance to the hospital.

Once outside, she looked up at the overcast sky, as if to glean some direction from it. There was only an impenetrable mass of gray cloud cover. She stood by the tall, white pillars of the hospital entrance for a moment, wondering which way to go. On an instinct, she turned left and went running down the street. It wasn't long before she saw her in the distance: a white-haired, elderly woman with aristocratically upright posture, progressing very slowly down New Scotland Avenue. Cordelia ran to catch her.

"Mrs. Rose! Mrs. Rose!"

The old woman turned around and squinted in her direction.

"Mrs. Rose! It's me! It's Dee!" She came face to face with the woman and impulsively took her by the hand. "Mrs. Rose, you can't leave the hospital like this. You're really sick. You need to come back with me and let the doctors and nurses take care of you."

"Dee, you're a sweet girl, but I can't go back there. I'm sorry. I have to go." She looked very nervous and agitated.

"But you're sick," repeated Cordelia. "You can't just wander the streets."

"Dee, I have to get to the bus station. I can't stay here."

"But I thought you wanted to come to Albany," said Cordelia. "I don't understand."

"I can't. I just can't do it." Mrs. Rose pulled her hand away from Cordelia's hand and started to cross the street as the traffic light turned green. Cordelia crossed with her. When they got to the other side of the street, they were at the entrance to Washington Park.

"Which way is the bus station from here, Dee?"

"This way," Cordelia said. "We go right into the park." She had no idea where the Albany bus station was, but she was pretty sure that going through the park was not the right way to get there. They walked together for a few minutes, passing a small pond in the park. The traffic noise from the road faded out as they got a little farther along.

"Please, Mrs. Rose, you really must go back to the hospital with me."

"I'm fine, Dee. I just have to get to the bus station."

Cordelia was still carrying the plastic bag of the woman's personal belongings. "Besides, you didn't even say goodbye to me, Mrs. Rose. You just left."

Mrs. Rose stopped and turned to Cordelia. "I'm sorry, dear. I wanted to talk to you, but I knew that you would try to keep me in the hospital."

"You just left," said Cordelia again, a bit surprised to realize how hurt she felt.

"I am sorry," said Mrs. Rose. "I really am sorry. I've enjoyed our little chats so much, Dee. You have no idea how much." She turned and started walking farther along into the park.

Cordelia stood where she was and held up the plastic bag she was carrying. "They found the rest of your belongings in the Emergency Room," she called.

Mrs. Rose stopped and turned around. "Oh, that's wonderful! I hope they found my glasses."

Cordelia approached and handed her the bag, and Mrs. Rose sat down on a bench in the park. Cordelia took a seat beside her. Mrs. Rose started to open the bag and examine its contents.

"I do hope they have my glasses in here." The old woman dug into the plastic bag and started pulling out a few items of clothing. She looked a bit less frantic, but still quite uneasy. "Now, where are my glasses? I hope they haven't lost them." She pulled out a sweater and a couple of skirts. "My glasses! They found my glasses!"

Cordelia watched Mrs. Rose putting on her glasses. She put them on, took them off to clean them with a stained handkerchief, adjusted them behind her ears, and then looked directly at Cordelia. Her face quickly lost its look of anxiety and reconfigured itself into an expression of amazement. She glanced at the name tag on Cordelia's blouse.

"Good Lord!" she exclaimed.

They sat looking at each other in silence. Mrs. Rose seemed to be studying Cordelia's face.

"This is Albany, you said. Right?" the woman asked.

"Yes, this is Albany."

Mrs. Rose pointed to Cordelia's name tag. "And your name is actually Cordelia? Not Dee? *Cordelia?*"

"Yes. I'm Cordelia." They sat again without saying anything, until Cordelia suddenly understood that the look in Mrs. Rose's face was a look of recognition. It took another minute before Cordelia could find the courage to speak her mind. "And your name isn't really Mrs. Rose, is it?"

The old woman began to cram things back into the plastic bag. Her hands were shaking, and she looked frantic again. "I can't! I can't stay here. I have to go." In her haste, she dropped several articles of clothing onto the ground: a sock, a blouse, a purple scarf.

Cordelia picked up the purple scarf and held it out to her. "Your real name is Kate Wunsch, isn't it?"

The old woman looked up at Cordelia for a moment. Her eyes pleaded for mercy. "I can't! I can't! I'm so sorry, but I can't do this."

"This is so crazy! You're actually my grandma!"

"Please stop! I can't do this. I have to go." The woman stuffed the purple scarf back into the bag and slid herself forward on the bench to get up.

Cordelia put her hand firmly on the old woman's arm to prevent her from standing. "No, Grandma, you can't go. You can't leave us again. You're going to stay here with us now."

49

An Unlikely Story

Cordelia sat at the nursing desk, barely able to get her words out quickly enough on the phone. "Dad! Dad! I found her! I found Grandma!"

Her father sounded puzzled. "That's what your mother just told me on the phone. She said to call you right away, but I don't understand, Cordelia."

"I found her! I found your mom!"

"I don't understand," he said again. "I'm here at the hospital in Syracuse, and she was just here until a few days ago."

"She's not in Syracuse, Dad. She's right here at Albany Medical Center!"

"I don't get it. That's a big hospital. How could you just happen to find her?"

The words came rushing out of her in an excited jumble. She told her father the story of the old woman who was admitted from the Emergency Room after hitting her head, so that she didn't even know what city she was in. She told him about how they would sit and talk together, and about the escape from the hospital and chasing her all the way to Washington Park with the bag of clothing that was finally returned, and about the glasses and the nametag and the kid-from-high-school-who-called-her-Dee so that her grandma never knew who she was talking to until she put on her glasses and saw her face and her name tag and then her-grandma-knew-and-she-knew-and-they-both-knew!

"Wait, wait! Slow down, Cordelia. I can't follow all this."

"Sorry, Dad, but that's what happened. I'm just trying to tell you what happened." Cordelia made herself stop talking for a moment. She tapped her foot restlessly, waiting for her father to speak again.

"Cordelia, I'm not sure you have the right person. Your grandmother's not using her real name any more."

"Right!" said Cordelia. "She calls herself Mrs. Rose. Catherine Rose."

There was a pause on the other end of the phone. "I'll be damned," he said. "It must be her."

"It's her, Dad! I couldn't believe it! She was trying to run away to the bus station, but I stopped her. After we sat in the park for a while, she finally admitted who she is. She told me that she traveled all the way across the country to see you, but then she got scared at the last minute. I think she's still pretty scared to see you." A longer pause ensued. "Dad, are you still there?"

"Well, I'll be damned," said her father again. "You found her. You found her, Cordelia."

Cordelia smiled proudly. "Right! It's her! But you and Mom and Gabe have to come see her right away because she's really, really sick, and the doctors don't think she has long to live. Her liver is all destroyed from drinking, and she sleeps a lot. She sits up and talks and acts normal for a few minutes, but then she just falls back to sleep."

"Well, your mom just told me that Gabe got sick to his stomach at basketball camp today. She'll have to stay home with him. But I'll come back from Syracuse right now."

"Okay, fine. I'll give you the room number, so you can write it down."

"All right, just let me get a piece of paper."

Cordelia gave him the room number and made him promise to drive carefully and *hurry!*

For the next hour or so, the old woman—Cordelia's grandmother—slept most of the time. Cordelia sat at her bedside for long stretches of time, hoping that she would live long enough for her father to arrive from Syracuse. Her grandmother's breathing was slow and regular. After a while, Cordelia felt less worried about her dying at any moment. She began to feel bored and restless, and she got up and took short walks in the halls. Sometimes she sat at the nursing station, and she told a couple of the nurses about how old Mrs. Rose was actually her long-lost grandmother. She told them about her father, who was on his way to see the mother whom he hadn't seen in many years. The nurses found the story fascinating, naturally. Over the next hour, she heard them talking about the volunteer girl on the ward who had found, quite by accident, the grandmother whom she had never met before in her entire life.

One of the nurses decided that the hospital's Public Relations department would love to cover a touching story like this. It would be great publicity for the hospital. Before Cordelia could stop her, the nurse called the PR department, and they agreed immediately to send a reporter to the floor to see the reunion of Cordelia's father and grandmother. The nurse then looked up at Cordelia and smiled, obviously pleased with her contribution to the big reunion. Cordelia politely thanked her, dreading to think about how her father was going to react to all this.

She looked up at the clock on the wall behind the long nursing desk. Syracuse was about two and a half hours away, and she had talked to her father about ninety minutes ago. He wouldn't be arriving for another hour or so. She went downstairs to the cafeteria to get a cold drink. She planned to get the drink and get back upstairs quickly, but she ran into Perry. He had heard the story already, and he wanted to know all about it. She told him about finding her grandmother, but as she talked, she became increasingly worried that her grandmother was going to die alone while she was down in the cafeteria getting a drink. She felt a pang of guilt at her selfishness; did she really need to buy the drink right now? Was she dying of dehydration? But she couldn't cut Perry short and get away from him, either. He seemed so needy and desperate to talk to someone. It seemed unconscionable to deny this poor kid a few minutes of conversation.

"I can't believe it, Dee," Perry said. "You were randomly assigned to take care of this old lady, and she turned out to be your own grandmother?"

"Right," said Cordelia. "I can barely believe it myself. But now I need to get back to her room. I don't think she has much longer to live."

"And your father is coming to see her?"

Cordelia was pulling impatiently on the strap of her purse. "Yeah, he's on his way. I really should get back up there."

Perry was undeterred. "How long has it been since your father saw your grandmother?"

"Years, years. I don't know how long exactly. But I really need to go. Nice talking with you, Perry."

He followed her out of the cafeteria, pecking at her with his questions until they arrived at the elevators. She was relieved to see the elevator doors come together and put a barrier between them. The elevator stopped at every floor while someone got on or off, and she thought she was going to scream at everyone for slowing her down.

When she finally got back to the ward, she rushed into her grandmother's room, fearing the worst. Still breathing and still sleeping. Thank God! Cordelia went back out to the nursing desk, where she heard two nurses talking about her grandmother. They didn't seem to notice her, and she lingered close by, just to hear what was being said. She was shocked by the distorted turns that the story had taken in such a short time. One nurse was telling the other that poor Mrs. Rose had accidentally gotten separated from her son during the Detroit riots in the 1960s. The lost little boy, too young to know his last name or his address, had been raised by another family, but he had been searching for his mother ever since. And Mrs. Rose, poor thing, had turned to alcohol to drown her sorrows when she couldn't find her child.

"But that's not true!" Cordelia exclaimed. "None of that is true!"

The two women turned to look at her, both of them seeming surprised and puzzled.

"You have to stop telling that story. It's completely untrue!" Cordelia felt thoroughly offended that these two women, who knew nothing about the situation, were sitting there and spreading this ridiculous, manufactured gossip about her family. It troubled her all the more because she didn't really know the whole story about what happened to her grandmother all those years ago. She couldn't stand there and let a bunch of strangers invent her family history, lest their fictitious version should become the world's accepted narrative before the truth could even have a chance to be known. "My grandmother just left. That's all. It had nothing to do with the Detroit riots. And my dad wasn't a little boy, he was a teenager. And she just left. And we don't know why. And that's that."

The women looked at her quizzically, as if they found her story far less plausible than the one they had been sharing. Cordelia went back into her grandmother's room and took her seat by the bedside. She decided that she would stay away from the nursing desk and maintain her vigil until her father arrived.

50

A Family Reunion

As Dan made his way down the hall, he saw Cordelia standing there and waving to him. There was a crowd of other people there, too, and this confused him. There were nurses and doctors and other people in hospital uniforms, and he couldn't understand why they were all standing there with Cordelia. She ran ahead to meet him. She started to explain about the nurse who called the Public Relations department, but he barely comprehended what she was saying. He was scanning the crowd of people in the hallway to see if he recognized his mother among the others.

Cordelia led him to the entrance of a patient room, but a tall, thin young man stepped into his path and introduced himself. He represented the Albany Medical Center newsletter, and he wondered if he could ask a few questions. How long had it been since Dan had seen his mother? How old was he when they were separated? Had he heard from her over the years? What was his reaction when he learned that Cordelia had found her? Dan absentmindedly offered a few very brief answers to the questions, but he was focused on trying to see into the room. A stream of nurses was trickling in through the doorway, and he could see them lining up around the perimeter of the room. He could see the foot of a hospital bed, but he still couldn't see who was in the bed because there was always someone in the way.

Cordelia interrupted the young man who was trying to do the interview. She took Dan by the arm and led him into the room. She stepped ahead of him and took one of the two empty chairs near the bed. Around the room were at least ten nurses standing against the walls. In the bed was an old woman who was sitting up wide-eyed and alert, but Dan could see that she was obviously quite ill. She looked terribly malnourished, and her skin had a yellowish hue. Her appearance was cruelly highlighted by the overhead light in the room. Even her eyes looked yellow. Still, Dan knew this old woman to be his mother from the first moment he saw her. The body was gaunt and frail, but something about her proud, erect posture sitting in the bed told him it was her. The hair was a tangled mass of pure white, but thick enough to remind him of the neatly brushed, thick red hair of the woman who had raised him. The eyes were tired and pathetic, yellow where they should be white, but they were still his mother's blue eyes. There were freckles on her face and arms. They were sparse compared to the freckles he remembered, but they were freckles nonetheless. There was apprehension in her eyes, too, and this was also familiar to him. She obviously knew him on sight. She reached out her arms to him.

He walked over to the bed and bent down to hug her. She wrapped her arms tightly around his neck, and he mechanically patted her bony back and then stood up again. He looked at Cordelia and saw that she was wiping tears from her face. He glanced around the room and saw that every nurse—every single one of them—was wiping tears away.

His mother spoke first. "Hi, Danny. It's really you!"

He said nothing. This was the moment he had been waiting for all these years, but it was all wrong. Sure, he recognized her as his mother, but she was also *not* his mother. She was some sickly old woman sitting in a hospital bed. All these years, he had dreamed about a dramatic moment, an overwhelmingly emotional moment, but this was a strange, empty moment of numbness. In his fantasy, there was always a young, vibrant, red-headed mom running down the corridors of an airport to throw her arms around him and cry tears of relief. He realized his folly. He had held onto a frozen image of her as she looked when she left in 1967: a forty-year-old woman, still beautiful and energetic, with a light step and a lively sense of humor. He knew that she would have aged, of course, but her aging was only an idea in his head, a concept that never had the slightest effect upon his mental picture of her.

His mother spoke again. "How are you, Danny? How are you?"

How was he? he asked himself. He felt confused and disoriented. Nothing in that room made any sense to him. The crowd of people in the room didn't match his reunion fantasies, which always involved only him and his mother. And here was his mother, but in a new version that bore the merciless signs of time and sickness.

So, how was he? He felt exhausted from the day. The two-and-a-half-hour drive to Syracuse, the chaos in the hospital there, the rush of hope followed by the crushing disappointment, the drive back with a second round of hope—all this had drained him. Nothing around him felt quite real now. In fact, he was starting to feel light-headed. In order to steady himself, he leaned on the back of the empty chair in front of him. He looked at his mother's desperate, yearning, frightened eyes, and he looked at Cordelia. His daughter was looking at him with an expression that implored him to answer his mother's question. What was the question? Oh, yes. *How are you, Danny?*

For a moment, his mind simply shut out everything around him. He heard his own words land heavily in the silence of the room.

"I'm hungry."

No one spoke. He looked around the room at the ring of nurses, then at Cordelia, then at his mother. They all looked blankly at him.

"My dad's just tired, Grandma," said Cordelia. "He traveled from Syracuse to get here." She gestured toward the chair he was leaning on. "Here, Dad. Come sit down."

He looked at the chair and then at his daughter. He could barely understand what she wanted him to do, but he could see that she looked worried. He knew that he was messing things up, and he struggled to fix it. He was supposed to say something else. Everyone in the room seemed to be waiting for him to say something else.

"I haven't seen my mother in thirty years," he said, glancing around at the nurses. A few of them nodded. He looked at Cordelia and he saw that she wanted more. He was supposed to say more. "I . . . I'm at a loss for words. . . It's been such a long time. There are no words to express how I feel right now."

He looked at Cordelia again to see if these words were better. She was smiling at him, but her smile seemed strained. He was still messing it up. But what else could he say? The words that came to mind would never do. *Why did you leave us? How could you do that to us? What in the world were you thinking? You should have just killed me before you left. You ruined my life.* But no. No, no, no.

These words would never do. He struggled for other things to say. What should one say in such a situation? He looked down at the sickly old woman in the bed. Her skin was yellow, like a faded old parchment document in a museum. She reached out and took his hand, gazing up at him with longing eyes. He looked at Cordelia, who seemed so worried and so kind. She was such a kindhearted child, he thought, and she had always been that way. He tried to think of better words, if only for Cordelia's sake.

"Welcome home, Mom." Maybe that would be better. He looked around the room. One of the nurses clapped tentatively, and then they all clapped. They clapped and clapped, and then they were wiping the tears again. All he could think about was how he was telling a lie. Albany was never his mother's home; Detroit was her home. He was telling a lie, but it seemed to make everything better. Cordelia was smiling a genuine smile at him now, so this must be better.

The nurses slowly filed out of the room. A couple of them patted him on the shoulder as they passed by. Their hands felt good to him, soft, warm hands, not old and cold and bony like his mother's hands. He wished they would come back and pat his shoulder again.

When everyone had left the room, his mother spoke again.

"Danny, come sit by me and tell me all about yourself and your family." But then she started to cough, and she couldn't speak any more. Cordelia gave her the handkerchief that was lying in her lap. The old woman held it to her mouth and coughed.

"Dad, pour Grandma a glass of water."

He reached over to the little bedside table and poured water from a pitcher into a glass. He felt grateful to have a task to do, a simple task that he could readily understand and complete. He gave the water to his mother, and she drank.

51

The Source of Clues

The family sat together in the old woman's room, their chairs placed on either side of the hospital bed. It was a hot, humid day in August, and he wondered why the air conditioning wasn't working well. Then he realized that they were in the older part of the hospital. The room was uncomfortably warm, and he kept thinking that all these people crammed into a small hospital room were not making things any better. He smelled disinfectant in the air, which only increased his desire to get out of the hospital and be someplace else with fresh, cool air.

The patient dozed off and on. Dan's wife Abby was there, along with their kids, Cordelia and Gabe. Aunt Molly, his mother's sister, had just arrived from Tucson. Other family members would be arriving over the next couple of days. There was the necessary medical talk for the first half-hour or so. Dan answered questions from Aunt Molly about what the doctor had told him. Yes, her condition was serious. Yes, it was definitely related to the alcohol. Yes, her time was short, very short. Cordelia chimed in when he forgot some detail about her grandmother's condition, because she had been with him when the doctor spoke with him.

Next, there was the family catch-up talk, which Dan always found a bit boring. Molly's grandson was graduating college in Arizona. Cordelia was leaving for college in a few weeks. Dan's sister Sarah was still at home in Detroit with her husband, who was recovering from hernia surgery. Her kids were doing well in high school.

Then there was a long silence, and they all sat together in the room. They were waiting for the old woman to die, Dan thought to himself. Once upon a time, she was a mother. Not just a mother, but also a wife, a sister, and a sister-in-law; she could have been a grandmother had she stayed put in her life. But now she was a sick old lady, and they were all sitting there waiting for her to die. He wasn't going to have the conversation that he had imagined all these years.

It was Aunt Molly who brought up the question. "Dan, how did you find out that your mother was here?"

He glanced at his mother lying asleep in the bed. She looked so frail and ill. All these years of waiting to see her again, and this is what he got: the chance to sit at the bedside of a dying woman who was unconscious.

"Well, it started with another clue," he said. He didn't need to explain what he meant, as he had discussed all the mysterious mailings with everyone over the past few months. Each time one of the clues arrived in the mail, he would call his sister Sarah in Detroit, then his Aunt Molly in Tucson, and finally his Uncle Jack in California. He wanted them all to know about the new clue, and he hoped each time that the newest evidence would trigger some connection in someone's mind and help solve the case. It was always another round of disappointments. "There was one last clue."

"But the clues never led anywhere before," said Aunt Molly. "They were always bits and pieces of her past. Old bits that were no help."

"This time it was different," said Dan, looking at his daughter. "First of all, it wasn't addressed to me. It was sent to Cordelia."

Cordelia smiled at Aunt Molly, looking pleased to be part of the story. "Yeah, a clue came addressed to me," she said. "I didn't even open the envelope at first. But then I heard my dad talking to my mom about my grandma, and I remembered the clues he had received. And I figured this must be another one. I opened it up, and there was a little note with the address of a hospital in Syracuse. She must be in Syracuse, I figured." Aunt Molly nodded. "So, I gave the note to my dad."

"But she wasn't in Syracuse," said Aunt Molly. "She was here in Albany."

"Well," said Dan, "she was in the Syracuse hospital for over a week, but then she left and found her way to Albany. And the strange thing is that Cordelia has been working here at Albany Medical Center as a volunteer, and she met her grandmother without knowing who she was."

"Really?" said Aunt Molly.

"Yeah, she didn't even know!" said Gabe.

"Right!" said Cordelia. And she repeated the story of the boy who called her Dee, and the patient named Mrs. Rose who was missing her eyeglasses. She told about the moment when Mrs. Rose put on her glasses and saw clearly her face and her name tag, and the two of them realized who was who.

"That's incredible!" said Aunt Molly.

Dan added that the doctor was impressed with the story about Cordelia searching for "Mrs. Rose" after she left the hospital. He told Dan that if not for Cordelia, his mother would probably have collapsed and died on the street. No one in the family ever would have known she was in Albany. Dan saw how proud his daughter looked when he told this part of the story.

"But wait," said Aunt Molly, looking puzzled. "My sister was using a false name. How did you find out that she had been in the hospital in Syracuse?"

Dan smiled. "Catherine Rose," he said. "After I couldn't find her under the name Catherine Wunsch, I called Abby and told her that my mother had never been in that hospital. But then I thought of asking for the room of Catherine Rose."

"Why Catherine Rose?" asked Abby.

"I was about to leave, but then I had a funny little memory about my mother. When we were little, she would love to sing along with records. She would sometimes pick up a lightbulb and pretend she was singing into a microphone. And she told us that she had always dreamed of being a famous singer, and one day she would use the stage name of Catherine Rose—her middle name was Rose."

"I remember that!" said Aunt Molly, wiping a tear from her eye. "I remember that she used to sing like that when *we* were kids. She would hold a light bulb and call herself Catherine Rose."

Dan paused and saw, for just a moment, his young mother singing along to the record player. He wondered if this would be his moment, the emotional moment he had been waiting for. Maybe he would feel very sad or very nostalgic or very happy. There was a glimpse of something, but it vanished in seconds. There was no big moment. He looked up and saw the family waiting for him to continue.

"So, I went back to the information desk and asked for the room number of Catherine Rose." He told the rest of the story while Aunt Molly nodded vigorously to signal her comprehension.

His Aunt Molly and Abby talked this over for the next few minutes, with occasional exclamations from Gabe. They talked about the amazing coincidence of Cordelia taking care of her grandmother in the hospital. They talked about Dan's search for her in Syracuse. And then the talk turned to the clues that Dan had been receiving. Why would this last clue be sent to Cordelia and not to Dan? And who had sent all these clues? Who in Fairbanks, Alaska knew anything about Kate Wunsch?

At that moment, his mother opened her eyes and looked around the room. She looked a bit bewildered by all the faces in the room, as if it was too hard to register them all at once, as if the transition back to consciousness was becoming more and more arduous each time she made the trip.

Cordelia took her hand. "It's okay, Grandma. We're all here to see you. It's just your family. It's all right."

His mother looked at Cordelia, and she visibly relaxed. "There are so many of you people," she said.

"That's all right, Grandma."

Dan's mother did a slow survey of the faces arranged around her. She looked at her sister Molly. She looked at Dan, Abby, and the kids.

"Sarah will be coming in a couple of days," said Dan. Just in case she was having trouble understanding, he added, "My sister Sarah. Your daughter. She'll be here in a couple of days."

His mother nodded. "I know my Sarah," she said to him firmly. She looked again into Cordelia's face. Then she seemed troubled and confused. "Jack," she said. She scanned the faces again, looking puzzled, like a woman doing a tally on a business ledger and coming up with the same deficit: "Jack."

Aunt Molly answered. "Jack's not here, Missy. He's home in California. Couldn't make it out here."

Dan's mother nodded her head thoughtfully, then looked at Cordelia. "I suppose he told you. That's how you found me, right? He must have told you I was coming."

"No, Grandma," said Cordelia. "Uncle Jack never told me you were here in Albany. I never even talk to Uncle Jack. I just found you by accident."

Aunt Molly leaned in toward her sister. "What did you just say, Missy?"

Dan's mother shook her head, looking disappointed. "Jack told you all, didn't he? I made him promise not to tell, but he must have told you."

"Jack never told me anything," said Molly. "But he knew? He knew where you were?"

Dan felt his face growing flushed. "Mom, what are you saying? Jack knew where you were?" His mind raced over the clues, the envelopes without a return address, the bizarre phone conversations with Jack, the final message to Cordelia.

His mother shifted her posture in the bed, looking disgruntled. She let go of Cordelia's hand. "I told him not to tell anyone. He promised me."

Everyone looked surprised and puzzled. Dan leaned forward on the edge of his chair. "Jack knew all along? But that's crazy! I talked to him on the phone a couple of times a year—more often lately—and he always claimed that he didn't know a thing."

"I talked to him, too," said Molly, "and he never said a word."

Dan looked back and forth from his mother to his Aunt Molly. "But the postmarks," he said. "The postmarks were all from Fairbanks, Alaska. How does that make any sense?"

His mother made a sour face. "Alaska? Must be that crazy woman he met in the rehab program. She dumped him and ran off to Alaska, but I suspected that he was keeping in touch with her. I told him not to tell anyone where I was. Not even her."

Dan stood up and wanted to speak, but no words came out of his mouth.

"Dan, please sit down," said Abby.

"Jack knew?" he finally said. "That crazy son-of-a-bitch knew?"

"Dan, please!" Abby pleaded.

Before anyone else could speak, Cordelia jumped up and took him by the arm.

"Dad and I are going to the cafeteria to get some coffee. Would anyone like something to eat or drink?" Before they could answer, she steered him out of the room and down the hallway to the elevator.

"I can't believe it," he kept muttering in the elevator. "I just can't believe it."

Once they were on the ground level of the hospital, Cordelia led him through the cafeteria line where they each got a cup of coffee, and she took him to a table in a far corner, away from other people.

"He knew where she was all these years. I would call him looking for information, and he knew all along."

"Dad," said Cordelia firmly, "your Uncle Jack is mentally ill. You told me yourself that he's really paranoid. You can't blame a mentally ill person."

He ignored her comment. "I would call him after every clue arrived and ask him if he could make any sense of it. I would plead with him to tell me something if he knew anything at all. And he lied every time. He just lied to me."

"But Dad, Grandma made him promise not to tell. He was only trying to do what his sister asked him to do. And he's not right in the head." Cordelia sipped her coffee, but Dan couldn't focus on the coffee in front of him.

"He knew! He sent me those useless, ridiculous clues, and he knew all along!" He heard his voice rising, and he saw a couple of people staring at him from another table.

Cordelia put her coffee down. "Dad, you have to stop."

"Don't tell me to stop! You have no idea what I've gone through. I ought to kill that crazy son-of-a-bitch!"

"Dad, that's enough! You're getting too loud. You need to be quiet."

"Don't tell me to be quiet! What do *you* know about all this? You disappeared for half the summer. You abandoned your family, and now you think you can come home and tell me how to handle this?"

Cordelia suddenly looked angry. She put her coffee off to one side of the table and put her palms down flat on the table, as if to signify her final position in the conclusion of a long negotiation with a difficult trading partner. "Now that's enough! I know that you're upset, but you're not going to start attacking me. And you might as well stop dwelling on poor old Uncle Jack. We're here because Grandma is dying, and that's the only thing you need to focus on. Your mother is dying."

Dan stopped and sat back in his seat. He was startled by how calm, clear, and resolute she seemed. This was not the hysterical teenage drama that she sometimes created when they fought. This was something more substantial, something planted on more solid ground. He looked across the table at his daughter and saw her in a different light. It was a moment—*the* moment—when a parent looks at a child and sees that childhood is no more. He saw that the transformation into adulthood had taken place for Cordelia, and it seemed like it had happened overnight. He saw a young woman sitting there, rather than a disobedient teenager. More: he saw a young woman who was completely in control of herself, and completely in control of the situation. He felt surprisingly comforted and calmed by her new-found ability to challenge him and stand her ground.

"You're right," he said quietly. "Your Grandma's dying."

"Your *mother* is dying," Cordelia said pointedly.

To which Dan said nothing.

52

Flashbacks

Kate saw her mother's face contorted in rage.

Dad, please! Don't let her hurt me!

Her father was lying on the couch asleep, the empty bottles on the floor nearby. Her mother stood over her with fists raised in the air.

Dad, please! she called.

I'll teach you a lesson right now, you little slut! her mother said.

Dad, wake up!

"It's okay, Grandma. You're here with us. Everything is okay."

Kate opened her eyes and saw her granddaughter sitting by her bedside. For a moment, she couldn't reconcile the frightening memory with the sight of Cordelia sitting there so calmly. The girl took her hand and stroked it.

"Dad and I are here. You're fine now. And your breakfast is here, too. Do you want some breakfast?"

It took another minute for the image of her raging mother to fade from view, and then she saw only the girl. Cordelia helped her put on her glasses. She marveled at the beauty of this child standing over her. Such a tribute to God's work that He created such a lovely young being! And she saw herself in this girl's face. Yes, there was no doubt about it. The girl looked like her, as she had noticed in the photos that Jack sent her over the years.

"So kind of you to come and visit me again," she said.

"Don't be silly, Grandma. *Of course* I'm here to see you. And Dad's here too."

Kate looked over to her left and saw her son Danny, sitting in a chair at the foot of her bed. He looked so distant, so far away. She thought of him as a boy. He was such a smart little boy, she thought. Smart and kind, but so sensitive, so easily hurt. Once, he had accidentally knocked a vase off the kitchen table, and it broke into bits. She was feeling drained and irritable from dealing with his little sister's tantrums, and she snapped at him. "Danny! What did you do?" She saw her mistake immediately. He looked so crushed, so devastated by her brief flash of anger. She hugged him and apologized at once, but looking at him now, the pain of that memory came back. She had hurt her little boy.

"You look tired, Grandma," said the girl.

Kate looked around the room and saw other faces. Her daughter Sarah was sitting there holding a shopping bag. Had she been out shopping? Danny's wife was there with their son. What was his name? Gabe? She felt her eyes closing again.

"That's okay, Grandma. You just rest. We'll be here."

Kate closed her eyes and slept for a while. But when she awoke, or was half-awake, she was immediately transported to the past again. And again, she saw her father passed out drunk on the couch.

Dad, please!

Shut your mouth, you little hussy! yelled her mother. She turned to her unconscious husband lying on the couch. *Your precious little angel here is just a filthy little slut!*

Dad, wake up! Please!

You shut your mouth or I'll shut it for you!

"It's okay, Grandma. Everything is fine."

It was the girl's voice again. Kate opened her eyes and saw Cordelia sitting there. The sun was still coming in through the window, so it wasn't nighttime. Was it still the same day? Yes, it must be the same day. How confusing these hospitals are! One can never tell what time it is.

Her mind went back to the memory. Had she really called out to her father when it happened? Probably not. No, definitely not. Saying anything only made things worse. Crying made things worse. Any effort to fight back or escape made things worse. Certainly, she didn't call for help that day, which was just one of many such days. How old was she at the time? Eleven, maybe twelve at the most. Hitting puberty.

She thought about another day, the day when she was fifteen and she came home from school to find her mother hitting her little brother Jack. Her mother had Jack pinned on the kitchen floor, and she was hitting and hitting. That was the day when Kate found her voice.

You leave him alone! Don't you touch my brother!

She realized she was bigger and stronger at that age, and she pulled her mother off Jack and pushed her down onto the floor. And she finally said what she had thought for years.

I hate you! You're a bitch and I wish you were dead!

She didn't punch her mother in the face, despite the urge, but at least she got her off little Jack. And for a moment, her mother looked afraid. That was a wonderful, powerful, and dreadful moment, to see her mother looking afraid of her. She stood over her mother with a clenched fist, ready to strike.

You're just an evil bitch!

"Grandma, you should eat something. Or at least have something to drink. Would you like some orange juice?"

She struggled to pull herself out of the memory. "Orange juice?" she said to the girl. "Sure, my dear. I'd like some orange juice."

Her granddaughter put the cup in her hand, and she drank the juice down gratefully.

"I brought something for us to do, Grandma," said the girl. "I got us a jigsaw puzzle." She brought the puzzle pieces over on a large board and set it on the bedside tray. "It's a puzzle of the Statue of Liberty." She held up the cover for her grandmother to see.

"Well, that looks like fun," Kate said. "That will pass the time until they can get the doctor to give me permission to leave this place."

"Right, Grandma, right."

For the next few minutes, Kate was able to focus on the puzzle, at least enough to watch Cordelia put pieces together. Her sister Molly entered the room to visit her. She did a few puzzle pieces, too. Kate wanted Danny to join them, but he said he was too tired.

"Have you ever been to the Statue of Liberty, Cordelia?" Kate asked.

"Oh, yes," said Cordelia. "We went there on a school trip once. It was really inspirational."

"I'm sure it was," she said. But she felt herself being pulled back to the memories, and she closed her eyes to shut out the Statue of Liberty.

She stood over her mother, who was still lying on the kitchen floor. She helped her little brother Jack get up. He was crying. Her mother then sat up, and Kate again had the urge to punch her. Or worse. She was standing in the kitchen, not three feet away from the silverware drawer. The thought crossed her mind: *I could kill her.* And maybe that would have been the best thing. Yes, she could have killed her. She could have ended it right there by reaching into the silverware drawer and pulling out her father's big carving knife. She didn't, though. Instead, she took Jack to the corner drugstore and bought him a vanilla milkshake.

Her mind jumped ahead to see a sequence of events in rapid succession: her father falling off the ladder at the start of her senior year, his coffin going into the ground, the relatives trying to comfort her hysterical mother at the funeral, and her brother and sister clinging to her on a miserably cold day in October. She saw herself graduating from high school the following year, with neither father nor mother in the audience to see her walk across the stage. She saw herself walking out the front door of her home, not yet eighteen years old, with a hastily packed suitcase, and she heard that terrible voice again.

You get out of here, you dirty little slut! Get out of my sight! No one wants you around here! No one! Don't come back!

She left, leaving poor little Jack to fend for himself, defenseless against that devil woman they got for a mother. She could have killed her—killed her with the carving knife, or maybe killed her with one perfectly justified punch—and it would have been better for Jack, who suffered so much ever since.

"It's okay, Grandma. Whatever it is, it's okay." The girl was there again when Kate found herself sitting upright in the bed, shaking uncontrollably. Cordelia was wiping the sweat from her brow with a cool washcloth. "Don't worry about anything. You're with us now."

Kate felt her chest heaving with each breath. When her breathing calmed down a bit, she looked at the girl. "Bless you," she said.

53

The End of Suffering

Cordelia was surprised that the doctor was so blunt when he spoke to her and her father. She thought that doctors were averse to telling families the truth, but he couldn't have been clearer. The end was near, and the sooner the better. If she lingered, there was a good chance that the bleeding would start again from the esophagus. That would be traumatic for her and horrible for any family members who might witness her vomiting up large amounts of blood. Better if she just slipped away in a "hepatic coma" due to her liver failure.

It had only been a couple of days since Cordelia followed "Mrs. Rose" into Washington Park, but her grandmother's condition had obviously deteriorated rapidly. Now she lay in bed sleeping, her dinner tray uneaten on a cart by the bed. It was already nine o'clock in the evening, and everyone else had gone home to get some sleep. Her father had refused to leave, so Cordelia stayed to keep him company. He went downstairs for a few minutes, reappearing with a copy of the *New York Times*. He sat on one side of her grandmother's bed, while she sat on the other. He opened his newspaper to work on the crossword puzzle. He turned off the bright overhead light in the room, leaving a couple of wall lights to illuminate the room more softly. Cordelia dozed in and out of sleep as she sat holding her grandmother's hand.

She awoke to a loud crash and jumped up in alarm. She saw her father rising to stand by his chair on the opposite side of the bed. For a moment, she couldn't understand what had made the horrific noise in the room. Then she looked at her grandmother and saw a woman entirely different from the one she had known so far. The old woman was sitting up in bed, looking wild-eyed and agitated. She picked up a small hand mirror and threw it hard against the wall, past the foot of her bed. It crashed against the wall and fell to the floor, where Cordelia saw the source of the original noise: a food tray, dishes, silverware, and the scattered remains of a hospital dinner.

"Leave him alone!" the old woman yelled at Cordelia. "I mean it! You leave him alone!"

A young nursing student walked into the room. She looked quickly from the patient in the bed to the mess on the floor. Obviously flustered, she said, "I'll call the intern so she can order some medicine for her." She left the room.

"Get away from me! Don't touch me!" her grandmother yelled in the direction of the nurse.

"Grandma, it's okay. Everything is okay."

Standing by the bedside, Cordelia reached out for her grandmother, but the old woman swatted her hand away. She looked like a cornered animal, frightened and dangerous.

"Here, Grandma, put your glasses on and you'll see that it's just me."

"Don't you come near me! You're an evil bitch!" She pointed an accusatory finger at Cordelia, who took a step back, stung by the reproach.

Cordelia's father spoke up. "Mom, stop it! Calm down!"

"You be quiet!" the old woman yelled at him. Then she turned to Cordelia again. "I hate you! I wish you were dead!"

Cordelia was caught off guard. She struggled to get control of her voice and fought back an urge to cry. "Grandma, it's me. Cordelia. You're just confused. Everything is going to be fine."

The old woman glared at her with an ominous look. She hissed in a low tone: "You evil bitch!"

Her father was starting to look angry. "Mom, be quiet! I mean it!"

"But Dad," Cordelia said from her side of the bed, "she doesn't know what she's saying. She's just mixed up."

"I don't care," her father said. "No one's going to talk to my daughter that way." He moved a step closer to the bed. "Mom, you need to stop it right now. That's enough!"

"Evil bitch!" yelled her grandmother at full volume.

Her father's face went crimson. "You just shut your damned mouth!"

"Dad, no! Grandma, calm down!" Cordelia turned toward the door. "Nurse! Can we get a nurse in here?"

"I hate you! I wish you were dead!" screamed the old woman, looking first at Cordelia and then at her father. "She's a bitch!"

Her father's expression was only slightly less scary to Cordelia than that of her grandmother. He glowered at the old woman and stepped closer to the bed.

"Who do you think you're talking to?" he said in a menacing voice. "You can't talk to my daughter like that! You're just a crazy old drunk who abandoned her own family!"

"Dad, don't!"

"Bitch!" shrieked her grandmother.

"Grandma, it's me!" said Cordelia, stepping closer to the bed. She held her palm up to her father on the other side of the bed as a stop sign. He took her signal and stepped back. She stood over the old woman and forced a wide smile. "It's me, Cordelia. You know who I am, don't you? It's just me."

The old woman looked at her with a contorted expression of fear and rage. Then, without any warning, she jerked up her right arm fast and punched Cordelia in the face. Cordelia staggered back, her hand coming to her mouth. When she held her hand a few inches away from her face, she saw blood on her fingertips.

Her father quickly moved in from the other side of the bed and grabbed the old woman's wrists. "How dare you hit my child!" he roared. "How dare you! You keep your hands off my Cordelia!"

The old woman had been sitting up, but now she fell back in bed, suddenly looking frail and frightened. Cordelia's father let go of her wrists.

At that moment, two women came running into the room, an older nurse and a young intern. The nurse turned on the overhead light, which seemed relentlessly glaring. Cordelia didn't want them to see her grandmother acting so crazy. She didn't want them to see her father's temper. And she didn't want them to see her bloody lip. The intern and the nurse talked about whether to administer oral or intravenous medication. They decided to try the oral medicine first, since their patient was currently quiet. The nurse left the room and quickly reappeared. She handed Cordelia's grandmother a pill and a cup of water. The old woman took the pill and soon drifted off to sleep. Cordelia was holding a hand to her throbbing lower lip, trying not to get blood on her clothing. She was also struggling to control her breathing and stop crying. The young intern left the room. The nurse turned to Cordelia.

"Are you all right, honey?"

"Yes, I'm fine," she said, her speech sounding thick as it tried to get past her swollen lip. "My grandma was just talking crazy, and she accidentally hit me. And my dad just got angry for a second, but we're fine."

"The intern says that your grandmother's in a state of delirium, probably related to her liver failure. She was in and out of delirium this afternoon before you came to visit. The medicine should help." The nurse then tendered Cordelia a fretful expression. "Let me have a look at that lip, honey. Oh, my! We'll have to get some ice on that." Then she turned to Cordelia's father.

"And you, sir?"

"Everything is fine," he said. "Just like my daughter told you."

"Do you need a break? Maybe you'd like to go down to the cafeteria and get a cold drink? We can keep an eye on your mother for you."

"We're fine, thanks."

"Okay, then." The nurse turned again to Cordelia, looking concerned. Finally, she left the room, shooting a suspicious look at Cordelia's father over her shoulder. In the doorway to the room, several security guards appeared. They positioned themselves in the hallway. The nurse stopped to talk to the security guards for a moment, and then she disappeared.

Cordelia went into the tiny bathroom that was part of her grandmother's patient room. She studied her face in the mirror. Her lower lip was split, bleeding, and swollen. She turned on the faucet, cupped some cold water in her hand, and brought it to her face. Her father appeared in the mirror behind her.

"Are you okay?" he asked.

"I'm fine, Dad. It's just a little nick."

"That looks awful," he said. "I'm really sorry that happened, Cordelia. I should have seen it coming."

"It's fine, Dad. It's not your fault."

"I'm really sorry," he repeated. "I'm so sorry."

Her father went back into the patient room. She could see him pacing back and forth in the mirror. The nurse reappeared with a plastic ice pack.

"Here, honey. Oh, my, you're going to have a fat lip there, aren't you? Let me see." She made Cordelia open her mouth, and she gently examined her with a hand-held light. "Well, it's only that one cut. And you don't seem to have any loose teeth. I guess you'll survive. Just keep the ice on it for a while." She patted Cordelia's cheek and left the room, throwing another distrustful look at her father on the way out.

Her father paced back and forth in the little room.

"Dad, why don't you sit down? You could work on your crossword puzzle."

"I'm fine," he said. He continued to pace, exhaling loudly once in a while. After a few minutes, he stopped pacing and started to clean up the mess on the floor at the foot of the bed.

Cordelia watched her father, carefully monitoring him for signs of more anger. He seemed to be calming down nicely, though. After cleaning the floor, he sat down with his newspaper again. She realized that she had been monitoring his moods for a very long time, and she was tired of it. For the moment, he seemed quiet and composed, so she could relax her vigilance. She noticed that the security guards no longer stood by their doorway, so they must have concluded that he was no threat to anyone. He settled into his crossword puzzle.

Cordelia thought about Martin. She hadn't had time to write to him in the last few days, so he didn't even know that she had met a sweet old woman named Mrs. Rose who turned out to be her long-lost grandmother. He certainly didn't know that she was now losing her grandmother. She couldn't wait to tell him that her grandmother became violently delirious and her father came to her defense. Now he was acting sweet and caring, like the father she used to have. She wanted to tell him all about this.

She also wanted to tell Martin that she was sad because she would never have the opportunity to talk with her grandmother about whatever drove the poor woman to leave her family, drink alcohol, date Don Juan, work in a plant nursery, join a convent, leave a convent, and so on. But maybe that didn't matter. She gently patted her grandmother's arm. "It's okay, Grandma. I understand." And she would explain to Martin that she did understand, at least somewhat. She would tell Martin what she hadn't told her father: that she called her grandmother's brother, her great-uncle Jack, in California. She made the call right after the family learned about Jack's involvement with the mysterious clues. It was a difficult conversation, since Jack kept crying about his sister's deteriorating health. And his thinking was so hard to follow. But in between the paranoid warnings about the government, she was able to piece together a few important clues to the early life of her grandmother—a terribly sad life, to be sure.

After that conversation, Cordelia felt that she understood her grandmother much better, and she couldn't wait to tell Martin about it. And she decided that when everything settled down, she would tell her father what she knew.

There was more that she wanted to tell Martin. She wanted to tell him what she was learning by sitting at the bedside of her dying grandmother. She was learning that suffering comes to an end. Her grandmother's suffering was coming to an end, so everyone's pain must ultimately end. Knowing this, she could endure the knowledge that suffering is a constant presence in the world. Here she sat, bearing witness to it, without feeling overwhelmed by it. She didn't have to turn away in anguish and hide from it. She didn't have to wish it away with grand fantasies of world peace. She could just endure it.

Her grandmother lay there with closed eyes. She was trying to speak. She spoke in a whisper, and Cordelia had to lean close to hear what she was saying.

"Our Father who art in Heaven . . ." Then she was quiet again.

"It's all right, Grandma. We're still here."

54

Cast the First Stone

She felt the girl holding her hand, wiping her brow. She opened her eyes and saw the girl sitting there, wearing a red T-shirt with "Marist College" written on it. Her lower lip was swollen. How did that happen? How did this lovely creature get a swollen lip? She closed her eyes again. She heard the girl's comforting words coming to her from the world outside, as she slipped back into her own world. And suddenly, the girl's words made all the torment stop. The sound of her words, the feel of her hand, the soothing presence of this granddaughter—it brought all her troubles to a halt. The frightening visions were gone, and she was filled with a quiet, peaceful feeling. The Lord's Prayer formed in her mind.

> **Our Father, who art in heaven,**
> **Hallowed be thy Name.**
> **Thy Kingdom come, Thy will be done,**
> **On earth as it is in heaven.**

"You just rest, Grandma. We'll be here if you need us."

Give us this day our daily bread.
And forgive us our trespasses,
As we forgive them that trespass against us.

She tried to open her eyes but could not. She knew that the girl was still there. How much time had passed? Minutes? Hours? Days? What day was it?

Forgive me, God, for I have sinned. I have lived my life in this temporal world of life and death, and now I feel myself slipping beyond the boundaries of it. But this is not what I expected. I find myself in a vast, peaceful stillness, a perfect everlasting moment with no fear, no regret. I find myself at peace in this strange matrix of space that I have never known, yet always known.

I was innocent once, but I have sinned. God forgive me, I have sinned. I abandoned my own family. What could be a more serious sin in His eyes? I left my husband and children, and now I will surely burn in Hell. Yet I have no sense that I am about to enter Hell, no sense that I am on the verge of eternal suffering. My eyes close and I am back in this Eternal Stillness. I am surrounded by God; I am in God. I view my temporal life with equanimity, and I see it for what it was: a life lived as a flawed mortal, an imperfect creature created by a perfect God.

There is no Hell here. There is no Hell! I can see what really exists now, and it isn't Hell. There is no Original Sin. What an absurd idea! How could a little child be born in sin? I can see the Timeless Reality from whence we all come, and it has nothing to do with devils and torment and Original Sin. This is a grace from God, surely.

She drifted off to sleep. Suddenly, there was no one else in the room, except for a strange shadowy figure at the foot of her bed. Afterwards, she couldn't be sure whether she had really been awake or she had dreamed it. Sometimes, it was hard to tell what state of consciousness she was in. Was she awake or asleep when she saw the figure? Was she dreaming or just hallucinating? Maybe she was hallucinating like she had done several times before when she was drinking hard and ran out of supplies. Was the figure real or imagined?

She heard the girl's voice again.

"It's all right, Grandma. Everything will be all right."

The girl disappeared, and the figure was there again, shrouded in darkness, standing motionless in the middle of her room. It wasn't a doctor or nurse, of that she was certain. She couldn't even discern for sure whether it was man or woman, although she thought it was more likely a woman. Was it her mother? A frightening thought, but the fear passed quickly. In any case, she could sense an attitude in this person, a distinctly adversarial disposition. This person was here to accuse her.

She closed her eyes—or dreamed that she closed her eyes. How could one be certain? When she opened them (or dreamed that she opened them), the figure was gone. She found herself composing a response to this intruder.

Who are you to accuse me? I was a mother. Do you know what it's like to be a mother? True, I left, but only because I was convinced that there was some essential badness in me, a badness that would destroy my child. I had to run away from him in order to protect him. Where is the judge, on Earth or in Heaven, who would blame me for that? I loved him, and I had to flee him. Suppose I were living in Medieval times, and I had fallen ill with the Plague? Should I put my arms around my little Danny and give him the Black Death? Would anyone blame me for leaving my home to protect my child from my illness? As our Lord said: Let him who is without sin cast the first stone. I loved my child, and I kept myself away from him in order to save him.

Yes, I was convinced that I was possessed of disease, of wickedness, of some kind of plague. And I was sure that it would kill my little boy if he were around me any longer. When he turned seventeen, I could stand it no more. I was certain of it, as certain as a mother could be.

You stand before me to accuse me, but hear this: I did not leave my child in order to find myself, or gain my freedom, or see the world. I left so I could spare my son and die alone of my affliction. I just never thought that the end would take so long to come. I ran away to die in Tucson, then I ran away to die in Denver; then I ran from town to town, always thinking that it was my last stop, that death would come for me soon. Often, I hoped that the alcohol would hasten the end, although I also feared death, as we all fear death. Why do we fear what must be the end for all of us? Why do we cling so desperately to these fragile bodies?

I loved Danny more than I loved his sister Sarah, and that is surely a sin, too. My love for that little boy consumed me like a fire, and there was nothing left of me for anyone else. I named him Daniel, for my father, and I loved my son completely, as I loved my poor, broken father.

I have sinned, but I loved that child, and perhaps that is the real meaning of my life. I loved! What could be more important in this earthly life? Why are we put here at all? What is it that we are supposed to do? Are we not meant to emulate God's love by loving one another? I stand before God as a miserable sinner who abandoned her family, yet I loved.

Now—and only now—I see there was no evil in me, no badness, no moral disease. I am a child of God, like everyone else. And God will surely forgive me my sins. Let him without sin cast the first stone at me.

"Hi, Grandma. It's Cordelia. Everything is all right. It's just me."

She became fully conscious again, slowly growing aware of the girl who sat close to her and held her hand. The girl was still wearing the same red T-shirt. It must be the same day. What seemed like many days must have been only a few minutes of time. Very confusing. But what a calming presence, this little angel! This girl, this Cordelia, was still sitting by her bedside and still holding her hand. Her voice was so kind and soothing.

For a moment, Kate Wunsch thought that perhaps she was already in Heaven.

55

Last Words

The nurses brought in a couple of comfortable recliner chairs for Dan and Cordelia. Dan looked over at his daughter. She was sitting on the opposite side of his mother's hospital bed, her lip still swollen from the day before. She hunched up her shoulders and shivered. The weather had shifted dramatically from intense August heat to a rapid cooling down, and there was a cool evening breeze blowing in through the window behind her. He got up and tried to close the window, but it wouldn't close. He went to the small closet in the room, where he found an extra blanket. Without saying anything, he wrapped it around her shoulders.

"Thanks, Dad."

Then he went back to his chair on the other side of the bed. He picked up his newspaper and resumed working on his crossword puzzle. His mother lay in her hospital bed sleeping.

"Multicolored," he read out loud. "Six letters across. Any ideas, Mom?"

His mother didn't stir. Cordelia gave him a questioning look.

"Your grandmother always loved crossword puzzles," he explained. "That's how I got interested in them."

"Oh!" said Cordelia. "I didn't know that."

"I guess I never told you," he said. There was so much she didn't know about her grandmother, and how could she know? He rarely spoke to her about his mother. He made himself a promise that he would tell Cordelia more about her after this was all over. "Let's see. Multicolored. Six letters. Any ideas, Cordelia?"

"Not really, Dad."

"*Motley*," he said. "But no, that doesn't fit the words going down."

His mother remained asleep. The clock said it was almost ten. Should they go home and get some sleep? The rest of the family had left the hospital long ago. He and Cordelia had stayed late last night, only to have his mother get delirious and hit his daughter. Maybe they should go home. But the doctor had been clear. It was impossible to be sure, but there probably wasn't much time left.

"Wait," he said. "*Calico*. That's it. Multicolored is calico. Six letters, and it fits perfectly."

He continued to work on his crossword puzzle, and Cordelia seemed content to sit on the other side of the bed with a blanket around her. She tipped her reclining chair back a bit, but she kept one hand resting on her grandmother's arm. Over the next few minutes, her eyes closed and her breathing settled into the deep, slow rhythm of an exhausted sleeper.

Not long after Cordelia had gone to sleep, his mother opened her eyes. She put on her glasses and turned her head to look at Cordelia.

"What happened to her lip, Danny?" she asked him.

"Oh, she bumped herself on the door," he said.

"Well, I hope the swelling goes away soon. Such a sweet girl you have, Danny."

"Thanks, Mom." He was surprised that she was speaking so clearly and calmly now, but that's what the doctor had predicted. In delirium, his mother could be confused and agitated at breakfast, but perfectly lucid at lunch. She certainly looked like she was back to her rational self now. Perhaps this would be his opportunity to talk with her—his last opportunity. Cordelia was asleep, and everyone else had gone home, but he still couldn't think of anything to say. After thirty years of imaginary conversations, his mind was a complete blank. Anyway, his mother's alertness quickly faded, and she lay there staring straight ahead with a dull gaze until her eyes slowly closed. Dan picked up his crossword puzzle again and worked at it for a few minutes.

"Let's see, let's see," he said. "One joule per second. Four letters going down. Oh. *Watt.* That one was easy, Mom."

"She hit me," his mother said, suddenly popping open her eyes again.

"What, Mom? Who hit you?" He thought that she might be lapsing into the delirium again, although she still seemed quite calm.

"She would hit me and beat me. And she beat Jack, too."

"Who are you talking about?" But then he knew before she could answer him. "Are you talking about your mother? My grandmother?"

"Yes, my mother. She would beat Jack, too. That was terrible. Just unbearable."

Was this true? He had never heard anything about it. Yet she seemed very calm and reasonable. And it felt true. She often spoke about her father when he was a kid, but never her mother.

He had always suspected that his maternal grandmother was a villain of some sort.

"I never knew that, Mom. It sounds awful." He put down his newspaper with the crossword puzzle in it.

"Awful, yes. Just awful. I couldn't protect Jack."

"But where was your father when she was doing all this terrible stuff?"

She raised her head off the pillow and spoke in a conspiratorial whisper. "On the couch. Passed out. Drunk!" Her head dropped back onto the pillow. She tried to lift her head again, but she seemed too weak to do it.

A nurse appeared in the doorway. "Do you need anything, Mrs. Rose? I mean, Mrs. Wunsch."

Dan turned in his chair to face the nurse. "Could you show me how to put the head of her bed up?"

The nurse showed him how to adjust the electric bed, and he raised the head until his mother was more upright. He propped a pillow behind her and moved his chair closer to the bed. Before the nurse even left the room, his mother continued to talk.

"I'm dying, Danny. Don't let the doctors here tell you otherwise. I'm dying."

"I know, Mom." He found himself leaning closer to hear her, as her voice was weak and faint.

They sat together in silence. He wasn't sure what to say to her. He didn't think that she knew the end was near, and he certainly hadn't expected her to talk about it. He should say something.

"Don't be afraid," he said.

"Oh, I'm not afraid of dying," she said. "I'll be with God soon. I'm sure of that."

"Well, that's good, Mom." He believed her about her attitude toward death and her faith in God, but she looked worried nonetheless. Her eyes seemed to be reaching out to him. There was another silence between them. He kept leaning forward, his face just inches away from hers. In his peripheral vision, he saw a nurse enter the room, look at them, turn around, and leave.

"I can check her vital signs later," called the nurse as she left the room.

A strange thing, Dan thought, to be in such close proximity to another person, eye to eye, but without talking. Most of the time, we're several feet apart and jabbering at each other constantly to fill the space.

His mother kept her eyes on him.

"So, you're an English professor," she said.

"Yes."

She nodded her head and tried to smile, but she twisted her torso back and forth, looking uncomfortable. Dan helped adjust the pillow behind her back. That seemed to help.

"Do you like it, Danny? Do you like being a professor?"

"Yeah, I like it," he said. He thought about the books in his office, and he had a glimpse of himself in front of a classroom full of students. "I love it."

"Good." She nodded again, but her face still looked worried. "Abby is so nice."

"Thanks, Mom."

"And you have two beautiful kids," she added.

"Thanks. They're good kids."

"They're so grown up, Danny."

"Yeah, they're growing up. Cordelia leaves for college soon."

His mother looked over at Cordelia. "I was away for a long time."

Silence again. He should say something else. She seemed to be waiting for him to speak. He studied her face. What did she

need him to say? The first thing that occurred to him was forgiveness. Maybe she needed him to say that he forgave her. Isn't
that what was supposed to happen here? She ought to apologize
first, and then he should forgive her. But she hadn't apologized.
And the forgiveness idea didn't quite feel right. First, he wasn't
sure that he was ready to forgive her. (Did he forgive her? He
had no idea.) Second, he wasn't convinced that she needed forgiveness. He almost wished that Cordelia would wake up. She
always seemed to know what to say to people. But he didn't really want her to wake up. He wanted these last moments alone
with his mother.

He tried to read what she wanted by studying her face. He
had an urge to touch her face, to run his fingers over the furrowed brow and read in braille what his eyes couldn't decipher.
He finally had a hunch.

"Nothing bad happened to me, Mom. Nothing bad happened
at all. I'm fine."

He was editing the original thought in his mind: Nothing
bad happened to me *after you left*. But he didn't want to hurt her
with those last three words. In either version, the statement was
a lie, to be sure. Her shocking disappearance was the worst thing
that ever happened to him; it was the disaster of his life. But telling the truth seemed like a cruel and foolish thing to do at the
moment. He had to find the right words to help her feel better
and die in peace. Cordelia would understand what he was trying
to do. She always knew the right thing to say to make a person
feel better.

"Nothing bad happened to me then, and nothing bad is going to happen to me now. I'm fine, Mom."

Her face began to smoothen, the forehead becoming less furrowed, the eyes relaxing their desperate reach. She nodded at him

again. He realized that he was on the right track. She didn't need his forgiveness. She just needed to know that he was all right. This struck him as amazingly unselfish. She didn't need him to forgive her so she could escape her own guilt. Her concerns were still about him, after all these years. At times, he had secretly accused her of being selfish. What could be more selfish than running away from one's own family? But now he saw her quite differently. She was probably always thinking of him, wherever she was, and she was still worrying now about whether he was all right.

Her eyelids drooped. She closed her eyes and opened them again several times. Each time she opened her eyes, he repeated his reassurance.

"I'm fine, Mom. Nothing bad happened to me. I'm all right."

And each time he said it, she gave him a weak little nod. She opened her mouth a couple of times, but she didn't seem to have the energy to speak any more. She was able to nod each time, though, and her face looked much more peaceful.

This is how it ends, Dan thought. She asked a few questions, he gave a few short answers, and that would have to suffice. And sure enough, she stopped opening her eyes. She lay there breathing for another hour or so, and then her chest stopped rising and falling. Her lips turned a dusky blue color. Her face bore a calm expression, and her hands were clasped together in her lap. Her suffering was over.

He looked at the shock of white hair and the few remaining freckles on her face. He tried to remember what she looked like as a young woman. He glanced over at his daughter, which made the task quite easy. But no, he told himself, Cordelia was not his mother. She was her own person with her own life. His mother was the old woman who had just let go of this life, with the help of a few words exchanged between the two of them.

He looked around to take in the scene in the hospital room one more time before waking Cordelia and going home. And what did he see? He saw his daughter asleep in her chair on the other side of the bed. She was keeping a vigil at her grandmother's bedside. Never mind that her grandmother had gone crazy and punched her in the face; Cordelia had obviously forgiven her already. She wanted to maintain the kinship connection with her long-lost relative. She was that kind of kid.

And he saw his mother, lying still and serene in her hospital bed. He saw the mother who had persisted in her determination to travel cross-country, despite being frail, exhausted, and critically ill. She came to see her son one last time before she died, just to make sure that he was all right. He looked back and forth from mother to daughter, and back to mother again, musing upon the mysterious and enduring power of family bonds.

He became aware of the cool night air still blowing in through the open window. He pulled the covers up over his mother's bare arms. Not that it would do any good, but it felt like the right thing to do. Then he stood up. After leaning in close to hear his mother's failing voice, his back sorely needed a stretch. He stood up tall and raised his arms over his head. He walked over to the window and looked out to see a full moon rising in the August night sky. After sitting in the small, dimly lit sickroom, the brilliance of it was startling. He felt sad to realize that amidst the relentless worries occupying his mind, he had forgotten the beauty of the moon.

Lightning Source UK Ltd.
Milton Keynes UK
UKHW021113100521
383425UK00007B/810